Jack Derringer
A tale of deep water

by

Basil Lubbock

Jack Derringer
A tale of deep water
by Basil Lubbock

Copyright © 2024

All Rights reserved.

ISBN: 978-93-62209-64-1

Published by

DOUBLE 9 BOOKS

2/13-B, Ansari Road
Daryaganj, New Delhi – 110002
info@double9books.com
www.double9books.com
Tel. 011-40042856

This book is under public domain

ABOUT THE AUTHOR

Alfred Basil Lubbock, MC, was a British historian, seaman, and soldier. He was a prolific writer about the last generation of commercial sailing vessels during the Age of Sail. He joined the Society for Nautical Research in 1911, served on its council from 1921 to 1924, and contributed to the periodical The Mariner's Mirror. He was born on September 9, 1876, in Rowley Bank, Arkley, Hertfordshire, as the second of five children. His father, Alfred Lubbock, and his mother, Louisa Wallroth, were married in 1875. Alfred senior served as an underwriter for Lloyd's of London and was a director of Robarts, Lubbock & Co, a private bank established in 1772. He descended from Sir John Lubbock, the 2nd Baronet. Basil Lubbock spent the majority of his early life with his uncle. He attended Eton College and was a member of the cricket team from 1894 to 1895. (His father had also attended Eton, where he was an accomplished athlete. Lubbock senior continued to play cricket into adulthood and was regarded as one of England's top batters). Lubbock junior learned to draw and paint using watercolours while at Eton. Some of his works were featured in his debut book. Others are in the collection of the National Maritime Museum in London. He was expected to follow family tradition and attend King's College in Cambridge. Instead, he decided to travel, leaving Britain by steamship for Canada.

CONTENTS

PREFACE

I have endeavoured in this book to paint sea life as it really is, as it can be seen on any deep-water sailing-ship of the present day, without glossing over the hardships, the hard knocks, the hard words, and the continual struggle and strife of it all. At the same time I have tried to hint at the glamour and fascination which the sea breathes into such souls as respond to its mighty call.

As to the queer collection of flotsam which found itself in the down-easter's foc's'le, I can assure my readers that this mixed crowd is in no way unusual; in fact, I am quite certain that the greater number of sailing ships "bound deep water" at the present moment are manned by crews of an even worse mixture of nationalities, trades, and creeds than formed the complement of the *Higgins*, which, for a ship sailing out of San Francisco, when seamen were scarce, was singularly lucky in finding so many bona-fide sailormen amongst her crew.

My reader may ask if the brutality described still goes on on American ships. All I can say is that several of the Yankee Cape Horn fleet are still notorious for it, their officers excusing themselves on the plea that only by the harshest measures can they preserve discipline amongst the hard-cut citizens of all nations who form American crews.

Many of the episodes in this book, including the cowpuncher's frontier yarns, I have taken from fact, and the treatment of the knifing dago by the bucko mate in Chapter IV. actually occurred in every detail.

As regards the moon-blindness, I have no doubt I shall have to bear with many scoffers and unbelievers, but this I know, that few men who have been used to sleeping in the open, whether sailors or landsmen, will be amongst them. Many a time have I hauled a sleeping man out of the glare of the tropical moon for fear of its direful beams, and many a time have I had the like service done to me. Few old seamen but have some strange yarn to spin anent the strange effects of the moon upon the human countenance exposed to its sinister rays: in most cases it is some hours' or some days' moon-blindness; sometimes it is a queer contraction of the muscles on the side of the face exposed; and I have even heard of cases of idiocy put down to the same cause. Certain it is that the cold beams of our world's satellite are not to be trusted. Why, do they not even poison fish or meat if left exposed to the mercy of their baleful glitter?

I must apologise for the sentimental part of this book, but apparently in a work of fiction a certain amount of sentiment is considered necessary, even in a sea yarn. However, if my reader finds it not to his taste, he can skip. We've all learnt to do that, some time or other.

BASIL LUBBOCK.

PART I

CHAPTER I
"THE YANKEE HELL-SHIP"

Bucking Broncho awoke to the familiar cry of "Roll out, roll out, show a leg!" and thinking it was the call of the Round Up Boss in the early morning, he opened his eyes and sat up.

The sight that met his gaze considerably astonished him, and the foc's'le, with its double row of bunks, its stuffy atmosphere, and its swinging oil-lamp, he mistook for some mining-camp shanty.

Slowly his half-shut eyes took in the details of the gloomy den, into which the grey light of dawn had as yet hardly penetrated.

Round him lay men in every condition of drunkenness, some prone upon the deck, others hanging half in and half out of their bunks, all apparently still in the stupors of a late carouse.

Stretched upon a chest right under his bunk lay a ghastly object clothed in greasy, blood-stained rags, which but for its hoarse rattling breathing he would have taken for a corpse.

From the bunk above him came a spasmodic grunt at intervals, sudden and unexpected, whilst opposite him a cadaverous-looking deadbeat in a miner's shirt whistled discordantly through a hawk-like, fiery-tinted nose.

As his eyes grew accustomed to the dim light he discovered other forms scattered in a variety of grotesque attitudes amongst the litter of chests and sea-bags on the deck, and through the open door he beheld a man, in a pair of overalls, sluicing himself with a bucket of water.

Then a gigantic form with a hairy face of kindly aspect blocked up the doorway, and in hurricane tones besought the snoring crowd to tumble up and man the capstan. Advancing into the foc's'le, this leather-lunged apparition coolly and methodically began to haul the insensible scarecrows out of their bunks, and to shake them until their teeth rattled.

"Say, stranger, whatever's the hock kyard to all this? What be you-alls aimin' for to do?" inquired Bucking Broncho in his soft Western drawl, as he watched the big man handling the drunks.

"Just you tumble out, my son, and get outside, or you'll reap a skinful of trouble. You'll get the hang o' things quick enough by-and-by," returned the other shortly.

"I'm clean stampeded in my intellec' complete," declared the cowboy; "but assuming you're the boss of this outfit, your word goes; I plays your hand, stranger, an' I rolls out."

The big, hairy-faced man was too busy pushing, pommelling, thumping, and hustling the rest of the inmates to take any more notice of Bucking Broncho, who, gaining the door, stared round in amazement as he found himself upon the deck of a large sailing-ship.

The cowpuncher, who had only seen "blue water" on two occasions in his life, had been shanghaied aboard the notorious Yankee skysail-yard clipper *Silas K. Higgins*, the hottest hell-ship under the Stars and Stripes.

The last of the wheat fleet, this vessel had been lying at anchor in San Francisco Bay for some weeks, delayed from sailing for want of a crew, which her bad name made impossible for her to get except by foul means.

With lavish hands her "old man" scattered his blood-money amongst the boarding-house runners and crimps, and then patiently awaited the result.

Slowly but surely his crew began to arrive, heels first to a man, some drugged, some sandbagged, some set upon and kidnapped along the water-front.

Night after night boats sneaked up to the gangway grating and deposited insensible bundles of rags, which the ghoulish traders in blood callously slung aboard.

But before signing the note, the experienced mate took care to ascertain if his new hand still breathed, for more than once in the past he had had dead men palmed off upon him. Then, if satisfied after his careful scrutiny, he ordered the watchman to drag the shanghaied man forward whilst he ticked off Able-bodied Seaman Jones or Smith, whichever name happened to come first on his list.

The *Higgins* had been waiting two days for her last man when Bucking Broncho fell a victim to the manhunters.

The cowpuncher, discovered in Chinatown busy celebrating his first night off the prairie, was pounced upon by these vultures as "an easy thing." Skilfully they drugged him, cheerfully they possessed themselves of his wad of notes, then, overcome by the humour of the idea, instead of substituting the trade rags for his clothes as usual in shanghai-ing men, they slung him aboard an hour after midnight in all the glory of chaps and spurs.

Thus, with her complement gained at last, the *Higgins* was about to get under weigh.

Wholly oblivious of the events of the past night, thanks to the strength of the dope, with buzzing head and half-fuddled senses the cowboy stood gazing stupidly at the scene before him.

"I'm shorely plumb locoed," he muttered. "What for of a play is this I'm into?"

Overhearing this, the man sluicing himself turned round.

"Bit muzzy still, mate——" he began, and then stopped in surprise.

This man formed a big contrast to the broken-looking crowd in the foc's'le.

As he stood there in the morning light, stripped as he was to the waist, he looked the beau ideal of health: the muscles on his arms and shoulders stretched the skin till it shone, and heightened the artistic effect of the beautiful Japanese tattooing which, in the shape of dragons, butterflies, Geisha girls, and other quaint designs, made a picture gallery of his body.

Six foot high at least, he stood lightly on his feet with the careless grace of one used to a heaving deck.

A peculiar look of devil-may-care good nature stamped his clean-cut, deeply tanned features, yet there was a keen glint of shrewdness in his blue eyes, decision in his firm chin and resolute lips, with just a touch of martial fierceness in the twirl of his small moustache.

No tenderfoot this man, though there was no mistaking his nationality. "A d——d Britisher" was written large all over him. Bare-footed though he was, in well-worn dungarees, with leather belt and sheath-knife, his birth was plain as his nationality.

In England they would use one word to describe him—the one word "rolling-stone"; but in the world not one but a dozen words would be required—frontiersman, sailor, soldier, gold-miner, cowboy, hunter, scout, prospector, explorer, and many more, all marked "dangerous" in the catalogue of professions, for the "rolling-stone" takes to dangers and hardships just as a city man does to dollars and comforts. And who shall lay the blame? It's all in the blood, whether you take your strain from Francis Drake the buccaneer or Shylock the Jew.

Such was the man who faced Broncho—just a British rolling-stone, a modern freelance, a sea rover.

As he spoke, Bucking Broncho gave him a keen look, and then cried out:

"I'm a coyote if it ain't Derringer Jack. Shake, old pard, you-alls ain't shorely forget Bucking Broncho?"

"Think I'd forget an old pal like that; no, Broncho, so sure as you remember me."

"Which I shorely does. I makes a bet I tells them brands o' yours on the skyline."

As they gripped hands Jack Derringer remarked:

"You've strayed a long way off your range, Broncho; shanghaied, I suppose? Well, you've run against bad luck here. It's a rough deal aboard this ship."

"What for of a game is it?"

"*Quien sabe?* Pretty tough, I expect, old man; you're a sailor outward bound ——"

"The hell you say!"

"Yes; I'll watch your hand as well as I can, but, mind you, Broncho, no gun-play whatever happens, or you'll reap more lead than if you'd got the whole of the Tucson Stranglers on your trail."

"I shorely notes your play, Jack; I'm the last gent to go fosterin' idees of bloodshed. This here deadfall draws the cinch some tight an' painful, but you can gamble I ain't going to plunge none before the draw; I'll just watch the deal a whole lot."

"That's *bueno*! Roll a small loop and don't stir up the range more'n you can help; trouble comes a-hooping and don't need looking for. How are you feeling after that poisoned grog?"

"Pretty rocky," replied the cowpuncher.

"Stuff your head into that," said the rover, pointing to the bucket of water which he had drawn a short while before.

"I guess you had better get out of those buckskins," he went on gravely, as Broncho tried the saltwater cure. "Bit of boarding-house runner's wit sending you aboard in them; but I'll fit you out. I expect you've only got the usual rag-bag, like the rest."

"Seems to me I've got my horns locked in a re-ather tough proposition. I shore aims to be resigned. The ways of Providence is that various an' spreadeagle that as a man of savvy I comes in blind an' stands pat," remarked the cowboy, as they retired into the foc's'le.

Perhaps before he gets rid of his cowpuncher attire for the blue dungarees of the 'fore-mast Jack, a short description might be welcome.

He was arrayed in full cowboy get-up, just as he had ridden into Frisco. He wore a fringed and silk-ornamented buckskin shirt, deeply fringed leather chaparegos, and long-heeled cowpuncher boots, on which jingled great Mexican spurs. Round his neck he had the usual gay silk handkerchief, and on his head a brand new Stetson hat.

A loose belt full of cartridges swung a 45-calibre revolver low down upon his hip. This had evidently been overlooked by the crimps, and, at a glance from Jack Derringer, he hastily tucked it under his shirt out of sight.

In appearance Bucking Broncho was a man of medium height, with good shoulders, none too square, but broad enough.

He was lean and muscular, with the firm flesh of a man in perfect health and training. There was not an ounce of fat on his whole body. His skin was darkened and toughened by long contact with wind, sun, and alkali.

His eyes were of that blue-grey so often seen in men of cool nerve, who, though used to danger and ready to dare anything, are yet long-headed and full of resource. He kept them half-shut from long squinting in the bright sun of the south-west.

His rather heavy moustache had been sunburnt and bleached to a raw gold colour.

It took but a short time to convert the cowboy into the sailor in flannel shirt and overalls, with a belt, minus revolver and cartridges, but with a sailor's sheath-knife instead.

Whilst he was changing his attire, being lavishly supplied with clothes from Jack Derringer's big sea-chest, his head was fast clearing and the drugging was losing its stupefying effect.

Calmly he reviewed the situation, and, used to the vicissitudes of the West, treated his change of fortune with the stoical philosophy of a frontiersman.

By the time that Broncho was arrayed afresh, the last of the poor drunks had been dragged from the foc's'le. Then, as Jack and the cowboy emerged, they came face to face with a big square chunk of a man, with eyebrows so thick and bushy that they almost hid his fierce, bloodshot little eyes.

"Up onto the foc's'le-head," he cried angrily. "Git a move on, yew blasted farmers, or yew won't know what struck yew."

It was Black Davis, the mate of the *Higgins*, one of the most notorious of buckos.

Broncho opened his mouth to reply, but Jack Derringer shoved him up the topgallant ladder with a grip of iron, and, directly they were out of earshot, said:

"That man with the eyebrows is kind of sheriff of this outfit—mate, sailors call it. He's a bad 'un from away back, but he's got the drop on us, old son, and we've got to jump around lively without any tongue-wagging, or he's liable to make things red hot."

"Gaud blimy, but h'I should sye so," remarked a cockney, who was shipping a capstan-bar close to them. "'E's a bloomin' devil from the word go, is that blawsted swine. H'I done a passage with 'im afore, an' I knows 'im, h'I does, the black-'arted 'ound."

They had no time for further reminiscences of Black Davis, however, for he now appeared on the foc's'le head in company with the big hairy bosun.

"Never see'd sich a crowd o' hayseeds—not two sailormen among 'em, I don't expec'," said the bosun.

"Deadbeats and hoboes, every doggoned one of them," growled the mate; "not a chanty in 'em, neither."

All hands were now tramping steadily round the capstan.

"Heave an' bust her!" sang out the big bosun. "Heave an' she comes!"

Presently a slim young Englishman with curly hair struck up the well-known chanty, "Away, Rio."

As the hoarse voices echoed over the calm waters of the bay, the crews of two large British barques came to the rail, hooting and jeering at the notorious hell-ship.

"Cut his black liver out, boys!" came a stentorian voice across the water.

"H'I bloomin' well will, one o' these fine dyes," muttered the cockney under his breath, with a murderous glance at the bucko mate.

Jack Derringer, who was a great exponent of chanties, followed the lead of the curly-headed one, and in a clean, strong baritone broke out with:

"As I was walking out one day
Down by the Albert Docks."

There were evidently more sailormen aboard than either the bosun or Black Davis had calculated on, for the chorus came with a roar: "Heave a-way, my Johnnies, heave a-way!"

"I saw the charming maids so gay,
A-coming down in flocks,"

continued Jack.

Then again came the deep-sea roar of—

"Heave away, my bully boys,
We're all bound to go!"

The shanghaied cowpuncher watched everything the while with a keen eye, and the chantying greatly pleased him.

"This is shore most elegant music," he said to Jack. "What for of a play would it be if I gives them the 'Dying Ranger.'"

"Wouldn't go, Broncho," replied the other. "These are sailors' working songs; they're to help the capstan round."

"You shorely surprises me, Jack. This here ship business is some deep an' interestin' as a play, an' you'll excuse me for ropin' at you with questions an' a-pesterin', but I'm cutting kyards with myself desp'rate as to this here whirlygig concarn we-alls is a-pushin' round."

"Why, we're getting up the anchor, Broncho. Do you hear that 'klink, klink'? That's the cable coming in."

"Hove short!" suddenly sang out the mate.

"Pawl her!" cried the bosun.

The tugboat now backed fussily up and took the hawser; the anchor was hove up to the cat-head, and the fish-tackle hooked on.

Then, whilst the anchor was hove in-board, a hand was sent to the wheel, and with a screech from her whistle the tug went ahead.

With a snort she began to move: the hawser sprang from her eddying wake, dripping and snaking as it took the strain; a ripple appeared round the *Higgins'* cutwater, and her bowsprit slowly swung round until it headed for the Golden Gate.

The mate went aft, and the bosun called out:

"That'll do, men; get your breakfast. You'll be turned to in half-an-hour."

CHAPTER II
"THE RULE OF THE BELAYING-PIN"

A shock-headed and tattered ragamuffin of a ship's boy crept off to the galley, and returned with a steaming kid of wet hash.

"Got no pannikin or plate, I suppose, Broncho?" asked the rolling-stone.

"I shorely don't reckon I needs them heretofore. I makes this trip some abrupt, as you-alls knows, an' I overlooks the same complete. Mebbe though I can rustle some tin-ware from the 'old woman.'"[1]

At these words a heavily-built, red-shirted man who had been sitting silently in the next bunk, looked up with a keen glance at the cowboy and asked:

"Say, stranger, was you on the Cross-bar outfit last fall? I seems to recall them feachers o' yours some."

"So?" returned Broncho politely.

"I was a-ditching on Hunker Creek," went on the red-shirted man. "You hits my camp a-trailing some horses which you allows some doggoned greasers has gone an' lifted. My name's Ben Sluice—Bedrock Ben they calls me down Arizona way."

"My mem'ry's plumb onreliable an' scattered this maunin'," replied the cowpuncher; "but I shorely recalls them greasers, now you speaks."

"And I'm sliding out chips you catches 'em all right?"

"Which we shorely does, mebbe two days later, an' swings 'em up to two cottonwoods without any ondue delays," said the cattle-ranger indifferently.

Then, turning to the tattooed Britisher, who had just managed to procure him a plate, pannikin, and cutlery, he inquired with a sly twinkle in his eye:

"How's that 'ere sun lookin' to-day, Jack?"

Now the rolling-stone was a keen watcher of the heavens, and in his chest he kept a big star telescope which, from the care he took of it, seemed to be his chief joy in life.

Many an hour of a hard-earned night watch below had he spent with his eye glued to that glass, and he was a mine of queer information and out-of-the-way knowledge on the subject of sun, moon, and stars, and with a certain air of pride and self-satisfaction he was wont to describe himself as an "astronomical weather-prophet."

At Broncho's question he threw up his head like a war-horse scenting battle, and replied with the gravity befitting such a serious subject:

"The sun rose well this morning, and I expect calm weather with light variable airs before we take the trades."

Ben Sluice the miner looked up in surprise at Jack's professional weather-clerk air.

"I presumes the 'old gentleman's' healthy, and ain't been a-developin' of measles none lately?" ventured the cowboy meekly.

"Well, Broncho, I'm afraid there is a small spot beginning to show faintly on the lower disk," declared the Britisher.

"You don't say? That 'ere luminary is shore misfortunate that away. You-alls recalls how he suffers so bad from that malady when we're out on the Circle-dot outfit together. I allow his grub is too heatin'," drawled the cowpuncher with a faint smile.

Meanwhile, sundry black bottles had made their appearance and been passed round. Voices began to be raised, Hollins, the irrepressible cockney, especially being full of talk.

"Well, byes, stryke me, but we're h'all in the syme boat. This mykes the tenth bloody time h'I've been shanghaied, but—oh lor! Black Dyvis! My crymes, byes, wait till you see'd 'im use a belayin'-pin; h'I've sailed with 'im afore, an' h'I knows——"

"The divil, but if it's a bastin' the rascal wants, I'll be after tryin' to oblige him ivery time," cried a wild-looking Irishman.

"'E'll give you h'all you wants at turn-to time, Pat, I tells ye stroight."

At this moment a slight diversion was caused by Jack Derringer unearthing the occupant of the bunk below his own, so that the cowpuncher could have it.

"Now den, what de hell——" began a big German as he found himself seized by the scruff of his neck and yanked out on to the deck.

"You scout round for another berth, Dutchy; this man here"—pointing to Broncho—"is going to have that bunk," said the rolling-stone coolly, as he seated himself on his big chest and began to fill a well-smoked briar.

"You tink you am cock o' dis foc's'le. Wait, mine fine fellah, you see different bresently," growled the Dutchman, picking himself up slowly.

But he took care to keep his distance from the muscular Britisher, and retired to the other end of the foc's'le, frowning ferociously as a general laugh arose at his discomfiture.

Suddenly the deck seemed to lift slowly; then there was a sidelong lurch and a rattle of falling tin-ware, as plates and pannikins slid off chests and fell to leeward.

A slight swell was beginning to make itself felt as the *Higgins* neared the entrance of the Golden Gate.

"The divil take you, ye rowlin' hooker," yelled Pat, as he dived after his pannikin.

"Motion affect you, Broncho?" asked Jack.

"My innards ain't presumin' none so far," replied the shanghaied cattleman calmly. "Barrin' it's some like the heavin' of an earthquake I once was in down San Laredo way, I ain't takin' no account of it"; and he took out a corncob pipe, cut a plug, and was soon puffing away quite at his ease.

"That's *bueno*," went on Jack approvingly. "When we turn to you'll have to go aloft; it's a bit of a hard graft the first time, but it'll soon come as easy to you as branding calves."

"If you-alls has to go up them rope-ladders, it's a cinch[2] that this here shorthorn'll be in on the deal, an' I'm willing to bet a stack o' blues I ain't none behind before the draw, neither. I ain't gettin' tangled up in my rope none as to this here climbin' game. I surmise it ain't none plumb easy, but if my old wall-eyed pinto can't pitch me into the heavenly vaults, it's a hoss on me if this here ship can."

"I expect there'll be the usual trouble when we turn to," continued the Britisher. "Mind your luff, old son, and don't hit back, or they'll lay you out."

"Do you-alls assert as how I'm to let that big hoss-thief come man-handlin' me without puttin' up some kind o' bluff."

"That's about the size of it; you'll only get the worst of it if you do. Take my word for it. Watch my play and whirl a mighty small loop."

At this moment the bosun's deep voice was heard outside:

"Turn-to, men, an' get them moorin' wires rolled up and the big lines below."

Slowly they began to shuffle out of the foc's'le.

"Snakes!" roared the black-browed mate, coming forward in three springs; "is this a funeral procession, or what?"

Armed with a belaying-pin, he sprang to the door of the foc's'le and showered down blows upon the head and shoulders of each man in turn.

"Jump, you packet-rats, jump!" he bellowed.

"Is it jump ye want?" cried Pat, and came out flying with one mighty leap.

Down went the pair of them, and this was the signal for the fight to begin.

As Pat and Black Davis struggled in furious embrace on the deck, a big red-headed English man came charging to Pat's assistance.

"H'it's slaughter from the word go!" screeched the cockney, and with the fiery tanglefoot tingling through his veins he dashed madly upon the second mate, a short but tough-built block of a man called Barker.

The scene now grew wild and furious, and as Broncho remarked afterwards:

"It shore were a jimdandy fight!"

The mates were buckos with a reputation to keep up, and whilst many of the crew were rendered half mad by the bad liquor which had been passed round at breakfast, several of them—such as Pat, Red Bill, who had gone to his assistance, Hank, an American, and one or two others—had their names to uphold as bad men.

Curses, yells, groans, and the thud of falling men resounded over the ship.

The fierce brutal mates, like wolves amongst a herd of swine, gloried in this exhibition of their strength, their animal natures revelled in the cruelty, and the lust of spilt blood was upon them.

With ponderous fists and scrunching belaying-pins they smote the hapless ones, who, weak from their shore debauch, with splitting heads and unsteady feet, yet with the courage of rage and bad liquor, offered a desperate resistance.

It was a struggle of savages. Old Adam, with his coat of civilisation torn off, let his primitive passions have free sway.

It was the barbaric test of survival by bodily strength. The whole question turned upon whether the mates were strong enough to rule their crew, and glorying in their strength, they stepped into the realms of brutality to prove their fitness and superiority over the men.

The greater the resistance the more they were pleased; they took a keen delight in exhibiting their methods of Yankee discipline. These violent methods they had reduced to such a deep science that they could fell a man with a belaying-pin in such a way as to cause no permanent injury.

Black Davis jumped with his heavy sea-boots full upon the ribs of the gross German, who lay gasping in the scuppers, and, strange to say, the result was nothing worse than a bad bruise.

But the sea is a hard master, and its followers must needs be tough to a degree to survive. Life on a wind-jammer soon weeds out the weaklings, who leave the lists worn out, broken, and spent.

Jack and Broncho tried their best to avoid being drawn into the vortex of the battle, but were suddenly confronted by the bosun as they prowled cautiously round the midshiphouse.

"What the devil are you two doing? Skulking, hey? Jump forrard an' help overhaul that port chain."

So back they had to go into the midst of the fray, where the two mates, surrounded by a yelling crowd, were fairly making things hum.

"Reg'lar New Orleans style o' towin' out!" gasped the cockney to Jack, as he skipped round the fore-hatch windlass to avoid the boot of Black Davis, whose eyes gleamed like those of a wild beast through blood and matted hair.

"Ho! ye murtherin' baste, ye, I have ye now," cried Pat with a wild Irish yell, and he sprang full on the mate from the top of the house, whence he had climbed by the iron ladder.

Down went the pair of them for the second time, and when the mate gained his feet one eye was closed, whilst Pat was spitting blood and teeth out of his capacious mouth.

As Jack bent down to lay hold of the chain, Barker, the second mate, sprang upon him, screeching venomously.

"I'll teach yew, me loafin' beachcomber; yew don't come it over Jim Barker none so easy, me pretty chanty-man."

The Britisher gave a peculiar smile—the little bruiser had grievously misrated his man.

Jack's easy smile drove him to a frenzy. His burly fist shot out straight from the shoulder, a knock-out blow aimed at the point of the rover's chin.

Jack grinned broadly as he jerked his head to one side. Then, as the second mate's arm shot over his shoulder into space, he seized it by the wrist with one hand. There was a quick half-twist, a slight pull, and the amazed bucko found himself lying on his back, trying to realise that brute force was of little use against the science of a Japanese wrestler.

But it was the only point scored against the mates in the contest. Jack turned calmly back to his work under the superintendence of the bosun, and Barker, scrambling to his feet, wisely decided to leave the "durned Britisher" alone, turning to wreak vengeance instead upon an undersized dago.

Presently a tall lean man was seen approaching from aft. He had the long hooked beak of a hawk, thin firmly shut lips, and a goatee chin-tuft, whilst from under shaggy grey eyebrows his steely blue eyes gleamed forth with a very sinister glitter.

It was Captain Bob Riley, the "old man," one of the most notorious of down-east skippers, a hard nut in sea parlance, but, like all down-east deep-water men, a fine seaman.

He arrived just in time to hold off a dago, who, with uplifted knife and a wild cry of "Me keela you, me keela you!" was springing upon the second mate.

The latter had not noticed the dago's approach, being busily engaged in punching a Chilean, whose "carrajos" were getting fainter and fainter.

The old man's nickle-plated revolver had the effect of cooling matters down.

The mates had had a good enough fight even for their appetites. Red Bill had a broken arm. Bedrock Ben, who had been to sea before and was a regular hard case, lay senseless in the scuppers, from the effects partly of belaying-pins and partly of poisonous liquor. The faces of Pat and the cockney were hardly recognisable, and even Broncho was hugging a damaged wrist, though, as he explained:

"I shore never goes nearer than the outskirts of the fight."

The ship had now passed through the Golden Gate, and the deep blue of the Pacific lay before her, stretching away to the indigo of the horizon, behind which lay the languid islands of the South Seas.

The glorious azure of the Californian sky was covered with fleecy white clouds, and a freshening breeze from the norrard was rippling the water into flashes of snowy foam, upon which the sun's rays sparkled and glittered.

Ahead the tugboat puffed away serenely, whilst the tow-rope, stretching between the two vessels, glistened with dropping beads of crystal as it alternately sagged and dipped into the blue, then rose again dripping and tautened.

Away to windward a beautiful little schooner bobbed gracefully to the swell under fore-staysail and mainsail, as it waited ready to take the pilot aboard.

And now the stentorian voice of the huge bosun rang through the ship:

"All hands make sail!"

Mechanically the men climbed up the ratlines and wearily crept out on to the yards to cast loose the gaskets and overhaul the gear.

As soon as the topsails had been loosed, the capstans on the maindeck were manned, and the ship resounded with the tramp of the men at the bars.

The cowboy followed Jack Derringer aloft on the fore to loose the sails from the skysail down.

The cowpuncher, cool and collected, managed very well for his first trip aloft, and found no difficulty in following out Jack's instructions; but up on the main two new hands who had never been to sea before got into hopeless trouble.

One of them, but a youngster, who had given his name as Jimmy Green, seemed to have had what little sense he once possessed entirely knocked out of him by the rough treatment on deck, and could hardly hang on, so scared and nerveless was he; whilst the other, a much-befreckled man, whom the cattle-ranger had at once nicknamed Pinto, still suffered so much from the effects of the black bottle that giddiness almost sent him headlong to the deck.

In misery of mind the two poor wretches clambered out on to the footropes of the upper-topsail yard and clutched the jackstay with trembling fingers, and the stalwart presence of the British bosun was required before they could be induced to move.

"Let go thet clew-stopper, yew chunk-headed hayseed," roared the battered second mate to another poor imbecile up the mizzen. "Are yew sayin' y'r prayers, or d'ye think that t'gallant yard's your sweetheart?"

Slowly the great topsails rose and the gleaming cotton bellied out to the breeze.

And now the tug cast off, and, with a long toot of farewell, headed back for Frisco, whilst a small boat from the dainty schooner removed the pilot.

By noon all sail had been set, and the men were mustered aft for watch-picking. A sorry crew they looked after the battle towing out.

First of all their dunnage was overhauled by the mates for revolvers and knuckle-dusters. Broncho's weapon, however, they failed to discover, as his knowing friend, the rolling-stone, had carefully hidden it.

Whilst the watch-picking went on, the old man paced silently to windward on the poop, and the steward took the wheel.

The two mates stood scowling over the poop-rail at the mob of well-battered and singularly tattered men, who clustered in a sullen, silent group on the maindeck.

The mate, taking the first pick, slowly threw his eyes over the crowd in hesitation.

Then he called out Hank, a long, tough Yankee already mentioned, who lurched leisurely to the port side.

A whirling belaying-pin interrupted his meditations, and Black Davis roared like an angry lion.

"Snakes alive, d'yew think we're goin' ter idle 'round all day while y're takin' a pasear? Skip, ye great, long, whisky-soakin' swab."

Hank did skip with remarkable agility as the pin whistled past him.

Then came the second mate's turn.

"Hyeh, yew, what's your ugly name?" he cried, pointing to Jack.

"Derringer, sir," answered the rolling-stone.

"Git over to starboard, Mister Derringer, sir!" he growled, and there was vitriol in his voice.

He had not forgotten that throw of Jack's whilst towing out, and there was murder in his heart as he glared at the Britisher.

Muller, the big German, was the mate's next choice, whilst Pat was taken by Barker.

Thus the watch-picking proceeded, but not without one or two further enlivening incidents.

Pinto reaped a black eye for not saying "Sir" when answering the mate, and Sam, a big buck nigger, was rolled in the scuppers for spitting on the deck.

To his great satisfaction the cowpuncher found himself in the same watch as Jack Derringer, in which were also Pat, Hollins, the cockney, Curly, the singer of the chanty "Away, Rio," who was a runaway English apprentice, Bedrock Ben, and the disabled Red Bill, the watch being completed by a man who called himself Studpoker Bob.

This last was one of those characters peculiar to Western America, who gain a living by dealing faro and studhorse poker in mining camp saloons. He had, of course, been shanghaied, and being a fatalist, like all gamblers, accepted his unpleasant position with apparent resignation. He was a long, scraggy individual with a thin, cadaverous face, shifty yellow eyes, and a huge jutting moustache.

In the port watch were Hank, Muller, Pedro, the Chilian dago, and his side-partner, Angelino, a Portuguee, Pinto, the freckled hobo, Jimmy Green, Sam, and the wretched ship's-boy, who answered simply to the appellation of "the kid."

Of the idlers, the bosun has already received attention. Chips was a quiet, harmless Norwegian named Hansen. There was no sailmaker; the steward was a nonentity and a tool of the old man's; whilst Lung, the cook, was one of those unfathomable Chinamen.

The starboard watch were now sent below until 4 p.m., and were speedily at work bandaging their many wounds, and putting their side of the foc's'le shipshape.

Red Bill went aft, and Captain Riley, an adept in such matters from much practice, skilfully set his broken arm.

Curly, being the youngest man in the watch, was appointed to the post of "peggy," and went off to the galley to fetch the dinner forward.

It was not very appetising, but, such as it was, was consumed eagerly, for the events of the morning had produced a hunger which did not blink at bad food.

Bedrock Ben, who looked a weird object with a great red handkerchief tied over his head and under his chin, started the conversation rolling with the remark:

"This is shore a red-hot ship, pards!"

"I'm surmisin' it were a some violent outfit myself," said Broncho reflectively.

"Bedad, an' ye're right, mate; this ould baste of a *Higgins* is after being called the hottest craft under the flag," put in Pat, with a shake of his fist towards Black Davis, who could be seen through the open door busily at work on the greenhorns. "But I'll be aven with ye yet, Mister Black Davis, be sure I will," he hissed.

Pat was feeling dangerously vindictive, for, with half his teeth loosened, his meal had been a source of pain.

"I don't know that she's worse than the *Frank N. Thayler*," remarked Jack.

"Well, I should smile! My crikey! W'y, the *Thayler's* a byby to this bloomin' 'ooker," grunted the cockney.

"Ever sailed in her?" asked Jack.

"No, thank Gaud!"

"Well, I saw her in Manila. Her decks were one mass of bloodstains; you couldn't get them out, either—holystoning only showed them up brighter. Her old man shot six men off the main-topsail yard. Some of her crew laid for him one day, and cut him open; but he recovered. That's what I call a hot ship."[3]

"I callate she's got to be some swift to rake in the pool against this craft, bloodstains or no bloodstains," drawled the gambler.

At this moment the sharp report of a Winchester rifle echoed through the ship.

Half the watch sprang to their feet with various exclamations.

"Gun-play, by all that's holy!" ejaculated Bedrock Ben.

"Some locoed critter goin' against rope," hazarded Broncho coolly, as they crowded to the door.

But the cockney did not stir from his bunk.

"Old man a-shootin' o' gulls, I h'expec'," he remarked; "'e's blawsted fond o' killin' them pore 'armless birds, the slaughterin' swyne."

Again a report came, and a gull wheeling astern fell dead in the frothy wake.

"He's shore a crackerjack with his weepon," commented Broncho admiringly.

The old man, who was a magnificent shot, soon scared away the following gulls, but not before he had accounted for three of them.

Well knowing what an impression his fine shooting would make upon his crew, it had become a regular policy with him on starting a passage to exhibit his marksmanship.

FOOTNOTES:

[1] "Old woman," a cattle-ranging term for the cook.

[2] *Cinch.* The *cinch* corresponds in an American saddle to the English girth. To cinch a girth up is to draw it tight by means of several turns of strap or rope between the ring of

the girth and a ring on the saddle, and from this the word has come to being used in a variety of ways; for instance, Cinch on to that—catch on to that; It's a cinch that—it's a certainty that; What a cinch!—what a good thing! what an easy thing!

[3] True.

CHAPTER III
"THE USE OF A SHEATH-KNIFE"

Contrary to the astronomical prophet's forecast, the *Higgins* was lucky in carrying the northerly breeze until she picked up the "trades," and the third day out all hands were turned to shifting sail.

By this time Broncho was beginning to feel his feet. He was fortunate in having such a useful friend as Jack Derringer, who showed him the right way to set about his work and saved him from many a trouble.

It is to be doubted if Broncho's untamed cowboy spirit would have put up with Barker's bullying and insulting tongue if it had not been for Jack's strong influence and keen common-sense way of viewing and explaining everything.

The rolling-stone, except for strange spells of melancholy, when he seemed to be lost in gloomy thoughts and was hard to get a word out of, had a way of looking at everything from a comic point of view, and his infectious smile and cool comments time and again turned Broncho's smouldering wrath into mirth.

The cowboy prided himself on his philosophical way of taking fate. His strong points were his virile manhood, his fortitude against misfortune, and his daredevil bravery, and in these traits he found an equal, if not a superior, in the cool, self-possessed Britisher.

Only once was the cowpuncher ever heard to discuss his friend, and that was in one of his queer outbursts of thought.

"This world is shore like a poker game. Some parties is mean an' no account, like an ace high or pair of deuces; some's middlin', an' has their good an' bad p'ints, like a pair o' bullets or two low pair in a Jack-pot; some gents outhold the rest as a general play, like three of a kind; but is likewise downed themselves by sech superior persons who, like flushes an' full houses, is bang full o' sand, sense, an' 'nitiative; but thar's only one sport I ever rounds up against who's got all the vartues of a four of a kind, an' that man's Derringer Jack—he's shore four aces an' the joker."

Shifting sail started off smoothly enough, chiefly owing to the bosun, who knew how to get work out of men without using a belaying-pin.

An old Blackwall rigger, he was the very beau ideal of what a bosun ought to be, and the sight of his spars and rigging was as good for the old man's liver as a ten-knot breeze astern.

One day the man at the wheel overheard Captain Bob commenting aloud to himself after a keen look round his ship.

"Me mates be all right as long as it's thumpin' men an' ship-cleaning as is the ticket; but when it comes to marlin-spike an' riggers work, that 'ere durned lime-juicer kin give 'em cards an' spades."

The bosun, however, was far from being popular with the bucko mates, as his methods of enforcing discipline were much too tame to gain their approval.

"Them doggoned lemon-pelters never could handle men; they coddles em an' spiles 'em. Human nature requires whippin', an' if them skulkin' 'possums don't get a sort o' warnin' pretty frequent, they're liable to get thinkin' they've got the bulge on us," remarked Black Davis to Barker one morning in disgust, as he watched the bosun, Jack, and Paddy chatting amiably together whilst they were at work patching a fair-weather topsail on the maindeck.

These two bullies spent their time looking for trouble. Their one delight seemed to be to haze the men and knock them about; they had already beaten every bit of spirit out of those two poor greenhorns, Pinto and Jimmy Green, whilst Sam, the great buck nigger, who topped Black Davis by at least half a foot, and Barker by more, fairly rolled his eyes in terror when either one of these worthies approached or spoke to him; they knocked the cowards about unmercifully, and even such gluttons for a fight as Pat and the cockney got their fair share of hard usage.

But neither Jack Derringer nor the cowboy had been touched since the towing out.

It was a mystery to all hands why Jack escaped so easily. It was not by reason of his muscle, which was not so apparent on the surface as that of the big nigger. It was not because they liked him, for any one could see with half an eye that the pair fairly detested him, and yet their mysterious fear of the rolling-stone seemed greater than their hate. It was not a ferocity of manner or a desperado air that caused this fear, for although Jack had a quiet way of taking the lead and ordering others about which had already made him cock of the foc's'le, his rule forward was far from being that of a despot; it was rather that of an easy-going, level-headed man, gentle but firm. Being also the only educated man forward except the young English apprentice, his advice and counsel were in constant demand.

Even he, however, could not understand his freedom from ill-treatment. Several times he complained in the foc's'le with a queer grin that he was not getting his fair share of belaying-pin soup. It actually seemed to annoy him, and he began to air his wit on the buckos in such an insolent, daring fashion that the men, hearing him, shook in their shoes at his temerity.

There was no mystery forward, however, about Broncho's escape from brutality.

It was known aft, of course, that he was a cowboy from the south-west, and Jack, with infinite cunning, had made Broncho out to the bosun a terrible desperado:

"One of the most noted 'bad men' of the West," he declared. "Known and feared from Arizona to the Kootenay, from Texas to the Pacific slope, with more notches on his six-shooter than years to his life."

This precious character, together with several blood-curdling episodes of his career, invented on the spur of the moment by the rover's fertile brain, was in due course passed on to the after gang, with the result that Broncho was treated with a strange deference by the buckos, much to the amusement of the hands forward who were in the know.

Barker took care that all the easiest work came the desperado's way, and often he would favour him in small ways, and even yarn with him, when the old man was below, in the hopes of hearing from his own lips one of his many deeds of blood. But all the time the bucko was nervous and ill at ease; his own gory record seemed mean and petty compared to the cowboy's wholesale butcheries. One night he buttonholed the cowpuncher whilst he was coiling up gear on the poop, and asked him to spin the yarn of how he killed the seven greasers at Tombstone, and Broncho had a chance of giving free rein to his inventive powers.

The nickname also of Bucking Broncho, which had long replaced the cowboy's real name, helped to promote the deception, which occasioned much unholy joy in the starboard foc's'le.

Thus it was that the buckos treated Broncho with almost servility, though they daily did their best to arouse every passion of hate, revenge, and murder in the rest of the ship's company.

But the sand in the time-glass of fate was nearly run out for one of them.

Whilst the bosun and some hands were busy bending the fore-topsails, the second mate went aloft on the main with Jack, Broncho, Ben Sluice, Pedro, and Sam.

They had just hoisted up the main upper-topsail ready for bending. Barker took his post at the bunt, Jack going out to the weather earing, with Broncho next to him, and Pedro inside next to Barker; whilst Ben and Sam went out on to the lee yardarm, where they were in a short time joined by Curly, who had been waiting below to let go the spilling-lines.

The head of the sail was spread out along the yard, the earings passed, and they were all busy making it fast to the jackstay.

Suddenly Barker, who had been watching for an opportunity to raise trouble, noticed that Pedro had skipped a roving.

"Yew mongrel skunk— —" he began, raising his fist to strike the dago; but the sentence was never finished and the blow never fell, for the hot southern blood, raised to boiling-point by long-pent-up passion, burst beyond Pedro's control.

With one flashing movement and a yell of fury, he plunged his knife up to the hilt in the mate's breast.

With a deep groan, Barker fell back against the mast, bleeding profusely.

Ben, catching the stricken man in his arms, vainly tried to staunch the wound; but it was all up with the second mate, who was too far gone even for speech.

As Ben held him there was a gurgle in his throat, and a stream of bright lung blood poured from his mouth.

"You've been an' gone an' done it this time," said the ex-miner to Pedro.

"Me keela lo gringo brute. *Carrajo, esta bueno!*" remarked the South American coolly, with a self-satisfied air.

"It's some obvious you've coppered his play," said Broncho.

"I allows he's done jumped this earthly game for good," he added, turning to Jack and indicating Barker, who already had the death-rattle in his throat.

"Yes, I'm afraid he's *pelili* [4]; these buckos are always looking for it, and they generally get it in the end," answered Jack quietly. "I heard him call Pedro by a name yesterday which it's suicidal to use to any of the Latin races, and one I've frequently seen cause gun-play in the West, as no doubt you have too."

There was a hush on the yard as they watched the dying man, who was already unconscious.

It was not a pleasant sight, but was viewed by Jack, Broncho, and Ben Sluice with calm eyes and level pulses. All three had been familiar with death in many strange and horrible forms, and their senses were blunted to the keenness of the horror.

But Curly, only a boy in years, hung over the yardarm white and sick and shaking, whilst Sam, the coloured man, drew back frightened and nerveless.

The dago, however, stared indifferently, as cool and unmoved as a Sioux Indian.

Suddenly death came! There was a spasmodic twitching of the limbs, a sudden gush of blood from the mouth, nose, and ears, the pupils of the eyes grew glassy, their whites showed, the head dropped back heavily on Ben's shoulder, and the complexion took on that strange appearance of wax as the bucko's spirit fled.

Shifting sail is a busy bit of work. The bosun and his men on the fore, with their backs turned, were busy stretching their sail to a chorus, all in ignorance of the tragedy which had just occurred; whilst Black Davis, with the rest of the hands, was in the sail-locker, putting away the unbent sails.

At this moment he appeared on deck, followed by a line of men shouldering a main course, which looked for all the world like a huge white serpent, coming along the deck on six pairs of legs.

It was a delicious day. The north-east trade wind was light, and the *Higgins* was sneaking along over the deep blue of the Pacific, doing hardly six knots.

The bright sun shone upon the gleaming cotton canvas, giving it the dazzling appearance of snow.

As the mate stepped forward of the mainmast, he glanced casually up at the men at work above.

The first thing to catch his eye was the red stain of blood on the bellying breast of the topsail, and then he noticed that the men on the yard seemed to be all crowded into the bunt.

"Brazen sarpints! What the tarnation hell air yew doin' up thar?" he roared.

"Second mate's got badly stuck, sir," replied Jack.

"Who stuck him?"

"Dat er dago, Pedro, sah," shouted Sam, who was not a special friend of the little Chilian.

Black Davis had seen many a fatality of this sort, and to his credit it may be said that, whatever the emergency, it always found him ready.

"Bosun!" he roared, "git down off thet yard an' fetch a pair er handcuffs!"

The whole ship was now awake to the fact that a tragedy had occurred.

The old man appeared through the companion-way with his Winchester crooked under his arm, and going to the rail of the poop, sang out to know if the second mate was badly hurt.

"He's done cashed in his checks, sir!" Ben Sluice roared back.

"Better send up a bosun's chair to get the body down on deck, sir," sang out Jack.

"All right, all right, not so durned full o' talk up thar," growled the old man.

An atmosphere of excitement began to pervade the ship, and all work was dropped. Those who were up the fore scrambled quickly to the deck, and began feverishly to discuss the matter with Black Davis's gang, in charge of the main course.

Black Davis, swinging himself on to the rail, slowly started the ascent of the main rigging.

"'Oo did they say stuck 'im?" asked the cockney.

"Yew bet it's thet dago cuss Pedro done carved him up. I see'd the devil stickin' out a foot outen them black eyes er his; I've just been waitin' ter see him get his claws into one of 'em," replied Hank, taking a mighty bite out of a plug of tobacco, which he proceeded to chew vigorously.

"Gee-up! gee-up! Pedro kill-um one piecee boss number two velly muchee chop-chop! Me heap flaid—no likee funee business; plenty muchee solly!" ejaculated Lung, looking out through his galley door.

"You thinks as 'ow it's goin' to raise trouble, does ye, ye bloomin' h'opium-slave?" remarked Hollins, with the insolent tone of one addressing an inferior being.

"And I ain't so sure the chink ain't right neither," put in Hank.

"Der teufel ish dode, und it serves him recht; he was lookin' for it," grunted Muller, the German.

"You're right, Dutchy. He were playing for a show-down an' the dago plumb euchred him," remarked the gambler, Studpoker Bob. "An' if thet other golderned bucko don't mind his little game some, he'll find himself up against the iron likewise," he continued in a lower tone, with an upward glance full of sinister meaning.

"I reckon he ain't easily gallied,[5]" said Hank. "It'll take a man with a mighty stiff backbone to heave that beggar to, an' you may lay to that."

"Begorr, but there's men in this foc's'le would be after batin' the eye-teeth out of him," burst in the eager Paddy.

"Not in the port foc's'le, son; yew bet he's got us all skeert."

"Be me sowl, but he ain't goin' to come it over us starbowlines none, or he'll get the divil's own larrupin'," said Pat fiercely.

"Who's goin' to do ther larrupin'?" inquired Hank scornfully.

"I'm due to get square with that ladybuck myself, bad luck to him."

"Holy Gee! but he'd fair eat yew, Pat, an' ask for more."

"Faith, an' would he thin. Well, he wouldn't be atin' of Jack Derringer none so aisy, anyhow. Be the Powers! but Jack could knock his d— —d head off."

FOOTNOTES:

[4] Kaffir word meaning "finished," "done."

[5] Whaling term meaning "scared."

CHAPTER IV "BARBARISM"

The bosun now appeared with the handcuffs, and they were speedily sent aloft with a bosun's chair. And now every eye was turned on the topsail yard to see Black Davis put the handcuffs on his prisoner.

To go up on to that yard, with a raging dago waiting to knife you as you stepped on to the footrope, required nerve, and the mate knew that he was in a ticklish position, and that he could expect no help from the other men on the yard.

Yet there was no hesitation about Black Davis; the man was so made constitutionally that he really did not know what fear was.

"Git the dago's knife an' sling it overboard," he sang out to Broncho, as he climbed out of the top.

At this Pedro bared his teeth like a tiger at bay, and turned upon the cowpuncher with knife ready.

"He shore has me treed," said Broncho to Jack. "I ain't organisin' to bluff that bowie o' his, or he has me p'inting out on the heavenly trail too prompt for words."

It was evident that Broncho was helpless against the desperate southerner, and was more than likely to get killed in his turn if he made the slightest attempt to wrest Pedro's knife from him.

"The dago has me out-held, sir; he's due to cut me open a whole lot if I makes a move," called Broncho to the mate.

At this, Black Davis, who was half-way up the topmast rigging, pulled out his gun, and pointing it at Pedro, sang out:

"Heave thet knife overboard, or I'll fill yew full of holes, yew dogasted West Coast beachcomber."

Quick as a flash Pedro turned and launched his knife full at the mate. It stuck quivering and shaking between the strands of the wire shroud, which, as Black Davis leant forward, was touching the top button of his waistcoat.

It was a close call!

Pedro, helpless without his weapon, snarled round like a wild beast; then, with wonderful agility, drew himself up on to the yard, and stepping on Broncho's hand, before any one could divine his intention, he sprang into the rigging on the opposite side to Black Davis, and in a moment was up over the crosstrees and running up the ratlines to the topgallant yard.

"Come de-own outer that!" roared the enraged and baffled mate. "Come down, or I'll perforate yew."

The Chilian gave a wild laugh as he reached over before swinging himself on to the topgallant yard.

The bosun sprang into the rigging and hurried aloft to support his superior officer.

Meanwhile, the old man looked on impatiently from the poop, fingering his rifle nervously, evidently debating what to do.

Then up went his Winchester. There was a heavy report, and the wretched Pedro, straddled with one foot on the ratlines and one on the footrope, spun suddenly round, threw up his hands, and dropped.

Just below him were the crosstrees, and on to these he fell, and, held there, lay senseless with head and feet dangling.

For a moment there was a deadly silence over the ship; then a low, menacing growl of rage rose from the crowd of men on the maindeck.

"Silence there, yew mutinous dogs! Silence, or, sure as my name's Bob Riley, I'll pump some lead into yew!" roared the old man, bringing the gun up to his shoulder again.

As he spoke the canvas began to shake; the helmsman had let the ship run up into the wind. Little wonder if, in the excitement of the moment, Angelino could find no time for glancing at the compass.

In a moment the ship was all aback.

"Darn my dogbasted skin!" raged the old man, turning upon the unfortunate Portuguee. "Hard up thet wheel! Quick, yew infernal lunkhead!"

Then, rushing to the rail, he roared:

"Down from aloft there. On ter the foc's'le head, some er yew. Don' stand gazin' round, yew moon-struck, mongrel crowd o' Bowery slush! Clap on to them weather jib sheets! Let go to loo'ard! Neow, then, round with them fore-yards—round with 'em!"

For a few minutes terrific confusion reigned. Excited men ran hither and thither, braces were thrown off the pins, and a medley of cries resounded over the ship, half drowned in the thunderous clatter of the flapping canvas.

Jack, Broncho, Sam, and Curly came sliding down backstays, leaving Bedrock Ben still with the dead man in his arms.

By this time the old man was half mad with fury, and dancing a regular war-jig aft. Words poured in a torrent from his mouth, cut off, distorted, and half senseless as they burst from his stuttering lips.

Certainly the facts of the case were enough to try the temper of any man as full of bile and ginger as a down-east skipper. His ship aback; a crew of lunatics running wildly about the deck, letting go sheets, lifts, spilling-lines, anything in their craziness; two dead men aloft, and with them his only remaining officers; last, but not least, two half-bent fair-weather topsails flogging angrily in the strengthening breeze, with every chance of splitting from top to bottom.

"Carpenter!" he yelled. "Carpenter, get them headsheets over! Sakes alive—bust me purple—what er mess! Hyeh, y' ravin' idiots, what y' doin'? Get on ter thet fore-brace. Come down, bosun. Jeerusalem, look at them t'p'sls! Hell an' damnation, who let go that sheet? Carpenter, ye mouldy wood-sawyer, can't yew thump 'em? Beat 'em, kill 'em, jump on 'em, man. Wal, I swow! What the blazin' flames o' hell d'yew think y' doin', yew bean-swillin', lop-eared Dutch swab——" and so he raged on.

What with the old man's scathing remarks and his own confused brain, the carpenter got in such a flurry that he hardly knew what he was doing.

Slowly things were straightened out, with the headsheets over to windward. On the advent of Jack and his gang from aloft, the foreyard was swung, and gradually the ship began to pay off under the influence of the backed headyards.

With the appearance of the huge bosun, calm and collected in the midst of the chaos, something like order began to prevail on deck. The *Higgins* was got on to her course, the yards trimmed, and whilst some of the hands were sent aloft to finish bending the two topsails, Ben Sluice and the body of the second mate were lowered to the deck in the bosun's chair.

The captain's bullet proved to have only grazed the forehead of the dago and stunned him, upon discovering which the mate had the senseless man roughly lowered down in a running bowline from the gantline block.

As Black Davis reached the deck, the old man, who was still fuming like a smouldering volcano, turned upon him with a withering glare.

"Hm, mister mate, an' a nice bunglin' yew made of it up aloft, lettin' a miserable little deck-swab of er Chilanean make a fool er yew like that. Ain't yew ever put the bracelets on a man before? Y'll have ter hustle round considerable mor'n this, or yew won't suit Cappen Bob Riley"; and with a final snort the irate skipper disappeared down the companion.

Mr. Bucko Davis turned back to his work in no very sweet frame of mind.

The body of the second mate had been placed on the main-hatch, and alongside it was laid the senseless form of Pedro.

"Hyeh, boy!" growled the mate to the kid, who was at work outside the galley, peeling potatoes for the cabin dinner. "Git er bucket er water an' see if yew can't wake thet dago up."

The boy drew a bucket over the side, and then, with shaking hands, tilted it gently over the face of the South American; but with his big brown eyes dilating with fright, the kid went very gingerly to work.

"Thet won't do, thet won't do," grunted Black Davis. "Give it ter me! Can't yew throw water yet?"

Seizing the bucket, with a true bosun's swing the mate hove the water over the unconscious man, with such skill that not one square inch of him from head to heel escaped the deluge.

"More water! more water! Neow then, jump around lively," called the angry demon impatiently.

With the sousing the mate gave him, Pedro could only do one of two things, either lie there and be drowned or come to his senses.

This latter he proceeded to do whilst the kid was drawing a fourth bucketful.

"Thought thet'd rouse the skunk," commented Black Davis; then, grabbing hold of the wretched man by the scruff of his neck, he dragged him off the hatch, and, dropping him on the deck, gave him three terrific kicks over the ribs.

"P'raps thet'll learn yew who's mate o' this ship, yew knifing beast; ther's one fer the second mate an' two fer me, 'count of all the trouble y've given me."

The miserable Pedro now broke out into low moans.

"Hm! Just like er dago! Cuts er man up an' then whines," went on the bucko, as he picked up the handcuffs off the hatch; then for a moment he stood hesitating, evidently turning something over in his mind.

Meanwhile the bosun had all hands busily engaged bending the main course. As the sail was stretched and the rovings passed, a subdued muttering went on, which in the present ugly humour of the men the bosun wisely took no notice of.

Presently there was a hail from the deck.

"Bosun, send me down er couple er them jailbirds o' yours."

A low, sibilant hiss of deadly venom ran along the yard at the sound of the mate's voice.

"Hm!" thought the bosun as he listened, "there's some of 'em pretty near ready for a word spelt with a big M."

He scanned the men on the yard for a moment in silence, and then carefully picked out two harmless ones.

"Pinto an' you, Green, get down on deck an' see what the mate wants."

With ludicrous haste these two worthies hurried down the ratlines, for they knew by experience what it meant to keep Black Davis waiting.

"Neow, yew two," said the mate, "skip forrard, an' if yew ain't got thet bosun's locker cleared out in two jiffs, thar'll be all-fired trouble."

They dashed off like a pair of frightened colts, and in record time reappeared with the statement that the locker was entirely bare.

"Left no blocks an' marlin-spikes behind, have yew?" asked the mate suspiciously.

"No, sir," came the reply in a hasty duet.

"Wall, I guess yew know what'll happen if yew have," he said with meaning.

"Neow, pick up the body of the second mate, take it forrard, an' lay it on the shelf," he went on.

"Aye, aye, sir!" came the hurried duet again.

As the two men rolled staggering off with the heavy form of the dead bucko, Black Davis turned to the dago on the deck.

"Know what I'm goin' ter do with yew, Mister Mate-killer? No? Wall, y'll soon find out. I reckon I'll have yew some tamed before I done with yew! Neow then, up yew git."

Except for a deep groan Pedro took no notice. At this the mate seized him by his shirt-collar and dragged him on to his feet.

For a moment the poor wretch swayed tottering, and then, with a great effort, collected his strength and retained his equilibrium.

"Oh, yew can stand, hey? Wall, neow, suppose yew walk forrard into thet bosun's locker."

Unsteadily Pedro lurched forward, dragging himself along slowly, followed by the bucko dangling the handcuffs.

The bosun's locker was small, and there was hardly room for the mate and his victim besides the dead man on the shelf; and as Black Davis entered, the miserable Chilian backed up against the bulkhead in doubt as to what was going to happen next.

"Hold out y'r hand," commanded the mate; and as Pedro obeyed, he snapped the handcuff on it; the other he slowly clasped upon the wrist of the dead bucko, whilst Pinto and Jimmy Green, standing hesitating what to do, watched him with eyes of horror from the doorway.

"I'll just see how yew like a night o' that, chained to a stiff of y'r own killing," said the demon, with a fiendish chuckle. "Wall, yew've got better company than yew ever had before. A pleasant night to yew!" and he retired, locking the door after him.

The bosun was now put at the head of the starboard watch, and the routine of the ship once more continued on its normal course.

Shifting sail was again in full swing, but the men worked listlessly in deadly silence; there was no chantying on the gantline, and they pulled and hauled without even the usual hee-hawing.

The bosun tried again and again to instil some life into the work, but in vain; all hands went at it steadily, but without a sound.

It is a very bad sign when a ship's crew work in silence, and even the mate ceased his hazing as he noticed the sullen humour of the men. You can bully and ill-treat a deep-sea crew as much as you like up to a certain point; but there is a limit mark, and if you step beyond that you begin playing pitch-and-toss with your own life.

The sea is not to blame for every missing ship. A steady-going, harmless man can be turned by continual brutality and ill-treatment into a desperate, iron-nerved assassin, and a good crew can be brought to such a condition that one accidental spark will set them afire; then, rendered half madmen, half fiends, they turn the ship into a shambles.

There is only one thing that protects the lives of American buckos, and that is that nowadays deep-water ships go to sea with such a mixed lot of nationalities in their foc's'les that they are totally unable to act together. The after-gang realise this fully, and work upon it, skilfully playing the men off against each other.

Whilst the ship's company were seething with passions which threatened to boil over at any moment, no sound came from the bosun's locker, where Pedro crouched alone with his victim.

At meal-times his food was passed in to him, in the presence of the mate; then the key was turned again, and he was left to brood anew with the blood-stained corpse attached to him like a Siamese twin.

At eight bells, 4 p.m., the decks were cleared up and the watches set once more.

At knock-off time all hands assembled on the foc's'le head, and a babble of wild, angry voices arose, in which the shrill squeal of Angelino, the Portuguee, Pedro's chum, mixed discordantly with the deep gutturals of the negro, the jerky sh's of the German, the twangy nasal accents of the Americans, and the misplaced h's of the cockney.

Grimy fists were waved and shaken furiously aft, and the venomous oratory of the long, vicious gambler, Studpoker Bob, was received with deep roars of approval.

Jack, Broncho, and Curly seated themselves apart from the wrangling crowd, and lit their pipes.

Curly, young, soft, and impressionable, was very indignant at the mate's callousness.

"It's enough to send Pedro off his head, chained in there all alone with that fearful corpse. It makes me creep to think of it. I shouldn't be surprised to hear screams from that bosun's locker before morning."

But Jack was not of his opinion.

"The dago's too near an animal for that. His nature's coarse-fibred, and though his blood is hot and excitable, his nerves are dull and only respond to the emotions of a brute."

"Which I concurs with them views entire," remarked Broncho. "I allows that dago's mighty familiar with corpses, an' no longer regyards them with respec'. That ain't no amature work, the way he uses his bowie; he weren't doin' no bluffin' on a four-card flush; the way he manip'lates his weepon shows he knows his game."

"Anyhow, it's a brutal shame, and from the way some of the men are talking I reckon Black Davis had better look out for squalls," cried Curly hotly.

"I don't think Davis is afraid of any man forrard; they talk too much. Listen to 'em now. He knows not one of them dare face him alone," said Jack.

"Still, I've seen marlin-spikes dropped from aloft, and on a dark night accidents easily happen," went on the ex-apprentice stubbornly.

"You bet, son, that ole pole-cat's got his ha'r-trigger fixed; he's plumb loaded with what you-alls call nerve, an' is due to make a mighty fervent play, however the kyards stacks up."

As Broncho spoke, the cockney's voice, loud and harsh, broke in upon them as he harangued his audience:

"H'it's a bloomin' shyme, byes, that's wot h'I calls it——" and the rest of his speech was drowned in the deep tones of the foc's'le bell, as the silent and suppressed kid, whose duty it was to keep time, sneaked up and struck eight bells.

CHAPTER V
"IN THE WATCHES OF THE NIGHT"

The starboard watch got slowly to their feet and tramped aft.

"Relieve the wheel and look-out!" called the mate.

It was Jack's wheel, and he was pleased, for he delighted in his night wheels, when, steering mechanically, like the born helmsman that he was, he allowed himself to get wrapped up in his thoughts.

The tropical nights always had the effect of stirring up half-forgotten memories in the breast of the rolling-stone, and after noting all his favourites gleaming above, he gradually lost himself in deep reverie.

The myriads of stars, studded like diamonds on the indigo robe of the heavens; the clear-cut moon, with its sparkling path of silver threads; the creamy wake, swirling astern in one blaze of phosphorus; the sharp outlines of spars, sails, and cordage, looking as if fashioned in ebony; the dreamy hum and soft caress of the gentle trade wind,—all these appealed intimately to the soul of the rover.

Forgotten were the stirring events of the day; he dreamed and dreamed in a paradise of his own, the beauty of the night recalling other such nights to him.

Once more he is mate of the rakish island schooner, lying lazily at anchor in some atoll lagoon, a bevy of flower-decked South Sea maidens dancing wildly on the maindeck to the soft tones of a guitar, the bright moon glistening on the swarthy faces of the Kanaka crew, seated round in squatting posture. The wild cries of the dancers are half-drowned in the deep boom of the distant surf and the rustling of the cocoa-palms rocked by the caressing breath of the steady-blowing zephyr.

Slowly the scene changes, the noise of wind and surf are hushed, the fairy dancers fade away, his luxurious hammock sinks to earth. He is alone, stretched at full length on the bare ground, a single blanket covering him; by his side is a trusty large-bore rifle, and at his feet a glowing camp-fire;

whilst around him, blocking out all but the sky, there stretches a thick entanglement of mimosa thorn.

Suddenly the silence is broken.

A deep, echoing roar rises on the night, swells and ceases, then breaks forth again, evidently nearer. He clutches his weapon.

His quick ear notes the uneasy whinny of his horse and the restless movement of the cattle. The king of beasts is looking for his dinner.

As he listens, the guttural notes of his Kaffir boy under the waggon whisper anxiously:

"Hark, Baas! Lapa! lapa! (There! there!)"

Again the scene fades, and he finds himself crouching in the smoky entrance of a teepee. Before him stretches the prairie, like a great, still ocean. In the foreground twisting lines of bent, naked forms hop and spring in fantastic figures, the moonlight glancing on their painted bodies. A discordant tomtom-beating mingles with wild whoops.

Gradually the ghost-dance grows quicker and quicker, the whooping redoubles, the dreary chant of a group of squaws swells in volume; then — —

Tink-tink! Tink-tink! Clear and sweet came the notes of the bell.

"'Ere, wake up, governor. You looks loike a bloke h'I once see'd a-walkin' in 'is sleep. Wot's the course?"

Jack started violently. It was the cockney come to relieve the wheel.

"South-a-half-west!" stammered the rover.

"South-a-'alf-west!" repeated Hollins, and Jack retreated forward.

And what were the thoughts of the murderer during that long night, as, hunched up with his back against the bulkhead and one nerveless hand held to the corpse, he crouched awaiting the dawn.

Was he thinking of life or of death, of the future or of the past?

Not he! His brain was vacant and his mind a blank; only his mouth was full, as he chewed steadily all through the long, long night.

Jack curled himself down under the lee of the main fife-rail, and, when the watch changed, returned there, preferring the open sky above him on such a perfect night to the frousy bad air of the foc's'le. Just as he was falling asleep, he noticed the small figure of the kid squeezing itself in behind the pump wheels.

The first hour of the middle watch passed without incident. Black Davis paced moodily to windward on the poop, the helmsman nodded sleepily over the wheel, and the look-out, trusting to luck in not being found out, was taking a nap on the foc's'le head.

Of the whole ship's company, perhaps the ragged urchin time-keeping was the only one thoroughly awake besides the mate.

But two bells had not been struck five minutes before every sleeper was aroused into wakefulness.

Suddenly a long, deep, wailing groan reverberated through the ship.

Dusky forms crouching under the lee of the bulwarks roused themselves, sat up, and looked round inquiringly.

The mate stopped in his walk and listened, the look-out sprang startled to his feet, and a hoarse murmur of gruff whispers broke out.

Again came the deep, mournful groan. It seemed to come from somewhere about the midshiphouse.

"What's thet noise forrard?" called the mate.

"Some one a-groanin' in the midshiphouse, sir!" hailed back the look-out.

The men nudged each other significantly.

"Poor Pedro!" came a loud voice from somewhere forward.

The mate frowned but said nothing, and the explanation evidently satisfied him, for he resumed his tramp.

Again the groan broke the stillness of the night.

There was something uncanny about the dismal sound. Full of superstition, like all deep-water Jacks, the men did not like it; several of the watch sprang to their feet, and there was a deep hissing of awe-filled voices amongst the dark groups of clustering men.

Suddenly a voice called from forward:

"It ain't the dago, sir; he says it weren't him."

"Who's that speaking?" roared the mate.

"Green, sir!"

"Come aft, yew; what yew doin' forrard in yer watch on deck?"

The man came running aft at a heavy, ungainly trot.

"Wall?" snapped the bucko venomously.

"Hearin' them groans, sir, I went an' listened at the door of the bosun's locker."

"Yes; wall? Go on, go on!" broke in the mate impatiently.

"I listens a while, sir, an' hears nothin'; then there comes a groan again, wery image o' Mister Barker's voice."

There was a renewed nudging and whispering amongst the group of men listening.

"Told ye so!" growled one. "Just wot I said!"

"By golly! dem is ghost groans, dis chile tell dat easy. No libing coon eber make dem noises, not on your life," grunted the coloured man, his voice shaking with fright.

"Silence there!" thundered the mate. "Go on, Green, spit it out 'fore y'r throat gits sore," he continued.

"Then I asks Pedro, sir, if it was 'im, an' he sez he ain't opened his mouth all night."

"All right, yew kin go," muttered Black Davis. "It's thet softy of a carpenter been eatin' too much!" he went on half to himself, half aloud.

Suddenly, right over his head called a voice:

"*I'm comin' fer yew, Davis, I'm comin' fer yew!*" Then, after a short interval, "*I'm burning! I'm burning! I'm burning!*"

The effect on the superstitious men was stupendous. The voice was the late second mate's to the life, and seemed to come from the mizzen-top.

Sam, the oracle on ghosts, threw himself to the deck, groaning in absurd terror.

"De ship am doomed! De ship am doomed!" he shrieked.

Angelino crossed himself nervously, and a shiver ran through the quaking crowd.

But there is not much superstition in a Yankee bucko, and Black Davis, tilting back his head, hailed the mizzen-top with a roar loud enough to wake the dead.

"Who's thet skylarkin' up thar? Come down, yew ratty hoodlum, or I'll break yew all ter pieces."

Dead silence!

"Up the mizzen riggin', some er yew swine, an' fetch him outer that!" roared the angry mate.

Not a man stirred.

Suddenly the tall form of the bosun appeared on the edge of the group of frightened men, awakened out of his light sleep by the commotion.

"What's up now?" he asked, as he shouldered his way through the men.

"Hell is up an' fizzlin'," burst out the exasperated mate. "Some d——d scowbanker monkeyin' aloft has got this crowd o' softies scared; but he ain't scared Black Davis—oh no! not by the Holy Pope—an' I pities him when he comes down."

"Jump aloft, bosun," he continued, "and see if yew kin rake him out by his eye-teeth; he's somewhere up the mizzen."

"Aye, aye, sir," replied the bosun in his deep voice, and turning, he swung himself over the rail into the rigging and went up the ratlines.

All heads turned upwards, anxiously watching him.

"He's a dead man," quavered one.

"Shut up, yew brayin' booby!" grunted the mate.

Up went the intrepid bosun. They watched him clamber out on the futtock shrouds and haul himself into the top; for a moment he disappeared behind the mast, and then reappeared, and with one hand on the topmast rigging, leant over the edge of the top and shouted down:

"There ain't nobody up here, sir. Are you sure you heard a voice?"

"Didn't I done tole you?" jerked Sam, his teeth rattling.

"Heard er voice!" howled the mate. "W'y, the swab called me by me name."

"It were Mister Barker's voice!" put in some one in an undertone.

"It were de voice ob de debble!" declared the darkey. "By gorry, dis bleedin' hooker am doomed!"

"Hell!" roared the mate. "If thet coffee-coloured Jamaica slush-bucket shoots off his bazoo again, I'll jump down an' whang his hide off."

This snuffed out any further assertions by Sam.

In vain the bosun searched aloft; he even shinned on to the skysail yard, and the fore and main were likewise searched, but without success.

There were no further utterances of the ghostly voice, and the matter remained an unexplained mystery.

Black Davis and the bosun did their best to thrash the matter out, but at last gave it up as hopeless.

"Must a' been some one foolin' on deck," suggested the bosun.

"But the voice came from aloft, man; the whole watch was hyeh with me. It weren't none er my crowd; I'll lay a hundred dollars thar's none o' them got the nerve to go monkeyin' with me like that," replied the mate impatiently.

"An' there ain't no parrot aboard. Well, it beats all my goin' to sea," muttered the other. "My crowd was all in the foc's'le 'cept Derringer, who was doin' a doss on deck, an' I see'd him standin' in your mob as I come along aft."

"Wall, then, if he was with my crowd o' hoodlums, it couldn't ha' been him, though if thar's any deadbeat aboard who's got the cheek ter do it, it's thet durned Britisher."

A curious grim smile appeared on Jack's face as his sharp ears caught the mate's remark.

Like the others, he had been awakened by the first groan.

As it ceased he heard a long-drawn breath, and looking round, spied the small white face of the ship's boy, outlined by the moonlight, as he crouched up against the mast behind the pump wheel.

Even as he watched he saw the small mouth open, at the same moment the groan broke out again, apparently by the midshiphouse.

Silently Jack gazed, marvelling. No sound seemed to come from the boy, but as the groan ceased his mouth closed, and he drew a long breath.

"Well, I'm jiggered," muttered Jack to himself. "The boy's a ventriloquist, and a wonderful one at that."

Then the kid threw his voice into the mizzen-top, and the words which had caused such consternation burst forth.

This time his mouth was nearly closed, and only a very keen observer could have detected any movement in his lips.

"Great Harry! If Black Davis were to catch the nipper at that game he'd kill him," mused Jack; and thinking that the performance had gone quite far enough, he drew himself under the fife-rail with the silence of a stalking Apache, and then suddenly pounced on the boy, clapping one hand over his mouth to prevent any cry of alarm.

"Hush, not a sound!" he hissed, as he took his hand from the kid's mouth.

"Don't split on me, Derringer, don't split on me. I'll never do it again, so help me bob," half blubbered the terrified urchin.

"Honest Injun?" inquired Jack.

"Honest Injun!" repeated the boy.

"Well, I'll pull you through this time; but don't breathe a word of this to another soul aboard," said Jack softly.

"Be sure I won't," whimpered the kid.

"Right! Now we've got to slip into that crowd there without them spotting that we've not been there the whole time; savvy, youngster? Keep your pecker up and mum's the word," whispered the rover.

"Hang me, but the lad's got nerve, and I like the look of him, too," he thought, as the pair of them stealthily joined the group of scared men.

"What's your name, kid?" asked Jack in an undertone, whilst the bosun was searching aloft.

"Jim," replied the boy; "I don't remember ever havin' no other."

"Where do you come from?"

"London. Fust thing I can remember was sleepin' in the parks; my, but it were cold sometimes."

"Got no father or mother?"

"No, I didn't have nobody; I wos just a street arab afore I went to sea."

"And how long have you been at sea, sonny?"

"Four year!"

"Pretty rough, eh?"

"Yes, mos' times, but I'm hard," replied the plucky boy.

"Well, see here, Jim," said the rover, gripping the boy's hand in his strong grasp. "I'm your friend from now on, and just you come to me when there's any trouble; savvy? Now you'd better skip along and strike 'one bell.'"

With tears in his eyes the boy stuttered his thanks before hurrying off to his time-keeping, and as he went he skipped along the deck for joy. His sad little heart had seldom known a kindness, and he had grown accustomed to bearing the hardships of his lot with a sullen apathy; but this offer of friendship and the protection of a strong right arm, coming as it did from the cock of the foc's'le, seemed almost too great a bit of luck to be true.

The boy felt a buoyancy within him which refused to be kept down, and his rising spirits, manifesting themselves in an attempted rendering of the hornpipe, all but brought him foul of the mate's heavy toe.

The excitement caused by the strange incidents of the middle watch sank all grievances for the time being. Like all deep-water men, the events which had put murder into their hearts one day were forgotten the next.

No longer did that sea-lawyer, Studpoker Bob, find an eager audience! Instead, authorities on ghosts and mysterious voices, such as Sam, gained the whole attention of the wildly superstitious crowd.

On coming on deck for the forenoon watch the mate made a visit to the bosun's locker.

He discovered the Chilian sullenly indifferent and serenely calm. The weird voices of the night did not seem to have troubled the man, or even aroused his curiosity, and he swallowed down hungrily the rough breakfast which the Chinese cook placed before him; after which he was released from the corpse, which was hastily sewn up in canvas, and, with half a dozen worn-out sheaves made fast to the feet, launched overboard.

No service was read over the body, for, as Captain Riley remarked to his second-in-command,

"In the fust place, I ain't got no doggoned prayer-book; an' in the second, I callate that Barker'll reach whatever port he's bound for quick enough, prayers or no prayers."

As the body took its dive, all hands rushed to the rail.

"So long, ye devil's spawn, a fair wind down under to ye. I guess they've their heatin' plant all fixed for ye," muttered Red Bill, of the broken arm.

"Solitary confinement on bread and water," was the old man's order *re* Pedro.

He was handcuffed, his donkey's breakfast and a blanket were tossed in to him, then the door was locked, and he was left to brood in semi-darkness, the only light being that which glinted through the ventilator in the door.

CHAPTER VI
"THE FATAL RED LEAD"

The trades failed close to the line, and all the troubles and trials of the doldrums began. They were a fine opportunity for Black Davis to take the steam out of his watch, for the wind, when there was any, came in short puffs from every quarter of the compass, and never blew for more than an hour or two in any given direction.

"Weather crossjack brace!" was the continual cry, and at night on the advent of each black squall there was a roar of:

"Stand by your skysail halliards!"

At one moment the rain would be coming down like a waterspout until the scuppers were full, and the next minute the wet ship would be glistening in the sunshine.

For five days the *Higgins* did not average twenty miles a day, and the whole of one baking Sunday she swung idly on her heel in the clutches of a Paddy's hurricane, whilst a stick of wood floating at her side would be sometimes ahead, sometimes astern.

Several of the men in their day watches below fished indefatigably from the jibboom, and Broncho soon had his first taste of albacore.

The flying-fish attracted him immensely, and he seemed never to tire of watching them as they flashed in and out of the water in glittering streaks of silver.

"I allows them fish has a high an' lavish time of it, a-pirootin' round permiscuous that-away. I shore wonders it don't exhaust them none, the way they hustles around," observed the cowboy to Jack Derringer, as they reclined lazily on the foc's'le head one afternoon watch below.

"A good time? Not much! Why, the albacore and bonita chase them out of the water, and the bosun-birds swoop down upon them in the air; they spend all their time flying from one enemy into the clutches of another."

"You don't say? It's shore some mean the way Providence cold-decks them fish that-away; yet they seem plenty numerous, notwithstandin' the way they're up agin the iron," drawled Broncho, as he slowly cut up some tobacco and refilled his corncob.

When within a few miles of the line the *Higgins* was put about for the first time.

This piece of seamanship was not executed without a vast amount of belaying-pin soup, even Broncho, the notorious desperado, getting his share in the heat of the moment.

The crew were raw and undrilled, and soon were worried into a hopeless tangle.

As the bosun had to attend to the crossjack and main braces in charge of the starboard watch, Jack was placed in command on the foc's'le, with Hank and Pat to aid him. This post is always reserved for the best men in the ship, for in a fresh breeze the men on the foc's'le have a most lively time.

From the moment that the helm was put down, the ship was in an indescribable uproar. The maindeck, littered with ropes'-ends, coils of braces, and handspikes, was soon in hopeless confusion. Braces jammed, tackles got foul, and the men ran aimlessly about, chased by Black Davis, who, like an avenging demon, was swearing as only a ship's mate can swear, whilst he fairly surpassed himself with his fist and boot work.

At the break of the poop the old man almost foamed at the mouth with fury. With clenched fists he raged up and down, roaring like a bull.

"Let go them royal an' skysail braces, yew mongrel rip thar, what in hell'r yew doin' of? Gol darn my etarnal skin if ever I see'd sech a inseck. Neow y've gone an' fouled thet brace! Snakes, yew ain't more use than a lot o' cawpses. Hyeh, bosun! Jump across an' thump thet hayseed, will yew?"

At the critical moment Sam, at the wheel, nearly had the ship in irons.

With one rush the old man was upon him.

"What in thunder air yew doin'? Y'll have her aback in a second, yew durned, sooty-faced heathen!"

And he gave the darkey a cuff on the side of the head which would have sent him to the deck if he had not clung to the wheel.

At last the yards were braced up on the other tack and the old man went below. Whilst the port watch cleared up the decks, the other retired to repair damages.

"I shore thinks I've been in some elegant skirmishes afore now," remarked Broncho, as he felt himself over for breakages in the foc's'le; "but

I'm an Apache if I'm ever into a fight that's more stirrin' an' eventful, not to say toomultuous. At one time I'm that tangled up in my rope I allows it's a whirlwind."

"I believe you, my bye," said the cockney, as he limped painfully across to the water-barrel for a drink. "I drors h'it mild when h'I sez it's chucks ahead of a bloomin' 'urricane."

"And you calls the play kerrect, Hollins. What with that old he-wolf a-howlin' in a mighty unmelodious way on the poop, an' Black Davis a-swarmin' all over me like a wild-cat, I shore reckons it's a heap thrillin'. Them two sports throws no end of sperit into their play."

"And thet ain't fosterin' no delusions; they're hot stuff, pard, an' they earns their reputations," said Bedrock Ben. "That 'ere Black Davis jumps me offen my mental reservation complete every time."

"When he gets a ship he ought to make a most successful master, if his training goes for anything," put in Curly. "I notice all the American deep-water skippers have the reputation of having been regular Western Ocean buckos in their time."

"That bloomin' roustabout'll never live to command a ship," grunted Red Bill from the opposite bunk. "He's too successful with his fists to live long. He'll get cut up one o' these days, like that other New Jersey tough."

"Yes, success isn't all jam," remarked Jack slowly. "It's got a remarkable habit of turning sour in your mouth, just as you are beginning to put on frills and throw out your chest."

"Them remyarks o' yours is shore wisdom, Jack," drawled Broncho in his musical Texan, as he blew a cloud of tobacco-smoke slowly through his nose. "What you-alls calls success don't always pan out so rich as you calculated it would. Often the kyards stacks up mighty contrary, an' when you're just about callin' for drinks round, blandly surmisin' in your sublime ignorance that you makes a winnin' an' is shore due to scoop the pot, that 'ere gent 'Providence,' who's sittin' some quiet an' unobstrusive whilst you raises the bet to the limit, just steps in an' calls your hand. Then it is that your full house goes down like an avalanche before his four of a kind, an' you, some sore an' chagrined, meanders off an' ponders on this vale of tears."

"You're some long-winded, Broncho," said old Ben Sluice, "but you're dead right. I've seen a hell's slew o' minin' pards go under just 'coss they'd struck it rich. They rakes in their dinero an' away they goes, playin' it high an' standin' the crowd, all the time a-consumin' o' nosepaint unlimited; an' the next thing you knows is they done jumped the track."

"H'I knew a real bang-up toff once," joined in the cockney. "'E wos a genelman, too, boiled shirt, shiny pants an' h'all, an' a dead smooth job 'e 'ad—just raked in the quids for doin' nuffin' but loaf 'round. You've all 'eard of the Scotch 'Ouse—leastways, h'any that's been to the little village h'I come from. Well, 'e was wot they calls 'shopwalker' there. H'I goes in there one day (h'I'd got a big payday comin', an' h'I thinks, thinks h'I, I'll be cute this time an' lay in a bang-up outfit). Well, h'in I goes an' h'up 'e comes as h'affable an' perlite as you please an' sez:

"'And what's yours, sir?'

"Well, h'I wos h'all took aback, gettin' sich a question from a puffect stranger. At last h'I stammers out:

"''Arf-an'-'arf, an' thank ye kindly, mister.'

"Well, 'e just smiles superior-loike, an' sez,

"'I mean, what do you want to buy?'

"Well, I thinks to myself, 'That's comin' it low on a chap.' It weren't the friendly touch, wos h'it? But h'I don' sye nuffin' 'bout it, but gets a rig-out an' skips.

"Next v'yage h'I comes into the West Indy Docks. I thinks as h'I loafs round, mebbe I'll go an' see if my rorty toff is still on top. Well, 'e ain't there, so I asts the cove wot I bought the duds from, when did 'e cut 'is 'ook? Well, wot d'you think, byes: 'e'd been an' committed sooicide. Stroike me good an' blind, but you could a' knocked me down wiv a feaver when I 'ears it."

"What's a dead cinch to one gent is jest an ornery layout to another," commented Broncho.

"I allows that 'shopwalker' o' yours don't accoomilate no joys from his duties. Mebbe he reckons them mighty low, not to say debasin', an' finally he gets that fretful an' peevish he jest throws up his deal in disgust, jumps on his war-pony, an' lights out on the death trail."

And now a pitiful incident occurred. That poor ship's drudge, the kid, with the exception of Jack Derringer, who was in the other watch, had but one friend and chum, which was the almost equally disreputable ship's cat—a gaunt, thin tabby.

These two shared their blankets and shared their grub. Scanty as the fare was, the kid always saved enough out of his daily whack to give the cat a good square meal.

As Broncho remarked,

"It's shore an example to humanity, the way that 'ere despised an' put-upon urchin hugs an' cherishes that cat; it's plumb touchin' as a spectacle."

Since the mysterious voice episode, Jack's friendliness with the ragged boy had caused some comment in the foc's'le.

Often these two were to be seen seated together talking in the second dog-watch. A notable change was beginning to show itself in the small urchin. He was no longer the dirty ragamuffin of yore; his shrill speech was not so full of oaths, and he ceased to shirk his work whenever he could conveniently do so.

The rolling-stone seemed to possess a wonderful influence over the boy, and in the dog-watch he grew into the way of giving the kid a short lecture.

These strange lectures proved a wonderful education to the suppressed urchin, who drank in every word of them.

"Jim," the rover would say, as he smoked lazily on the fore-hatch, "your language is a sight too foul for a kid of your age. You just take a turn with that small tongue of yours, and go easy on swearing. I know it's hard, specially at sea, but I'll give you a tip. Now you've seen the Spanish inscriptions on cigar-boxes, haven't you? Yes? Well, suppose something happens—you stub your toe over a ring-bolt, or slip up on some slush by the galley—you want a harmless, inoffensive word to express your feelings. Well, there's your word in top-weight Spanish on the cigar-box. 'Claro!' you say, short and quick in an annoyed way, 'Claro!' Well, you do it again; this time you're feeling a bit hotter, and you want something the least bit stronger. 'Maduro!' you say, and put your feeling into the 'u.' But you go and stub your toe a third time; it's getting to be a bad habit of yours, and you really want something strong this time to get the proper flavour in your mouth. There's the word ready for you on the cigar-box. 'Colorado!' and the worse you feel the more you roll the 'r,' until you can make the word howl with pain. Listen——"

Jack frowned ferociously, and then from the back of his throat threw out the terrible oath:

"Color-r-r-r-a-a-a-do!!!"

The rolling-stone's lectures were certainly original, to say the least of them, and they generally had their amusing side.

One Saturday night Jack lay on his back watching his beloved stars, whilst the boy was busy at the pump washing off his weekly allowance of dirt in preparation for Sunday.

This was a new habit of his, set going by his star-gazing friend, who, finding that the boy did not possess any soap, had presented him with a dozen pieces, saying,

"Jim, here's some soap for you. If there's any of it left by the time we're in the North Atlantic, there'll be trouble."

As the boy finished his toilet the rover called to him, and pointing upwards, said:

"Do you see that star, Jim? That's 'Aldebaran,' the eye of Taurus, the bull, the second sign of the zodiac. Doesn't he shine plain? He's easy to see, isn't he? But suppose he was all coal-dust and dirt! We shouldn't be able to see him, should we? In the same way, if you're all dirty and covered with coal-dust, instead of being well polished by soap and water, how do you expect your guardian angel to watch over you? Why, he'd lose you amongst all the other specks of dirt on this earth, and never find you again; then you'd be an easy thing for the old gentleman with a forked tail, eh, sonny?"

"I'm afeard then, Jack, my guardian angel ain't never see'd me since I was born, for I don' ever remember bein' clean 'ceptin' lately," said the boy mournfully.

"Well, cheer up, old son! I expect he's got his eye on you all right all the same," declared the other heartily, alarmed by the seriousness with which Jim took his remarks.

Then, searching round for an idea whereby to soften his statements, he spied Sam.

"Don't you be down-hearted, Jim," he went on. "Look at Sam. How would you expect his guardian angel to see him? Yet he does, notwithstanding his colour."

"But Sam do shine be-e-autiful when he's hot," declared the boy.

This last was too much for Jack; he lay back and roared, whilst Jim's big brown eyes watched him in wonder.

But the men forward were rather huffed by Jack's friendship with the boy.

"Fust time h'I ever see'd the cock o' the foc's'le pal up with the ship's boy," grunted the cockney one day.

"You just be keerful what you say, Hollins," said Red Bill. "I just gave the little nipper a clout on the jaw t'other day for giving me sauce, when up jumps Derringer.

"'Leave that kid alone,' sezzee.

"'Mind yer own bloomin' bizness,' sez I; an' before I knows where I am, I'm lyin' on my back on the deck with a bump the size of a two-sheave block on the side of my head."

"'E calls 'im Jim, too," went on the scandalised cockney. "Might be bruvers, the way Jack spiles 'im. Kids want kickin'—h'it's the on'y way ter teach 'em."

But to return to the cat.

It was close on eight bells in the afternoon watch. The *Higgins* lay rolling in a heavy swell, with her courses hauled up; the sun was obscured, and heavy rain-clouds hung over the horizon.

There was not the slightest breath of wind, and the ship echoed with the slating and flogging of her sails as she rolled.

A continuous stream of water gushed in through her ports, and poured in a cascade first one way and then the other across the maindeck.

The port watch were on deck, busy "sand and canvassing" the main and fore fife-rails, preparatory to revarnishing.

The fore-hatch had just been chipped, and was resplendent in bright patches of red lead. The fates were rapidly arranging a holocaust for poor puss, for, as if obeying some unseen hand, he suddenly roused and stretched himself where he had been coiled up asleep on the foc's'le head; then, with the slow, graceful movement of his tribe, he descended the ladder and deliberately went up and rubbed himself against the fore-hatch. But alas! the eagle eye of Black Davis was upon him, and the red lead betrayed him, for it had left its marks upon his brindled coat; too late he tried to lick it off.

"Terantulars, yew dirty sneakin' beast. Rub my paint off, would yew?" roared the mate.

With remarkable swiftness he clutched poor puss in his iron fist, and a second later the cat was adrift on the swell and hidden from sight.

With a scream of fury and distress, the kid, who had been at work on the fore fife-rail, flung himself upon the bully, biting, kicking, and scratching.

Broken words burst from his mouth in a torrent, and, Jack's lecture forgotten, he raved and swore as only a boy bred to the sea can swear, raining a very shower of blows with his little fists upon the big mate.

Catching him by the scruff of his neck, Black Davis flung him aside.

The poor boy was hurled across the deck, to be brought up by the iron combing of the hatch, which caught him upon the left brow as he fell.

Jim dropped stunned, and lay motionless, bleeding copiously, whilst the fatal red lead with sardonic irony smeared itself in mockery upon his cheek and shoulder.

There was a low growl of suppressed anger from the watch, and if looks could have killed, Black Davis would not have lived long.

"Git on with your work, yew scrapin's o' hell, or I'll soon knock the bile out o' your gizzards," he roared; then, walking up to the senseless body of the boy, he kicked it twice heavily on the ribs.

"No shamming, yew little devil! Up yew get, or I'll make yew smell hell."

But before he could lift his foot again the stalwart form of the rolling-stone stood between the mate and his victim.

"Drop that, you d——d child-murderer! Come on and hit a man your own size."

The words fairly hissed from Jack's firm mouth, and there was a devil in his flashing eyes no one on board had ever seen there before.

Planted lightly but firmly on his legs, he squared up to the bucko with clenched fists and furious, quivering lips.

"Come on!" he raged, taking a step forward. "Come on, you devil!"

The port watch stared, open-mouthed, half expecting the heavens to fall in their amazement at Jack's daring.

Black Davis's glance fell before the fury of Jack's eyes. His big fist, half-raised, dropped to his side again; he took a step backward, then, muttering something indistinctly between his teeth, he slowly turned on his heel and walked aft.

Jack stared, the anger in his eyes changing to a look of blank surprise.

"Well, I'm blowed!" he muttered.

A half-muffled cheer broke from the port watch and many of the starboard who had jumped from their bunks in anticipation of a royal set-to.

The rover turned and snapped out,

"Fetch a bucket of water, one of you."

A dozen men rushed to obey.

Bending over the senseless urchin, Jack gently wiped the blood and red lead from the little white face; then, with the tenderness of a woman, he picked the boy up in his arms and carried him to his bunk.

There he skilfully doctored the long cut on the boy's forehead, first washing it, and then drawing the edges together with sticking-plaister zigzagged across it, whilst the starboard watch looked on in admiration of his handiwork.

Luckily for the poor little waif, his short life of hardship and want had so toughened him that, with the exception of a bad bruise, his ribs were intact.

"Poor old Dandy!" were the first words the kid spoke after coming to, and the tears rushed to his eyes as the lonely feeling of his loss came over him.

"Never mind the cat, sonny. I reckon Jack Derringer's done saved your life; if it hadn't been for Jack, you'd a' been hittin' the trail after Dandy yourself," said old Bedrock Ben.

"And that ain't no bloomin' josh. Jack put the skybosh on the 'ulkin' bully, and no mistyke. Crikey, if it weren't the 'ighest old rig to see Black Davis spifflicated.

"''Ow's that, umpire?' sez I.

"'W'y, h'out, er course!' and away walks 'is bloomin' lordship, fairly 'oodooed."

Thus the cockney, with a chuckle of delight.

"Did Derringer save me from the mate? I don' remember nothink. Black Davis slugged me, didn't he?" the boy asked faintly.

"If standing up between the mate an' you lying senseless, and daring Black Davis to touch you, isn't saving you, I don't know what is," said Curly hotly.

"Oh, shut up, you fellows, and leave the boy alone," growled Jack. "It's just eight bells, and Jim's going to lie quiet and get some sleep.

"Do you hear that, Jim?" he continued; "you're not to stir from your bunk till I give you leave. Green'll do your 'peggy' for you, eh, Green?"

The man nodded nervously in assent.

"That's *bueno*! Now shut your eyes, sonny, and take a siesta."

The boy's brown eyes glowed with a wealth of gratitude and a dog-like look of adoration as they rested upon Jack's stalwart figure; but the rolling-stone was a martinet of a doctor—not a word would he allow above a whisper in the foc's'le until the kid was asleep.

It was the cockney's wheel when the watch changed, and at four bells, six o'clock, he came forward, his face eloquent with news.

"H'I've found 'im out, byes, h'I've found 'im out!" he shouted incoherently to the group of men seated yarning on the fore-hatch and spare spars, and he pointed wildly at the rolling-stone.

"What's he done now?" rumbled half a dozen deep voices.

"Wyte, me bloomin' ole shellbacks, lemme tell the yarn."

"Well, pipe ahead; we ain't stoppin' ye," growled Red Bill.

"Jack," said the cockney, suddenly darting upon the rover—"Jack, me bloomin' lovy-duck, does you know w'y Black Dyvis wouldn't stan' up to yer?"

"Maybe I do, maybe I don't," laughed Jack.

"Well, h'I do, then, so now. I 'eard the ole man spin the bosun the whole blessed yarn; an' believe me, byes, h'I wos that tickled to death, before I knoo where h'I wos the bally 'ooker wos two p'ints off 'er course."

"Heave ahead, mate, heave ahead; you're all aback. Swing yer fore-yards an' get sail on to yer yarn," broke in the impatient Red Bill again.

"Orl right, cocky, orl right. Dye yer 'air. That red 'ead o' yours mykes ye in sich a blawsted 'urry, you'll get jumpin' inter yer coffin one fyne dye afore ye're dead."

There was a laugh, for Red Bill was notoriously hasty and impulsive in his actions.

"Well," began the cockney impressively, "h'it were this wye. The bosun wos a-leanin' agin the rail to windward er-scannin' o' things in general, an' allowin' mebbe 'e'd take a pull on the weather braces, w'en h'up comes the ole man from 'is grub. 'E goes over to ther bosun an' 'e sez:

"'What sort of er'and is that man Derringer?'

"'Best man wiv a marlin-spike h'I've see'd fer a long time,' sez the bosun.

"'Well,' goes on the ole man, speakin' slow an' solemn-loike, ''es the man as did up Slocum on the *I.D. Macgregor!*'

"Byes, h'I could er dropped. Slocum, mind you, the bigges'-fisted lump of a two 'undred an' fifty pound bucko sailin' the seas—the man as can 'old a six-foot Noo Orleans buck nigger, one in each 'and, lift 'em off the deck, an' bash their ugly black 'eads together; h'I've see'd 'im do it——"

"That's so, mate," broke in Hank. "I were in Iquique wi' him when he killed er man—picked him up an' kind er bumped 'im agin the boat skids an' broke his head; the ole man put some lie in the log, an' there weren't no more heard of it."

"Well," continued the cockney, "the skipper 'e spins the bosun the yarn, an' h'I jest absorbs h'it likewise. Seems Cappen Summers told 'im 'bout it, an' 'e spots you, Jack, from them tattoo-marks o' yourn.

"Well, byes, this ere grinnin' cuckoo 'ere, 'om I'm pra'd to shipmytes wiv, 'e 'as words or somethin' wiv Mister Bucko Slocum, syme wye mebbe as 'e 'ad wi' Dyvis, an' they ups an' 'as it out.

"Well, they fit an' fit an' fit, Cappen Summers an' the 'ole bloomin' ship's comp'ny er-lookin' on. My crikey, but it must er been the 'ighest ole rig! Fer two hours they fit by ole man Summers' ticker, till they wos h'all blood an' rags. Then Jack, 'e up wiv 'is fist an' lets drive. Oh Lord! Weren't it er knock-out! That swot Slocum, 'e just flies back'ards, lands on 'is 'ead on the quarter-bitts, an' lays there, reglar broke up; didn't come to till nex' mornin'.

"Ole man Summers tho't 'e were killed, an' gives Jack 'is job on ther spot.

"That's w'y Dyvis weren't 'avin' none!" concluded the cockney solemnly.

"'Sthat true, Jack, 'sthat true?" shouted half a dozen voices.

"Better ask the old man," laughed the rover.

In a moment Jack was circled by a crowd of eager men, all bawling at once.

"Lord lummy, Jack, you must be a bruiser," called one.

"Did Black Davis know this, d'you suppose?" asked Curly.

"'Course 'e did, you h'ass!" cried the cockney scornfully. "W'y, 'e ain't put a finger on 'im th'ole passage, not even towin' out."

"I reckon Black Davis was some scared he'd lose his job if Jack downs him, same as that other fire-eatin' miscreant," mused Broncho. "No, he were dead agin playin' your hand, Jack; he weren't hankerin' to be your beef— he's too keerful of his skin that away."

"Gaud blimy! Wot er scrap h'it would er been," lamented the cockney.

"It shore would ha' been some lurid, but I pities the mate. He was due to emerge a totterin' wreck. Jack was just a-moanin' for blood an' oozin' with f'rocity," asserted the cowpuncher.

"He did look a heap grim," remarked Bedrock Ben.

"But what if Black Davis had downed him?" inquired Pinto.

"Sich thoughts is figments," said Broncho contemptuously. "I'm puttin' up chips Jack'd have that rancorous hold-up too dead to skin. Jack weren't aimin' to put no delicacy into his play, that time."

"Green, if you don't *tcha-tcha* [6] and strike eight bells, you'll have the mate on your trail," broke in the bucko-downer, anxious to cut short the conversation.

And a few moments later the silvery note of the bell announced that the first watch had begun.

FOOTNOTES:

[6] *Tcha-tcha*, "hurry up" (Zulu).

CHAPTER VII
"IN THE SECOND DOG-WATCH"

All through the tropics, Pedro, under the influence of his solitary confinement, had been becoming more and more morose and despondent.

He hardly touched the wretched fare which was placed before him, and had wasted to a shadow of his former self.

His fierce black eyes glittered out of a sallow, heavily-lined face, upon which the lowering scowl daily became deeper and deeper.

His ragged moustache was broken and torn by chewing, whilst his lower lip hung sore and bleeding from the constant gnawing of his teeth.

"It's a cert," remarked Broncho, "that that bowie-whirlin' dago is due to go flutterin' from his limb one o' these days. He's lookin' 'bout ready to break camp for the etarnal beyond; his vittles no longer gives him joy, an' he just sets thar an' wilts."

"Weevily hard tack and dirty warm water wouldn't give anybody joy," replied Jack. "He wants air and exercise; they should let him out for an hour on deck every day."

"Gate an' seat checks for the realms o' light is about what he wants, I reckon," retorted the cattle-ranger.

And Broncho was right. One morning they found him too late; he was lying in a pool of blood with a small piece of broken wood in his clenched fingers. With this poor weapon the Chilian had managed to tear open a vein in his arm, and so bled to death. Thus miserably ended the poor little bucko-killer.

His death brought the superstitious members of the crew to the front again. Pessimistically they prophesied all sorts of evils, and Sam, the chief authority, openly proclaimed that Black Davis, with the death of the ship's cat upon his soul, would be the next victim of the ghostly avenger.

In the south-east trades easy times reigned in the starboard watch. For nearly a week not a sheet, brace, or halliard was touched, except for the usual pull on the braces and general "freshening of the nip" every evening.

In the second dog-watch the men would collect on the foc's'le head, and exchange yarns with eager faces and vehement gestures.

Every man forward had seen life in its more unusual phases. Paddy, Hank, Jack, and the cockney had all been shipwrecked more than once; and even Jim had had a strange crop of experiences crowded into his short life.

One evening Jack had just related a yarn of how he had been wounded in an affray in the New Hebrides, when mate of a "blackbirder," as the schooners recruiting Kanaka labour for the Queensland plantations were called.

"Any money in thet layout?" inquired the gambler.

"Used to be," returned Jack, "till the missionaries and opposition in Australia broke it up."

"Thar's many a cinch in the South Seas," observed Hank. "Copra an' curios ain't bad, nor yet pearls, speshully if yew kin strike a preserved patch when thar ain't no gunboat knockin' around."

"Smuggling opium's good, too," reflected Jack musingly.

"Yew bet! Ever tried it?"

"Aye."

"How did it pan out?" inquired Bedrock Ben, somewhat eagerly.

"So-so!" grunted the rover. "Did three good trips. Then we got caught napping in a typhoon, and the old junk went to the bottom."

"Close call, eh?"

"Yes; only three of us saved—two Chins and myself."

"H'I tell ye, byes, smugglin's good gear h'all round," broke in the cockney.

"Begorra, an' I'm after knowin' that same. Weren't I in the *Admiral Tronde*, a bruck-up little one-gunned stame-kettle runnin' guns fur them Urriguay sports," cried Paddy excitedly.

"Were ye, Pat? Bully for you," went on the cockney. "I done some gun-runnin' too up the Persian Gulf; but h'I 'ad ter quit—the screw were good enuff, but the 'eat wos a knock-out. Lord love ye! W'y, we biled our cauffee on the shanks o' the anchors; s'elp me, but they wos allers red 'ot. An' th' ole man, 'e don' ever wear nuffin' but a bloomin' gal's night-gownd — —"

"Heat don't worry me," interrupted Hank. "It's cold calls the turn on me. I was up the Behring once sealin' an' got my bellyful."

"Much ice?" inquired Jack casually.

"A pretty considerable mush of it."

"I was two months in the ice to the south'ard once in the *Cairngorm*," declared the rover.

"The hell yew war? 'Member speakin' the *I.P. Rakes* off the Dyeego Ramerrez? Yew had ye jibboom gone an' nought above the lower-mast forrard. Your ole man sent a life-boat aboard us fur spuds—said y'd got scurvy bad. By Davy, I allers allows thet were the dirtiest sea I ever see'd a boat live in."

"It was bad," agreed Jack. "We got stove in trying to get aboard again, and lost three men."

"Thet's right! I see'd yew wi' these very eyes, smashed to staves yew were; an' yew were in thet boat, eh?"

"Yes," said the Britisher quietly. "I was second mate of the *Cairngorm*, and had charge of her."

"Phew!" exclaimed Hank, drawing a long breath; "an' whar did yew larn thet trick o' handlin' a boat? Been whalin', I s'pose?"

"No; all the boat-work I know I picked up in the Islands."

"Ever seen Siwash squaws run a birch-bark through rapids?" asked old Bedrock Ben. "That's what I calls boat-handlin'."

"Squaws 'andle a boat! To 'ell wiv ye!" burst out the cockney disdainfully. "What d'you know 'bout h'it? W'y, you ain't never seen the Boat Ryce."

"What boat race?" grunted old Ben.

"Lord lummy, byes, listen to 'im! Sech h'ignorance is bloomin' well a disgryce."

"What's this here race you-alls alludes to?" inquired Broncho in his polite Texan drawl.

"Oh, 'ell!" gasped the cockney, and sank back in a state of collapse.

"I see'd the Boat Race onct," suddenly put in Jim's small voice, "an' I ain't never forget it."

"I ain't no use fur racin'," growled Red Bill. "I does a v'yage once in one o' them tea-clippers, an' that were enuff racin' to last me my time. What wi' carryin' on when it's blowin' great guns an' muckin' around in the tropics with royal stuns'ls, save-alls, water-s'ls, ringtails, an' sech-like superfloous pocket-handkerchers, it ain't no game fur a white man."

"What was your ship, mate?" inquired the rover, looking up with interest.

"*Titania.*"

"I came home from Australia once in the *Cutty Sark*," said Jack slowly.

"Lose any men?" asked Red Bill sharply.

"Well, off the Horn we did. Helmsman lost his head—let her run off, whilst we were at the main braces. We shipped a big sea and lost nine men overboard—two of them washed off the foreyard."

"I believe you, son," snorted the fiery-headed Bill. "That's the way wi' them packets. Men's lives is nuffin' so long as they makes a good passage."

"Men's lives!" growled Jack disdainfully. "Red Bill, you talk like a softy! What do you come to sea for but to take the rough with the smooth? When a man begins thinking of his life at sea, it's about time he stopped ashore and turned counterjumper, ink-squirter, or hayseed— —"

"Go easy, mate, go easy!" put in Hank mildly.

"Well, I've got no patience when a man begins talking about his precious life."

"Look 'ere!" began Red Bill hotly, "you jest take in the slack o' that jaw-tackle o' yours, Jack Derringer. You're a sight too free wi' them insinnivations. I ain't afraid o' you for all ye prize-fightin' tricks, so go slow, or there'll be a slogging match."

"Bill," said the rolling-stone, with that catching smile of his, "shake hands. You're a white man, and I take it all back. It was just you talking of men's lives that roused my dander. I don't like to hear good sailormen talk about their lives like so many frightened land-crabs. I once went a yachting trip with three brass-bound, useless, chicken-hearted clothes-props, and I tell you I got a sickener of 'my precious life' talk.

"Things went well enough at first, when there was only just enough wind to keep us moving—though I had my hands full, what with cooking, steering, and doing all the dirty work; for though they were all three big men, they were so fat and flabby they couldn't pull their own weight on a rope or even hit a dent in a pat of butter; but we got a bit of a blow heading over to the French coast from Falmouth, and if ever I saw three badly scared, nerveless citizens, it was that crowd.

"The boat was a snug little yawl, and as I was pressing her through it pretty hard, things naturally got a bit wet, and now and again some green water lopped aboard.

"Well, after they'd had their first experience of a big dollop, they all turned on me.

"'Isn't it getting dangerous?' began the first uneasily.

"'Haven't we got too much sail for safety?' quavered the second.

"'Wouldn't it be risking our lives to go on?' stuttered the third. 'I'm afraid——'

"'Any fool could see that,' I broke in, as I shoved her nose into a lump of green water to cut short their chorus.

"After a good deal of spluttering they recovered sufficiently to give tongue again.

"'I'm wet through,' whimpered one. 'I must go below and change my things or I'll catch cold. D'you think it safe for me to leave the deck?'

"'I guess the deck can take care of itself all right,' I answered.

"'No, I don't mean that,' he said solemnly. 'I mean, if the boat turned over when I was in the cabin, I should lose my life, I should be d-d-drowned.'

"'By Jove, so you would!' I exclaimed, as if struck by the gravity of the idea.

"'D'you really think it would be more dangerous below than here?' put in another of the boobies anxiously.

"'You're all insured, ain't you?' I asked with a wooden face.

"'Yes,' they gulped as a spray took them; 'but for God's sake turn the boat round and go back.'

"'Can't; too dangerous to run before this sea,' I declared, making a big bluff.

"They were getting too much for my patience altogether, so with a wild cry of 'Look out!' I shoved the helm over and soused them again.

"This time I had them all as limp as a wet swab, and as the wave hit them they screeched like so many frightened women. But directly the water cleared off there was more tongue-wagging.

"'My God! I thought we were gone,' gasped one.

"Then the second booby let fly:

"'What an escape! A second longer and I should have been drowned——'

"'How terrible!' I put in brutally.

"'Terrible? Yes, you're right. Isn't the sea awful? I've never been in such danger in my life before.'

"'Nor ever will be again if you can help it, I expect,' I sneered.

"But their minds were too overwrought to take any notice of my brutal speeches.

"'I thought I should burst— —' began the fattest.

"'I've often thought you'd do that,' I cut in cheerfully.

"' — —from holding my breath so long,' he finished, eyeing me dismally.

"Well, the end of it all was, I got the unhappy trio below, battened 'em down, and weathered it out by my lonesome. Twenty-seven hours at the tiller! Ever since that cruise, whenever a man begins to talk about his life being in danger, I begin to get hot in the collar."

"Land folk is certainly queer that way an' easily scared," commented the pacified Red Bill.

"Gettin' scared is easy. The bigges' fire-eatin' son of a gun is scared some time in his life; but it's givin' away your hand an' showin' you're scared that gets you logged down as plumb nerveless an' no account," remarked old Ben sagely.

"You're shore right, Ben," agreed Broncho. "It's the white-livered coyote who can't keep his mental fears corralled who goes to drawin' his gun when there ain't no need, an' gets over shootin' an' pluggin' the wrong gent."

"Thet's so, pardner," grunted the gambler. "See this scar?" pointing to a livid streak on his cheek-bone. "I gets that from a tenderfoot back-east puppy as acts the way you mentions."

"He sartinly makes a greevious mistake that time," returned Broncho ambiguously.

"He shore would ha' had a depitation o' thanks from his grateful pards if he'd hit the bull's-eye, I reckon," rumbled old Ben in a loud aside.

At this moment the bell went, and the watch on deck got hastily to their feet, caught up caps, and knocked the ashes out of their pipes before going aft.

Sometimes Broncho and Jack would sneak into the bosun's little berth in the midshiphouse. Here the three of them, with pipes smoking like chimneys, passed many a pleasant hour.

Over the bosun's bunk was the worn and faded photograph of a very pretty girl. This picture seemed to attract the rolling-stone in some strange way, for often he stared fixedly at it with a faraway look in his eyes, as if he were peering back into the past and trying to recall some half-forgotten memory.

One night, noticing his rapt gaze, the bosun remarked casually:

"Yes, she's a nice-lookin' gal, ain't she?"

"I beg your pardon!" said Jack hastily, the dark red flushing through his tan. "I didn't mean to be rude, but that photograph reminds me of somebody."

"Well, bein' as we're all good mates here," observed the bosun, "I'll tell you the yarn. I never ain't married—I ain't that lucky, though I walks out with scores o' gals in my time; but I on'y ever has one real sweetheart, an' she was a clipper. She was——" He broke off, and then resumed slowly, "That's 'er photo—she was second 'ousemaid to Lord Arrendale" (Jack gave a sharp start of surprise).

"That's away back ten years or more," continued the bosun reflectively; "then I goes off on a v'yage out East, thinkin' as how with a big payday a-comin' I'd get spliced when I gets home again. But my luck's dead out. I gets wrecked among the Islands, an' precious near ate up, an' it's over four years afore I drops my mudhook in the old cottage. Then I found my gal had gone an' left her place an' disappeared." The strong man's eyes grew misty, and the deep voice shook. "Well, I ups anchor an' beats up and down the whole country, but I never meets up with my gal no more; so I goes to sea again, and I ain't been ashore more'n two months all put together in the last ten years.

"And do you think I ever forgets that gal o' mine? No, sir; she's as dear to me, an' more, than she was in them days when I was a-courtin'. I often envies folks that I sees married, all so comfort'ble in their little bit o' home with the kids an' all. The likes o' them never don't seem to realise their luck. It's us fellers who 'as no wife, nor 'ome, nor kids—who's in Shanghai one minit an' off the Horn the next—it's us who spots their luck."

The bosun ceased and looked keenly at Jack.

"Ben Cray," said the latter earnestly but simply, reaching out his hand and seizing the bosun's burly fist, "I'm sorry!"

Broncho stared; he had only heard the big Britisher addressed as bosun, and did not know his real name, and he also thought that Jack was in like ignorance up to that evening.

There was something going on behind the scenes which he could not even guess at. He was a keen observer, and had noticed the blush on the cheek of his friend.

"He's a hard-cut citizen, is Jack," thought the cowboy. "It takes a lot to jump him offen his gyard."

"Ben," continued Jack, "you're a real white man. I remember her now, poor little thing, and you too."

"I spotted you fust day you comes aboard, sir!"

"I didn't know, bosun; I've never been home since I went to sea, and that was just before you went on that unlucky voyage."

"I see'd the ole lord last time I was back," began the bosun with some hesitation; and then stopped, as if he would have liked to say something more, but dared not.

"Hm!" muttered Jack indifferently, with mask-like face; but the keen-eyed cowpuncher noticed a singular gleam in the rover's clear blue orbs.

For a few moments there was silence, and then Broncho broke in:

"Talkin' of marriage, you shorely recalls my Juanita, don't you, Jack?"

"Certainly I do."

"Well," went on the cowboy, "I never gets my brand on to her, though I near has the hobbles on more'n once."

"I'm very sorry to hear that, Broncho. I thought you were in double harness long ago."

"Well, I never does fasten somehow, though I ropes at her continuous; then one day she goes curvin' off with that ere miscreant Montana Joe, which has me plumb disgusted. I just chucks a pair o' blankets across my saddle, stuffs a wad o' notes in my war-bags, an' lights right out. Finally I makes Frisco, where I gets to drownin' dull care with nosepaint; an' I makes sech a success of that ere undertakin' that I presently finds myself as you-alls knows."

"Sidelights out, hand on the look-out!" roared Black Davis from aft.

"Aye, aye, sir!" came back the answer, and night began.

The following evening Jack, Broncho, and the boy Jim were yarning together on the foc's'le head, when a terrific uproar broke out on the deck below them. There was a hurricane of deep-sea laughter, and the next moment the small form of the cockney disengaged itself from the crowd, and came dashing up the topgallant ladder.

"Jack!" he cried, "Jack, wot's a genelman?"

"Why, Jack is, er course," burst out the boy.

"I mean, wot mykes a genelman?"

The rest of the crowd were on his heels, and Curly, thrusting his way through, burst out hotly.

Jack Derringer | 69

"Hollins says a gentleman is a man with shiny pants and a stove-pipe hat. What do you say, Jack?"

"Bedad! I on'y knoo one gintlemen," cried Pat, "an' he weren't one at all at all."

"I see's a gentleman once," said Red Bill, "an' he had a bit er glass stuck in his eye."

"When you-alls says gentleman," drawled Broncho, "you mean the real brand, I surmise; for there's a greevious number o' gents a-waltzin' around puttin' on frills an' bluffin' they're the thoroughbred article, which same soon bogs down in one's eestimation as plumb low an' ornery. What you-alls call gentlemen is gettin' 'most rar' as buffaloes in these here widespread an' high-flung times; but when you does cut their trails, you can bet a whole team you're goin' to be duly impressed tharby."

"A gentleman's a cove wi' clean 'ands, 'coss he don't work," shouted Jimmy Green excitedly from the edge of the crowd.

"You shut yer dirty 'ead! 'Oo asked you ter talk when able seamen's around?" roared the cockney furiously. "Give that byby-face er clout, will ye, Ben?"

Jimmy Green got his clout and retired from the contest.

"A gentleman's a sport who can sit down to a game o' poker an' lose his dollars smiling," asserted the gambler.

"A gentleman's a tenderfoot who trails round buyin' salted claims," pronounced old Ben.

"I meets a shentlemans vonce vot I yumps a bag along vor, an' he give me two bob; you bet dat's a shentleman's, my schmard fellers," grunted Muller.

"A gentleman has shiny boots," put in Pinto from the background, with a nervous glance round as if he were taking a liberty.

"That's wot I sye," cried the cockney approvingly; "'e's a toff wi' shiny pants an' shiny boots — —"

"And a boiled shirt, I hope?" interrupted Jack, laughing.

"Well, h'I don' mean to insinnivate nuffin' agin you, Jack. We h'all knows you is a real bang-up 'eavy swell when you've got your shore togs on."

"I meets a genelman one time way down to Saint Louis, bigges' genelman eber I see'd, an' he gib dis chile a clout on der ear an' say, 'Get out ob my way, yo dirty nigger,'" announced Sam.

"Well, 'ave you h'all done, for Gaud's syke?" inquired the cockney loftily.

"Wall," said Hank slowly, "I calculate a gentleman's a cuss as is some perlite. He don't spit on the floor— —"

"Bedad, what does he do, thin?" broke in the astonished Pat.

"Why, spits in the spittoon!"

"Er course," agreed the cockney. "W'ere wos you brought h'up, Pat?"

"Seein' as 'ow each member o' this 'ere committee-meetin' 's 'ad 'is sye," he went on, "h'I arise ter propose that we asts the opin'on o' Jack Derringer, h'as bein' er h'expert on the subject."

"I shore seconds thet proposal," said Broncho, "though I nurses certain views tharon which no expert is goin' to stampede me out of."

"Well," began Jack, as they all waited round silently, "it's a pretty big subject; but my idea of a gentleman is a clean man who minds his own business and'll go the limit for a pal—a man who plays his cards straight and keeps a stiff upper lip."

"Thet ain't no gentleman, thet's a white man," exclaimed old Bedrock Ben, with a shake of his head.

"Same thing, ought to be," replied Jack.

"Well, see 'ere, cocky, does you mean ter tell me a man can be a genelman wivout no shiny pants nor nuffin'?" asked the astonished cockney.

"Every Siwash is a gentleman when he's got his store-clothes on, 'cordin' t'you, Hollins," said Hank with contempt.

"What in hell air yew broken-down gin-soakers doin' forrard? Relieve the wheel, yew scum, or I'll come an' knock yer durned ugly heads off."

It was Black Davis on the rampage. The foc's'le head committee-meeting broke up like a swarm of disturbed ants, and as they crowded down the ladder the cockney called out:

"There's a genelman for ye, byes, a real genelman."

CHAPTER VIII
"ON THE FOC'S'LE HEAD"

One Sunday afternoon in the south-east trades the foc's'le indulged itself in another of those excitable debates which sailors on deep-water ships love so much.

It was a superb South Pacific day, with a glinting sea and a sky full of those fluffy white billowy clouds which painters so delight to seat cherubs upon.

The upper strata of these sheep-backs moved faster than the lower, as if engaged in a heavenly steeplechase, signifying an increase of wind.

On the *Higgins*, for a wonder, peace reigned, for the old man and Black Davis were both below taking a "stretch off the land," whilst the bosun held the deck.

Forward both watches were assembled on the foc's'le head—some stretched on their backs with eyes shut, others propped up against the capstan or bitts pretending to sew or read.

Studpoker Bob, true to his bent in life, was rapidly appropriating Hank's payday by aid of a very dirty pack of cards and a game known as "Casino."

Close by sat Jack Derringer, patching a pair of oilskin pants, with the cowboy prone beside him, a paint-covered, disreputable slouch hat which had once been a "shore-enough Stetsin" hiding his face from the glare of the sun.

Leaning against the port lighthouse, old Ben Sluice, with the aid of a gigantic pair of spectacles perched on the tip of his nose, laboriously spelt out a yellow-backed English society novel.

The cockney, with his head buried in his arms, lay face down on the deck in the attitude beloved by the British Tommy Atkins, snoring like a tired cross-cut saw; whilst Paddy at his side bent a wrinkled brow upon a gigantic volume entitled, *The Drainage of Europe*.

Below on the maindeck Curly and the boy worked steadily upon a mass of singlets and shirts, with the aid of the wash-deck tub.

Suddenly old Ben Sluice dropped his book, gave a slow look round, and, catching Jack's eye, spoke:

"Jack, you've been learnt—eddicated as they say. What breed o' coyote air these here book-sharps? What does they allow is their long suit? Does this here benighted burro reckon he knows 'hoss'? He don't know 'hoss' from 'jackass,' nor 'mewel' from 'dogy'; he's green an' juicy a whole passel, like a fool-kid suckin' eggs an' actin' smart."

"What's the trouble, Ben?"

"Why, look-a-here; this buckaroo clean gets me, fur a fact. I cain't throw a squaw-hitch over his idees worth a cent. He has me driftin' like lost sheep——"

"What cuts you, old son?" broke in Broncho, from behind his sombrero.

"Wall, it's this way. Thar's a long-nose coon the book-sharp calls Lord Edward, who didn't oughter be allowed round. He's a big auger, too, way up on the trail.

"He goes buttin' round the landscape, a-hittin' it up high, a-discardin' his dinero like as if he's a mine-boss an' a-soakin' up tanglefoot to beat a sheepman; an' he's roped up a wife as pretty as a peach, whom he don' pay no more attention to than if she's an empty bottle.

"He jest neglec's her complete 'cept with his tongue, which is that mean an' ugly it gets her hot in the collar every time. Wall, she jest sets thar an' wilts, an' don' pay no heed to nothin', though thar's a whole mob o' softies floppin' round her like gapin' trout-fish, sayin' as how hers weren't no dago dream o' paradise, till they gets mushy an' maudlin' over her white face an' big eyes; an' thar ain't one of 'em, with their soft talk, who's got the sand to up an' shoot the white outer the high-falootin' eye of Lord Edward.

"Chucks! It makes me tired. Is they men or wax figgers? An' this here book-sharp allows they're first-class broncho-twisters. But if they is low-down skunks, the wimen bar this here put-upon Lady Beatrice is shore rattlesnakes from away back, they're that venomous; an' they fires out words at this here Lord Edward's wife as'd make a jack-rabbit curl his tail, which same words carves out wounds in the pore female like mushroom bullets. I'm a single-footer myself, an' ain't cut the tracks o' many wimen bar squaws; nor yet want to, unless this here book-sharp's brand o' female is a fake, which I shore reckon it is."

"Women is mighty various," drawled the cowpuncher meditatively. "Some is sweet as molasses, some's all venegar. One kind'll stampede at the drop of a hat, another'll get balky an' jest set thar. No, you can't play no system on women—the deal's a sight too blotched."

"Then you allows this here book-sharp shows savvy in his idees?"

"Has these here rattlesnake females you discourses on many rings on their horns?"

"Wall, I reckon their lustre is some faded, if that's a high kyard in the deal."

"Which it shore enough is, for it's this way. When we-alls starts along this mortal trail we're like colts friskin' about, allowin' it's a case o' jam an' doughnuts cl'ar through. We shore sooner or later butts into trouble, gets bogged, and is yanked out, an' goes on gettin' bogged an' bein' yanked out till it gets to be a habit. But wi' wimen it's different. Gettin' bogged that-a-way frets 'em, till they're feelin' as ugly an' mean as Government pack-mules, an' they jest hankers to shoot off their bazoo till they has some one howlin'; an' the more rings they has on their horns the more they frets an' sets in to pull the props out from under the fresher fillies an' side-track them into the bog of disrepute."

Jack listened to this speech with half-shut eyes, and then half muttered to himself:

"Men are a queer kind of beasts and women a queer kind of angels."

"I allow Broncho piles it on too thick," declared old Ben stubbornly, not noticing Jack's remark.

"Bedad!" chimed in Paddy, roused from his book by the miner's deep voice, "but my old woman's after bein' 'the pole o' me tent,' as they say in the Seharey. Her spuds'd make the mouth o' the divil wather sufeecient to put out old Mother Nick's galley-fire."

"Lawd, you surprise me, Pat!" exclaimed the cockney, rolling over on his back and rubbing his eyes. "A bloomin' Don Juan like you spliced? W'y, you're a disgryce."

"Be aisy, be aisy, an' don't call y'r brither names. What's a Don Juan, any way?"

"A Don Juan is er sort er——" and Hollins broke off and scratched his head for want of the proper word.

"I'll be after Don Juaning you with a black eye the minit before next," burst out Paddy fiercely, the suspicion breaking into his brain that he was being insulted.

"Oh, go slow an' don't be so bloomin' gay," drawled the cockney disdainfully. "You ain't the on'y lydy-killer on the beach, if you 'as got an old Dutch peelin' spuds on yer h'ancestral mud-bank."

"The hen-breed is smooth goods s'long as yew don't get married none; then they're sure p'ison," suddenly broke in Hank, with the sad but self-satisfied look of a man of big experience in such matters.

"Thar, you're shore way off the range," exclaimed Broncho emphatically. "A female which ain't hitched up in double harness is as wo'thless in the game o' life as an ace which ain't drawed nothin'. Her locoed parents is plumb chagrined to death, when, after chippin' in a blue stack or two for the draw, they can't rake out even a hen-ranche tough or a paper dude to yoke her up to. And, again, say you-alls is a-aimin' to throw your rope over some high-steppin', head-tossin' filly; what with you prancin' out in y'r store-clothes every time, an' the dinero you-alls has to paw down in your war-bags for to soothe her frettin's for doughnuts an' sech eadibles, it shore makes your wad o' notes look some flat an' shrunk up. An' all the time you-alls is a-frettin' an' a-frothin' an' feelin' chunked up, mebbe, one minit, an' flatter than a flapjack the next. No, you draws no dividend on women onless they're married. It's them yoked-up longhorns like Paddy who gets a rake off the pot in this earthly game."

"I'm puttin' up my payday agen that deck-swab that yew ain't married none, Broncho," returned Hank sourly.

"That's so, son, I ain't that lucky," drawled the cowpuncher. "I've taken tickets more'n once, but I never ain't drawed nothin' I'm near makin' a winnin' play with."

"I'd rather hev' had a blank than the winning number o' the lottery I raked in my old woman with," growled the disillusioned Hank.

"Mebbe she reckons she ain't owin' Providence nothin' fur bliss gratis when she gets down to the bedrock o' your vartues," remarked old Ben Sluice, with a slow grin.

"Is that meant?" snarled Hank, rising to his feet. He was not in the best of tempers—those who played cards long with Studpoker Bob seldom were. "I'll soon show yew my vartues, my all-fired smartie," he growled, advancing on Ben in a menacing attitude. "I guess them vartues'll raise some pretty considerable bumps on y'r ugly figger-head."

"It's a foight, bedad!" exclaimed Paddy, delightedly. "Go it, ye spalpeens! Git a move on your bump-raisin' operations, Hank, me broth of a boy."

"Jest you backwater some," said Ben coolly, pulling out a capstan-bar from the rack as Hank squared up to him.

Hank drew back uncertainly, for there was a nasty gleam in the old miner's eyes.

"Crikey! but 'e's got the bulge on you, Hank, proper," grinned the cockney appreciatively.

"I would shorely like to savvy what for you two lunattics is a-howlin' for blood?" drawled Broncho, as he slowly proceeded to fill his pipe.

"This half-baked sluice-robber has the hell-freezin' nerve to insinnivate that my old woman don't bank none on my vartues," explained the injured benedict ferociously.

Jack had been holding himself in up till now well enough, but this last was too much for him, and, doubling up, he burst into a roar of laughter, in which old Ben joined heartily, taking for granted that the laugh was on his side of the deck.

"I guess Ben wouldn't think it so durned funny, if he'd drop that handspike an' stand up like a man," snarled Hank.

"Book-sports allows as how it's women as causes mos' of the skin-ticklin' in this ornery globe, an' I reckon they shore hits the bull's-eye this time," remarked Broncho, sagely.

"What's the row?" broke in Curly excitedly, coming up the topgallant-ladder in two bounds.

"W'y, swipe me if ole Ben ain't been an' hurted Hank's delikit feelin's," explained the cockney.

"It's a cert, son, as how Hank ain't out to have his back scratched that away. A wounded grizzly is mild an' dreamlike compared to him," added Broncho, with a slow droop of his left eye.

"Vy don' you blunk 'im?" grunted the Dutchman's heavy voice, addressing itself to Hank.

"Hell!" burst out the exasperated man. "If thet Dutch son of a carrion-crow gives me any durned chin-chin, I'll ram his ugly pig's-eyes outer the back of his head"; and Dutchy withered into his shell again.

"Look-a-here, partner, ain't you had 'bout enuff o' this low-grade dust-raisin'," inquired Ben loftily; still, however, clinging to his trusty capstan-bar. "'Cos thar goes four bells an' it's my wheel."

"Air you goin' to take in the slack o' them insinnivations?" demanded Hank, with dignity.

"You jest step outer the trail an' let this outfit pass, or I reckon you'll be shy considerable epidermis in another minit," growled old Ben angrily, as Hank blocked his way down the topgallant-ladder.

"Wall! Dog my cats if I stand to that!" roared Hank, and he made a wild rush at the old miner.

Ben lunged out furiously with the handspike, but the long, wiry down-easter dodged the formidable weapon with catlike activity, and the next moment they were "in holds," in the parlance of the prize-ring.

Clutched in each other's arms, they reeled across the foc's'le head like hugging bears, and then down they came with a crash on the deck.

"I'll learn yew to miscall a free-born American citizen, yew long-ha'red dump-thief," screeched Hank, as they rolled over and he came on top.

But with a desperate effort Ben reversed the positions, and as his horny fingers gripped the other's hairy throat he growled like an angry grizzly.

"You reckon you's ugly, but this child's uglier."

Hank tried hard to gurgle out a suitable retort, but his effort sounded like the choke of a ship's pump. Wildly he clutched at the iron hands on his throat, but in vain; he could not budge them. His breath began to come in short gasps, his face to flush purple beneath the deep tan, and his strength to leave him.

Both watches were now gathered round the two combatants, a ring of excited faces.

The gambler was perched up on the capstan, and as he remarked afterwards in describing the fight to Red Bill, who was all this time waiting to be relieved at the wheel,

"I jest sits back in the peep-chair an' follows the run of the cards, like it were a faro game."

The cockney, his face working with excitement, hopped up and down like a cat on hot bricks, crying out,

"Sock it to 'im, Ben, sock it to 'im! Starboard watch fur ever!"

"Chucks! but Ben has him in one spin o' the wheel," remarked Broncho to the rover. "This here's a freeze-out for Hank; he's beginnin' to unwind melodies o' despair."

For Hank, in his effort to breathe, was groaning and grunting and choking.

"Go easy, Ben; I think Hank's had about enough," interposed Jack, leaning over and trying to drag him off the prostrate down-easter.

"Sticks to Hank closer'n bacon-rind," observed Broncho, watching Jack's unavailing efforts.

"Help me get him off," panted the rover. "He'll choke the man in a minute."

"That's some obvious—that 'possum ain't doin' no roll-over an' playin' dead," drawled the cowboy composedly, as he lent Jack his aid.

"A man's finish is his own," put in the gambler, objecting to the interference of the two friends.

"You jest hold your hand, my lively one-horse-saloon bottle-washer, or I suspicion I'll have to tame you some," said the cowpuncher contemptuously.

Then, with a terrific heave together, Jack and Broncho pulled old Ben off Hank on to his feet.

Ben just stood there and looked at his victim, gasping on the deck.

"Mebbe that'll learn you some, mister; Ben Sluice don't allow no Yankee wolf to come yowlin' blood round him without puttin' up a breeze o' some sort"; and he turned on his heel, clambered down the ladder, and went aft to relieve the wheel.

"Wake up, old son, an' take a new hold," said the cowpuncher kindly, as Hank gave no signs of life except to roll his eyes and breathe in harsh, jerky groans.

"Get us a bucket of water, Jim," called the rover.

The water had the desired effect. Hank's face assumed a more healthy colour; he drew a deep breath and sat up.

"I'm feelin' some considerable used up," he muttered slowly; and then he began to swear in that vivid, forcible way which obtains at sea. Presently he rose to his feet and stood staggering, then lurched forward like a drunken man and headed for the topgallant-ladder.

"He's shore as wobbly as a tenderfooted cow-hoss in a patch o' cactus," remarked Broncho, as he noted Hank's tottering steps.

"I was all choked up in a minit; that minin' tough's fingers are like iron clamps," threw back the other, as he carefully clawed his way down on to the maindeck.

"And that h'ain't no josh, neither," declared the cockney feelingly. "'E nearly 'as you garrotted inter dead meat, s'elp me bob."

"I allows Hank has all he wants," pronounced Broncho. "When women is the theme o'discourse, gents o' savvy cash in an' quit; thar's no knowin' which way the cat will hop. You're liable to get creased or reap a skinful o' lead whichever way you plays your hand."

And thus the argument finished.

CHAPTER IX
"THE GLORY OF THE STARS"

That evening, Jack, the astronomical weather-prophet (as he laughingly called himself) took advantage of the magnificence of the stars, undimmed by the moon, which was still below the horizon, to bring out his big telescope.

Eight bells had gone and the starboard watch were below until midnight. The greater number of them, preferring the fresh night air to that of the stuffy foc's'le, had brought their blankets up on to the foc's'le head. Here they lay about in attitudes peculiar to sailors, and in which only sailors could sleep.

Only one man lay at full length, flat on his back, his pipe between his lips, as he puffed steadily, a vacant look in his open eyes as he rested his brain as well as his body. This was Red Bill. Near him lay the cockney, curled up like a dog and snoring tunefully, his pipe on the deck by his cheek, where it had fallen from his mouth. A sailor always lights his pipe to go to sleep with, and generally falls asleep smoking. A habit which is supposed to be very dangerous to landlubbers, but which, so far as I have heard, never caused an accident at sea.

Paddy sat jammed between two bollards, his chin sunk upon his chest, in a position which looked the reverse of comfortable, and yet he was sleeping peacefully.

Up in the bows reclined Jack, with the cowboy and Curly. These last two were taking turns to peer through the telescope, whilst Jack discoursed upon the wonders of the heavens.

"Now, just you look at that fellow there, Broncho," said the rover, pointing along the cowboy's line of sight. "That's the planet Saturn."

"You don't say!"

"Yes, have you got him? Now, do you see his rings?"

"Which I do for shore. Whatever be them rings, Jack, an' why does this here Saturn trail round with 'em. I notes he's the on'y star with them appendages."

"They're supposed to be rings of gas or vapour. It's been said that our world once had rings like that, and that they burst and all fell upon the earth at once, which produced the flood."

"Say, but that's kinder strange. However scientific sports onravels them mysteries an' rounds up them facts shore has me bogged. Mebbe Providence devastates this here Saturn with floods right now. If them rings is rain-clouds they're bulky a whole lot, an' liable to swamp this Saturn planet if they plays a steady game; an' if I were an inhabitant thar I'd be hittin' quite a gait for the high spots, or pawin' in my war-bags for the price of a birch-bark."

"Of course, you know the signs of the zodiac, Curly," went on the amateur astronomer.

"No, not all. Spout 'em out, Jack, and show 'em to us."

"Why, don't you remember the rhyme:

The Ram, the Bull, the Heavenly Twins,
And next the Crab, the Lion shines;
The Virgin and the Scales,
The Scorpion, Archer, and He-Goat,
The Man that holds the water-pot,
And Fish with glittering tails."

"Whar's the Bull you mentions?" exclaimed the cowpuncher eagerly. "I jest itches to throw a rope over him."

"Well, do you see that V with a big red star?"

"Red star—why, shore, I savvys that V since I were a kiddy."

"That's the head of the Bull, and that rose-red star is Aldebaran, the eye of the Bull. That's a star you'll find useful some day, Curly, when you're captain of a ship and want to take night sights."

"Why ever do they call him 'Aldebaran'?" asked Broncho.

"It's Arabic, meaning 'the follower,' because it follows the Pleiades."

"I know the Pleiades," said Curly, pointing aloft proudly.

"Many a night I saw the Pleiads,
Rising through the mellow shade,
Glitter like a swarm of fire-flies
Tangled in a silver braid,"

quoted Jack.

"The Pleiades," he went on, "were the seven daughters of Atlas, and are in some mysterious way connected with the flood. The ancient Egyptians celebrated a festival in November at the culmination of the Pleiades, which they directly connected with the flood.

"The same thing seems to have occurred amongst the Hindoos, the Persians, the Druids, and in the South Seas. The Japanese Feast of Lanterns is also supposed to commemorate this event, whilst the ancient inhabitants of Mexico had a tradition that the world had been destroyed at the midnight culmination of the Pleiades. This is all mysteriously borne out by the fact that Taurus, the Bull, whom you have just looked at, shows only his head and shoulders; he is supposed to be swimming."

"That's shore interesting as an idee," commented Broncho. "But do you-alls regyard this here flood superstition you recounts as a likely play?"

"It's only a theory, Broncho, with maybe nothing in it."

"Theeries is theeries, an' facts is facts. I meets a gent once way down to Tombstone, who allows he's the bigges' full-blooded wolf in Arizona. He's shore a tough citizen a whole lot, carries a six-gun with the stock full o' notches an' the trigger tied back. Wall, this here Tombstone sport, which his name is P'ison Dick (an' he's shore p'isonous as a t'rantler) cherishes the theery, an' gives it out premiscuous as a hoss-back opinion, that a 45-calibre bullet ain't able to worry him none; if he accoomilates one he allows he assimilates it into his system, an' don't take no more account tharof. That's his theery, an' as mebbe you-alls shrewdly surmises, it bogs down in the dust before facts—an' it's this way; he's been a-loafin' around Tombstone mebbe hard on the hocks of a year, an' the camp's shore full to bustin' with his goin's on; and I ain't wonderin', for there ain't a moon goes by without Tombstone's shy a citizen an' mebbe a greaser or two, all corpses o' this P'ison Dick's layin' out.

"Wall, it's 'bout sundown, one day in the early fall, when a stranger comes lopin' into camp on a played-out pinto pony, which he halts up before the 'Gold Nugget,' old Konkey Bell's saloon, an' proceeds to dismount tharfrom like as if he's some wearied an' bone-tired. I notes this through the door, from where I'm buckin' a faro game, an' likewise takes in a pair o' big black eyes an' a smooth face. 'It's a boy,' I remyarks casual to myself as I coppers my bet, an' the next minit I sees this here black-eyed foreigner up agen the bar, a-swallowin' a drink 'longside o' P'ison Dick. It ain't manners none to take a drink alone that-away, an' is liable to make a gent too conspicuous to be healthy; but seein' he's a stranger and without many rings on his horns, it passes. P'ison Dick scowls, but says nothin'; then *poco tiempo* tells the bar-keep to set 'em up again.

"The bar-keep slams down a glass before the stranger, who pushes it away some careless, an' allows he's done finished lubricatin'.

"P'ison Dick's eyes kinder narrowed like a snake's.

"'I'm askin' you to hev' a drink, stranger,' he says, colder'n ice in hell.

"You-alls may surmise the rest of us is some taciturn, not to say mute a whole lot, an' some foxy longhorns is already takin' cover.

"The stranger smiles kinder queer at Dick—jest a mouth twist, his eyes lookin' a heap grim; an' he stands thar for mebbe the length of a drink o' whisky, then snaps out in a sorter shaky screech, 'To hell with yer drink!' an' before you can turn a kyard over, he ups an' has the glass bruck on P'ison Dick's crimson beak.

"By this move he has Dick some disgruntled an' gains more time to draw; then, bang! go the gatlin's a'most together, an' Dick's theery cuts adrift from him without strainin' itself none. He's dead meat that sudden, he don't even have time to emit a groan.

"The stranger's hit too, plumb through the lung, an' pretty soon cashes in likewise; but, where the game comes queer is this way. That 'ere black-eyed party whom I allowed was a boy is a woman, an' a mighty pretty one at that, though her spirit peters out 'fore we is able to corral any reasons for the game she plays; an' as I pulls my freight next sun-up I never does accoomilate no knowledge tharof. Anyway, P'ison Dick gets his medicine an' lights out that sudden for the heavenly pastures I reckons the angels, or more likely it's them fork-tailed miscreant collectors, is some surprised to see him bulgin' in an' defilin' the scenery o' their sperit-ranche."

"Well," observed Jack slowly, "astronomy's a science which gives a wide fling to the imagination, and without those theories you despise is liable to lose a great deal of interest. But let's look at Orion, the finest constellation in the heavens. He's the greatest hunter the world has ever known—Nimrod, who, with his dogs, has been placed up in the heavens to hunt the Bull.

"D'you see that reddish star? That's Betelgeuse—Arabic *beyt al agoos*, 'the old man's house.' Betelgeuse is a sun like our own, but a cooling one, and represents the left shoulder of Orion, Bellatrix, supposed to be a lucky star for women, being the right shoulder. Those three bright stars in a line are the hunter's belt, whilst below is Rigel—Arabic *rigl*, 'a foot'—being Orion's left foot.

"That big star of a delicate green is Sirius, the blazing dog-star, Orion's great hunting dog."

"So!" drawled Broncho with a slow smile. "Smell-dawg or tree-dawg?"[1]

"Sirius," went on Jack, taking no notice of Broncho's facetiousness, "is the brightest star in the heavens, though not the biggest. Canopus, though only half as bright, is immeasurably bigger; but if it were as near to us as Sirius I expect it would shine in the sky with as great a brilliance as our sun.

"Now, at the least computation, Sirius is fifty billion miles off, or five hundred and thirty-seven thousand times as far from the earth as the sun; and since light diminishes as the square of the distance increases, the sun, if as far off as Sirius, would give us two hundred and eighty-eight thousand million times less light than it does now.

"The character of Sirius' spectrum shows that, surface for surface, its brightness is far greater than the sun's, and as Sirius is some twenty times the size of the sun, Sirius is reckoned to shine some seventy times as bright as the sun. This is putting the calculation at its smallest. Good authorities put Sirius at twice that distance off, and calculate the star's brilliancy as two hundred and eighty-eight times greater than the sun's.[7] Now, when you come to contemplate Canopus——"

"Hold on, son! Hold your horses there!" burst out Broncho, drawing a long breath. "Sirius is a size too large for this child. My brain's dizzy an' wobblin' with them Sirius calc'lations o' yours, an' if you turns your wolf loose on this Canopus star, compared to which you allows Sirius is merely a puny picaninny, you'll shore have me that locoed an' brain-strained, tryin' to size up them measurements o' yours, I'd be liable to dislocate my mental tissues an' stampede away into a lunatic complete."

"Well, you needn't worry; astronomers are beaten by Canopus."

"If you-alls aims to surprise me by that statement, you don't succeed. I bet a stack o' blues them astronomy sharps goes locoed or beds down in their coffins 'fore they has time to round up the tally o' Canopus," declared the cowpuncher.

"He's so far off," continued Jack impressively, "that if they used up all the oughts in the world, they couldn't get his distance down on paper."

"Tell us some more about Sirius," said Curly, his eyes bulging with Jack's stupendous statements.

"Well, there is another queer thing about Sirius. He's got a big companion-star fussing round him, which gives such a dim light it can only be seen by the very biggest of astronomical telescopes. There is no reason why there should not be many invisible as well as visible stars in the firmament. As Bessel said, 'No reason exists for considering luminosity an essential property of stars.'

"Just imagine, then, that it is quite possible that the heavens are not only full of those bright globes we see night after night, but besides them a multitude of dim, ghostlike stars, unseen by us, but there all the same, are pacing along their allotted paths like the rest."

"Are these invisible, unlighted stars allowed by scientists, Jack?" asked Curly, in a subdued voice of awe.

"Hinted at, hinted at," returned the rover carelessly. "But I'll tell you something more wonderful to think of than that—the systems of double, treble, and quadruple suns. Now, our solar system is at the bottom rung of the social ladder in the heavenly world. We just have a plain white sun, which we revolve round with regular seasons and fixed day and night; but take a system that revolves round a double star, and thus has two suns, and say these suns differ in colour,—as is often the case, for every star has a colour of its own—Sirius is a pale green, Aldebaran rose-red, Betelgeuse orange-red, Rigel a blue-white, Capella a pearly white, and so on.

"Suppose, then, one of these suns is red and the other blue. Imagine, if you can, the combinations of colour that ensue, not to mention the variations in day and night and in the seasons.

"At one time both suns will be high in the heavens at once, one shedding rays of red, the other rays of blue; and as they set in different corners of the horizon, two gorgeously coloured sunsets simply overwhelm the sky with beautiful colour-effects.

"At another time, perhaps, one sun will be above the horizon for half the round of the clock, the other taking the other half—no night during that period, simply so many hours of red and so many hours of blue light, and perhaps the sunrise of the one coincides with the sunset of the other. Ye gods! What a prospect! But how much further does a quadruple system carry us—four suns glaring down upon one; no nights at all now (the people in those systems no doubt have reached a stage in the evolution of the body—if, indeed, they have bodies at all—when sleep is no longer required), just days of every hue, of every grade of colour—pale blue days, brilliant red days, gorgeous yellow days, violet days, green days——"

"Good night, Jack," broke in the cowpuncher softly. "I guess I'll quit. You're one too many for me; you have me beat to a stan'still. My head'll burst if I accoomilates any more astronomy. It takes up too much space in my brain-cells an' don' settle down none, but jest rampages 'round stampedin' my intellec's out into the cold, till I wonders, has I a headpiece at all or has it blowed off like a rawcket?"

This broke up the astronomy party, and the three rolled into their blankets; but Curly, when he was turned out at one bell, complained of a dream in which the devil, with a face of variegated colours, had been grinning at him through Saturn's rings, whilst the grim shades of ghost stars pranced before him in all manner of fantastic shapes, headed by the monstrous fiery apparition of Sirius, whose flames, spread out in great tentacles—a twisty, creepy, crawly mass of claw-ended arms—sought to drag the terrified dreamer out of his blankets.

FOOTNOTES:

[7] It is now known that these figures *re* Sirius are much overstated.

CHAPTER X
"STUDPOKER BOB'S MALADY"

Like most wooden ships, the *Higgins* had to be pumped out twice a day, once in the morning watch and once in the second dog-watch.

A ship's pumps are worked by handle-bars on heavy flywheels, and it is probably the finest exercise in the world for your back muscles, especially if you have a bucko like Black Davis to watch over you and keep you doing sixty revolutions to the minute for half an hour without a spell.

The bosun was not such a keen muscle-developer, and in consequence the starboard watch only averaged thirty-five to forty revolutions a minute, and also had a spell-ho after fifteen minutes.

Notwithstanding this, Studpoker Bob, who had a horror of any sort of form of muscle-developing, used to let his arms go round with the brakes, and so managed that, instead of his arms pulling the brakes, the brakes pulled his arms.

This man was fast beginning to show up in his true colours.

As Broncho observed to Jack:

"That ere kyard-sharp don't surge back on a rope suffeecient to throw a calf. He's shore regyardful of his health that-away; yet he's a-distributin' views in the foc's'le like as if he's the most put-upon gent in the ship, which same views is shore fomentin' trouble."

"The man's a real waster," replied the rover. "I watched him dealing a brace game last night against Hank, Ben, and those two tenderfoots, Jimmy Green and Pinto. I believe he's got notes for most of the men's paydays already, and now, as you say, he's trying in a sneaky, underhand way to rake up trouble; but sailors always will walk blindly into the ditch, and won't be warned."

"Which his mood is shore ornery an' he's plumb wolf by nacher; but as you-alls sagely remyarks, them misguided shorthorns won't believe it none, an' listens to his howlin' like he's the President of the United States. It has me plumb wearied," and Broncho sniffed disdainfully as he slowly filled his favourite corncob.

But matters were rapidly coming to a head. The *Higgins* had lost the south-east trades, and was plunging into a heavy head sea under topgallant-s'ls, whilst a succession of sprays turned the forward part of the ship into a shower-bath, and ever and anon a green sea tumbled aboard and roared aft.

The wind, a dead muzzler, was slowly increasing in strength, with an edge to it which was a good foretaste of the "Roaring Forties."

To windward the sky had a dirty look, and untidy, threadbare storm-clouds swept across it, whilst in the west the sun sank into a greenish, sickly sea through a variegated mess of yellow tints.

The watch no longer went about bare-foot in thin dungarees; instead, oilskins and sea-boots were the order of the day.

At four bells, 6 p.m., the port watch went below, and as they came forward some of them presented a very curious appearance. Sam, the coloured man, had supplemented his rags with odd bits of dungaree and canvas, tied on to his body with numerous pieces of ropeyarn; whilst Jim, the boy, swaggered along in an old blanket coat of Jack's, which made him a good-sized overcoat.

The cockney went aft to relieve the wheel, a somewhat comical figure in some Piccadilly masher's discarded town coat, with velvet collar and cuffs, whilst the rest of the watch were turned out to man the pumps.

They started briskly to work at a cry of "Shake her up, boys," from the bosun.

Studpoker Bob, in his usual style, took special care lest he should inadvertently put some weight on to the brakes, and was succeeding, he thought, very well.

Jack, of course, was not the man to let the opportunity go by without a chanty, and started off with:

"Were you never down in Mobile bay?"

The whole watch thundered in the chorus with the exception of the gambler, who kept all his breath for his mutinous talk in the foc's'le.

As they swung the bars, deep came the note:

"John, come tell us as we haul away."
(Jack) "A-screwing cotton all the day."
(*Chorus*) "John, come tell us as we haul away.
Aye, aye, haul, aye!
John, come tell us as we haul away."

Then Jack went on:

"What did I see in Mobile Bay?"
(*Chorus*) "John, come tell us as we haul away."
(Jack) "Were the girls all fair and free and gay?"
(*Chorus*) "John, come tell us as we haul away.
　　　　Aye, aye, haul, aye!
　　　　John, come tell us as we haul away."
(Jack) "Oh! This I saw in Mobile Bay."
(*Chorus*) "So he tells us as we haul away."
(Jack) "A pretty girl a-making hay."
(*Chorus*) "So he tells us as we haul away.
　　　　Aye, aye, haul, aye!
　　　　So he tells us as we haul away."

So the chanty ran on gaily verse after verse, the chorus raised high above the moaning of the wind and the groaning of the ship.

"Give us another!" was the general cry as the last verse finished, and away went Jack again with "A-roving":

(Jack) "In Amsterdam there lives a maid—
　　　　Mark you well what I say—
　　　　In Amsterdam there lives a maid,
　　　　And she is mistress of her trade.
　　　　I'll go no more a-roving from you, fair maid!"

(*Chorus*) "A-roving, a-roving, since roving's been my ruin,
　　　　I'll go no more a-roving from you, fair maid!"

This also ran its course, then Curly struck up "One more day for Johnnie":

(Curly) "Only one more day for Johnnie."
(*Chorus*) "One more day!"
(Curly) "Oh! rock and roll me over!"
(*Chorus*) "One more— —"

Then the bosun most rudely interrupted the music.

Biff! Bang! Thud! "You d— —d sodgering hound!" Whack! "I've watched you loafin' long enough!" Thump! and Studpoker Bob, lifted clean off his feet by a sudden muscular grasp upon his collar, was held at arm's length and fairly battered by the bosun's brawny fist. Crash! an eye closed up.

"Mercy! mercy! you're killin' me!" whined the miserable wretch.

Bish! his nose began to bleed.

"Had enough yet, you d— —d Yankee tough?" growled the bosun.

"Yes, yes; lemme——"

Crack! and his two front teeth were loosened.

"By gum! that were a sockdologer!" commented Bedrock Ben.

The men had stopped working and watched the gambler getting his gruel with appreciative eyes.

"Now, then, put your back into it and no more sodgerin'!" said the bosun, as he released his iron grip.

"I'll get even with you, you durned Britisher," snarled the card-sharper, as soon as he was released, his anger overcoming his caution.

"Give me lip, will ye?" roared the bosun. "Threaten me, would ye?"

Again he seized upon Studpoker Bob, and this time did not desist from his chastening until the man dropped to the deck, beaten to a jelly and hardly able to move.

At the wheel the cockney hopped up and down with excitement, straining his neck in his eagerness to see the gambler get his hammering, and a grim smile of amusement came into Old Man Riley's keen visage, as he watched the performance with the eye of an expert from the poop rail.

Letting his victim lie where he dropped, the bosun turned to the pumps and called out, "Tune her up again, boys!" and presently came the welcome cry, "That'll do the pumps!" and the watch trooped forward.

Studpoker Bob, who had lain all this time groaning on the deck, made shift now to get to his legs, and made tracks for the foc's'le.

But the bosun was on to him again.

"Here, you there," he called, "go up an' overhaul them fore an' main t'gallant buntlines."

And up the man had to go.

It was now two bells, and Red Bill trudged slowly aft to relieve the cockney, as he owed him a wheel, and the second dog-watch being considered one of the worst wheels, the cockney had gladly consented to take an hour of that instead of the whole trick at any other time.

Diving through a curtain of spray, the rest of the watch reached the foc's'le.

Hanging up their oilskins, they proceeded to make themselves comfortable. Some crawled into their bunks for a short spell; others, with pipes alight, sat round on the chests, then yarns and chaff began to fly round.

Without it was cold and wet, nearly dark and with every prospect of a dirty night.

The wind could be heard moaning and crying, whistling and screaming through the rigging.

The ship groaned and creaked beneath the sledge-hammer blows of the heavy head sea.

The sprays rattled outside, and all was dismal and comfortless. What wonder if the watch below is one of the comforts of a sailor's life.

"Golly, byes!" burst out the cockney, as he dashed in dripping. "Poor ole Bob, didn't 'e get it socked to 'im. 'E weren't 'ollerin' for more when the bosun got through with 'im, were 'e? Sykes alive! but it were a h'awful lickin'!"

"Begob! but it takes the divil an' all to tackle that big hefty brute of a bosun; an' now he has the poor varmint overhaulin' buntlines. Be me sowl, but Bob's fair up agin' it!" said Paddy.

"And serve him right. The amount of work he does wouldn't bother a child," remarked Jack scornfully.

"Oh, Bob's orl right. 'Is trouble is weakness. 'Ow can 'e work? That bloke ain't got more strength than a 'edge-sparrer; 'is 'ealth is give h'out."

"Who told you that?" asked Jack.

"'E did 'imself, 'bout two days back."

"And whatever is the malady of this here weak-kneed kyard-sharp?" inquired Broncho, in his slow, polite way.

"'E sez as 'ow h'it's consumption which 'as 'im in its gruesome clutches."

"I ain't heard him kaufin' none," remarked the cowboy suspiciously. "I cuts the trail one time of a gent who cashes in from that cawpse-makin' complaint, an' he shore coughs a heap plentyful, an' that loud an' wideflung you couldn't bed-down in the same teepee with him an' make any sort o' success o' slumber. His kaufin' that-away shore puts a bull-moose to shame."

"Now, see 'ere, ducky, I ain't er-sayin' as 'ow that ain't the general racket; but Bob, 'e sez to me, sezzee, 'I'm past the korfin' styge; h'I just spits up my lungs in chunks; h'I ain't the strength to korf,'" returned the cockney doggedly.

"I ain't in line for no sech flapdoodle as that," drawled Broncho. "He ain't goin' to fool this old he-coon none that-away. Why, consumption can no more make a play without kaufin' than smallpox can without spots."

"'Ave it 'ow you loike—h'I just tells you what 'e sez, that's h'all," retorted the cockney angrily.

"Thet's right, pard; but I reckons Broncho calls the deal correct when he says that consumption ain't no more than a low-grade malady without kaufin'. It's kaufin' that makes it the clean-sweep disease that it is," joined in old Bedrock Ben.

"Bedad thin," commented Pat, "Bob's sick with consumption, but the disaise ain't after makin' him ill at all."

"The man's as strong and well as you or I," exclaimed Curly hotly, poking his head out of his bunk.

"I ain't sayin' but that if Studpoker Bob's got consumption prowlin' around him, it ain't been an' staked out its claim an' started in to work diggin' out his innards by now, after the energy the bosun displays on him," went on Ben.

"And that ain't no bluff, neither. The bosun shore puts a heap o' zest into the game, an' after bein' upheaved an' jumped on that-away, I reckons Bob don't get so much bliss as he did," agreed Broncho.

At this moment, Jim, who had just been to strike one bell, dived in glistening with wet.

"It's blowin' up hard; it'll be 'All hands to the crojjick' at eight bells, the bosun says," he announced.

"What's that, sonny? All hands at eight bells? An' it's our first watch below! Hell take the sea, anyhow," growled old Ben.

"We're in for a night of it. Listen to the wind," observed Curly.

There was a general rush for oilskins and rubbers.

"You'll want lashings on your oilskins to-night, Broncho," remarked Jack, as he knotted a deep-sea lashing round his waist.

"An' what's the aim in life o' these here lashin's?"

"Ter keep the bloomin' water out, er course," jerked out the cockney, as he struggled with a sea-boot.

"Where's that 'ere sufferin', consumption-stricken gent, Studpoker Bob, all this time?" asked old Ben, looking round the foc's'le.

"He's warmin' an' repa'rin' himself in the galley, and havin' a chin-chin with Lung," returned Jim.

"And he calls himself an American citizen," grunted Ben, in great disgust. "I'd sooner exchange views with a pra'rie-dog or a gopher than one o' them heathens from the Orient. They're all right to wash clothes or toss flapjacks or sech-like plays, but to shake dice with 'em—no, sirree, that's what I calls plumb degradin'."

As he spoke the thundering voice of the bosun was heard.

"A-l-l h-a-n-d-s s-h-o-r-t-e-n s-a-i-l!"

Sure enough it was about time, for the wind was shrieking through the rigging with more strength every minute, and at every plunge the heavily pressed vessel sent the sprays right over her. The lee-scuppers were full, and a succession of dollops poured over the weather rail.

CHAPTER XI
"THE STORMFIEND"

"Crojjick buntlines and clew-garnets!" roared Black Davis.

The men stumbled clumsily round the fife-rail and groped about in the darkness for the right ropes; then, like sundry tug-of-war teams, stood waiting for the word.

"Ready with your tack there, bosun?" called the mate.

"Aye, aye, sir!"

"Haul away!" came the order.

"Hoo-oop, come in with her! Ho-yah, an' she must!" sang Jack, giving time to the hauling.

"Hand over hand, hand over hand!" yelled the bosun.

"Yo-ho-yo-ho-oh-yo-har!"

Swish! and a green sea tumbled aboard, washing the men at the clew-garnet off their legs.

"Bedad, an' it's could!" gasped Pat.

"Thet'll do, y'r weather buntlines; haul away to leeward!" called the mate.

"Hy-ei-ei-ei-ei-ei!" came the swelling chorus, the note rising at each pull.

"Now, then, what ye crowdin' up like that for? Spread out! How can you haul if you ain't got room?" holloaed the bosun. "Up with her, boys, lively now, lively!" he cried sharply. "Oh ho! Two-block her!"

Suddenly from aft came the old man's voice, rising above the roar of the gathering gale.

"Belay all that! Git them t'gallant-s'ls in, Mr. Davis, quick!"

"Aye, aye, sir!"

There was no time to lose. A nasty-looking heavy black cloud with torn, ragged edges was racing up to windward.

"There's dirt in that," said the bosun to Jack, as they manned the t'gallant clew-lines.

"Haul, yew mutton-faced haymakers, haul!" bellowed the mate.

The ship resounded with the cries of the men and the thunder of the flogging canvas.

As the *Higgins* lay over, it was almost impossible to stand on her gleaming wet decks, and to leeward the men on the spilling-lines were up to their waists in broken water.

"Sweat her up, my barnacle-backs!" yelled the bosun encouragingly, standing out a very tower of strength in the midst of the panting, struggling men.

"There's snow coming," jerked out the rover to Broncho, as he sniffed to windward.

First the mizzen topgallant-sail was clewed up and four light men were sent aloft to make it fast; but it was touch and go whether the fore and main topgallant-sails would be clewed up before the approaching squall was upon them, and the men had only just got out on to the footropes and started to fist the sails when it swooped down upon the ship with a furious roar, accompanied by a mixture of snow, hail, and sleet.

The driving snow thickened the darkness into the density of black mud. The sleet spattered and hissed and the hail rattled, pounding on the wet decks like dancing pebbles and beating with blood-drawing force upon the grim, weather-worn faces.

Upon the yards, headed by the bosun, the men fought furiously with the maddened canvas. Crooked fingers scratched despairingly at the rigid curves, bleeding knuckles struck ragingly at the stubborn, iron-like folds. Wildly-shouted commands, cut off by the hooting wind, flew to leeward unheard.

The face of the bosun at the bunt of the main topgallant-sail grew twisted and distorted with grimaces in his vain attempts to make the men understand, unseen in the smothering darkness of the squall even by the man next him; vainly he waved and gesticulated; again and again his mouth shaped the words:

"All together! All together!"

The footropes swung violently as the savage sail jerked them, in a vain attempt to dislodge the struggling men.

The *Higgins* lay over and over and yet over under the strength of the blast; the covering-board disappeared, then the dead-eyes and the topgallant rail; the sheerpoles were dipped, the fair-leads smothered, and a hissing cauldron of seething white water boiled up to and over the hatch tarpaulins.

Minutes passed and she lay steady, her lower yardarms spiking the whirling smother to leeward, right over, pressed down and overwhelmed by the fearful strength of the screeching tempest.

Then there came a lull. The gallant vessel gave a desperate quiver as she struggled to rise, then slowly she brought her spars to windward and shook herself free, the water pouring off the maindeck and dragging the gear off the pins in a hideous tangle.

"Now! now! now!" screeched the bosun, his voice strained to cracking point, and ten sets of hooked claws from ten burly fists fastened upon the swelling breast of the main topgallant-sail.

A few inches were gained and stuffed between the groaning yard and the straining, perspiring bodies. Again the aching finger-tips caught hold; a foot came in this time, then another, and the men at the yardarms fumbled for the gaskets.

"Catch a turn! catch a turn!" bellowed the bosun.

The cockney to windward, his sou'wester gone, his long hair streaming in the wind, and his thin, comical face working furiously with his efforts, managed to get the yardarm gasket passed.

One more heave and the sail was muzzled, and the worn-out men clambered slowly down from aloft.

Meanwhile, Jack, Broncho, Hank, and the gambler were having the time of their lives on the fore.

Jack, at the bunt, with a grim smile on his streaming face and eyes gleaming with a kind of strenuous joy, leant far over and watched like a prize-fighter for an opening.

Broncho and Hank, on each side of him, plucked furiously at the tightly stretched canvas without success.

Like the bosun, Jack saw his chance in the short lull and grabbed a fold, but it was too strong for him and tore itself free; again he dived at it, but the sail, which had not been properly clewed up, behaved like a fiend.

It bellied up in front of him and above him in raging protest, and battered him mercilessly against the mast, whilst it nearly sent Broncho and Hank headlong overboard.

The cowpuncher made a wild clutch at the man-rope as he was hurled backward, and hung there, his muscles strained and cracking as the canvas beat its weight upon him.

Hank, with both arms embracing the bunt-line, swung on the footrope with head and shoulders buried in the shaking folds.

Unsuccessful in its murderous attempt, the sail dropped back and the battle began anew.

Fiercely, enraged by the dastardly behaviour of the vicious sail, the three deep-sea musketeers leant forward to the attack again.

Again and again the sail broke away from the clawing hands, staining itself red with the blood from torn finger-nails and skinned knuckles, until at last they got a firm hold.

Up it came, inch by inch; their arms groaned under the strain, their curved fingers throbbed with fiery pains—still with gritted teeth, they hung on.

Bending over, Jack drove his strong teeth into the sail where his left hand had a grip; then with the weight on his jaw, he shifted his hand and groped for the bunt gasket, whilst Hank hurled furious profanity at the frightened gambler, who was hanging on to the jackstay to leeward, terrified, half-demented, quite useless.

The card-sharper made no attempt to move from his position, and whilst Jack and Broncho passed the bunt gasket, Hank slid out along the footrope and, grasping the jackstay with his left hand, hit fiercely with his right at the face of the shirker.

There is a grim work sometimes aloft in the raging of a gale, the work of heated blood and feelings overwrought by the cruel stress of the moment.

The gambler flinched from the vicious blows and whimpered miserably.

"The cur's no use, anyhow!" shouted Jack disdainfully, but Hank in his mad rage heeded him not.

At last the sail was overcome; they swung themselves into the rigging and slowly descended, struggling against the fury of the wind.

Each gust pinned them down as if spreadeagled, and it was a work of difficulty and arduous labour shifting their feet from one ratline to another. When they reached the deck they were streaming with perspiration and nearly dead beat with their terrific exertions, but the keen, chilly wind soon put new life into them. Paying no heed to the buffeting of the storm, the flying spume, or the pattering hail, they hastily hauled themselves along the weather rail in the pitch darkness, knowing by long experience of night work the geography of the ship.

They found the rest of the crew gathered round the main fife-rail, about to haul up the main course.

The lull had passed and the wind was once more shrieking over them in its mad turbulence. Hail, snow, and spindrift flew across the straining vessel in solid sheets, whilst on every side the torn-up sea lashed itself into smoking soap-suds, and in rushing breakers hurled itself to leeward.

The ship, too heavily pressed under whole topsails and two courses, ploughed her way straight through the rising seas, taking whole mountains of green water over her weather rail forward which, pouring aft, kept the maindeck continually awash.

A bright shaft of light from the carpenter's lamp suddenly flashed forth upon the wild scene, illuminating with its rays the group of sorely spent men amidships. Then it went out before the onslaught of the furious wind, and the darkness seemed greater than before.

Muller, the German, was just slacking away the main-tack when a furious gust came; he lost his head at the wrong moment and the tack took charge.

In a second pandemonium reigned. A frightful slating arose from the released sail, and the heavy block raged about at random, threatening death at every spring, whilst the great ninety-foot mainyard buckled like a bamboo cane.

The confusion for some minutes was indescribable, and by way of improving the situation, the bosun and four of the best men were washed from the clew-garnet into the lee-scuppers.

At the break of the poop the old man danced and screamed with rage, swinging his arms and beating his fists on the rail in a very whirlwind of passion.

Black Davis, hanging on with one hand and grasping a belaying-pin in the other, clawed his way skilfully along the weather bulwark and pounced upon the unfortunate Dutchman.

"Hell an' furies!" he screeched. "Yew infernal, stockfish poundin' Dutch son of a shark, yew slab-sided, bean-swillin', dunderhead yew, what yew think y'r doin', hey? Want ter carry away the mainyard, yew slush-brained numskull?"

Crack! crack! crack! went the belaying-pin on the wretched man's head.

Suddenly, in the midst of it all, the wind lulled again, and the bosun, crawling up the sloping deck on hands and knees, gave tongue lustily:

"Haul away there, haul away, haul away, haul away!"

Once more backs were bent and arms stretched out. Slowly the buntlines came two blocks under the frenzied efforts of the half-dazed men.

"Away aloft an' make it fast!" came the command.

The stumbling, panting crowd pushed and shoved and tumbled over each other as they struggled to the rail and swarmed over it into the rigging.

Headed by the untiring bosun, they raced up the ratlines and scrambled out along the footropes.

"Dig your fingers in and on to the yard with her, boys. All together, now, ay-hay an' up she comes!" roared the bosun from the bunt. "Make a skin! make a skin!" he went on sharply.

"It's shore none easy," muttered Broncho.

"Now you have her! now you have her!" came the bosun's overstrained voice again. "Roll her, boys, roll her!"

"She's a-comin'!" gasped some one, and with a last great effort they got the sail on the yard.

"I'll sit down on the footrope, whilst you swing the gasket to me," Jack called to the cowpuncher, leaning over and putting his lips close to the other's ear.

"I surmise as how a diamond-hitch ain't needful in these heavenly regions," grunted Broncho to himself as he passed the gasket.

"Don't haul on it with both hands," suddenly cried the rover from the footrope below him. "Keep fast hold of the jackstay with one hand. Never trust a gasket, or one day you'll take a header to the deck."

"You can bet your moccasins I'll be a heap regyardful of what you-alls advises. I'm none anxious to come flutterin' from my perch that-away," observed Broncho, as he took Jack's advice.

Hardly was the main course fast before the wind shifted suddenly into the west-south-west, and began to blow harder than ever.

The men were trooping off to man the fore and mizzen upper-topsail spilling-lines, and Black Davis and the bosun were at the halliards; but as the wind came astern, the old man thundered out:

"Hold all fast there! Weather crojjick brace!"

"Weather crojjick brace!" echoed the mate. "Let go o' that gear!" and he crossed the deck to slack away the lee braces.

As the helm was put up and the ship went off, a heavy westerly sea came up on each quarter, and soon converted the maindeck into a raging flood, which made squaring the yards no child's play.

"Now you're going to see what a Cape Horner's maindeck is like in heavy weather," remarked Jack to Broncho, as they took hold of the brace, ready to haul away on the word of command.

"I ain't hankerin' after no sech spectacle," replied Broncho. "I've had the vividest scrimmage of my life, an' I'm some jolted up an' chewed from the effects tharof."

"Haul away!" roared Black Davis.

Hardly had three pulls been taken before the top of a sea fell upon them, and the whole watch lay on their backs submerged and hanging on to the brace for dear life.

Two or three unfortunates let go their hold and were washed helplessly away, head under, at the sport of the mighty, swirling mass of water. Bruised, battered, and choked, they were rolled over and over and hurtled mercilessly forward in the cruel grasp of the raging torrent.

As the water gradually drained off, Black Davis, who was clinging to the lee crojjick brace, with which he had taken a rapid turn round the pin, felt a heavy bundle of gasping humanity bump heavily up against his sturdy sea-boots.

Long habit caused him to draw back his toe and deliver a shrewd kick at the object.

A muffled yell broke forth.

"Oh, it's yew, is it, yew lump o' Dutch grease? Git up!" he snarled as he repeated the dose.

Half senseless, chock full of salt water, breathless and bruised, with sore head and sore ribs, the luckless Muller contrived to scramble giddily to his feet and blunder hurriedly out of range.

As he once more took hold of the brace, the German gritted his teeth and muttered ferociously:

"Vait, mine fine mister mate, I dink I vill my knife stick into you von dark nacht; yah, mine Gott! Den you no more kick me, ain't it? Yah!"

Then other unfortunates gathered their scattered faculties together as the thundering voices of the mate and bosun mingled with the roar and the scream of the stormfiend.

Pinto disengaged himself from the rough embrace of the fife-rail and crawled up on all fours. Studpoker Bob, who had clung wildly to the poop-ladder after the first mad rush, appeared grumbling in his usual surly fashion, and Jimmy Green limped painfully forth from behind the hatch.

"Haul away!" roared the bosun.

A bright whisp of a moon now appeared, soaring like a flashing scimitar into the eye of the wind, and it was very welcome as it shed its cold beams upon the wild scene.

The wet, glistening decks, the mass of curved cordage bending to the blast, the line of toiling men, the clear-cut figure of the old man swaying at the break of the poop, the raging sea which rolled in great snow-capped mountains of ink, the scudding ragged clouds, and the rounded bosoms of the straining topsails—all these its silver rays showed forth in rugged, strongly touched relief.

The wheel was now too much for the strength of little Angelino, and though he worked furiously, heaving it up and down with all his might, he was always too late in meeting her; the compass card grew more and more unsteady in its movements, and the ship began to swing a couple of points on each side of her course.

The result was that the tired men at the braces spent most of their time under water.

"Somebody'll be overboard directly, if Angelino goes on letting her run off like that," grunted Jack to the bosun, as they hung on, dipped to their waists in the surging flood, and waited for the maindeck to clear itself.

"This old *Higgins* is a bit of a wet ship, I'm thinkin'," reflected the bosun. "She's as bad as any iron ship that ever I was on. Call 'em diving-bells an' half-tide rocks—these here wooden Yankees are just as bad."

Presently an extra big monster came along, and broke aboard high over the men's heads, sweeping across the maindeck with a deafening roar, and taking every man on the braces away in its furious embrace.

This was too much for the old man. For a few moments his whole crew disappeared from sight in the flood; then, as the water began to pour off over each rail in turn, he caught sight of an odd leg or arm poking out of the torrent for a second, like derelict boughs tossed about in a swollen mountain stream.

With a furious imprecation he turned and pounced upon Angelino.

"Oh, it's yew again, is it? What in hell d'yew think y're doin', spinnin' tops er what? Snakes! d'ye want to have her broach to? Hard up, yew scattermouch, hard up! Thet's enuff! Neow then, meet her as she goes off. Gol darn my skin, yew ain't got more strength than er cockroach! Heave her down, man, heave her down——Gaul bust my boots, down, I said—don't yew know down from up yet? Jeerusalem, y're enuff to make the Archangel Gabriel bawl blue hell."

Then, giving the little dago a cuff on the ear, he rushed to the break of the poop, bellowing,

"Lee-wheel, hyeh, send a lee-wheel along, Mister Davis, an' send a man to relieve thet dago; he ain't more use than a bad egg."

By the time the yards were squared and the starboard watch allowed to go forward, all but an hour of their watch below had passed.

"Well, Broncho," said Jack with a queer note of gaiety in his voice, as they stripped off their oilskins, "this is something like, eh? This is the weather to wash the mud out of a man and keep his blood from getting sluggish and clogged." And he sang softly,

"See how she buries that lee cat-head;
Hold on, good Yankee pine!"

The foc's'le presented a dreary interior, and seemed more calculated to produce melancholy and sourness than gaiety; yet, as the light from the lamp fell upon the rover's face, there was a look of exultation upon it; his eyes glittered and beamed with a great content, whilst the corners of his lips curved and his mouth opened with a bright, unconscious smile.

A born fighter, the blood of battle was surging in his veins, roused by the tempestuous strife with the elements. The queer fascination of danger gripped him; he gloried in the desperate struggle with those two mighty ones, the wind and sea, in all the grandeur of their fearful passions.

It is not given to every nature to feel this strange delight in battle, this glorious uplifting of the soul in moments of great stress or peril, this queer, sweet sensation of sheer personal joy which tingles through a man's blood and converts it into electric fluid, whilst it cools his nerve, clears and sharpens his brain, and enables him to take no heed of hunger or thirst, heat or cold, bruises or knockdowns, but to accomplish prodigies of strength, endurance, and valour with a cold, icy courage and unwearying muscles.

Broncho stared at the rover with wondering eyes, then glanced round as if to see wherein lay the cause of this strange joy.

On the floor of the foc's'le three inches of water washed steadily backwards and forwards at each heave of the tumbling vessel; from a line overhead suspended a row of yellow oilskin coats and pants, which swayed gravely to the rolling like so many headless bodies. Everything seemed damp and miserable; the air was close and foul and the wet clothing steamed; a mess of debris and wreckage washed wearily to and fro on the flood; tired men with aching limbs lay silent between their damp blankets, whilst that great comforter, the pipe, sent out great clouds of smoke from each pair of lips.

Outside, mingling with the crash of the seas, the stormfiend could be heard playing his great oratorio.

"We shore seems to be havin' a mighty strenuous time of it," replied Broncho slowly, "though how you contrives to accoomilate joy an' delight tharfrom has me a heap surprised. What with the way this here locoed ship's a-buckin' an' pitchin' worse'n the meanest cayuse that ever wears ha'r, an' the waves like stampeded landslides a-pourin' over one an' a-heavin' one around without consultin' nobody's opeenions on the proposition, it's shore toomultuous an' is due to have me some ravelled an' frayed if it keeps up this vigorous high-flung gait."

"*Waache eein bietje!*" laughed Jack. "This cattle stampede's merely beginning; it's just taking a preliminary pasear. Wait till we get into the clutches of a Cape Horn snorter."

"A cattle stampede is low down an' ornery compared to this here fatiguin' disturbance," returned Broncho in disgust.

"It bogs down as plumb dull an' no account before this impulsive whirlwind, which I states emphatic is a whole team an' jest raises Almighty discord from the heavenly vaults to the bottomless pit as easy as winnin' a Jack-pot with four aces."

"Douse that glim," growled a voice, and soon the foc's'le resounded with the deep, heavy breathing of tired men asleep in a foul atmosphere.

CHAPTER XII
"A CALL FOR NERVE"

At midnight it was Jack's wheel and Broncho's look-out.

"How's she steering?" asked Jack, as he took the wheel from Hank.

"Oh, not so dusty. They've got the relievin' tackles rigged, an' she only wants watching. Ain't yew got no lee-wheel with yew, though?"

"No, I guess I can manage."

"Waal, I reckon yew can tiew, though it'll come heavy on yew, durned heavy."

It was now blowing a strong, steady gale, with squalls at intervals—a good fair sample of "running easting down" weather.

The sky was almost clear, and the great Southern Cross gleamed high up in the heavens.

The *Higgins* required careful watching to meet her in time as she was hurled from mountain to valley. Down, down, down into the depths, down she dropped until the foresail began to shake; then up, up, up she went again, staggering desperately to reach the top as, like a beast of prey, a great hill of whirling liquid with a seething crest of foam swooped upon her.

High up above the helmsman it reared its raging top, a nerve-shaking, a terror-giving sight as it threatened to overwhelm the struggling ship with its huge bulk and roll her over and over, broken, waterlogged, sinking— only one more ship to be posted as missing, gone to an unknown grave in the vast depths of the mighty Southern Ocean. But up swung the stern of the gallant clipper as, held steady by Jack's cool hand, she ran dead before it, and the great roller rushed by harmless and fell with a deafening clatter upon the flooded maindeck.

In such a sea everything depends upon the helmsman, and the bosun kept handy to the wheel, ready to give his powerful aid should the emergency arise.

But the rolling-stone needed no help—he was thoroughly in his element. A magnificent helmsman, a few spokes either way and he kept the *Higgins* steady on her course.

The thought that the safety of the vessel and the lives of his shipmates depended upon his skill and nerve was pure bliss to him. He rejoiced in it, and mocked at the vainly pursuing seas.

The helm was heavy, however, for one man, and all his strength was needed; yet he felt it not. His muscles rebounded to the call upon them, and he threw the wheel up a turn with easy grace, where another man would have been straining with cracking muscles.

With legs firmly planted on the grating, he stood to windward, swaying easily with the motion of the vessel, whilst with keen eyes he steered by a star at the yardarm, hardly taking a glance at that deceiver, the compass.

This, this was life, strenuous, stern, full of fearful hardship, yet wonderful bewitching joy—the life which sharpens the faculties, quickens the wits, and hardens the backbone of a man, producing at the same time a self-reliance not to be come at by any other method.

It is the strife, the struggle, the fierce endeavour which, once experienced, make the quieter, more tranquil paths of life seem dull and insipid.

It is the sense of safesty in this life which palls upon men and drives adventurers forth into the world, seeking anything that will arouse their natures, grown sluggish and torpid in the monotony of the modern daily round.

Some go and shoot big game, others climb mountains, a few explore, and some rush gaily into foreign wars, all for the same reason, to shake off the choking folds of security's sombre cloak and feel the thrill of danger.

What is there to compare with this exulting feeling, this tasting of the juice of peril in realms where the spice of life, the sweets of a hard-fought victory, are known to the full?

In these realms the qualities of nerve and pluck are at a premium, and he who has not sufficient goes under, broken and tossed aside in swift defeat. In these realms a man is thoroughly tested and tempered in the fire, and he must be "clean strain" or he won't survive the ordeal.

Jack gazed with a look of defiance into the heart of the storm.

"Fight me, you raging sea and howling wind," he cried in his exultation; "overcome me, if it is so fated, but I will give you a stiff battle. All my cunning, all my nerve, all my endurance are ready to my call. Exhaust them if you can, break them down, but first you have to break my spirit, strain it, tear it, beat upon it, crush it down; and if you are able to destroy it, you can take my useless body also. Blow, ye winds; smite me, O sea, for I am ready!" And he hummed the famous chanty:

"Blow the man down, Johnny, blow the man down!
To my aye, aye, blow the man down!
If he be white man or black man or brown,
Give me some time to blow the man down."

Meanwhile, on the foc's'le head, Bucking Broncho trudged up and down, five paces to windward and five paces back in a vain attempt to keep himself warm.

"This here seems a pretty tough game I'm into," he mused. "It shore needs sand to make a winnin' against the kyards these tempestuous elements holds up, an' a gent can't drop out o' this game the fates drags him into. He's got to stay with it from his first sun-up to his last moon-rise, for if he lays down an' quits he leaves this mortal game for good, which no critter with the smallest grain o' sand is goin' to do without puttin' up some sort of a fight; yet when Providence begins to crowd the play an' get action this-a-way, it's shore a hard, deep crossin'.

"I never allows I'd have to dig up the hatchet an' go on the war-path with any sech ragin', blisterin' proposition as this. It kind o' shakes the grit out of a man an' makes him feel small an' petty."

As the *Higgins* rushed madly before the blast, she buried her nose to the cat-heads in each huge comber. At each plunge she threw great masses of spray full fifty feet away from her dripping cutwater to port and starboard.

The wind roared in a voice of thunder out of the foot of the foresail, but with the exception of the fore-topmast staysail the head sails had been made fast, and the long bare jibboom stabbed viciously into the smother as each overtaking sea rushed onward.

Broncho, as he looked ahead with straining eyes, submitted to a strong feeling of awe as each gigantic sea went foaming by, leaving a white curtain of spume and froth in its train as it roared past at headlong speed.

The majesty, the might, the stupendous power of the furious sea, its insolent treatment of the strong ship as it raged around her, its fury, its superb grandeur—all these appealed to the wild soul of the cowboy, and the charm, the fascination of the Great Waters was beginning to wrap itself around him.

It is this great power of fascination and attraction which the sea possesses that gets to the root of men's hearts, and, once there, can never be exorcised.

Suddenly, as Broncho watched the furious battle and meditated thereon, at a moment when the *Higgins* balanced giddily on the top of a sixty-foot "grey-beard," he caught sight of a ship hove-to on the port tack under lower-topsails, lying right across the down-easter's bows.

"Ship right ahead," he yelled. "We'll be clean over her as we're goin'."

Before he could say more the stranger lay close aboard on the crest of the last roller, in plain view of all.

She was an iron Clyde-built barque, with painted ports, and made a grand picture in the moonlight as she lifted gracefully to the top of the great hill of water. Helpless, unable to move out of the way, she lay at the mercy of the *Higgins*, and a collision in that sea would mean the loss of both ships with all hands.

"We'll hit her plumb on the port quarter," cried the bosun to Jack. "Down with your helm, down with it, even if we have our decks swept bare," he roared.

To bring the sea on either beam would mean the grave danger of broaching to, with the chance of a capsize and the certainty of having the decks swept fore and aft.

Jack, cool and collected as ever, hove the wheel down a few spokes.

"Right down!" yelled the bosun, who was hanging on to the mizzen backstays. "Right down, or you won't clear her."

"If you leave it to me, I'll clear her all right," said the rover coolly, his eyes glued on the barque.

"Have it your way, have it your way," returned the bosun, giving in to Jack's calm confidence.

"Better order the hands aloft, or some one'll get taken overboard," went on Jack quietly; "and you might hand me the end of that boom-guy."

As Jack hurriedly lashed himself to the wheel, the bosun's deep voice broke through the noise of the gale like a foghorn.

"Aloft, all hands!" he thundered. "Away aloft for your lives."

The men needed no second bidding, but raced up the ratlines, for a gigantic roller was raising its head above them to starboard as it tore down upon the *Higgins*.

It was a moment of terrible peril. Would they go clear of the barque? Would the huge "grey-beard" destroy them? Two heavy chances against them. Everything depended on Jack's skill, his keen eye, his strong arm, and his nerve—above all, his nerve.

The elements had taken up his wild challenge with a vengeance. He had swung the *Higgins* four points off her course and stood braced ready for the shock, for that terror of sailors, a pooper, was approaching at terrific speed.

The bosun, half way up the mizzen rigging, yelled wildly to him. He caught something about "hanging on," but the rest was lost in the roar of the gale.

Over his shoulder he caught a quick glimpse of the approaching sea, a great wall of water, black and forbidding, which, as it raced in pursuit of the flying clipper, grew momentarily more mountainous, until, having reached the limit of its growth, it burst its whole length of summit into boiling, hissing white water, which gave it more than ever the appearance of a snow-capped ridge of solid earth.

As Jack turned his eyes resolutely away, he realised how the inhabitants of Herculaneum must have felt the moment before Vesuvius poured its molten lava upon them.

Still he stood erect, head up, without a flinch. It was a position sufficient to scare the stoutest heart, and freeze a man's brain into idiocy. Yet his nerve never failed him, whilst the watch clung aloft, shaking with sheer fright, and with wavering eyes stared wildly from the helpless barque to Jack, and from Jack to the swooping demon of a sea, which, roaring and raging in pursuit, lifted its foaming head on a level with their blanched faces.

Broncho, hanging in the fore-rigging, gave his chum up for lost.

"He's shore due to cash in this time," he muttered sadly. "Even if we-alls go clear o' that ship, he'll come through the racket a drowned cawpse. Poor old Jack, standin' thar game as hornets, no more fretted than if he's coolly sittin' down to a poker game."

Jack gave one last look astern at the approaching sea, and then a keen glance at the hove-to Scotchman.

"We'll do it by the skin of our teeth," he murmured, as he put the helm up a few spokes to steady her as she went.

And now the mountain of water was upon him. Catching the *Higgins* on her starboard quarter, it hit the mizzen-mast half way up to the crossjack yard, and with a fearful din went raging over everything.

It washed over the poop until the spanker boom was hidden; the two quarter-boats were smashed into staves, and there was a crash of splintered glass as the windows of the afterhouse went in.

Jack wondered, as it fell upon him, whether the terrific force of the comber would not tear the wheel up and carry it with himself overboard.

But the stout wheel held, and Jack was crushed furiously against it until all the wind was beaten out of his body, and his ribs almost stove into his lungs.

Still he kept his senses, and never lost his presence of mind. Grimly he grasped the spokes and waited for the end, wondering how long he could live under water without becoming unconscious.

A hideous pain in his chest gradually overcame his will-power, and caused a drowsiness in his brain, which echoed one word again and again.

"Loyola!" it said, "Loyola! Loyola!"

But it is slow work drowning. His eyes shut in agony, there was a rushing sound in his ears, and his head felt as if it would burst. With clenched teeth he fought the growing feeling of insensibility. Seconds would decide it now.

"Goodbye, my darling, goodbye!" cried his fading senses.

It was his last conscious effort. Was this the end? Would the water never clear off? Indistinct pictures of his past life flitted through his dazed brain like blurred dreams.

The notes of a long-forgotten tune tingled in his ears, then suddenly changed to a bugle call; the Reveille was sounding, clear and shrill, to be broken in upon by the deep boom of Big Ben striking the hour; then he heard nothing but a wild moaning, and a sound as of the flapping of countless wings. Flames flashed on his eyeballs; blue, red and green, purple and yellow sparkled before him like a myriad of precious gems; then all was black, a hideous, piercing black.

With a sickly roll the *Higgins* freed herself, and the tons of water, pouring to leeward, washed over her rail in a smother of foam; then, with a jerk, the gallant vessel gained her level once more.

The breath of the keen westerly gale put new life into the half-drowned man, as he hung crumpled up and stupefied in his lashings, his hands still grasping the spokes with contracted muscles.

Slowly he opened his eyes and gasped for breath like a fish out of water. His scattered senses returned to him, and his keen brain revived with a wonderful vitality; but whilst his mind, recovering rapidly, grasped the situation, his overstrained body remained weak and helpless.

Dimly his dazed eyes perceived the Scotchman rising ahead on the crest of the wave which had just swept over him. He heard wild cries from aloft, but could distinguish no words.

Instinctively he exerted his last pound of strength to meet her as she fell off, and then collapsed into unconsciousness.

And now the *Higgins* flew upon the stranger with the swoop of an eagle.

All hands but the senseless helmsman gazed fascinated at the nearing peril, whilst the bosun scrambled hastily out of the mizzen rigging and made for the wheel.

But Jack had done his work. It was touch and go, but he had judged the distance exactly. As the *Higgins* surged past, her bow wave swamped the poop of the barque and poured over her rail.

The Scotchman was close enough to toss a biscuit aboard, and a weird chorus of yells arose from her crew, who had swarmed into her rigging. The *Higgins'* starbowlines replied with a ringing cheer, and the next moment the barque was almost out of sight astern, only her topmasts showing from behind a big sea.

The bosun ground the wheel up, and the *Higgins* was put on her course again.

But what a sight were her decks! The two boats were matchwood, the doors of the bosun's locker and carpenter's shop opening to windward were burst in; the heavy poop-rail of brass was bent and twisted into all shapes, whilst the standard compass box lay forced over by sheer weight of water to an angle of forty-five degrees.

The cabin was nearly full of water, which had poured in through the smashed windows, and the foc's'le and midshiphouse were both badly waterlogged. The maindeck was a hideous tangle of gear washed off the pins, and the top of the midshiphouse had been swept bare. Galley funnel, harness casks, rolls of wire, all were gone; whilst of the poop ladders, one lay over-turned, clean wrenched from its supports.

The mate now appeared, followed by the old man and the steward.

"What in hell er yew been doin' with my ship, bosun?" roared the old man, and the bosun started in to explain.

Meanwhile, with tender hands, the senseless form of the rover was unlashed from the wheel and carried forward to the foc's'le, and the old man, on hearing what had happened, had the grace to send the steward along with a stiff glass of grog.

In the foc's'le Jack quickly regained his senses, the men contending eagerly for the honour of attending upon him.

A buzz of conversation went round as the port watch, who had been washed out of their bunks by the big sea, eagerly asked question after question.

Suddenly the bosun stood in the broken doorway.

"How are you feeling, Jack? It were a pretty close call, weren't it? Smite me pink, but you've got the pluck of the devil, an' I'm proud to be shipmates with ye. Your hand, mate," and he grasped the rover's hand in his great paw with a grip of iron.

"I'll be as right as can be, directly," said Jack weakly.

"Well, you just stay where you are and don't think of moving," replied the bosun. "Now then, the rest of you starbowlines, out you come! There's heaps of work to do"; and he retired aft, followed by the watch.

The carpenter was routed out, and whilst some of the men helped the steward in the cabin the rest were kept busy nailing up weather-boards over the broken windows of the afterhouse.

CHAPTER XIII
"THE MAN WITH THE GUN"

"Seven bells! Tumble up, starbowlines, an' show a leg. There's burgoo for breakfast."

It was Jim calling the watch at 7.20 a.m., so that they could get their breakfast before going on deck at eight bells.

"Burgoo? Who said burgoo?" cried Red Bill, sitting up excitedly at the announcement of this luxury.

"I've just seen Lung cooking it," declared Jim. "The steward says there's to be burgoo for breakfast from forty to forty."

"Then we're in the Roaring Forties all right," observed Jack.

"Did you see that ere chink a-cookin' of it, did you say, kid?" inquired old Ben Sluice.

"Yes, I did," replied the boy.

"Well, I'm glad I didn't, or I couldn't have ate it, for sure," returned the ex-miner with a grunt. Like many westerners, he considered the pigtail tribe as "rank p'ison," and he never lost an opportunity of deriding the *Higgins'* cook.

"How's that ere boisterous party, the weather, a-conductin' himself this maunin'?" asked Broncho. "I'm hopin' he's got his fur some smoothed since last night, when he's shore more pesky than a croger[8] with the indigestion."

"She's hummin' pretty strong yet," Jim replied; and then inquired softly, "How you feelin' this mornin', Jack?"

"Fit enough to put the gloves on with Sullivan, and as hungry as fifty Siwash Indians," replied the latter gaily, vaulting out of his bunk.

"Fur a bloke as wos as near drowned as you wos, h'I bloomin' well thinks you tyke the cyke," exclaimed the cockney. "W'y, my gills is still flappin' fur air an' me stomich gurglin' wi' salt water after that ere washin' around we gets squarin' 'er in las' night."

"Be Jasus, ye're roight, me son o' London Town, an' I've been after dramin' I was a fish an' couldn't get into the wather. Shure, it were a crool drame after spendin' the blitherin' night sprainin' me nose with tryin' to get it out of the wet. Ah, the wather! I ain't after havin' no use for it onless it's a weak solution in a glass of ould Oirish," said Pat in disgust.

"'Allo, Pat, 'old 'ard! I'm a bloomin' swot if you ain't given yer jibboom a bigger hoist," burst out the cockney with a note of concern in his voice.

Pat's nose was very much what society papers call tip-tilted.

"Arrah, now, with yer bamboozlin'," cried Pat.

"Wot you sye, byes?" pursued the cockney. "Ain't 'e been an' cock-billed that yard of 'is?"

"You shore has her p'intin' so as an angel with a spy-glass can look down your nostrils," remarked Bedrock Ben, solemnly, amidst laughter.

"Fetch the grub along, there's a good chap," said Curly, whose duty it was, but who was vainly struggling to get a pair of wet rubbers on over damp socks, to Jim.

"Right you are," said the boy cheerily, and he started off cautiously for the galley for two reasons—the one to avoid the succession of dollops which poured over the rail, the other to escape the vigilant eye of the mate.

He found the industrious Lung busy burnishing up his pots and pans, and though several inches of water were washing over the floor of the galley, it was as clean as a new pin.

"Starboard watch's breakfast ready yet, Lung?" asked Jim.

"You wait one quallah minit; burgoo no done yet," returned the celestial.

"What kind of a time did you have in the galley last night?" inquired the boy.

"Me heap 'flaid. Tink-um dlown chop-chop. Plenty muchee water top-side galley. Big sea come, tink all smash, China boy tink-um all-e-same dead. No can see, no can do, no likee, velly bad time."

"I don't wonder. The water must have poured in through the chimney-hole and nearly filled you up," Jim admitted.

"Water him come, heap big flood; bime-by him go 'way, hey? Lung no savvy nuttin' plenty long time——"

"Nearly drowned, eh?"

"Lung tink-um pletty soon dlown. Plenty muchee solly! Want um first-chop coffin, no have got; no loast pig, no China blandy, no funelel. Tink-um lose face, heap 'shamed. Bime-by come one-piecee boss, him talkee-talkee.

"'You allee-lightee, Lung?' him say.

"'No can tell,' me say. 'Tink-um China boy plenty muchee sick, plaps him die pletty soon.'

"'No sick, no dead if can chin-chin,' him say, an' go 'way."

"Was that the bosun?" asked Jim.

"Yass, him bosun," replied Lung, as he handed Jim a kid of steaming burgoo and a big tin of a coloured concoction known at sea by the name of "ship's coffee."

Jim started warily for the foc's'le, but the eagle eye of Black Davis was upon him, and he was fairly caught.

"Hyeh, yew kid! What yew doin'? Is this y'r watch on deck or ain't it?" roared the mate from aft.

"Come hyeh, yew whelp!" he bellowed.

Jim went bravely up on to the poop and faced the bully, expecting nothing less than a knockdown; but Black Davis, though boiling with rage, controlled himself with an effort.

Shaking his fist in the boy's face, he burst forth:

"Yew little skunk, I'll half kill yew one o' these days, loafin' an' sodgerin' around! Git out quick, or I'm liable to let fly an' jump your ribs in."

Then, as Jim moved hurriedly away, he roared,

"Wait, doggone ye! Who told yew ter go, yew Whitechapel mudlark? Jump up, overhaul an' stop them main-tops'l buntlines, an' turn to at one bell on the poop brasswork. I'll teach yew, yew Bowery refuse, thar ain't goin' ter be no skulkin' while Davis is mate o' this packet. Away with ye!"

On coming on deck at eight bells the starboard watch were all sent aloft, each man with a bundle of rovings and rope-yarns.

Now that the *Higgins* was getting near the stormy cape, all preparations had to be made for the tempestuous weather which is always encountered whilst turning the last corner of the world, as rounding the Horn is sometimes called.

For great "Cape Stiff" never disappoints one. He keeps an unlimited supply of bad weather about him, dealing out his great sixty-foot greybeards, his terrific hail-squalls, and his furious southern blasts with no niggard hand.

To withstand the boisterous southern wind, the sails had to be lashed as securely as possible to the jackstays, which run along the top of the yards. This the watch were sent aloft to do.

As the *Higgins* tore along before the gradually slacking westerlies, a swarm of Cape pigeons, molly-mawks, and Cape black hens swooped about her stern, whilst three or four majestic albatrosses sailed in their stately manner in the wake of the clipper, occasionally with a graceful sweep stooping to pick some tit-bit off the water.

Presently a sail was sighted right ahead, and the *Higgins* overhauled her hand over hand.

In an hour the stranger was close alongside. She turned out to be one of those famous craft, which are fast disappearing—a South Sea whaler.

She was truly an interesting sight as she rolled heavily on the long westerly swell, lying hove-to under bare poles, with nothing but a tarpaulin in the mizzen rigging.

She was evidently a real old-timer, for as she rolled you could see that she was as round as a barrel, with a square sawed off stern and an apple-cheeked bow, surmounted by a long jibboom with a great hoist to it.

She had no yard above the main-topgallant but the crow's-nest—a huge barrel from which the look-out, with skinned eyes, searches the ocean for the longed-for blow of the whale—hung on the main-topgallant mast, looking heavy and bulky enough at that height to carry away the slender spar.

But this same crow's-nest was empty. The whaler had a well-seasoned and weather-stained appearance. As she heeled over she showed a bottom covered with long weed and barnacles. Her rigging had a slack and unkempt look about it, being a mass of bights and Irish pennants; whilst her yards were badly braced and cocked at all angles.

Only two men could be seen on her decks, and they seemed to pay little attention to the *Higgins*.

There was no one at her wheel, but as she was hove-to a helmsman was not necessary; for all that, she had a strange appearance of desolation about her.

The two men visible seemed busily occupied, whilst squatting on their hams, at some mysterious work, and an object stood on the deck between them which was too small to be distinguished, but seemed to be giving them a great deal of thought, for they looked to be both staring fixedly at it.

"Come yew hyeh!" called the old man to Jim, who was busy polishing the compass case. "Come yew hyeh, boy, an' help me with these flags."

"Neow then," he went on, hauling the Stars-and-stripes out of the flag-locker, "run 'Old Glory' up to the monkey-gaff."

"Aye, aye, sir!" replied Jim.

But though the old man tried to have a flag-talk as he went by, the stranger made no response, the two men on her deck making no movement, much to his indignation.

"The infarnal son of a gun! Ain't he got the civility even to dip to the Stars-an'-stripes? Gaul bust my etarnal skin!"

"Kin yew read her name?" he sang out to the mate, who was ogling her stern with an ancient-looking ship's telescope.

"The *Ocmulgee* o' Nantucket, I make it, sir."

"Why, thet's ole Ebenezer Morgan's boat! Terant'lers, air they all asleep, er what? A goldarned, barnacle-backed South Seaman, an' he won't have a gam! Jeerusalem, but thet beats all my goin' to sea," growled Captain Bob Riley in tones half angry, half puzzled.

"Hyeh, yew boy," he went on, turning to Jim, "jump below an' ask the steward fur my gun. I'll poke his fire for him,[9] I'll wake up his oil-soaked intellec', I'll stir his blubber, or thar's no sech things as snakes an' pumpkins."

On Jim handing him the Winchester, he went to the break of the poop and let drive two or three shots through the rigging of the whaler.

As the sound of the report reached them and the whistle of the bullets went "Theu, theu!" overhead, the two men on the deck of the South Seaman jumped about six feet into the air, then rushed below and were seen no more.

"Seemed to scare 'em some, anyway," remarked the old man coolly, as he pumped another cartridge into the barrel.

At this moment Black Davis, spying round to see where he could find trouble, caught sight of Jack, Broncho, and Studpoker Bob all on the lee main lower-topsail yardarm, at work putting in rovings—at least, Jack and Broncho were at work, but the gambler on the inside was loafing as usual; and thinking that the old man and mate were too busy watching the other ship to notice him, whilst the bosun was forward with his back turned, he had calmly lit up a pipe, a most heinous offence during work hours at sea.

This was too much for the bucko mate altogether. For a second he glared at the delinquent as if mesmerised, for the man was out of reach of his terrible boot or even a well-aimed belaying-pin; then, with a roar of fury, he pulled out his ever-ready six-shooter and fired.

The shot narrowly missed the gambler and cut the lanyard of a marlinspike, which he had slung round his neck.

The heavy spike dropped, and hitting Black Davis, who was standing just underneath, on the shoulder, felled him to the deck.

The incident, seen from the poop, looked as if Studpoker Bob had deliberately dropped the spike with intent to hit the mate, and such the old man believed to be the case.

Without a second's hesitation he brought his Winchester to the shoulder and fired at the card-sharper, who, hit clean through the back and lungs, threw up his hands and dropped forward over the yard; then, as the vessel pitched, he fell headlong to the deck.

The whole affair was so sudden and unlooked-for that it took Jack and Broncho, who were carelessly working with both hands, completely by surprise; and the jerk, caused by the sudden release of the gambler's weight on the footrope, upset their balance before they could catch a hold. At the same time the ship gave a heavy roll to leeward, and they both fell into the sea.

Immediately all was confusion. Whilst the old man thundered out orders from the poop, the bosun bellowed for all hands, and Jim rushed wildly to the stern, and, cutting loose the three life-buoys, sprang over with them into the swirling wake; and so quick was the boy, that Jack and Broncho, both good swimmers, came to the surface close to him.

The three scrambled into the life-buoys, and even in that short space of time the *Higgins* was nearly half a mile away.

Meanwhile on board of her there was trouble. As the port watch rushed wildly aft at the bosun's call, the first thing they saw was the broken body of Studpoker Bob, which, with crushed-in head, was lying crumpled up in a pool of blood, within a few feet of the senseless form of Black Davis.

The carpenter stood waving his arms at the door of his shop, shouting,

"Man ovairboard! Man ovairboard!"

The starboard watch came sliding down backstays from aloft in frantic haste. All hands were speedily in a wild state of excitement and indignation.

"Steady, boys, steady! Stand by yer lee braces!" called the bosun quietly in his deep voice.

"Hard down the wheel!" roared the old man. "No, hold hard, as yew were! Hold on all! Keep her as she goes!"

"Ain't you goin' to try an' pick 'em up, sir?" asked the bosun indignantly.

"What kin I do, bosun, what kin I do? We ain't got no boats! Snakes, what a 'tarnal mess! But thar ain't nothin' ter do. Send the port watch below," cried the old man unsteadily.

There was a roar of indignation from the crew at these words, and a storm of groans, hoots, and hisses broke forth.

"It's murder, begorr, black, bloody murder!" screeched Pat.

"Ain't you goin' ter give 'em a chanst?" cried the cockney with his shrill squeak.

Things began to look nasty. The men gathered round the main-hatch. Some of them drew knives, others pulled belaying-pins from the rail, and fists were shaken wildly at the old man as he stood at the break of the poop, roaring:

"Git forrard, yew rakin's an' scrapin's o' hell an' Sing-sing, git forrard, or I'll blow the guts outer some o' yer," and he lifted his Winchester threateningly.

A belaying-pin whirled and nearly knocked it out of his hands, whilst Angelino's knife stuck quivering in the rail before him.

"Jump up hyeh, bosun!" he jerked rapidly. "Steward, whar' are yew?"

"Here, sir!" called the steward at his back.

"Fetch my pistols an' git the hell of a gait on yer."

"Here they be's, sir," said the steward meekly, thrusting them forward.

He was a well-trained steward, and had been through this sort of business with Captain Bob Riley before.

"Better get forrard, boys," said the bosun soberly. "It's too late to do anything now, an' you ain't foolish enough to go buckin' against guns, are ye? We're short-enough handed as it is, without any more lame ducks."

The bosun's sensible words had their effect, and so did the old man's glittering nickel-plated six-shooters.

There was a murmur of consultation amongst the men, and two or three of the cowards began to sneak to the rear of the group.

"Wot er we goin' ter do?" asked the cockney. "St'y w'ere we are an' get plugged, rush 'im, or retryte. I ain't afryde of 'im an' I'm feelin' dyngerous."

"He's got the drop on us, pard. It ain't no manner o' use that I ever see'd, takin' liberties wi' six-shooters," declared old Ben gloomily.

"I'm gyme ter sock it to 'im, any'ow. I'll stand in ter jump 'im. Wot you sye, fellers?"

The cockney was as pugnacious as a cock-sparrow, and far from lacking in courage.

"Bedad, an' I'm with ye!" sang out Pat.

"It vas too lade, anyway; der ole man vas too schmard vor us," grunted Muller heavily.

"Dat am what I done told you," put in Sam.

"Wot er you w'inin' 'bout there, you good-fer-nothin' nigger," sneered the cockney. "You ain't no bloomin' use, any'ow, so shut yer jaw."

"Brazen sarpints!" broke in the old man again, "what's all this powwow about? Air yer goin' ter git forrard, or shall I slam her loose?"

What the outcome of the matter would have been it is difficult to say, but at this interesting point a big sea interrupted the discussion most effectively. Toppling aboard amidships, it overwhelmed the mutineers and washed them helter-skelter in every direction. So the trouble finished, and Yankee discipline once more reigned supreme.

Black Davis was taken below with a badly broken collar-bone, whilst the remains of Studpoker Bob, the gambler and sea-lawyer, were got ready for burial.

For a few days the absent ones were discussed in the foc's'le, until the advent of Cape Horn weather drove all other thoughts out of the minds of the short-handed crew.

But Curly went heavily-hearted about his work, whilst the big bosun also felt their loss in his own fashion.

And before the westerly gale flew the *Higgins*, leaving two men, a boy, and three life-savers to the mercy of the great southern rollers.

FOOTNOTES:

[8] A cougar or mountain lion.

[9] An expression meaning to stir up a whale's inside with a lance. When a whale spouts blood from his blow-hole, his chimney is spoken of as being afire.

PART II

CHAPTER I
"ADRIFT"

All three castaways were close together, and floated easily enough in the life-buoys with head and shoulders above water.

"Thrown your life away, Jim," jerked out the rover, as he skilfully avoided a big breaker. "The old man won't round to—no boats."

"Ain't there no chance o' gettin' aboard the whaler?" asked the boy. "She's dead to windward, an' seems to be driftin' down our way."

"I allows as thar's p'ints in Jim's remyarks," observed the cowpuncher, floating with his back to wind and sea. "But say we-alls gets alongside: if this here sea butts us up agin her, we're shore liable to emerge tharfrom a heap busted an' unstrung."

"Look out!" broke in Jack hurriedly, as he faced to windward, and the next moment the broken top of a sea rolled them over and over.

Jack and Broncho both came out of the clutches of the roller without any damage, but poor Jim's life-buoy brought him to the surface upside down, and the rolling-stone only just rescued him in time.

"Lord, I thought I was a gorner!" gasped the boy, as all three in the midst of a smother of bubbling froth floated down into the calm hollow behind the breaker.

"That wave does mighty near call the turn on you that time, Jim. This here is drawin' the cinch some tight, an' I ain't hankerin' after any more hurdygurdies o' that party's sturdy physique," remarked Broncho, conversing in his usual quaint, off-hand way, his gentle southern drawl in no way affected by the terrible circumstances in which he was placed, for the chances of being picked up by the Nantucket barque were very slim.

As they rose to the top of the next wave, all three anxiously turned their eyes on the whaler.

"Shall we reach her?" asked Jim, with trembling voice.

"Drift right on to us in an hour or two. Keep your pecker up and feet down," declared Jack cheerily.

"I will if I can, you bet your life," replied the plucky boy, regaining his courage at Jack's reassuring words. "Why, look! The old *Higgins* is nearly out of sight. I expect there's hell to play on her now," he went on.

"An' I ain't none sorry to quit her," drawled Broncho serenely, "that's presumin' we-alls escapes boggin' down in this here quicksand."

"My God! Look out for yourself, Jack!" suddenly cried the boy in accents of horror.

A huge albatross was swooping down upon the rover.

These birds are the terror of a man overboard in the Southern Ocean. With their great curved beaks they attack the eyes of the castaway, who, from his position in the water, is but poorly placed for defending himself, and nearly always succumbs, his strength failing him in the unequal combat.

"Your knives, boys!" sang out Jack heartily, as if this new danger were nothing much to bother about.

Then with a lightning stroke he almost severed the great bird's head from its body.

With a splash it struck the water, and, after one wild flurry, lay motionless, floating on the wave with its head under.

"That's fine bowie-work as ever I sees," remarked Broncho. "That bird gets all he wants; he ain't askin' for more. He shore makes a sperited play, but he notes now as how he can't bluff Jack none."

"Bold, vicious bird, that!" commented Jack.

"One down, but there are hundreds more," groaned Jim.

"Three's too many for 'em. I don't think any more will attack us, except perhaps an odd old one," declared the rover.

"I corrals your remyarks with gladness, Jack," declared the cowboy; "for I was shore some dubious about the play. If they rounds up together an' charges in a mob, it's on the kyards one or other of we-alls emerges from the battle shy an eye."

Presently another albatross made a descent upon them, and after a fierce fight retired from the contest, bleeding and disgusted; but he had left his mark on Broncho's hand, which was nastily torn.

"This here abandoned conduct of these debauchees of birds has me plumb weary," remarked the cowpuncher, as he wiped his blood-stained knife on his sleeve. "I feels like a spring lamb on the pra'rie up agin an eagle. That ere profligate bird was shore hungerin' for blood, an' I feels kind o' comforted when I dirties his shirt-front, an' he, carolling forth a squawk, jumps out an' pulls his freight. No, Jack, thar's nothin' timid about these here albatrosses; they're bold a whole lot, not to say f'rocious an' gore-thirsty."

"Our combination's too strong," grunted the latter optimistically.

But though Broncho discussed the danger in his off-hand way, and Jack seemed cool and undismayed, Jim hung in the life-buoy, his little, thin face white and drawn.

The desperate fight with the fierce birds had almost been too much for his young nerves, toughened though they were, and he felt sick and faint.

But the cold was now beginning to make itself felt, and this was really the chief danger to the castaways; for the wind had been falling steadily all the morning, and had become very faint, whilst the sea ran in long oily ridges, only one of which here and there broke with any strength. The boy's lips were blue, and his teeth chattered, though he tried hard to keep them clenched.

"Bit cold, Jim, ain't it? How're you feeling?" asked Jack, observing the pinched features and chattering teeth with inward concern.

"I'm all r-r-right! Go-go-goin' strong."

"More'n that riotin' albatross is," remarked Broncho, pointing to the dead bird, which still floated close to the rover. "He ain't stuck his head out of water since Jack downed him."

"He's d-d-d-dead, isn't he?"

"I ain't right certain he ain't foxin'," returned the cowpuncher. "Give him a poke with your bowie, Jack, an' see if you can't rouse him some."

"Not I," objected Jack. "Let sleeping dogs lie."

And so time passed as, slowly, very slowly, the whaler drifted nearer.

The sea was bitterly cold, and occasionally a breaker knocked the breath out of them, but no one of the three showed any signs of weakening.

Hovering round them were several albatrosses, besides black-hens and molly-mawks, all squawking loudly, and evidently trying to summon up sufficient courage to attack the dauntless trio.

"Them birds is shore organisin' for war," observed Broncho, as he watched them. "They're beginnin' to whoop an' beat their tomtoms a whole lot. I've a theery that six-shooters would be good argyments with them feathered sports. I regrets most sincere our havin' to leave our weepons on the *Higgins* that-away, Jack; I just loathes hittin' a new trail without packin' a gun along."

"No time to pack our trunks," grunted Jack disgustedly. "Left my baccy, and want a smoke bad."

"Wall, you shorely goes the limit a whole corralful for sheer, blisterin', hell-freezin' coolness. You'd light a seegyar whilst you were prospectin' the bottomless pit, Jack."

But Jack was watching the gathering birds.

"Union is strength," he said musingly. "Closed ranks defence against an open order attack. Let's tie the life-buoys together."

"Sech observations is plenty sagacious," commented Broncho approvingly, "an' I votes we acts tharon instanter. You bushwhack in here, Jim, between us two. This here hand has got to be played with care, if we-alls is goin' to avoid gettin' cold feet."

Jack and Broncho still had their bundles of rope-yarns and rovings thrust through their belts, and with these they soon lashed the life-buoys securely together in the form of a triangle.

"Now, let 'em all come!" cried Jim defiantly.

"They're shore makin' war medicine," observed Broncho; "but I ain't in no frenzied hurry to begin the battle. Let 'em sachey around an' take their time."

"Here comes a scout, boys," cried Jack, as a great, white-headed bird swooped gracefully towards them.

"Take your seats, gents, the performance is about to commence," remarked Broncho coolly.

But the albatross only circled slowly round, evidently rather diffident about beginning the attack.

"He's cuttin' kyards with himself as to whether he'll jump in an' skeer us up some, or lope back an' make a report on our poseetion," was the cowboy's interpretation of the bird's actions.

"He's going," exclaimed Jim, with a long breath of relief.

"He's wise! It's just the tenderness of hell saves him from our bowies that time," drawled Broncho, with a grim smile.

For nearly an hour they floated with knives drawn, but the fierce birds never came within range of the flashing steel again, though they kept wheeling round the castaways in a manner which was very trying to the nerves.

About 2 p.m. the old whaler was only about a hundred yards off, and drifting right down upon them.

"Let's give 'em a shout," proposed Jack. "A whaler would think nothing of launching a boat in this sea."

"Whoopee!" yelled Broncho; but there was no sign of any one moving on the barque.

"Co-oo-ee!" sang Jack; but still no result.

"I'll soon wake 'em if they ain't all dead," declared Jim, and putting a finger in his mouth, he emitted an ear-piercing whistle, which swelled and sank like a siren.

"That shore takes the pot for the shrillest, most searchin' whistle I ever hears," exclaimed Broncho. "It plumb near deafens me, an' I bet the limit it scurries up those sharps aboard there a whole lot."

And Broncho was right, for now two heads appeared above the rail of the barque, and an arm was flourished.

"Hurrah! we're seen," cried Jim.

"Whatever species of men are they?" exclaimed the cowpuncher excitedly, as he scanned the distant heads with his keen, prairie-trained eyes.

"Do you-alls notice anything strange about them whalers?" he asked of Jack.

"Seem to have very blotchy faces."

"Blotchy faces? Wall, I should gamble," drawled Broncho. "Why, their physio'nomies is cut up in black an' yellow squares like a checker-board, an' may I be locoed if the one without a sombrero ain't scalped."

"Stickin'-plaster, p'r'aps," suggested Jim, "some whale they've been scrappin' with done it."

"Something's queer aboard," mused Jack. "Those are the two scattermouches we saw this morning. Query, where's the rest of the crowd? South Sea whalers carry a big crew."

"Stand your hands thar, boys; thar's somethin' wrong on that packet or I'm a jack-rabbit. Seems to me we're prancin' down too rapid an' heedless on that ere outfit. We're liable to overplay our hands if we don't go some slower," said Broncho solemnly, as with knit eyebrows he watched the nearing whaleship.

"Maybe it's the phantom ship or the haunted whaler, *quien sabe?*" remarked Jack. "Anyhow, it's better than cruising off the Horn in a life-buoy. *Que quieres hombre*, Broncho—cross the road and let 'em go by, or politely inquire if they've got measles aboard?"

"That's all right, that'll go for humour this time," retorted Broncho, with keen irony.

"S'pose they have got somethin'," put in Jim. "Berri-berri, or scurvy, or Java fever——"

"Go it, Jim," laughed the rover. "What else? Plague, eh? And leprosy? Or I have it—Yellow Jack, of course; that would account for the yellow, blotchy faces."

"I ain't s'picious o' no malady," asserted Broncho. "No, it's ambushes or some sech cawpse-makin' plays I'm some doobersome of; an' I'm allowin' we-alls had better have our bowies out when we meets up with them speckled parties. They shore looks to me like redskins painted for war."

"Why, they're Kanakas!" declared Jack, as they got nearer.

"What breed o' dawg are Kanakas?" asked Broncho.

"South Sea Islanders."

"Cannibals!" gasped Jim. "I see our finish."

"Long pig, eh, Jim?" laughed the rover.

"Them cannibals is some like redskins, ain't they?" inquired Broncho, taking no notice of Jack's levity. "Cold an' p'isonous as rattlesnakes, an' the way they've daubed themselves shows they're plumb ready for the thunderbolt of war."

"Tattooing," explained Jack; and as soon as they were close enough he sang out, "Ship ahoy!"

One of the Kanakas waved his arm, but the other jumped up and down, evidently very excited, and gave vent to the most weird cries.

"He's throwin' off some mighty high-flung whoops. What's that ghost-dance he's evolvin' thar? Do you savvy, Jack, if that's his wardance?" inquired the cowboy.

"Oh, Lord!" groaned poor Jim dismally. "Here we are right into a horde of man-eatin' savages."

"Stick your spurs in, sonny, an' we'll stampede right over 'em on the top of the next wave, so as they won't know if it's a landslide or a cloud-burst that devastates 'em," said Broncho heartily.

"Stand by to heave us a rope," hailed Jack again.

The silent one waved, then disappeared, and presently bobbed up above the rail with a coil of harpoon-line in his hand.

"Heave away!" yelled Jack.

The rope's-end came snaking out over the water, and Jack, leaving his life-buoy, made a dive after it.

"Who'll go first?" he asked quickly, on getting hold of the line.

"Can't we-alls go in a bunch," inquired Broncho. "It would be a safer play that-away. I ain't hankerin' on playin' a lone hand agin them two tiger-lilies. Where's the rest of the band? The deal seems some queer to me."

"We must go one at a time. Which is it, quick?" asked Jack shortly.

"Pass me," returned Broncho distrustfully. "You take the first deal, Jack; you've been acquainted with them tattooed gents before, an' mebbe will make a better play of it, breakin' the ice, than either Jim or me."

"Yes, go ahead, Jack—if you think it's all right," added the boy uneasily.

"Well, here goes then," and watching his chance as the barque rolled, he shouted, "Haul away!" and at the same time kicked out lustily towards the ship.

The sea swung him right up to the rail, and catching hold quickly, with the aid of the Kanaka he managed to scramble aboard, and a few seconds later Broncho and Jim were likewise hauled over the bulwark into safety. And as they lay on the deck rubbing their cramped and chilled limbs to restore the circulation, they gazed around anxiously; but except for the two Kanakas, who stood regarding them silently, the decks seemed to be deserted.

CHAPTER II
"THE *OCMULGEE*"

"Where are the rest of the crew?" inquired Jack of the Kanaka who hove the rope, as he looked round the empty decks.

"All gone dead!" responded the South Sea Islander laconically.

"All dead?" burst out the former with a start.

"All dead!" repeated the Polynesian mournfully. "De coral him splead, de palm him g'ow big, but man him die all-e-time!"

The speaker was a magnificent specimen of manhood, standing six foot, with limbs of perfect proportions.

He was dressed in the dungarees of the sailor, with leather sea-boots. The clothes hung loosely on his emaciated form, and he had the appearance of a strong man worn out by long hardship and privation.

A gigantic harpoon in his right hand and the hideous tattooed gridiron on his face gave him a look of ferocity directly at variance with the expression in his big brown Polynesian eyes, which contained that wonderful liquid softness shown chiefly in the eyes of deer.

The other Kanaka had resumed his squatting position on the deck in front of a little ebony image, which he gazed at with a fixed stare.

The *Ocmulgee* was a regularly old-timer, and her decks were ornamented with various trophies of the whale-hunt.

The companion entry was made through a part of the huge skeleton lower jaw of a sperm whale; the wheel, which was inlaid with mother-of-pearl, had spokes of sea-ivory beautifully carved, each in the shape of a human arm with closed fist. The fife-rails were likewise decorated and fashioned, whilst the compass could be seen through the grinning teeth of a sea-lion, marvellously worked in polished ebony. Even the worn running gear of this dandy whaler travelled through ivory blocks.

Her bulwark rail was studded like the jawbone of some huge monster with the long teeth of the cachalot, which did duty as belaying-pins.

Four magnificent whaleboats swung from stout wooden davit legs, whilst her decks, which were flush fore and aft and stained by much oil to the deepest mahogany, were singularly spacious.

Amidships were the brick-built tryworks, and forward a small galley, or what used to be called in the old buccaneering days a caboose.

"Geewhittaker!" ejaculated Broncho, as he cast a look of inspection round the deck. "What's this we-alls have strayed into? This here barque seems to me to be a cross between a dime-museum an' one o' them flash saloons. I recalls a saloon one time, way up in the Spokane, they calls the 'Golden Dollar.' Say, boys, but she were a beaute, with a bar-counter a-glitterin' with twenty-dollar gold pieces, let in betwixt mother-o'-pearl, an' opals big as pigeons' eggs, an' that stuff scientific sports calls chrysolite."

"Look at that cannibal worshippin' his idol," said Jim in an awestruck voice. "Ain't he a ferocious-lookin' savage? There's somethin' deuced uncanny about this queer-lookin' ship, an' I'm beginning to wish I was back in the life-buoy."

Meanwhile, Jack, who could patter several of the island dialects, perceiving from his tattooing that the Kanaka was a Marquesan, had begun to put questions in that language, to the evident pleasure of the native.

"What does this here tattooed party say?" inquired Broncho. "That lingo you-alls converses in is some strange to me, an' onlocated in my realms o' larnin'."

"These two Kanakas," said Jack in explanation, "come from the Marquesas Islands, the most noted cannibal group in the South Seas— —"

"O-o-o-oh, Lo-o-ord!" began Jim in a scared voice; then, gathering courage as he saw the quizzing smile in the rover's eyes, "Thank goodness that, though I'm young, I ain't tender."

"This man's name," continued Jack, "is Tari, and the other, bowing there before the image, is Lobu. He is a little touched in the head from a blow of a cutting-in spade— —"

"These here two Cimmarons, you-alls says, is man-eaters, an' one of 'em is locoed," interrupted Broncho solemnly. "Wall, I'm shore thankful a whole lot they ain't more numerous. Mebbe, though, these two Marquesas sports have done roasted an' eaten the rest of the outfit—they looks hungry enough to chaw up a whole bunch of Navajo bucks without battin' an eye nor yet fallin' victims to indegeestion. I reckon they regyards humans the same as we-alls do pra'rie hen, ba'r stakes, terrapins, an' sech-like high-flung eadibles, as bein' plumb full of relish. They don't look to me as if they'd pass up their hands or quit s'long as thar's an uneaten cawpse idlin' around; no, siree, they jest sharpens their carvin' knives an' sits right into business."

"They used to be cannibals; they are not now," went on Jack. "These two men are harpooners. Tari here knows Big Harry, whose mate I was for three years trading among the Islands— —"

"You don't say!"

"He says the *Ocmulgee* has been out three years with only three hundred barrels of oil to her credit. She lost her mate and three men in a fight with a solitary bull-whale in the Japanese seas; then scurvy broke out whilst they were away to the south'ard; and, to make matters worse, they got jammed in the ice the whole winter. When they finally got clear there were only the captain and five men left. The captain bore up all he knew to make northing. They had a long spell of foul weather; then he died, and the other three men and these two have been alone on the ship for a whole moon, drifting under bare poles."

"Wall, I reckon as how they've been sittin' in pretty dirty luck; but do you-alls mean to relate as how Destiny allows these here tattooed, man-chewin' pagans to win through, whilst white men has to go donnin' wings or tails, harps or hot pitchforks, as the case may be, in the etarnal beyond? Fortune shore deals a queer gsame."

"That's about the size of it," said Jack.

"Can this here aboriginal speak English?"

"He can talk Beach-le-mer, a kind of pidgin English of the South Seas."

"Same as that flapjack-tossin' Chink, Lung?"

"Pretty much the same."

"Wall, I surmise he regyards that 'ere hunchbacked, ebony mannikin as havin' pulled him through this devastatin' holocaust, scurvy, which downs the rest of the band so free an' easy," remarked the cowboy musingly.

"What are we goin' to do, Jack?" asked the boy, with chattering teeth. "Can't we rout out some dry duds? I'm near froze standin' here talkin'."

"That's certainly the first thing to be thought about," agreed the rolling-stone. "Then, when we've overhauled the ship below, we'll have a powwow."

Leaving the two Kanakas on deck, they descended the companion-way, and found themselves in a fair-sized cabin, with doorways opening out of it.

In the centre was an inlaid mother-of-pearl table, and the bulkheads were hung with curios of every description—spears of all shapes and sizes, fantastic-looking bone-studded clubs, various harpoons, some twisted and bent, evidently the relics of by-gone battles, swords of sharks' teeth, ships' models in bottles, specimens of skrimshander, rare shells and Japanese nitchkies in cabinets, carved cocoanuts, feather cloaks and war head-dresses; and last, but not least, some fearfully-grinning Japanese masks.

Catching sight of these, Jim gave an exclamation of horror.

"Mercy, look at those devil-faces!" he gasped.

"Devil-faces—which that ain't no compliment to the devil, an' I reckon he's plumb mortified at sech remyarks. Them feachers is that fearful they're suffeecient to promote silence in a hoot-owl," remarked Broncho solemnly.

"This cabin is surely the dime-museum you were talking about," said Jack, with a laugh.

"It's shore liable to give a gent who's been some free with the nosepaint the jimjams in a highly variegated form. It would knock him offen his mental reservation quicker'n a bullet out of a Winchester."

After searching through the berths, Broncho and Jack managed to find clothes which fitted them; but Jim had to close-reef the legs of his trousers and the ends of his sleeves before he could get his hands and feet to appear.

Clad once more in dry raiment, they then made a descent upon the deceased captain's stateroom, and overhauled the log-book.

It was a gloomy perusal.

They found the statements of the Kanaka Tari to be correct, and the log had been written up to within the last month.

The entries were a series of tragedies. Solemnly Jack read them out, picking the more important items:

"*Oct. 2nd.*—William K. Budd, 1st officer; James Rake, harpooner; John Coffin and Pedro Gonzalez, able seamen, killed by a whale in Lat. 43°25 North, Long. 136°15 East.

"*Feb. 16th.*—Henry Gaul, cooper, died of scurvy.

"*Feb. 23rd.*—Simeon Bennett and Henri Rochey, able seamen, died of scurvy.

"*May 2nd.*—Shut in by pack ice in Lat. 69°12 South, Long. 140°63 West.

"*May 15th.*—Ezekiel K. Scruggs, 2nd officer, died of scurvy."

So the sad entries ran on until the last, which was entered in a very shaky hand:

"*Oct. 3rd.*—Only six of ship's company left, including myself; all of us, except two Kanakas, in the last stages of scurvy. Cannot last many more days. Strong westerly winds with snow squalls increasing in force. Unable to take sights. Ship hove-to on port tack."

"That's shore a heap melancholy. I surmise he cashes in *poco tiempo* after them observations—his luck's that mighty rank, not to say demoniac," was Broncho's comment.

"The first thing we'd better do," said Jack, as he closed the old sharkskin-bound log-book, "is to examine into the provisions. I expect they're liable to be pretty bad."

"I'm goin' to hunt up some fishing-lines," announced Jim. "Eating deep-sea fish is better than living on food which has killed a whole crew with scurvy."

"Which I think your proposeetion is as full of sense as a rattlesnake in August is of p'ison," remarked Broncho approvingly.

Then, whilst Jim went after the fishing-lines, Jack and Broncho made their way into the lazarette, and started to overhaul the stores.

"Just as I thought," muttered the former, holding aloft an old binnacle-light which he had discovered and promptly brought into use, and peering round the gloomy interior. "Condemned Government stores, and the cabin truck run out."

Two or three barrels were standing already broached, with a few pieces gone out of each, as if an attempt had been made to pick out the best bits.

"This here pork an' beef is plenty lively for its years," declared Broncho, his hand to his nose. "I reckon it has over a hundred rings on its horns; but you can bet your moccasins it goes pawin' 'round in a man's inside until it has him oozin' with p'ison from his spurs to his sombrero. I ain't none surprised it makes a winnin' agin them onfort'nit' whale-huntin' sports."

"And look at the hard-tack," said Jack, as he shook a handful of weevils out of a biscuit.

"It's shore inhabited a whole lot. I allow them Kanakas has insides like goats."

"Well, there's no time to be lost. The sight of that grub means cracking on for the Islands," grunted Jack, as he hurriedly made for the door.

"Can you locate us at all, Jack?" asked the cowboy, as they once more breathed freely in the dime-museum cabin. "Ain't thar no blazed trail we-alls could jump on to, so as to lope into Frisco some quicker'n we've been comin' out?"

"'Fraid not; Frisco's a long way off, but I don't think we're more than a week's sail from Pitcairn Island. This breeze'll let her head up within a point of north. I'll get the latitude if I can catch the sun to-morrow, but I'm afraid the longitude will be mere guess-work, as the chronometers have both been allowed to run down."

"Wall, you play the hand, Jack; you're up in this ship's game. I just come in blind an' leave it to you, bein' what you-alls might call an amature."

"We'll just have a powwow with the Kanakas and then get to work," said Jack, as they left the cabin.

On gaining the deck they found the elements still moderating.

The *Ocmulgee* floated high out of the water as buoyant as a cork, and her deck, except where the rollers slopped through the bulwark ports, or an occasional saucy-crested comber popped over her topgallant rail, was quite free of water.

At the stern was perched Jim, busily watching three fishing-lines, whilst amidships Lobu still sat gazing at his ebony *tiki*.

From the caboose came a thin wreath of smoke, which blew down to leeward in a long streamer. Tari was within, doing all he knew to make a fat lump of rancid pork more or less eatable.

Jack gave a long look round the heaving horizon, but no sail broke the monotony of rushing sea and sky. He then went and sounded the pumps, and was well satisfied.

"An hour's work will pump her dry," he remarked to the cowpuncher. "We'll get sail on her first, though."

Then, "All hands make sail!" he sang out cheerily, dropping naturally into the position of leader.

"Jim, you're an active nipper and quicker than the rest of us; jump up an' cast the gaskets off the main-topsails."

"Aye, aye, sir," returned the boy, with a twinkle in his eye and an emphasis on the "sir."

But Jack never noticed it. He was too busily employed trying to make Lobu understand that he had to get off his haunches and add his weight and muscle as they mustered at the lower-topsail sheets.

"Warble out one o' them chanties o' yours, Jack," called the cowboy. "They helps a man to brace back on a rope a whole lot."

Thereupon Jack struck up an old sea legend about a drowned sailor, who married a mermaid and had an unpleasant habit of climbing up ships' cables and frightening their crews.

Taking the upper-topsail halliards to a small capstan aft, they tramped round strongly to the weird sailor song, in the wild chorus of which even Tari joined:

"And it's blow, ye winds, heigh-ho!
Blow, ye winds, heigh-ho!
Blow away the mist and snow!
And it's blow, ye winds, heigh-ho!"

Before dark the *Ocmulgee* was plunging heavily along under two lower-topsails, main upper-topsail, reefed foresail and staysails, close hauled on the port tack.

The spanker was also set, without the head being hauled out.

By this time all hands were pretty well wearied, besides being very keen set, and some of Tari's cooking was demolished with many grimaces.

Then, leaving Jim at the wheel, they turned to again to rid the ship of water, and it was close on two bells in the first watch before the cheerful sound of the pumps sucking greeted their ears.

Leaving Lobu to resume his religious duties before the ebony image, the rest of the small ship's company assembled round the wheel, and held a counsel of ways and means.

"Wall, Jack," said Broncho, opening the debate, "you-alls bein' the old he-coon of this outfit, we awaits your remyarks as to what trail you allows we'd better pull our freight on to. We-alls wants to be posted as to how the kyards are stackin' up, an' how we're to play our hands to emerge victors out o' this here onexpected racket."

"I reckon we ought to be somewhere near Pitcairn or the Paumotus in less than ten days," replied the rover easily.

"At Pitcairn we can get fresh fruit and vegetables. From there we can jog across to Papeete, the port of Tahiti, hand the *Ocmulgee* over to the American consul, and take schooner for Frisco."

"The way you puts it, this here bill o' fare seems some easy to chew on," commented the cowpuncher, looking keenly at Jack. "Mebbe, though, it ain't sech a cinch as I surmises. Ain't we-alls some scarce as an outfit to keep this here ship from stampedin' 'way offen the trail? Do you-alls reckon we is numerous enough to ride herd on her."

"Well," returned Jack slowly, "we are rather short-handed, and that's a fact. Still [with a smile], we're enough to keep the ship from milling.[10] Tari and Jim can both steer; and you, Broncho, must have your first lesson as soon as possible. We three will have to take watch and watch, as I don't like to trust the ship to the Kanakas."

"And who'll ride first night gyard?" asked Broncho.

"You two both look pretty fagged out. Suppose you jump below and turn in; Tari and I will keep the middle watch."

"I ain't tired—I'm as frisky as can be," objected Jim. "I might as well take the first trick now I'm at the wheel."

"And I'm as full of buck as a corn-fed cow-pony," put in Broncho. "You're lookin' some weary an' overplayed yourself, Jack; just you prowl down in your blankets whilst Jim and I deal the game."

"I think we'd better elect a captain first," said the rover casually, "or it'll be a case of too many cooks."

"Bein' as you savvys the game, Jack, I concloods you-alls is elected onanimous; thar shore ain't no candidate for the opposition. You're the range-boss o' this round-up."

"Why, 'er course," affirmed Jim.

"Well, then, you two obey orders and turn in until further notice," returned Jack, with a laugh.

"You guileful ole terrapin!" growled Broncho, as he reluctantly made for the companion-way, followed by the boy.

FOOTNOTES:

[10] Going round in a circle, as cattle sometimes do when frightened or restless.

CHAPTER III
"THE BURNING OF THE SOUTH SEAMAN"

The night passed without incident, and dawn found the *Ocmulgee* jogging along with the yards just off the backstays.

The wind had steadied down to a fair south-west breeze; the sea was much quieter, and matters were looking up all round.

Broncho was taught to steer, and Jim fished indefatigably, but beyond catching a huge molly-mawk, which had swooped on the bait, he had not had much success.

Tari, however, the skilled harpooner, had managed to spear several dolphins, and dolphin stew made a welcome addition to the poor fare.

So the days passed.

Except for Lobu, the madman, who caused some anxiety by his queer behaviour, all hands were pulling together well.

Tari proved to be invaluable. He had a soft, gentle nature and worked like an ox, his disfigured countenance aglow with beaming good temper.

He cooked, he steered, he was ready for everything and toiled away unceasingly with wonderful endurance. The man was untiring in his efforts to please, and Jack especially he seemed to take to.

"You my *pleni*," he had announced to that worthy in his soft Polynesian tones.

Pleni means "friend," and has a peculiar sentimental significance in the South Seas, and after this announcement Tari waited upon Jack like a slave.

This behaviour seemed to impress the cowpuncher greatly, and about the third day on board he commented on it to the rolling-stone.

"That 'ere Tari, whom you-alls say by his tattooing is a big chief, behaves as if he's your nigger, Jack, an' he shore hungers to please you. You sartinly has his affections roped, tied down, an' with your brand on to 'em that-away. I watches him eyein' you with them big antelope orbs o' his same as if you're some kind o' god, an' it's plumb touchin' as a spectacle."

"That's the custom, Broncho, in the South Seas. The natives are like affectionate dogs, and when a man announces that he is your *pleni* it means that from then on you are his first consideration in this world," replied Jack. "It's a far, far stronger affection than that which lovers hold to one another in the Society and Marquesas groups, passionate though they are."

"Wall, I reckon a pagan Kanaka shore calls the turn that-away on redskins. Tari's a different breed entire to them yellow snakes. I ain't never seen the redskin's eye I'd trust, but Tari's I'd jest as soon stack upon as any white man's."

"How do you like the *Ocmulgee's* tobacco?" asked Jack, as he lit his pipe behind his hands.

"For smokin' it'll about run in double harness with tea, which same is puttin' it some mild; but for chewin' it makes me as peevish as a sick infant, it's that rank, an' shore gives a gent a ja'ndiced view of life."

During this conversation they were seated round the cabin skylight in the first dog-watch.

Suddenly Lobu, who as usual was engaged in mysterious confidence with his black baby-god, sprang to his feet, and with a wild cry seized Tari's harpoon, which was resting up against the fife-rail; then, before any one of them could make a move, he had the weapon poised for a terrific lunge at Jack.

Like a wild thing, Jim, who was steering, flung himself in front of his hero. At the same moment, Tari, making a wonderful shot with a belaying-pin, which he had snatched from the rail, dashed the harpoon to the deck, and before the infuriated madman could pick up his weapon, all hands had scattered for safety.

"He's running amuck! Look out for yourselves!" roared Jack, as he dodged round the companion.

Broncho made a break for the tryworks, whilst Jim, springing on to the main fife-rail, went hand-over-hand up the port lower-topsail sheet.

Foaming at the mouth and jerking forth queer, wild guttural cries, Lobu, with weapon raised on high, hurled himself round the companion after Jack; but the fleet-footed Britisher was too quick for him.

Foiled here, he suddenly turned and launched his weapon at Jim, who was swarming up the purchase with the agility of a monkey.

Nothing but a sharp roll of the ship saved the boy, and the harpoon stuck quivering in the mainmast.

Meanwhile, Broncho, with the ready resource of a frontiersman, had seized the coil of line from a boat tub, and hastily making a running bowline, crept up behind the unsuspecting Kanaka.

Lobu now stood hesitating, and gazing stupidly up at Jim above him.

With a quick twist of the wrist the rope snaked from the cowboy's hand, and the loop dropped neatly over the insane man's head and shoulders. With such an expert at roping and throwing as Broncho, it was but a moment before Lobu lay on the deck, securely bound and helpless.

"My! That was close!" panted Jim, as he slid down to the deck.

"Jim, shake!" said the rover, breathing deeply and with the smallest tremble in his voice. "I won't forget what you did to-day as long as I live."

The boy blushed vividly with pleasure, and stammered out something which was quite unintelligible, whilst Broncho said heartily:

"Good for you, son! It shore were a clean strain play o' yours, an' plumb full o' sand as the Mohave desert."

Then Tari came in for congratulations and thanks, and the way Jack gripped his hand made the Islander beam with pleasure and wince with pain.

"Fine shootin', Tari, as ever I sees," commented Broncho. "Black Davis is plumb childlike with a belayin'-pin compared to you."

The question now was, what was to be done with Lobu, who lay on the deck panting and spent, and apparently sane enough again, though rolling his eyes in wide alarm.

"I believe he thinks we are going to cook and eat him," observed Jack. "The Marquesans always used to eat the captured amongst their enemies."

"I'm feelin' some hungry myself," asserted Broncho, with his slow, quiet drawl, which always grew slower and more serious the lighter and more flippant the remark he was making happened to be.

This was the way with the cowboy. On serious or more important subjects he assumed a lightness and indifference in his speech which he was very far from feeling, whilst he brought out a joke with more solemnity than a Chancellor of the Exchequer introducing the budget.

"We'll shore have to skin him," he went on. "Eating a gent unskinned when he's tattooed that-away would give folks delusions that they're consumin' of boa-constrictors, which same is liable to give palp'tations round the cartridge-belt to a gent who's been used to beans, salt pig, an' air-tights, bein' some rich an' high-flung as an edible."

Jack and Tari proceeded to have a long consultation together in the Marquesan dialect, at the end of which the former turned to the others and said:

"Tari wants us to set him loose. He says he'll watch him closely, and give us warning if he looks like having another fit of man-hunting. What do you say, boys?"

"Wall, you can bet your moccasins I'm goin' to pack 'round a six-shooter in future. That 'ere Lobu springs his little game on us that headlong an' sudden, an' puts sech fervor into it, that he comes near callin' a show-down on the crowd; an' in the event of his scoutin' off on the war-path again, I reckon I'll plant some lead amongst his idees, an' sober him some," pronounced Broncho.

"He don't look any too safe," said Jim, as Lobu, having recovered his breath, began to scowl and mutter to himself.

"I'm an Apache if he ain't hungerin' to begin his butchery again," drawled Broncho; "he's shore due to inaug'rate a holycaust if we turns him loose."

"Heart no bad! Head bad!" said Tari sadly.

"Mebbe, son, mebbe. But he ain't sedentary enough to go skallyhootin' 'round onfettered; he's a heap too vivid an' high-sperited, an' is liable to crease one of us mavericks."

"Better put him in the forepeak and clap the hatch on over him," proposed Jack.

"He's cert'nly too apparent on the scenery where he is," declared the cowboy.

Jack's idea was finally acted on. Lobu and his ebony idol were relegated to the forepeak, and once more serenity prevailed.

With sunset the wind died down considerably, and the long swell caused the *Ocmulgee* to roll heavily.

Night descended. The sky became one sparkling mantle of stars, and the sea, in heavy black ridges, lumbered in from the westward, slow and dignified, the last relics of the Roaring Forties.

At each lurch of the vessel her canvas thumped against the masts and rigging, giving forth a sound like the cracking of an Australian stockwhip.

The dark form of the cowboy at the wheel swayed slowly backwards and forwards across the glittering moonlight as the vessel rolled.

The flare of the galley fire peeped forth forward in shafts of yellow light. The silent decks were striped with cold moonbeams and inky shadows, weird and eerie-looking, the great whale-jaws at the companion giving a grotesque appearance to the after part of the barque.

Occasionally the top of a roller would slop in through a port, and ripple across the sloping deck like a stream of shining silver.

Reclining on the locker which ran round the cabin skylight lay Jack Derringer, pipe in mouth, lazily watching his beloved stars.

Forward the Kanaka Tari could be seen flitting backwards and forwards across the shaft of light from the galley, busily engaged in gathering fuel from the fore 'tween-decks.

Presently he went forward, and lifting the hatch of the forepeak, looked down into the gloom, where lay the poor madman.

As he bent over the hatch a heavy volume of smoke poured forth, enveloping his face and causing him to cough.

Hastily withdrawing his head he rushed aft, crying in his strange, broken English:

"Shippe burn! shippe burn! Lobu settee fire shippe!"

Up jumped Jack, quick to think and quick to act.

"Leave the wheel, Broncho, there's not enough wind to hurt. You, Jim and Tari, get the quarter-deck buckets forrard. Follow me, Broncho—sail-locker, spare t'gallants'l."

Short and sharp came the words, and Jack was gone.

In an incredibly short space of time Broncho and the rover reappeared with the sail on their shoulders.

Meanwhile, Tari and Jim had succeeded in hauling the senseless form of Lobu out of the forepeak, and were hard at work throwing water on to the smother of smoke.

It was a slow process, however, as the water had to be drawn over the side, there being no pump on board.

Rapidly the sail was dipped overboard and spread out.

"Pass it down to me, boys," called Jack; and before any one could divine his intention, he had descended the ladder into the midst of the smoke.

With hurried hands the sail was lowered down after him, and for a few minutes it looked as if the fire was going to be smothered.

With redoubled vigour they turned to the buckets, and, in a constant stream, the water was sent sousing down.

Suddenly Jack's head appeared, soaking wet and blackened with smoke, at the top of the ladder.

"An axe!" he gasped out. "The bulkhead's caught!"

"An axe! an axe!" repeated Jim aimlessly.

But Tari, with two bounds, reached the caboose, and snatching up the weapon with which he had lately been chopping wood, dashed forward and handed it to Jack, who once more descended, having tied a red silk handkerchief over his nose and mouth.

Then the sound of blows could be heard below, as the rolling-stone battled with the flaming bulkhead.

Suddenly the chopping ceased, the dense clouds of smoke were redoubled, and a second later flames were perceived.

Meanwhile, no signs of Jack.

The bucket gang began to grow anxious.

"Hey, Jack, cut loose outer that, or you'll get straddled," called Broncho.

In response, a faint cry as if from a long way off came floating up.

Still no Jack.

Moments passed, and it was plain to all that the fire was rapidly gaining on them.

"Come up, Jack, come up!" cried the boy wildly.

"No use, Jim," growled the cowpuncher. "You can't ride him—no, not with buckin' straps an' a Spanish bit."

No responding cry was heard this time.

"My God, where is he?" exclaimed Jim with alarm. "He'll suffocate and lose his senses if he stays down there any longer."

"I guess I'll just scout 'round an 'see how he's playin' the game. Mebbe them flames makes a winnin' against him," said Broncho leisurely, in his most indifferent tones—the very carelessness a sure sign that he was deeply anxious.

"Lemme go, lemme go!" urged Jim, his voice strained and overwrought.

"No, son, it's my bet," said the cowpuncher, as he slipped a rope's-end over his shoulders. "Now, you-alls cinch on to the end o' this, an' if I don't show up on the scenery in five minutes, just yank me out, an' don't use no mildness neither"; and down went Broncho.

A minute later he reappeared, followed by an object whom they had some difficulty in recognising as Jack Derringer.

He was black as a sweep. His clothes were in tatters and smouldering in places; most of the hair on one side of his head was singed off, and he was evidently very exhausted.

On reaching the deck he swayed unsteadily, and then toppled over in a faint.

"One o' them locoed critters who don't know when they've got enough," growled Broncho, as he soused a bucket of water over the inanimate form.

"You go to blazes!" came in faint tones from the senseless man, and two rows of gleaming white teeth appeared in the blackened countenance of the rover, as his lips curved in a smile and he slowly opened and shut one eye.

Jack was only overcome by the fumes of smoke, which had got into his lungs, and the fresh air and cold water rapidly revived him.

Presently he sat up.

"It's no use," he exclaimed. "The ship's saturated with oil, and will be in a blaze fore and aft in half an hour."

And the flames and smoke, which were now bursting through the scuttle, gave point and emphasis to his remarks.

"Which is the best of the whaleboats, Tari?" he continued.

"De starbo'd boat on de quarter."

"Well, jump's the word, boys. Hustle, we've got no time to lose. Broncho, you and Tari fill the water-breakers belonging to the boats; Jim and I will get the grub on deck."

Working with a will, they got the whaleboat over, and whilst Tari and Jim jumped into her, Jack and Broncho passed the provisions along.

She was a magnificent boat, a fine specimen of New Bedford handiwork, and held a vast amount without any overloading.

The four boat-breakers were passed in, a keg of biscuits, and enough salt horse to last close on a month with care; then a huge tarpaulin, a spare mast and sails from one of the other boats, four Winchester rifles and ammunition, whilst the three white men each buckled on a revolver and belt of cartridges.

This armament was Jack's forethought, for he knew that possibly they might find themselves amongst the Paumotu or Low Archipelago of atolls, which had got a very bad reputation and lay right in their course for either Tahiti or the Marquesas.

The sextant was not forgotten, or the chronometer; and even oilskins, blankets, and spare clothing were handed aboard. Whilst the small ship's company worked hard to provision the whaleboat, the old oil-sodden *Ocmulgee* was blazing furiously.

The whole of her, forward, was now a mass of flame, which with long yellow tongues went licking out to the end of the jibboom and up the tarred shrouds aloft. The foresail and topsails soon caught fire, and, with the blazing jibs and rigging, lit up the scene until the castaways were working as if by daylight.

At two bells in the first watch the fore-topmast came down with a crash, a mass of sparks like a St. Catherine's wheel; then, plunging into the sea with a loud hiss, it lay dead, a blackened, charred wreck.

By this time the main rigging had caught, and the ship was like a gigantic beacon.

"We'd better shove off clear of her at once," cried Jack, as he appeared out of the cabin entrance, his arms full of odds and ends.

"What you totin' along, Jack?" inquired Broncho, from the boat.

"Tobacco, matches, bull's-eye lantern, hammer, saw, packet of nails, two towels, a housewife, fishing-lines and hooks, spy-glass, nautical almanac, chopper——"

"Ain't you forgot somethin?" broke in the cowpuncher, with gentle irony.

Lobu had already been placed in the boat securely bound. He had recovered his senses, and sat quiet and sphinxlike on the floorboards.

As they were preparing to shove off, Tari rushed forward, and presently reappeared with his beloved harpoon.

"All aboard!" now sang out Jack lightly. "Any more for the shore?"

He was a most cheery person to be shipwrecked with. His spirits rose with the danger. Desperate situations, hardships, the near approach of death, all seemed to act upon him as a tonic and instil him with an infectious gaiety.

He jumped lightly into the boat and they shoved on.

"*Kaoha, nuir!*" muttered Tari, as they pulled away from the burning ship.

It was a friendly farewell, for the words, roughly translated, meant, "We part in friendship!"

Jim hummed the famous chanty:

"Leave her, Johnny, leave her,
It's time for us to leave her."

"*To fa*,[11] old ship!" called Jack. "The luck's against you. Kismet, always Kismet!"

"Yes, the kyards is stackin' up against you, an' like many another clean-strain gent, you bucks against them without weakenin'. Finally, you cashes in, back to the wall, boots on an' your gun empty. Old *Ocmulgee*, I looks towards you, you're dyin' game." Thus Broncho.

It was a melancholy sight as, lying on the swell about half a cable's length off, they watched for the end.

She was now in flames fore and aft. Every rope was a thread of fire. Even where they lay to windward they could hear it roaring and hissing as it wrapped the poor old barque in its furious toils.

The sea sparkled in the reflection. The smoke fell away to leeward in a huge bank of black, blotting out the stars.

The faces of the boat's crew showed red and yellow in the glare of the fiery blast—Tari's sad and downcast, Lobu's sullen and indifferent, Jim's wide-eyed, the cowboy's keen and interested, and Jack's dreary but resolute.

In silence they watched the end, each wrapped up in his own thoughts.

Tari wistfully wondered if he would ever see his beloved island home again, with its breadfruit trees and cocoanut palms, its surf-beaten shores and rocky headlands, its sandy inlets and crystal streams; and not least, its light-hearted, flower-decked maidens. He was weary and worn with this tragic voyage, tired of this buffeting by the Fates about the rough world, and longed desperately for his own *paepae-hae* once more.

Jim, who had never known a *paepae-hae*, whose only home had been a ship's foc's'le, whose playground had been that rough one the wide world, recalled tales of open-boat experiences with a feeling half of dread for the future, half of excited anticipation, the glamour and fascination of uncertain fortune making itself felt even in his small but romantic breast.

Broncho pondered upon the strange freaks of Dame Fortune, the streaks of good and bad luck, called by some "Providence," which go to make up men's lives.

Jack stared with the bright glare of the flaming ship full in his eyes, yet saw it not. His mind was far away. His memory was crowded with strange events, perils overcome, dangers met and conquered on the battlefield, in the bush, on deep water, and on mountain top, and his courage rose high— that courage which, in conjunction with iron nerves, great strength to suffer, and absolute fearlessness of death, made the rolling-stone such a difficult man for the Fates to trample upon.

Well he knew the terrors which were likely to be before them, the terrors of an open boat alone in mid-ocean—the torments of thirst and hunger, the growing weakness of mind and body, the aching, cramped limbs, the perils of storm and calm, the gradual feeling of despair, the long days of helplessness, then the feverish senses full of distorted views as mind and body grew more diseased, and, last of all, the wild, raving delirium. Well he knew them. He gave himself a shake and braced his mind to fight the coming battle.

All night the *Ocmulgee* roared, hissed, and crackled. All night the yellow tongues flared in fiery coils about her.

At six bells, eleven o'clock, the mainmast went by the board; then the mizzen tottered, swayed, hung for a moment like a flaming Tower of Pisa, and then slowly, deliberately, plunged into the sea.

A smother of foam burst forth, the sparkling white enveloping the flickering yellow and extinguishing it.

In the black background of smoke the red sparks gleamed like myriads of fire-flies.

And now, as the flames broke out over the hull, the salt-incrusted timbers turned the yellow tongues into weird blue and green flares, which in all the shades of the rainbow flickered and flourished.

Still the gallant old ship floated, and it was not more than an hour before dawn when at last, being burnt down to the water's edge, the *Ocmulgee* had to give up the fight.

All this time the castaways lay off, waiting to see the last of the burning ship.

Suddenly Jim sprang to his feet, shouting excitedly,

"She's going! she's going!"

Slowly the *Ocmulgee* lifted her stern into the air; her weather-worn rudder rose dripping from the ocean; then her keel showed, foot by foot, draped with long streamers of seaweed, as if with a shroud.

She gave a heavy lurch forward, a plunge, and was gone, leaving nothing but a swirling eddy of tossing white water.

FOOTNOTES:

[11] "Goodbye" (Samoan).

CHAPTER IV
"THE OPEN BOAT"

Morning broke and showed the whaleboat floating a mere speck upon the heaving blue of the Pacific.

At daylight they hoisted the lugsail, and steered north-east before a fresh south-westerly breeze, heading for Pitcairn Island.

Jack, with pencil and paper, worked out his dead reckoning, and calculated the distance to the island; but his great hope was being picked up by a passing vessel, as he was so uncertain about his longitude.

Having got his position to the best of his ability, he arranged a scale and regular allowance of food and water, which he personally served out, the others trusting themselves entirely to his judgment.

The whaleboat darted swiftly and buoyantly over the long swell, making good northing, and all hands were in cheerful spirits.

Lobu, who seemed quiet enough again, was allowed to have his hands free; but one ankle was padlocked to a thwart, whilst all weapons were removed from within his reach.

He sat silent and meditative in the bottom of the boat, gazing intently at his little black *tiki* which Tari, with kindly forethought, had removed from the ill-fated *Ocmulgee*.

Aft sat Jack, the steering-oar in his hand, a boat's compass between his feet, whilst Broncho and Jim reclined at their ease against the stroke thwart, and Tari slumbered peacefully at full length in the bows.

Four days passed thus peacefully, and then the good south-west wind slackened, wavered, and finally died away, leaving the whaleboat floating motionless on the long, never-ceasing Pacific swell.

The sun shone fiercely with an eye-wearying glare; a thickness of steamy mist gathered and obscured the horizon. The atmosphere was heavy and suffocating, with a moist heat; the sky was a pale sickly blue, and the deep stillness grew oppressive and aroused a feeling of depression and apprehension.

The castaways lay silent. Not a breath stirred the air; everything seemed motionless with the exception of the long, stately swell of the restless ocean.

Suddenly the universal quiet was broken. Over the water came the quaint wild cry of a Mother Carey's chicken, and two or three of these small flitters were perceived hovering around.

"Mebbe there's some island hereabouts with them birds so handy," suggested Broncho, aroused out of his lethargy by the queer note.

"I'm afraid not," replied Jack. "I don't like to hear a Mother Carey's chicken give tongue, though; it generally means a long spell of calm weather."

"Why, oughtn't we to pick up the south-east trades directly?" inquired Jim.

"Never can tell nowadays; we may have more than we want of the doldrums. The current seems to be setting us to the westward, also."

"It certainly is some lackin' in wind," muttered Broncho sleepily, as he stretched himself in the shade of the sail for a snooze.

The drowsy afternoon passed slowly. Forward the two Islanders slept peacefully; Jim nodded, curled up against the rover's knees; and the latter sat idly handling the steering-oar, puffing meditatively at his pipe. Only the wild cry of the restless harbingers of calm broke the stillness.

Occasionally a flight of startled flying-fish burst forth from beneath the shadow of the whaleboat, and, skipping along the surface, presently plunged out of sight again with tiny splashes.

Once a line of porpoises passed, leaping forth each in turn with steady regularity, their polished black bodies gleaming as they curved in and out.

Slowly the sun approached the horizon and the darkness crept over the east. Still not a breath of air moved.

Two long scorching days passed, and still they lay becalmed. Even the swell had subsided, and the ocean resembled a vast sheet of quivering glass. Things began to look serious.

The water was running low. Jack had had to cut down the allowances to half a pint per diem, and the dread torment of thirst was beginning to take hold of them.

The close heat was becoming unbearable, and the air stifling with the damp steaminess of a hothouse.

The castaways lay panting, and though dry and parched within, without they streamed with moisture.

The three whites in their shirt-sleeves, and with ducks or dungarees rolled up to their knees, were tanned as dark as the Kanakas, and their hard-worked muscles strained beneath the shrinking skin, giving their arms and legs the yellow gloss of burnished copper.

Jim tried to whistle for a breeze, but his tongue was too swollen from want of water, and the undaunted boy gave it up with a careless laugh.

"My penny whistle wants oiling," he said.

"I reckons we all want lubricatin' some," observed Broncho. "I shudders when I thinks of all the nosepaint I've put into my system so careless an' easy, without the remotest idees of what you-alls call economy or thrift."

"Don't talk about it," grunted Jack, with a queer grin. "I'm thinking of all the fresh-water baths I've had."

Undismayed, they joked lightly in the face of a terrible death, though each word was a stab in the throat and their voices grew huskier and weaker every minute.

"Speakin' o' baths," pursued Broncho, "I callate I'll take a swim right here. Mebbe the liquid is due to ooze through my hide an' lay the dust some, even if it ain't deep enough to drown a mosquito."

Jack silently pointed over the quarter to where the long fin of a shark was visible, almost motionless in the water.

"Third day he's been there," muttered the boy, with an irrepressible shudder.

"Soaking one's clothes is a small relief. Let's fill one of the empty breakers," proposed Jack.

"Shower baths! That's a jimdandy idee," said the cowpuncher approvingly.

They were soon scattering salt water over each other, and after this they found some small comfort by keeping their clothes wet.

The following night Lobu broke loose from his padlock, and springing to his feet with a blood-curdling yell, dived overboard, and started swimming up the shining wake of the moonlight.

"Out oars and after him!" cried Jack, springing to the stroke thwart and shipping the long, pliant ash-stick.

Tari ran the other oar out, and before Broncho had struggled clumsily to his feet, the two were pulling strongly after the madman.

"Sit down, you two," called Jack calmly. "We'll catch him."

But even as he spoke there rang out a wild shriek, and the next moment the boat was floating over a swirl of troubled water, which gradually grew still again; but the white sheen of the moonlight was mingled with the red of poor Lobu's blood.

"The shark!" gasped Jim in horror, and broke into the wild, sobbing laughter of hysteria, which shook his poor little frame in sudden pitiful jerks.

Jack bent down and tenderly lifted the boy on to the thwart alongside him, and putting his strong arm round him, held the twitching hands in a grip of iron.

Ha! ha! ha! ran the wild hoarse laughter, echoing through the still tropical night, and followed abruptly by long, choking sobs, which burst broken and husky from the dried-up throat.

The big brown eyes grew glassy with a fixed, unconscious stare; the laughter died down into whispered chuckling horrible to hear; foam gathered on the lips, which bared clenched teeth, and the whole small body shook as if with ague.

"Water, quick!" cried the rover.

"Him de las'!" said Tari quietly, as he handed across a pannikin half full of muddy fluid.

The breaker was empty.

"It may save the boy's life—he's not as strong as us men," pleaded Jack. "It's only his wonderful pluck that's kept him up as long as this; if his nerves go, he's done. We're strong; we can pull through, but the boy can't. May I give it him—it's his last chance?"

"Why, you durned old chipmunk," broke in Broncho half angrily, "d'you think Tari and I are sech low-down, ornery cattle as to up an' jump Jim's claim that-away."

"No dam fear! Oh hellee, no," jerked out the heroic Kanaka, vehemently in his turn.

"Thank you, boys," returned Jack; "I didn't mean to insult you."

"Put it in the diskyard," spoke forth Broncho, with one of his expressive poker slang expressions.

Tari remained silent, gazing, with his handsome but disfigured features full of pity and concern, as Jack, forcing open the clenched teeth, slowly trickled the precious water down the unconscious boy's blackened throat.

The effect was instantly perceptible. With a deep sigh and a relaxation of his rigid limbs, Jim rallied, and consciousness crept into his haggard eyes.

"Where am I?" he stuttered faintly.

"It's all right, old son," declared Broncho cheerily. "You just lie quiet an' slumber some."

Jim looked wonderingly round at the three faces, and then a wave of remembrance swept over him.

"Poor Lobu!" he murmured.

"Lucky Lobu!" said Jack to himself, thinking of the slow, suffering death from thirst which probably awaited them.

"Now, Jim," he continued aloud, "you've got to turn in. It's your watch below."

"We'll all be on watch below soon, I suppose," said the boy slowly, in a low tone.

"Me tink rain to-mollah!" suddenly put in Tari. The Kanaka knew well that the sky never looked more settled and less like rain, but with kindly nature he tried to instil hope.

Broncho, sitting in the stern, looked at the Marquesan and slowly lowered his left eyelid.

"You bet Tari's right. I sorter feels somehow as if we're goin' to have a regular deluge. These here tropical downfalls is that swift an' powerful, they're liable to swamp the boat a whole lot," he remarked, with the quiver of a smile.

Jim lay back on the blankets, but his nerves had been too shaken for sleep; and, as Jack watched the boy's wide-open, feverish eyes, staring vacantly at the brilliant lamps of heaven, he shook his head sadly. Then, determined to prevent the boy from pondering on their gloomy future, he began to relate the story of the heavens in a low, husky voice; and so successful was he with his old legends, that for the greater part of the night he had Jim and Broncho listening with eager attention, wholly oblivious of their desperate position as they searched the skies for a particular constellation, and then drank in Jack's half-forgotten classic yarns.

The sun rose, a great red ball, into the unhealthy blue of the heavens, and found the castaways nearer their end.

All through that baking day Jim rambled in the realms of fancy, speaking so thickly in his sufferings that the disjointed, wandering sentences could not be understood.

Tari lay motionless and resigned. Jack and Broncho conversed occasionally upon their position with slow, difficult words.

Though a certain amount of salt junk and hard-tack still remained, Jack did not attempt to serve it out, as suffering from thirst as they were, it would have been impossible to swallow any solid.

Towards sundown, after a long silence during which even the babbled mutterings of the poor boy had been inaudible, Broncho, lying in the bottom of the boat, croaked out to Jack, who sat stubborn and erect in the sternsheets, his emaciated hand still gripping the useless steering-oar:

"Say, old son, the deal's near finished. Jim's about through, an' I'm feelin' pretty near the '*Adios!*' myself. I guess our last chip will be raked in before maunin'. So long, if my senses jump the track an' go stampedin' off in the night."

"Die hard, Broncho!" was all the other replied, but he shut a pair of swollen lips with a snap of determination, and his eyes shone with the bravery of his spirit.

Then, letting go of the steering-oar, he took the sheath-knife from his belt, and slowly cut a notch in the stock of his revolver, which was still slung at his hip as he had hurriedly slipped it on when leaving the barque.

"This makes the eighth day," he muttered.

"Bite on the bullet, Broncho. We're not beaten yet," he said aloud; and called to the Kanaka, "How you, Tari?"

"Dam fine."

But the weakness of the voice gave the lie to the brave words.

Of the castaways, Jack seemed to be the strongest. Whether it was due to his indomitable spirit or his wonderful endurance, he certainly bore up better than the others.

Rising slowly and somewhat unsteadily to his feet, he peered round the shining horizon; then, dipping a pannikin over the side, he began pouring the refreshing liquid over the three prone forms—first soaking Jim and Broncho as they lay together amidships, and then crawling forward and performing the like service on Tari.

"T'ank you, my *pleni*" whispered the tender-hearted Marquesan, pressing his cracked lips to the rover's hand.

Jack's eyes grew very bright at the warm proof of affection.

"*Tiakapo*, Tari," he said softly in the Gilbert dialect, gripping the Kanaka's brown fist.

He did not like to say goodbye, but he felt that this was the last time his strength would allow him to come forward.

"*Moee-moee ariana!*" ("Go to sleep by-and-by!"), said Tari meaningly in Tahitian, and then very softly he muttered the Samoan goodbye, "*To fa!*"

The sun set in a blaze of colour, and darkness rushed upon them. Soon the lamps of heaven began to sparkle forth in all their brilliancy, and Jove's great binnacle-light, the silver moon, appeared above the horizon.

With the exception of poor Jim, who babbled hoarsely with but small intervals of silence, the occupants of the boat lay motionless, quiet and still, breathing with difficulty through their blackened, dried-up throats.

Jack alone still sat erect, grasping the oar.

During the earlier part of the night, Broncho, unable to withstand the temptation any longer, had surreptitiously been dipping a finger over the side and then sucking it.

Then for some time he lay still in the bottom of the boat by the side of the unconscious boy, too weak and exhausted to raise himself.

Suddenly, about midnight, he sprang to his feet, shouting with delirium, and caused the boat to rock violently.

Jack staggered up and grasped hold of the madman, fearing that he would fall overboard, and Tari made a gallant attempt to crawl aft from his position in the bows, but fell back overcome by sheer weakness.

"Steady, old man, steady!" called the rover, in his thick, hoarse voice.

"Lemme go, lemme go!" shrieked the madman, "an' I shorely devastates this hold-up a whole lot. He's a size too small for game like me"; and hurling Jack to one side, he drew his revolver and plumped all six shots at an imaginary foe, whom he seemed to see out on the placid waters of the great Pacific.

"Ah, I reckon I perforates his innards some that time," he continued, and broke into a horrible, blood-freezing chuckle.

Then, as suddenly as he had broken out, the cowpuncher became quiet again, and, seating himself on the midship thwart, idly started to twiddle his empty six-shooter round his forefinger, whilst Jack watched him with anxious eyes.

Presently he moved again, and crouched down cautiously in the bottom of the boat, taking infinite care to keep under the shelter of the boat's side, as if fearing an attack of some sort from the sea.

Then, clutching Jack by the arm, he pointed out to starboard with his cocked revolver.

"The Apaches, Jack!" he whispered, "the Apaches!"

"They're only squaws and papooses," said Jack quietly, wishing to humour him.

"Squaws an' papooses? Air you locoed? Why, they're all bucks an' out on the war-path! Chucks! thar's nothin' peaceful about them redskins; they're painted for war an' is shore out for blood."

"Perhaps you're right, Broncho," returned Jack, in his weak voice. "We'll lie low below these rocks," pointing to the boat's side. "They'll go right by us if we lie quiet."

"That's the only play, I allow," assented the cowpuncher as he lay motionless alongside Jim. "Though if they hit our trail," he continued, indicating the path of the moon, "which our tracks is easy for a twelve-moon babe to read, they won't give no notice, but just jump in with war-whoops and bullets toomultuous, which same deal is mighty likely to relieve us of our scalps complete."

Then he relapsed into silence, concentrating all his attention upon the imaginary Apaches, as he crouched in supposed concealment beside Jim, the empty revolver in his hand.

So the night wore on. Jim rambled with husky whispers as he tossed restlessly, unheeded by the light-headed cowpuncher, who occasionally communed with himself in a hoarse undertone.

"Thar's that ha'r-brained shorthorn Derringer Jack juttin' his chunky body over the skyline. Some gents ain't got the savvy of a pra'rie-dog, but I always allowed Jack had sense enough to come in out o' the wet, though he's some prone to overplay his hand by prancin' into trouble too gay an' heedless."

A grim smile crossed the face of the rolling-stone as he listened.

For a few minutes Broncho remained silent, then broke out again oracularly with the single sentence,

"Let every gent skin his own eel!"

Then all of a sudden he thought he was out on the plains again, vainly trying to stop a cattle-stampede.

"Turn that muley, Texas; throw a gun in his face! Hey, you point-men, what in hell'r you doin'? Hold 'em, can't you? Now, Larry, stop actin' smart like a fool-kid. Jump in an' hustle. This here's the hell of a run! Ride, boys, an' drift 'em together!"

Broncho was back again, the hard-working foreman of a trail outfit.

"Jimminy! here's a mesquite thicket!" he went on, and bending his head low between his shoulders, he clasped the thwart with both arms; for a second he remained thus, and then rambled on:

"This here star-faced sorrel is shore burnin' the earth, he's that speedy. Whar's that chuck wagon, I wonder? The herd's some scattered. Dick's down! Poor old Dick! The old passel of 'em right over him—nothin' left but blood an' mush, same as that Bee County Texan last fall. That's shore a raw deal for a cowman."

Again he was silent, then shouted wildly,

"Rowel an' quirt, boys, rowel an' quirt!"

Suddenly Tari's hoarse voice broke in from forward:

"Big rain come soon!"

The Kanaka was right. A large black cloud was coming swiftly up astern, which had not been noticed by Jack, taken up as he was by Broncho's ravings.

Hastily Jack and Tari with weak, desperate efforts managed to spread a sail to catch the precious fluid.

Jack gently pushed Broncho to one side, but this roused the madman's ire.

"If you reckons I allows a pullet like you to come man-handlin' me, you're shore saddlin' the wrong hoss. No deadbeat ain't goin' to come pawin' this longhorn 'less he's organised for war instanter——"

"Only me, Broncho! Don't you know Derringer Jack?" broke in that worthy sadly.

The delirious man stared wildly.

"Jack!" he muttered. "Why, it's Jack!" Then, overcome by the growing weakness, he sank back in the bottom of the boat, but he never took his haggard eyes from the rover.

The tropical squall approached rapidly; the stars faded away before it, as it climbed the heavens; then, with a burst of wind, the rain fell upon the boat's crew and lashed the calm sea into white as it pounded all around them.

In a moment all hands were soaked, and Jack and Tari, refreshed and wonderfully strengthened, were soon busy pouring the life-giving liquid down the parched throats of the two delirious ones.

When day broke the boat was running northward before a light breeze, and both the boy and Broncho had recovered their senses again. The water-breakers had all been filled, and a small quantity of beef and biscuit served out by Jack. A renewed cheerfulness prevailed, and a hopeful confidence that they would win through animated all.

Broncho, on being told of his night's behaviour, was very disgusted with himself.

"The way I conducts myself was shore scandalous," he remarked with keen self-reproach, "not to say low an' ornery. I'm plumb 'umiliated with my outrageous goin's on. Whyever didn't you down me, Jack? A man as weakens that-away an' goes locoed when things merely seems a bit rocky ain't worthy to live," and he gave a long grunt of contempt.

"Why, this here piccannine, Jim," he went on, "has more sense an puts me to shame. He ain't that pifflin' an' foolish as to go shootin' up spectres, not to speak of scarin' the whole outfit with delusions about Apaches an' cattle stampedes."

And Broncho relapsed into silence. He was indeed sore about his short spell of delirium, which he considered as a sign of want of grit on his part, and nothing the others could say seemed to comfort him.

Presently, as Jack notched his revolver for another day, the cowpuncher observed with keen irony against himself:

"Put away your weepon, Jack, or I'm liable to emit a screech at the sight tharof, and drop off into a swound, like a female I meets up with in Dodge one time, when I, aimin' to be polite, pulls out my six-shooter an' hands it to her, thinkin' mebbe she'd like to overhaul it like them towerist folks does, an' perhaps try a shot at the telegraph post in front of the Long Branch Saloon, which same post is that full o' lead I wonders it remains erect."

As the sun approached the meridian the light breeze died away, burnt up by the fierce heat of the tropical rays.

The sail was spread and lashed to four upright oars as an awning, and beneath its grateful shade the four castaways dozed through the afternoon.

After the scanty evening meal, still very weak and worn, though much revived and strengthened, Tari, Broncho, and Jim lay down on the blankets which covered the floorboards, and, protected from the glare of the moon by the sail, fell into a deep, heavy sleep, whilst Jack sat in his usual position in the sternsheets. For some time he lost himself in dismal reverie, and gave himself up to that deep melancholy which seemed to attack his courage at times, and brought that look of weary hopelessness to his face, so strangely at variance with the whole tenor of his nature. Often had his observant friend, the cowboy, noticed these fits of sadness in his friend, and wondered what was the cause of them. Some time in his past the rolling-stone had been badly knocked over, argued Broncho, and the wound was still unhealed; it was the only explanation he could imagine to account for this awful depression which weighed upon his friend.

However, whatever it was which weighed so heavily upon the rover's mind, it was presently overcome by a drowsiness born of lack of sleep. His gloomy reflections merged into dreams, his head dropped back against the gunwale, and, in a position in which only a sailor could, he slept.

But, alas! his face lay outside the protection of the sail, and the full strength of the moonbeams fell upon his closed eyelids.

CHAPTER V
"THE SPELL OF THE MOON"

Dawn broke, and the sun rose into the windless sky and turned the vast blue of the ocean into a glittering sheen, which it hurt the eyes to look upon.

Of the sleepers, Tari was the first to rouse himself, and as he gained his feet and took an eager glance round the horizon, Broncho and Jim awoke, but Jack slept on.

"Don't wake him," said Broncho in a low tone. "Rest is shore needful to Jack after the way I disturbs his slumbers lately with my rediclous, rannikaboo idees on the subjects of holdups an' Apaches."

So Jack was allowed to remain huddled up on the after-thwart in the uncomfortable position in which he had fallen asleep.

Broncho served out the rations, and whilst they munched their hardtack Jack stirred and opened his eyes.

"Awake, are you, old son?" remarked the cowpuncher heartily; "you've had a jimdandy sleep. Here's your chuck all ready for you," and he passed over Jack's allowance.

"By Jove! It's dark!" exclaimed the latter; "but why are you fellows having your chow in the middle of the night?"

"Middle of the night——" began Broncho, and then stopped, a look of consternation in his eyes.

"My God! he's off his head!" whispered Jim.

"Never seen such a dark night," went on Jack. "Can't see a yard!" Then, as he felt the warm rays of the sun on his face, "Why, what's happened? Where are you all?"

Slowly the terrible truth broke upon him. For a long minute no one spoke, whilst Jack fought with all his courage and strength of will against an overpowering desire to give way and break down.

This last calamity, coming on top of all the late trials, threatened to overcome his iron nerves, which, sorely tried and weakened by anxiety and privation, were strained to their utmost.

In silence he sat, shaking all over as if with ague, the others watching him with fixed, blank, expressionless eyes, as if hypnotised.

Not a muscle moved amongst the three onlookers of this cruel struggle.

No sound was heard but the lapping of the water against the boat's side and the creaking of the steer-oar in its crutch, jerked by the fierce grip of Jack's shaking right hand.

Presently he spoke, slowly and deliberately, pronouncing each word with care in the great effort to keep his voice steady.

"Boys, I'm blind, stone-blind!"

"Hell!" ejaculated Broncho, with a long breath, and there was a world of feeling in the utterance of that one word.

Suddenly Jim broke down and burst into long, deep sobs, which shook his little body fiercely as they tore themselves forth.

Then Tari, the poor savage, sprang forward, and kneeling at the blind man's feet, seized his hand, patting and caressing it.

"You no mind, Jack. Me your *pleni*, me your dog, my eyes good, see dam long way. Me see for you, me look eberywhere, all-e-way you want; tell you what Tari see, then you no want eyes."

"It's all right, boys," said Jack cheerfully, the sound of Jim's sobs and Tari's low pleading acting like a tonic on his manhood. "It's all right. I guess I'm moon-struck, that's all; it's my own fault—I fell asleep in the full glare of the moon. Don't you worry, boys, it'll pass off in a few days."

"Ain't thar no remedy for this here malady?" inquired Broncho. "It's a cinch we-alls ain't goin' to allow this here dissolute moon to deal sech a low-flung play without copperin' his bet. He ain't goin' to bluff us on sech a debased an' dark-evolvin' deal without bein' raised to the limit. I propose we-alls has a powwow as to how to euchre his little game."

"There's no remedy that I ever heard of," said Jack meditatively, in a low, quiet voice.

"Every disease leaves a trail, an' it's by scoutin' along that trail that we-alls hits the remedy," declared Broncho. "Mebbe your eyes is some painful, Jack?"

"Only a very slight throbbing."

"Can you locate this here throbbin'?"

"Seems to be along my eyebrows."

"What for of a play would it be if we-alls ropes an' ties down these throbbin's you mentions with a bandage o' sorts?"

"Might try a cold-water bandage," returned Jack doubtfully, "though I'm afraid only time will cure me."

"As to cold water, that's some difficult to round up, bein' most scarce as ice on this range. Why, this here ocean's as warm as new cow's milk."

"How about a hot-water bandage?" put in Jim, who was listening eagerly to the cowboy's proposals.

"Why, thar you euchre me again, son. We-alls can't light a camp-fire to heat a billy in this here boat; it's liable to bust the bottom out o' her."

Eventually Broncho, tearing off some strips from a flannel shirt, dipped them over the side till they were well soaked, and then bound them X-fashion across Jack's eyebrows.

"It's a poor hand," muttered the cowboy, "but we plays it for all it's worth."

Jack was made to lie down on the blankets under the awning, and all three vied with each other to make him as comfortable as possible.

The blindness made the strong man feel as helpless as a child. Jack's captaincy was over and he became a passenger in the boat, whilst Broncho took his place.

The cowboy, seated in the sternsheets, talked without ceasing in the desire to keep Jack from brooding. He recalled cunningly many a mirth-provoking experience which the two had gone through together in the past, and again and again he had his audience laughing uproariously at some quaint yarn. Even Tari, who understood very little of Broncho's queer cowboy and poker slang, joined in with a will.

"Do you mind how that tenderfoot Britisher downs Texas out with the U-bar outfit last fall, Jack?"

The cowpuncher stopped and smiled meditatively.

"Yes," he went on, addressing himself to the Kanaka, "Britishers is shore oncertain in their play a whole lot. As I daresay you-all notes, Tari, they mostly acts contrary to all idees o' wisdom, an' yet wins through on the game, an' it's a mighty difficult proposeetion to locate their play or cinch on to their system.

"Jack's British an' so's Jim; but they've trailed around that wide-spread through diff'rent countries that thar ain't much o' the Old Country paint an' varnish left on 'em. It all don' get rubbed off.

"I meets up with a pretty hefty mob o' Britishers, moseyin' 'round one way an' another. Some's green an' juicy, an' that tender you'd think they didn't oughter ha' left their mammy's apron-strings. But them shorthorns don' never pan out jest how you-alls imagines. They interdooces new idees into the play. It ain't all bluff, neither, an' as they accoomilates wisdom an' absorbs the many an' variegated systems in which life is played, they frequent emerges tharfrom as hard as granite and as knowin' an' crafty as a she-grizzly.

"When I paws back in my mem'ry I rec'llects quite a corralful o' strange plays these here British shorthorns makes.

"One I minds spechul; he's no more'n a kid, his eye-teeth bein' hardly growed. It's San Antonio whar he butts in on the scenery, w'arin' dude clo'es an' lookin' that soft and innocent I'm mighty dubious 'bout his not meltin' into a cawpse 'less he pulls his freight for milder climes. But I notes a clean-strain look in his eye, kinder open an' free like'n eagle's, which same eye gives me a faint surmise as how he ain't so tender and lamblike as he appears.

"I runs agin this here shorthorn first, a-takin' a pasear in his dude clo'es. Next I meets up with him over a faro game, an' I sees he has the fever on him shore 'nuff; his eyes is a-glitterin' an' his jaw clenched like he's desp'rate. He shore loses a heap, an' I notes his war-bags a-saggin' in and in, till presently they is plumb empty an' devoid of contents entire. Then he r'ars up on his hind-laigs, gives a laugh 'most like a wolf-howl, an' vamooses.

"'Bout an hour later he swarms in on the scenery again, but he's a mighty dissolute lookin' hobo now. His dude clo'es is gone—I reckons he's done pawned 'em—an' he's a-caperin' 'round in a p'ar o' overalls, nought but squares o' variegated colours wi' patchin', an' a shirt which is 'most all ventilation. He's bar'-foot an' bar'-headed.

"Wall, this here youthful scarecrow wanders kinder thoughtful up to the kyard-sharp who deals the faro game which roped in his dinero, an' slammin' down a twenty-dollar gold-touch, allows he'll cut kyards for it.

"That 'ere kyard-sharp kinder smiles slow an' satisfied, like a wolf wi' a strayed calf or a b'ar wi' honey, an' then cold-decks him some careless an' easy.

"But the boy cinches on to his play; his eyes sparkle, an' he cuts loose some loud an' fierce:

"'You're a damned cheat!'

"The faro-sharp ain't fretted none. He jest pulls his Colt an' p'ints it 'cross the layout, sayin' sorter glacial-like:

"'Do you-alls savvy the meanin' o' that word. Mebbe bein' some recent an' ignorant o' manners, you don't.' He pauses an' takes a chew slow an' delib'rate, his gun still p'inting in a line wi' that British infant's breastbone; then he resoomes, frownin' f'rocious an' grittin' his teeth: 'Wall, I aims to larn you. Car'less words is the downfall o' many, an' has to be c'rrected, or are liable to breed trouble. That word you-alls uses means "Death" in Texas.'

"But the boy, who I can see is some fretted an' impatient, breaks in here with his queer coyote laugh; then, flingin' himself forward over the layout, he rams his forehead plumb up agin the cold muzzle o' that Colt, and warbles out soft an' sweet like he's some pleased wi' himself:

"'I say you're a d——d cheat!'

"Great snakes an' creepin' reptiles! But it were a nervy play to make!

"The silence is that thick you-alls could pick it up an' chew it, an' you could hear the flies walkin' about! We mavericks who has the front stalls even cinches on to our breath an' corrals it in our innards, till we're as distended an' blown out as a dead steer in a coullee.

"An' the shorthorn shore bluffs this frothy kyard-sharp clean an' easy. For a moment he looks kinder dubious an' mystified; then he lowers his gun, kaufs up the Britisher's double-eagle, an' chucks it over to him, a-sayin':

"'Here's y'r dinero, an' I'm advisin' you, stranger, to pull your freight an' git. You-alls is too d——d tough for Texas."

Broncho stopped, and then broke into a yarn which he told with much droll solemnity, ending up with:

"This here's meant to be humourous. Mebbe it ain't, but it's allers had humour cinched on to it an' it's got to be a custom, so I allows we'll have to let it go at that, bein' as it's tagged an' labelled that-away, though I shore reckons it's mighty grim an' doleful as a funny play, and it more often has me winkin' water than throwin' off onrestrained guffaws."

It was a gallant fight, this of the plucky cowboy, desperately pitting old yarns and jokes against the present blackness; but through all the laughter his serious, anxious eyes kept watching his blind shipmate with an almost pitiful look.

Perhaps, of all the occupants of the whaleboat, the calamity to their leader hit the cowpuncher the hardest. The strongest natures feel the most, especially for others, and no one could say that there was any strain of weakness in Bucking Broncho.

Jack's bandages were constantly renewed, and fresh soaked in salt water. He proved a good and tractable patient, and no one heard any complaint leave his lips.

Only an occasional fleeting look of agony in his sightless eyes showed the chafing of the restless spirit within.

Soon after midday, Jim, who was standing up in the bows taking a glance round the horizon, suddenly gave a shout of surprise.

"Land ho!" he cried.

Right ahead, where the horizon grew indefinite and seemed to melt away into the midst of the tropical heat, there lay an island, clear cut and distinct. The black reef, the low beach, the very palms showed up in dark clusters of straight stems and bushy foliage.

"Hurrah! An island right ahead!" he went on.

Tari and Broncho scrambled up and clambered forward.

After a long look, Tari said quietly,

"Dat am ghost-island!"

"Ghost-island? Precious little ghost about that," asserted Jim confidently.

"It's an atoll, I expect," called Jack from under the awning. "Surely we can't have drifted as far north yet as the Paumotus! By my reckoning the nearest island is over a hundred miles off."

"It's a coral island—I can see the cocoanut trees," the boy sang out excitedly.

"I'm afraid Tari's right, son," said Broncho, after a long scrutiny. "It's a mirage!"

"A mirage?" exclaimed Jim incredulously, in tones of deep disappointment.

It was a wonderful sight. There lay the island, plain to see, and no one but a trained observer could have detected that it was a sham.

But Tari and Broncho were right. Many a mile had the cowpuncher ridden in chase of just such a lifelike image on the prairie without getting any nearer.

"These here mirages is just a deadfall, an' many a poor cowman has panned out through trailin' after them," observed Broncho.

"Well, the island that mirage reflects is somewhere down under the horizon," said Jack. "Just take its bearings, one of you, and we'll shape our course for it directly the wind condescends to blow."

"It's north-a-half-west," said Jim, after a look at the compass.

All that long afternoon, whilst they drifted helplessly, the fairy island hung over the horizon in the north.

Soon after darkness had fallen Jack startled the whole boat's crew by saying very quietly,

"Boys, it's my watch on deck now. I've got my sight back."

There was a wild, hoarse cheer, a buzz of congratulations, and night set in.

CHAPTER VI
"THE ATOLL"

During the night the south-east trades came upon them in a squall, and the whaleboat was soon bowling along merrily.

In a short while they found themselves in the midst of a choppy, foam-flecked sea, making good headway before the gradually strengthening breeze.

As daylight crept over the east, Jack, with a horrible sinking feeling of dismay, felt his returned eyesight gradually fail again.

As the deep indigo of the night gave way before the rosy beams of the morning sun and the moon lost its glitter, Jack saw a mist of grey slowly spreading before him; then, as the light of day increased, the grey merged into a black, which grew darker and darker, until the rover felt as if he was being pressed down by an awful pall of ink, pierced by tiny shafts, glinting flickers, and hovering waves of flashing, scintillating light, which splashed through the black curtain for all the world like the Northern Lights.

Great was the distress of his companions on hearing of this return of the evil.

Jack took his misfortune very quietly, and stretched himself in the bottom of the boat with a great show of fortitude and resignation.

"Keep a look-out for the island," he murmured, and then lay silent with closed eyelids, which he found afforded him some relief from the shafts of light which leaked in through the black shroud of his blindness and burnt his aching eyeballs.

A heavy feeling of depression weighed down upon the boat's crew, and Broncho's many attempts to break it only served to increase it.

Jim felt cowed and frightened; Tari, always of a singularly silent disposition, remained mute in the bows, and whilst Jack tried hard to respond to Broncho's sallies, his tortured brain refused to follow the thread of the discourse, and he found himself answering at random and listening without hearing.

About noon, Jim, who was on look-out duty forward, sang out excitedly that he saw something ahead, sticking out of the sea.

"Looks like a ship's mast," he cried, "but there don't seem no yards or sails on it, 'cept what looks like a flag flying at the truck."

Eagerly they all, except Jack, strained their eyes on the distant object.

"Appears to me like one o' them Sitka Indian totem-poles," called Broncho to the rover. "It's a cert it ain't got no fixin's."

"No hull in sight yet?" asked Jack, with the low, subdued voice which had come upon him with his blindness.

"Nary a thing. It shore looks some queer an' lonely out thar, a-stickin' out o' the scenery like a burnt pine."

Suddenly Jim began shouting with all the strength of his lungs.

"Land ho! Land! Land! Land! Hurray! The island at last!"

Sure enough the boy was right. Away a point to starboard of the mysterious mast a long clump of palms was appearing in view.

"Him Low Island" asserted Tari, after a short look.

"An atoll, certainly," said Jack from aft; "but we're rather far south for the Low Archipelago. It must be one of the Gambier group."

"Why, it's quite close," cried Jim. "I can see the surf now all along, and the mast is sticking right out of the middle of it."

"Inhabited, then!" exclaimed Jack uneasily. "Get those Winchesters loaded, Broncho. One can't trust Paumotu Islanders; they're a treacherous lot, and have cut off many a ship before now."

Swiftly the rushing whaleboat approached before the strong trades.

Here and there to right and left the white water, flashing in the sunshine, swirled and thundered on half-covered reefs, round which countless numbers of shrieking, swooping seabirds hovered and darted as they fished.

Round these reefs the deep blue of the Pacific changed to a translucent emerald green, such as is given to the submerged part of an iceberg when the bright sun is upon it.

The island was evidently but the smallest of coral reefs, studded with a thin growth of cocoanut palms, which seemed thickest at the point where Jim had first sighted them.

Like all atolls, its highest point was but a few feet above the sea-level, and it hung, but a floating speck of shining white sand and green foliage, in the midst of the immense space of blue sea and sky.

But for the screaming birds, no sign of life showed, no habitations, no smoke, nothing but the green brush, the gleaming sand, and shining, flashing surf.

And yet, set in the very midst, rose a gigantic palm, bare as a ship's spare topgallant mast, entirely denuded of its cluster of yellow fruit and waving, fernlike branches.

From its top fluttered a small, small flag, undistinguishable at the distance, but without possible doubt a signal of some importance, put there by human hands.

As the whaleboat drew nearer the hoarse grumble of the surf could be heard as it cast itself in long rollers upon the narrow, fragile strip of beach, with the whole weight of the Pacific behind it.

And now, as every feature of this fairy isle unrolled itself before their anxious eyes, keenly they surveyed it all, watching grimly for the dreaded human.

"Nary a sign o' man thar," muttered Broncho. "It shore looks lonesome a whole lot."

"The inhabitants of atolls always live on the lagoon," explained Jack. "They shun the sea strand and consider it the abode of evil spirits and devils."

"Can we land through that surf?" asked Jim uneasily, as he scanned the boiling white water ahead.

"Want a Pitcairn Islander to take us in if it looks as bad as it sounds," declared the rover.

"Me boat-steerer, go in allee-lightee," said Tari quietly.

"We'd better skirt round the island first, and see if we can't find an opening into the lagoon," advised Jack.

The boat's head was turned, and skimming along just outside the breakers, they commenced to circle the island.

All of a sudden as they came opposite the big palm, a man appeared through the brush and walked slowly on to the beach.

He stopped at the water's edge, and stood there watching them, his form standing clear-cut and lonely against the dazzling whiteness of the sand.

Jim drew his breath with a long hiss of apprehension, and Broncho fumbled his Winchester uncertainly as he gazed at the apparition.

Tari, at the steering-oar, gave a queer grunt of alarm, and with a rapid gesture, murmured in dialect to the rolling-stone, who, helpless in his blindness, lay silent and worried.

"Carryin' a war club!" exclaimed the cowpuncher significantly, in a low voice.

It was a moment of great suspense. Who knew what lurking savages lay hid behind the ambush of that brushwood, ready as the boat's keel grated on the shore to shower a flight of poisoned arrows upon the strangers?

What would be the next move of the decoy in the foreground? Was he about to entice them ashore with friendly gestures? What blood-thirsty design had he planned for their entrapping? They could not tell. They could only trust to Providence and await the issue.

Suddenly the solitary figure moved, flourished an arm, and hailed them.

"Boat ahoy!" came thundering down the wind.

The effect of the two English words was electrical.

Jim sprang wildly on to the thwart and cheered. The cowpuncher laid down his Winchester, and bent his eagle eye upon the man with renewed keenness.

"He's white, shore enough!" he exclaimed, and burst into a strange laugh of relief.

The Kanaka gave a short, expressionless grunt, whilst Jack clambered to his feet, and with one hand round the mast to balance himself, shouted out the question:

"Can we get into the lagoon?"

"No; better land here. Look out for the surf, though. Where you from?"

"Shipwrecked!" replied Jack.

Acting on the stranger's advice, Tari turned the boat's head shorewards. The sail was lowered and mast unstepped, whilst Jim and Broncho shipped two oars and prepared to pull or backwater, according as the Kanaka should direct.

Skilfully Tari ran her in, and then waited just outside the broken water for a good opportunity.

Picking out the last of three big waves, he signed to Jim and Broncho to give way, and off went the whaleboat, swooping forward on the crest of the roller.

Straight as an arrow Tari kept her head, and the boat danced along without shipping more than a cupful or two of water; then, judging his time to a nicety, the Kanaka backed her off as the breaker toppled and fell crashing; again, with wild cries of encouragement, he bade them pull, and the boat was hurled towards the beach in the midst of a raging mass of foam, which kept Jack busy baling as it boiled around and lipped in over the gunwale.

The beach shelved gradually, and the whaleboat was carried far up it before the undertow began to take hold.

At a word from Tari, all hands leaped overboard, and, helped by the big stranger, who had run into the surf to their aid, they ran the boat high and dry.

Weakened and cramped by their long spell of hardships and privations since leaving the *Ocmulgee*, this last effort used up every remaining ounce of strength, and utterly exhausted, the castaways threw themselves full length upon the sand and lay there.

Before them stood the stranger, tall and muscular. His burly figure and square, resolute face were those of that unmistakable type, the British bluejacket, and he hardly required the bell-bottomed navy trousers to identify him.

Virile strength, trained and disciplined to a fine perfection, showed in every line of his active form.

"You're on British soil, lads," he began, squatting down beside the worn-out boat's crew, and he jerked his thumb up at the small flag straining in the strong breeze from the top of the bare palm.

They now perceived it to be a very minute Union Jack, faded and somewhat ragged.

"This island is called H.M.S. *Dido*," he went on. "I named her after the gunboat I belong to. My name's Bill Benson, bosun's mate. I fell overboard about a month back. Got picked up by that black-'arted scoundrel 'Awksley, of the *Black Adder*."

At these words, Jack, who was listening indifferently, suddenly leant forward to attention with a strange new look on his tired face; noticing which the man exclaimed,

"Know him, governor?"

"I do," returned Jack slowly, with a deep note of sternness in his voice.

"Know no good, I'll be bound; but he's ashore here somewheres. His blighted crew o' yellow-skinned beachcombers got fed up with him, an' they just popped the three of us ashore 'ere—marooned us, as they say."

"Who was the third, do you say?" broke in Jack again, a strange excitement in his eyes.

"Why, that pretty little wife o' his to be sure, who's a mighty sight too good and 'andsome for the likes of 'im. We've been 'ere more'n a week now. That's my yarn, an' when you've had your siesta, I'll hear yours. Your landin' party was a kind o' surprise-packet to me, an' I just piped to clear decks for action when I see'd you fust; an' you can bet I just sweated pure joy when you hailed back in the old chin-chin."

"Wall," said Broncho slowly, sitting up and looking round, "you shore had us shorthorns some fretted an' scared likewise when you jumps out on the scenery so gay an' easy; but it's that 'ere flag o' yours which has us some distrustful an' on the scout for ambushes at the first turn of the kyards."

"Oh, that's my pocket 'andkercher. I shinned up that old palm, trimmed his spars offen him, an' nailed it wi' wooden pegs to the masthead, when I fust takes possession o' the island in the name of 'Er Majesty, so as there shouldn't be no international hankypanky diplomatin' round later," the navy man explained calmly.

"Where's this Hawksley gone to, do you say?" asked Jack, trying hard to hide the excitement in his voice.

"Why, I h'expec' he's divin' in the lagoon fishin' up oysters, a-lookin' for pearls; 'e puts in mos' of his time that way."

"And his wife?" queried Jack again, his voice shaking for all his efforts to control it.

"Moonin' round somewheres, poor thing. I reckon he's mighty near broke 'er heart. She don't seem to take no 'eed o' nothin', an' just navigates along plumb indifferent; dumb as a bloomin' Thames barge, with the look of a beaten dog in 'er big, mournful eyes."

A deep, half-smothered curse burst from Jack's pale lips, and springing suddenly to his feet, he wandered off unsteadily with bent head along the beach, feeling his way by the edge of the breakers.

The others watched him wonderingly. Jim got up, meaning to follow him; but Broncho motioned him down again, saying:

"Let him be, sonny!" Then, turning to the bluejacket, explained, "Our mate's blind, an' it kinder hits him on the raw at times."

But the anxiety in the cowboy's eyes robbed the easy tones of their indifference. The man received his explanation with a nod of the head.

"Sorter moody, eh? An' I don't wonder— —"

"Seein' as you-alls wants to savvy why we comes a-pirootin' in disturbin' the ca'm salubrity o' your peaceful layout so abrupt an' precip'tite-like," broke in Broncho hurriedly, with a sudden change of conversation, "I'll just paw round in my mem'ry an' enlighten you some."

"Navigate ahead, governor, me ear-valves is open," said the bosun's mate politely.

"It's this way," drawled Broncho. "My bunkie there"—pointing to Jack's receding form—"me, an' the boy goes a-weavin' offen a ship into this here toomultuous sea without stoppin' to count the chips, we're in sech a hustle—some like the way you-alls vamooses the war-boat, I surmise. That 'ere event occurs away down south, crowdin' hard on two moons back. We-alls goes floatin' round in the swirlin' vortex o' them tempestuous waters, till things begin to look scaly; but finally we makes a landin' on what you-alls call a whaleship.

"It's there we meets up with Tari here, and another saddle-coloured gent who's locoed. This same saddle-coloured gent, which his name is Lobu, puts up sech a fervent play that we-alls has to corral him in a kind of calaboose forward; but it shore don't give him no bliss, an' he's that enraged an' indignant that he starts in to light a camp-fire down thar, allowin' as how he'll call the turn on us that-away, an' he mighty near rakes in the pot with that desp'rate play o' his. Though we-alls busts in an' tries to down the flames with wet sails an' liquid goods, it ain't no use; the deal goes agin us, an' we has to make tracks.

"We saves our skins by scoutin' off in this here boat, which same play has that paltry Lobu plumb disgusted to the core, an' he finally allows he'll shore pull his picket-pin for good an' quit this vale o' tears.

"A-promotin' o' which idees, he goes jumpin' off into the sea, an' though we-alls makes a sperited play to obstruct his little game, it's no use; we're too late, an' the last the outfit sees of him is his blood, whilst he goes p'intin' off under water a-wrastlin' with a shark.

"Right in the tracks o' this eepisode we-alls near bogs down likewise, bein' some scarce in liquid refreshments, not to say entirely lackin' in the same—our canteens havin' run out, an' things lookin' ugly an' desp'rate, when rain comes.

"But we ain't out o' the wood yet, for Derringer Jack yonder, who's all the time doin' range-boss an' playin' the leadin' hand with both sand an' savvy, goes buttin' his head agin fate, an' one maunin' emerges outer the racket plumb moon-blind.

"It's shore a low mean play the Fates puts up agin poor old Jack, but I ain't out to give you-alls no sarmon tharon, nor yet to bewail the abandoned an' ornery conduct o' Destiny.

"It's a paltry play it makes, for shore, a-debauchin' itself on Jack that-away, an' plumb mortifies the whole outfit to death; but to resoome this here narrative, it's yesti'd'y we-alls sees your island in a mirage an' capers off on its trail, with what result you-alls knows."

"I'm a flat-foot if you unfort'nit jossers ain't been jammed in a clinch proper," commented the naval Robinson Crusoe, as Broncho ceased.

There was a short pause, and then Jim broke in:

"Got any fresh water here?"

"I ain't see'd none; but there's milk, er course."

"Milk!" ejaculated Broncho in astonishment. "I don't see no cows around."

"No, there ain't no cows a-muckin' around; but the milk here grows up aloft, on them trees."

"Cocoanuts!" exclaimed the boy eagerly, with a watering mouth.

"That's what," replied Bill Benson heartily. "Like one, young 'un?"

"Aye, that I would."

At which the bosun's mate got good-humouredly to his feet and strolled off into the low brush. Presently he reappeared with his arms full of ripe, juicy fruit.

"Wot oh, Aunt Sally!" he cried cheerfully. "Two shies a penny! 'minds one er 'ome, don't it?"

In a few moments they were all quenching their thirst with the delicious milky juice.

"My! that's somethin' like a drink!" sighed Jim, drawing a long breath.

"It shore beats any bug-juice I ever pours down my throat," commented Broncho appreciatively.

"It 'as its good p'ints," observed Bill Benson. "You can lap it down till y'r back teeth are awash without acquirin' a cordite mouth, but it falls considerable flat on the palate after a week o' nothin' else. There ain't no bite to it. It's good enough for babbies, but I'm gettin' that sick of it I'd as soon suck bilgewater."

CHAPTER VII
"LOYOLA"

Meanwhile Jack wandered off along the shore with bent head and stumbling feet, not knowing nor caring where he went, for his brain was seething in a ferment.

The news which Bill Benson had given him racked the distracted man almost beyond the limit of endurance. His heart leaped at one moment to a fierce, delirious joy, to be cast down the next into the very depths of despair.

Then a rage seized him, a wild, ungovernable fury, which shook his weak, overstrained body to the very core, till he was forced to sink upon the sand from sheer physical inability to remain erect. Hot, passionate words rushed in a low, hoarse whisper from his cracked lips; the blind eyes sparkled with a gleam of almost madness, and the emaciated hands clenched and unclenched ceaselessly.

Slowly the paroxysm passed; a look of dreadful sadness came into the eyes, and a long, dry sob broke huskily from his lips.

"What shall I do? Oh, God! what shall I do?" he wailed miserably.

"Kill the devil!" whispered a voice within him.

"No! no!" interposed another. "Let him be. It's none of your business. She made her bed and must lie on it. She cast you aside, and now you have no right to interfere."

"But she loved me—I know she did. Even at that last meeting, when I like a fool lost my temper, even then I saw the love in her eyes," he whispered softly; then with a deep, bitter groan, "My God! why did she do it? Why did she do it? And that beast, of all men. And now—what now, I wonder?"

The rover sat silent in an unnatural calm. He was hidden from the group of men round the whaleboat by a clump of cocoa-palms, jutting down on to a sort of promontory from the main grove.

Suddenly his ears, sharpened by his blindness, caught the sound of approaching footsteps. With his head on one side in the attitude of listening, he waited, cool without, but a very whirlwind of excitement within; for as they drew nearer he recognised the soft tread of those unknown feet.

Yes, it was! At last she was coming! This one thought filled him and set his heart beating to suffocation. The strangeness of the meeting on this lonely atoll of the two who had separated under such tragic circumstances, he did not realise at the time.

A great, overpowering longing to see her and touch her filled the blind man. How slowly she was approaching! Would she never reach him? What if she did not see him—should he shout? No, that might bring the hated Hawksley from the lagoon, which would never do. Jack desired of all things that this first meeting between the two should be private. Besides, he mistrusted himself with Hawksley; he knew there was murder in his heart crying for accomplishment, and at the very thought his fingers crooked significantly.

No, assuredly it would not do to risk drawing Hawksley's attention.

Should he rise to his feet and stumble forward to meet her? The knowledge of his blindness struck him like a blow. He dreaded the moment when she should find it out. "How would she take it?" he wondered miserably. No, he dared not blunder upon her like a drunken beachcomber. His manhood rose in rebellion. He desired most fervently to hide from her this tragedy which fate had put upon him, this fearful calamity which destroyed his strength and nerve and scourged his pride through his utter helplessness.

So the sorely-tried man waited, crouching on his knees.

Coming slowly through the clump of palms was a white woman, clad in a creamy dress of some silken texture, with a wide-brimmed panama perched upon a wavy mass of dark brown hair, which shone like gold where the sunbeams kissed it.

Her face was of a dead white, and the beautiful features were thin and drawn, whilst her brown eyes, ringed in black circles and filled with a look of piteous sadness, seemed too big for the rest of the face.

As she reached the edge of the sand and espied the rolling-stone, an involuntary cry broke from her lips. For a second she stood stock still, whilst a look of amazement crept into her eyes.

Then, satisfied that her vision was playing her no trick, she advanced into the open, restraining with difficulty a passionate desire to rush forward and throw herself at the blind man's feet.

And then, as she drew nearer to this man whom she had treated so badly, though from no fault of her own, but through sheer force of circumstances, a strange hesitation filled her. Her heart, beating suffocatingly, urged her forward and yet dragged her back at the same time; her feet lagged, then hurried, then lagged again, whilst her hands twined themselves together nervous and shaking.

At last she stood before him, looking down upon his haggard, storm-lined features, from which the blind eyes stared up vacantly with an expression which even in her agitation she could not help but notice.

"You, Jack—you?" she began softly, and her voice trembled in spite of a great endeavour to keep it steady.

"Yes, me, Loyola," came the reply; but how dull, how indifferent, how hard and cold were the well-known tones.

An icy chill crept shuddering down her back at the sound of this strange new voice, so different to the one she had been used to in the old happy days, now so far away, so long ago, though not in time.

The pallor of her face took on a greyish tinge and the sadness in her eyes deepened.

There was no forgiveness, as there was no hope. Why should she expect it? Ah! but what a difference it would have made to her! How it would have helped her to bear her fate!

For a second she tottered on the verge of a breakdown, and then rallied, drawing upon that splendid woman's courage which enables such as her to stand and bear with fate where others would fall and be crushed.

Bravely she forced herself to continue, beating down the misery and despair which the cold tones of his voice had raised within her.

"And what are you doing here, Jack?"

"Tossed ashore by the capricious sea. I might ask you the same question, had I not already heard your story."

"Not from—Hawksley?" She stumbled miserably over her husband's name, and then with a sudden fear cast an uneasy look over her shoulder.

"No; the bluejacket," said Jack's even voice, and he got slowly to his feet.

"Won't you—won't you even shake hands, Jack?" pleaded the woman in her low, sad voice. "I know you won't forgive me, and I don't expect you to; but——"

It was the "but," the misery, the despair, the utter hopelessness, and yet the passionate entreaty in that last little word which conquered Jack's iron-bound soul and swept away his righteous indignation at a treatment which had spoiled his life.

He was touched; that "but" weighed down the scales on the side of his love, till his grievance, his outraged feelings, and the resultant misery leaped from him lightly as a feather.

"Why, of course I will. And as for forgiving you, I've forgiven you long ago."

The new warmth in his voice brought a bright flush of pleasure to the woman's face.

"Oh, Jack," she began; but stopped, watching with slowly growing amazement whilst the blind man tried to find her outstretched hand.

What was the matter with Jack? Why did he paw the air in that uncertain fashion, instead of grasping the hand she extended to him?

Anxiously she looked at him, unable to fathom his strange action; then took his wavering hand in hers and held it, a great comfort and a new joy springing up within her.

What surer sign of friendship, of love, of deep understanding than a firm hand-grasp?

His bony fingers closed on her slender ones with a grip that made her wince, and a sudden light lit up his dull eyes.

And so they stood for one long minute of time, hand in hand.

The sun played upon them, lighting the woman's hair with sparkles of yellow fire, and warmed the tired bodies with its tender glow, just as the content of this tardy but complete reconciliation warmed their tired souls.

The long rollers boomed a deep note of approval as they surged shorewards in snowy foam, and the gentle breath of the trade wind touched them caressingly with its invisible fingers.

The very sands flashed their delight up at them, and the swaying palm-tops rustled with a drowsy murmur of satisfaction.

Often thus does nature seem to tune herself in accord with the feelings and emotions of mankind.

In that moment the sinister barrier of misunderstanding, which for so long had stood gloomy, forbidding, impassable, had been removed from between their hearts, and the very air, the sea, the earth, the waving foliage, the shining sand rejoiced thereat.

But as the cowboy would say, "You can't buck against destiny."

Destiny had tied a knot—a huge, cruel, untieable knot—which held the lives of these two apart, set though they were in the same web of fate.

Bitterness, doubt, misery had been the direct result; but now, by the aid of that little winged cherub who plays such pranks with most lives, the bitterness, the doubt, the misery, all had been swept aside—only the knot remained.

With a long sigh of thankfulness Loyola murmured gently,

"You do forgive me, Jack?"

"I do, I do, child," he replied, the hardness all gone from his voice. "I don't know why you did it. Only this I know, it was no fault of yours. Fate in some way stepped in between us, and—and—and I can feel it in the air"—he lifted his head and drew a long, deep breath—"I feel that we are still the friends, the——" he stopped, hesitating, flushed, and a tender light glowed in the blind eyes.

"Yes, Jack?" she whispered, longing to hear the word he had left unspoken.

"Who used to be so fond of each other," he ended lamely.

"But," cried the woman eagerly, "I must tell you why I did it. I did it——"

"Don't tell me, Lolie; I don't want to hear. I know now you must have had some good reason, that is enough for me. We can still be friends."

"But I must, I must. I did it to save Big Harry, poor old dad. He was caught in Hawksley's clutches and I sold myself to save him, and—and—and it was all no use," she sobbed. "He had cheated the pair of us. It broke dad's heart, and he died two months after you left the schooner."

"My God! If I had only known!" groaned the man, with miserable self-reproach. "And that's why! and that's why! I might have guessed something of the sort if I hadn't been such a cursed, jealous fool."

"I treated you shamefully, Jack," she whispered brokenly. "I ought to have given you a reason, but I couldn't. Shame held my tongue, and I let you go away without a word; but—but God knows I've been bitterly punished. No one could imagine what I have suffered with that demon—aye, and must continue to suffer."

"Can't anything be done, Lolie?"

"I must brave it out to the end, I suppose, as others have done before me," she muttered drearily.

"Something shall be done!" cried Jack cheeringly.

His old confidence was coming back to him. Now that the mystery of Loyola's strange marriage was cleared up, and he was no longer in doubt that she still loved him, a mighty flood of gladness was surging up within him.

For the present this newly gained knowledge was sufficient. Who knew what the future might not bring forth? At any rate her love was his; that, Hawksley could have no part in.

As for Hawksley, he despised Hawksley. Let the ruffian take care. Snakes were only fit for stamping on, and Jack began to see himself stamping on Hawksley with a keen satisfaction.

So the rover mused, whilst Loyola stood by his side, watching him.

"And now," he proposed, "I'll give you a sketch of the events which landed me on this coral spit, after which we'll plan out the future."

And, standing there in the glaring sunlight, Jack plunged into a recital of his late adventures, whilst Loyola listened without comment until he came to the part the moon had played.

At the news of his blindness an involuntary cry broke from her, the shock of the quiet announcement struck her like a blow. Her Jack, dear old Jack of the happy *Moonbeam* days, blind? No, it could not be! Fate was cruel, as she well knew, but not as cruel as that. Leaning forward, she placed her hands on his shoulders and peered into the blind eyes, as if she would reassure herself by their appearance.

She saw no difference in them, no difference from the eyes she used to know. It could not be! Jack was mistaken, and yet, how could a man be mistaken as to whether he could see or not?

Again she peered desperately, her face within an inch of his. Jack could feel her soft breath on his cheek; her lips, half opened in her excitement, seemed to be touching his moustache; the slightest movement forward on his part and they would be against his.

Never had the man been so tempted. At the same moment a wolfish head poked stealthily through the brushwood, and a pair of cruel, cunning eyes glared forth angrily upon the scene.

CHAPTER VIII
"THE FIGHT ON THE SANDS"

"Ho! ho! ho!" laughed a high, sneering voice "A pretty picture, upon my word—and the good, saintly Loyola, too! Where does hubby come in, I wonder?"

The pair sprang apart as if struck by a thunderbolt, and as Jack faced round the ruffian recognised him.

"Oh, it's you, is it? Big Harry's dandy mate spooning with my little wife! Well, I am surprised! What a shocking world it is, to be sure!"

"You devil!" hissed the rolling-stone furiously.

"Don't like being interrupted, eh? Well, that's not to be wondered at. Unfortunately"—and the scoundrel's tones took on an air of insolent importance—"I happen to be the husband of that lady who was hugging you so fondly."

Poor Loyola sank back upon the sand, and hiding her face in her hands, crouched down in an attitude of absolute hopelessness.

"Come on, you limb of Satan!" roared Jack, his voice shaking with passion. "She shan't be your wife for long, if I can help it. In less than five minutes she shall be your widow, if I swing for it."

"Not so fast, my valiant lover, not so fast. Tom Hawksley's too leery a bird to have salt put on his tail so easy. How do I know you haven't a gang of beachcombers waiting handy to pounce out on me? You didn't come here alone, did you?" and the cunning eyes leered round the beach uneasily.

"I tell you there's no one within hail," growled Jack; "and if there were they wouldn't interfere. I mean to kill you with these hands," he added, a very world of piled-up hate in his voice.

"Oh, ho! that's the time of day, is it? Feeling nasty, eh?" sneered the marooned ruffian coolly.

"Come on, you coward!" thundered the rover, furious with impatience and yet not daring to move on account of his blindness.

He knew that if Hawksley once realised that he was blind the game was up—he would be at his mercy; and he trusted entirely to the scoundrel venturing within his reach, knowing that once he got a grip the victory would be his.

"Come on yourself," cried Hawksley cunningly.

"I mean to fight on the open beach, and not in the scrub," said Jack coolly, with a sudden change of tactics. "I've got plenty of time. I'll wait till you are ready"; and he sat down.

Hawksley, for all his cool sneers, was as raging within as his enemy, and longed to wreak a terrible vengeance upon the hated stealer of his wife's love. Not that the man cared twopence about his wife. He had thought nothing of herding her into a crowded harem of native girls aboard the schooner; he missed no chance to insult her; he knocked her about, despised her, and yet inwardly feared her, such was the strange twist in his mean nature; but above everything he valued her as his possession, the prize of the South Seas, to play with and torture with a cruelty which he delighted in. Thus, to find her in another man's arms, as he supposed, seeking a sweet consolation for all his brutality and devilish treatment, was gall and wormwood to him.

He would have preferred a chance to accomplish his purpose by some mean treachery rather than by risking himself in a stand-up fight; but what could he do? He possessed no weapon. So, trusting in a knowledge of every low fighting trick known from the coasts of Japan to Sydney and from Hongkong to the San Francisco water-front, he decided to give battle.

Slowly the ruffian crept out from the protection of the trees and advanced upon the blind castaway.

Jack, with only his ears to trust to, listened with all his might at the approaching footsteps; but it is difficult to judge distance correctly by the ear, and he jumped to his feet, meaning to spring upon his opponent, thinking he was but a few feet away when in reality he was several yards.

Only just in time Loyola looked up, and, noticing the crouching attitude of the two men, in a moment divined what was going forward. "How could her lover, blind as he was and worn with privation, hope to overcome Hawksley?" she wondered fearfully. Yet she knew Jack too well to attempt to interfere, and she had implicit confidence in his powers. Once, long before, with one arm broken by a revolver bullet, she had seen him administer a terrible licking to a giant negro. Still, she racked her brain to know how she could help him. She saw him about to spring, and his object flashing upon her without a moment's hesitation, she cried sharply, "Too far, too far!"

Jack understood and waited, whilst Hawksley, puzzled by these tactics, came on still more slowly and cautiously. Then, gathering together all his over-tried strength, the rover sprang furiously like some wild beast in his blindness, his hands held out in front of him ready to seize whatever they touched.

But though the rapidity of his movement was such that Hawksley had no time to jump on one side, the direction was not so good, and only his left hand got a grip as he flew past the surprised scoundrel.

Instantly his fingers hooked themselves into Hawksley's coat-collar, and held on desperately; but the impetus of his spring carrying him forward, and the drag to it being all on one side, he spun round giddily, vainly striving to keep his balance by the aid of his loose right arm; then down he came on the sands, dragging the sorely puzzled Hawksley with him.

For a moment there was a wild mix-up of struggling limbs, and then Hawksley tore himself free from his antagonist, whose strength, overstrained by the late hardships, was to his dismay fast leaving him.

The still puzzled Hawksley, rolling out of Jack's reach, got on to his feet, and watched his opponent with amazement in his eyes.

Jack was on his knees with head cocked on one side, pawing round the sand as if he thought Hawksley was some sea-shell lying hidden somewhere close to him.

The sight of the blind man feeling around him with such cautiousness was almost uncanny to his opponent, who was fast coming to the conclusion that Jack was mad; but to poor Loyola, watching him with tear-stained eyes, the piteousness and horror of it was absolutely heartrending.

The very helplessness of his motions brought hot, scalding tears to her eyes, and her love surged within her to the exclusion of every other thought, except that somehow she must manage to protect her blind lover from the scoundrel who called himself her husband.

All the mother's feeling for her child welled up in the woman's heart as she watched, and unable to stand the bitter sight any longer, with a wild, choking cry, she sprang to Jack's side, and, falling on her knees, threw her weak right arm over his shoulders with an indescribable air of loving protection.

"Where is he, Lolie, where is he?" hissed the rover between his teeth; whilst Hawksley, infuriated afresh by her loving action, yelled venomously:

"Get away, you she-devil, get away, or I'll do for you as well," and he began to creep forward with that strange slinking motion of his.

"You coward!" cried the woman, in ringing tones of utter scorn. "You coward, to fight a blind man!"

Then, springing to her feet, she took a stand between her husband and her lover in a posture of splendid defiance, with head thrown back and flashing eyes. At the same moment she snatched a tiny stiletto from the bosom of her dress, a weapon which she had long kept ready for the moment, that moment which so often had nearly arrived, when a steady thrust of the sharp point would be her only escape from what was worse than death.

A sparkle of light glittered on the steel as she held it firm, point outwards and ready for action, with a deadly menace.

"Ho! ho! The little tiger!" sneered Hawksley, stopping in his advance and laughing sardonically.

The news that Jack was blind let a light upon his actions, which had been causing the suspicious scoundrel some uneasiness, and with a relieved mind the latter decided to take his time and play with his victims in that cat-and-mouse style which he delighted in, from the sheer cruelty of his nature.

"So the pretty boy is blind, is he? How sad, how very sad!"

But Jack was not the man to remain inactive whilst his opponent taunted him, however blind and weak he might be. In a moment he was on his feet again and rushing wildly upon the sneering voice, and if Loyola had not jumped nimbly to one side he would have bowled her over in his headlong gait.

Hawksley, chuckling like an amused fiend, stepped quickly out of the blind man's path, and stretching out a leg, tripped him up with an easy carelessness.

The latter fell heavily, but recovering himself with a desperate effort, whirled round on his knees in the sand and pounced upon the over-confident ruffian's foot, his hands falling upon their object by a bit of sheer good luck.

Down went the discomfited Hawksley on his back with a shrill cry of surprise, and there ensued a fearful struggle as the two bodies rolled over and over together, each man striving with all his strength to gain the upper hold.

But Jack's strength was nearly spent, and recognising this, Hawksley, by a sudden jerk, broke his hold and freed himself; then, scrambling quickly out of the blind man's reach, rose to his feet with a hoarse laugh of triumph.

Rousing himself from a growing lassitude, and with a strange giddiness in his head, Jack attempted to follow his example. Panting heavily in short, quick sobs, with gritted teeth, he vainly strove to rise, but with a fog creeping over his brain he had to sink back again, and it was only by sheer will-power that he saved himself from fainting.

Again Hawksley advanced upon him, deeming this the right moment to finish matters; but before he could reach him, Loyola, with a wild scream for help, rushed forward and flung herself with all her strength upon her husband's back, and clung there desperately, twining her arms round his neck in a heroic attempt to hold him off his prostrate enemy.

With a snarl of fury Hawksley tore off her grip and cast her from him, and with a moan of despair she fell on her face in the sand.

The sound drew a groan of helpless anguish from the rover, who again tried vainly to regain his feet. The next moment the ruffian was upon him and locked two sinewy hands round his throat. With a muffled gurgle Jack fell back, and, kneeling upon his prostrate body, Hawksley proceeded grimly to choke the life out of him.

Again the woman, a wild terror in her eyes, flung herself upon the demon and attempted vainly to pull him off her lover, sending forth scream after scream for help.

Jack, with a terrible knowledge of his absolute impotence, felt his senses leaving him as those horrible, muscular claws sank deeper and deeper into his neck and shut off his windpipe.

His face became suffused, the veins swelling in his temples to bursting point, and the purple tint of suffocation began to creep over his features.

Paying no heed to the hysterical attempts of the weak woman, Hawksley held on, chuckling to himself with satisfaction as he watched his victim weakening.

Seeing that her endeavours were absolutely without avail, the distracted woman rushed off for the stiletto, which she had dropped in the sand when surprised by Jack's wild rush past her. At the same moment, the castaways, headed by Broncho, burst through the clump of palms in a headlong charge, drawn to the rescue by Loyola's screams.

The cowboy, on perceiving the two struggling forms on the beach, without a second's hesitation stopped in his stride, and drawing his revolver, let go with unerring aim; much practice in a land where one's life depended on the quickness of one's draw and the sureness of one's aim had made him an expert in revolver-play.

The bullet pierced through the fleshy part of Hawksley's left arm, and with a cry of rage he let go of his victim's throat and sprang to his feet, facing round with his venomous snarl like a wild beast at bay.

"Hands up!" roared the cowpuncher, covering him with his weapon. "Hands up!"

The ruffian gave a rapid look round in vain search for a way of escape, and then, as his shifty eyes met Broncho's stern ones, full of a steely glitter of held-in anger, with a gesture of overdone indifference he brought his hands together over his head.

Whilst the cowboy covered his prisoner, Tari sped back to the boat for a length of rope, and Loyola and Jim knelt anxiously over the prostrate form of the rolling-stone.

"If he's killed him," began the boy hoarsely. "If he's killed him——" and there was murder in the small voice.

"No! no! no!" wailed the woman, as she chafed Jack's hands feverishly.

The thoughtful bluejacket, who had rushed to the water's edge after one glimpse of the purple face, reappeared with his cap full of water.

"We'll put life into him in less than no time," he exclaimed heartily, scattering the water over the rover's suffused countenance with a vigorous heave.

Tari made quick time to the boat and back, and he and Broncho between them trussed the discomfited Hawksley in a most scientific manner.

In vain his cunning tongue pleaded eloquently on his behalf. They paid no heed.

"I found that man kissing my wife," he began, a whole world of outraged justice in his oily tones.

"We found you stranglin' a blind man," replied Broncho sternly, as he clove-hitched the seizing on his prisoner's wrists.

"I swear to God I didn't know he was blind," declared Hawksley vehemently. "When I saw him hugging my wife I went for him, as any man would. I was only going to teach him."

"Teach Derringer Jack a lesson?" drawled Broncho. "Wall, I surmise he had to be blind an' starved an' near dead o' thirst, or the rope would have been round your horns, mister."

"I'm bleeding. Ain't you got the humanity to bind up my arm?" whined the wretch, seeing his first line of argument had no effect.

"I'm shore a whole lot sorry it was your arm an' not your black heart I put a bullet through," returned Broncho sourly, without any offer to doctor the wounded member.

"Loyola, you wench," cried the exasperated Hawksley, "ain't you got no sense of duty? Would you let your husband bleed to death?"

The woman rose slowly to her feet from Jack's side, and without a word tore a strip off her skirt; then, with a look of the most utter aversion in her face, deftly bound up her husband's wound.

"What are you going to do with me?" he asked again of the silent cowboy.

"Depends on my bunkie thar," replied the latter sternly. "Mebbe string you up to the nearest cocoanut palm."

"It'd be murder!" whined Hawksley, now thoroughly cowed and frightened. "I was within my rights."

"Thar ain't no rights for skunks," growled Broncho, his eyes watching the efforts to restore the senseless man with but ill-concealed anxiety.

At last Jack opened his eyes and gasped faintly, "Water! water!"

The half of a cocoanut, full of the creamy juice, was thrust to his lips.

He drained this with a sigh of satisfaction and a hoarse murmur of,

"I'll soon be all right, boys."

Then, stretching forth his shrunken, sun-browned hand, he whispered softly,

"Lolie! Lolie!"

The woman kneeling at his side seized the rover's fingers in hers, and with big tears of thankfulness in her eyes, pressed them reassuringly.

Little Jim, with a strange lump in his throat, turned his head away quickly, whilst the bosun's mate found a sudden interest in the contemplation of their captive.

For some minutes Jack lay quiet, fumbling the woman's small hands in his with a clumsy weakness. The very touch seemed to fill the spent man with renewed life. Tenderly he stroked them, lovingly he caressed them, whilst his brain slowly cleared.

Then he was picked up and carried into the shade of the palm-grove, close to where the whaleboat had been hauled up.

Here he lay through the long afternoon, slowly regaining his strength, with Loyola, Jim, and Tari by his side.

A few yards off sat Hawksley, securely bound to the trunk of the great palm, whilst up and down the beach paced the cowboy and Bill Benson, deliberating as to the fate to be meted out to their prisoner.

Broncho, recognising how things were between Jack and Loyola, wished to cut the Gordian knot by the short, decided methods of Arizona. A rope and a good tree was what he advocated for Hawksley.

But the bluejacket, used to the stern justice of a British man-of-war, wished to carry the ruffian before a court of law, knowing that he was wanted by every cruiser in the South Seas for illicit blackbirding, girl-stealing, pearl-poaching, and a host of other offences, which up till now had gone unpunished owing to his remarkable slimness and the sailing qualities of his schooner, the *Black Adder*.

"But your brass-buttoned British sheriff wouldn't hang him," objected the cowboy. "He'd round him up in some crazy calaboose, an' the next thing we'd hear that the varmint had gone an' jumped the track, an' mebbe come bulgin' in interferin' with my pard Jack's domestic affairs agin. No, siree; thar ain't a shade o' horse-sense in that bill o' fare."

"And if we swings the blighter off, it's two Roosians to a heathen Chinee that some fool-head will go an' blow the gaff — —"

"As how?" demanded Broncho, half-angrily, not liking Benson's insinuation at all.

"No offence, governor, no offence," exclaimed the bluejacket; "but we most of us has a bust occasional-like, an' that's the time these here state secrets get blown; and then there's the Kanaka."

"Tari's white cl'ar through an' is Jack's dawg. I ain't frettin' he'll stampede our cattle none."

"Any'ow, I votes we pospones the execution o' justice till to-morrer," observed the bosun's mate cautiously. "Mebbe the gal oughter have a say."

"I guess nit! Gals is shore to make a wrong play when a lynchin' is the game. They're too soft-hearted an' mushy that-away."

"What erbout y'r mate?"

"Jack's an interested party, an' so is barred from the jury," declared Broncho uneasily.

The cowboy knew well enough that Jack would not countenance such downright methods of justice as a lynching. Everything depended on it being done without the rover's knowledge, and by hook or by crook Broncho was determined that this snake in Jack's path to happiness should be removed somehow; he relied greatly, however, on being able to bring the bluejacket round to his way of thinking.

Over and over again he bitterly reproached himself that he had not aimed to kill, when he let fly the bullet which creased Hawksley's arm.

Now that he knew Jack's secret and the reason of those long fits of melancholy, he was set upon removing the cause of them.

The man deserved death, he argued; he was a notorious scoundrel, and the fact that he had nearly succeeded in killing Jack was quite reason enough to satisfy the justice of the drop, in the cowboy's easy Western code of laws.

However, giving up the discussion for the time, the two agents of justice returned to the group under the trees.

"How are you makin' out, mister?" asked the bosun's mate of Jack, as he threw himself down lazily.

"First rate," replied the rover cheerily. "By the way, I seem to recall your voice. Were you on the China Station five years ago in the *Diadem*?"

"I was that."

"Coxswain to old Typhoon Blake?"

"Why, that's so."

"Remember rescuing a man from a sampan one day up the Shanghai River."

"Had a bag of dollars with him? The two Johns tried to lay him out, an' he up-ended one of 'em?"

"Yes, that's right. Remember me now?"

"W'y, blawst me but you 'as the cut of his jib; but—he weren't on the lower deck, mate. That blighted josser was a reg'lar copper-bottomed swell, an' took 'is chow with old Typhoon."

"Well, my name's Jack Derringer."

"That's so, that were the name right enuff. I 'eard number one speakin' about 'im. Well, it's a queer old giddy-go-round, this bloomin' world; you gives me ten dollars then, an' now I tips you a drink outer a bally cocoanut."

The afternoon passed slowly, Hawksley, scowling and gnawing his lips, lay apart, coining new words to his extensive vocabulary of oaths.

Jim and Tari went off on a tour of exploration round the island, whilst Broncho and the bosun's mate sat well out of earshot, a pair of conspirators arguing heatedly, with Hawksley's life hanging on the result.

Jack and Loyola under the palms talked fitfully in low tones, with long silences in which an uneasy melancholy and a deep mutual feeling of sad helplessness reigned.

CHAPTER IX
"THE LYNCHING"

With darkness the explorers returned, and also Jack's strange eyesight, much to the amazement and delight of Loyola.

The first use the rover made of his recovered vision was to gaze long and earnestly at the woman by his side, and his eyes brightened from a look of keen criticism to a warm glow of deep, hungry tenderness.

"Well?" asked Loyola's low voice, as she sat with downcast eyes before the overpowering longing of his gaze.

"My God!" burst out the rolling-stone, "and to think that you are tied to that villain."

"You have my love—what else matters?" she whispered shyly.

"I want you, you, you!" he hissed. "Oh, child, you don't know how hateful my life has been without you."

"We can only hope," she said bravely.

"Lolie, there is murder in my heart when I think of it all. Aye, murder, crying, begging, moaning for its victim," he cried hoarsely.

"Oh, Jack, you mustn't talk like that."

"I can't help it, child, I want you too much!" groaned the rover dismally.

Her small hand crept into his with a mute sympathy and perfect understanding. The very touch soothed him. No need to speak. Each knew the other's thoughts, and with wistful, tender glances they sat hand in hand, snatching a sweet comfort in being together.

Whatever the future held for them, whatever fears or black forebodings each held in his or her heart, they put away from them, determined to let nothing cloud the sweetness of the moment.

It might all be very wrong, but they were but human and both had suffered much.

And now Broncho approached and insisted on lighting an immense camp-fire, though the night was quite warm and the trade wind mild and gentle.

"It's shore a heap cheerless an' doleful rustlin' your chuck an' beddin' down for the night without a fire," he explained. "It's plumb comfortin' to lie in the smoke and kauf, an' minds me of old times, though I shore misses the song o' the night gyard ca'min' down the cattle an' the yowlin' o' the coyote huntin' his grub."

Presently food was served out from the scanty store landed by the marooners, for while that lasted the *Ocmulgee's* awful salt junk and hard-tack were placed on one side, with many a sigh of relief from the whaleboat's crew.

Loyola insisted on taking Hawksley his allowance with her own hands, for which she received a choice lot of carefully picked insults by way of thanks.

With bent head and her hands to her ears the woman writhed under the lashing tongue, each hideous, sneering sentence cutting her to the heart. With all her misery revived, she staggered back to the others white and shaking, and sank down by Jack's side in an attitude of utter despair.

The rover bit his lips in a desperate effort to control his feelings, but there was a wild look in his eyes which the observant cowboy noticed with a kind of grim smile.

"*Poco tiempo!*" he muttered to himself with a grunt of satisfaction. "*Poco tiempo!*"

The bosun's mate, stretched by the side of his fellow conspirator, desperately strove to rally out of a growing despondency. His eyes roved round restlessly, and he fidgeted as if unable to remain quiet for long.

What had been the result of Broncho's eloquence? Even Tari seemed to be affected by the general uneasiness, whilst the boy could not keep his eyes from the clear-cut shadow of the prisoner, silhouetted inkily on the moonlit sands.

With a furious shake the bosun's mate attempted to banish his gloomy thoughts, and turning to Broncho, remarked with a suspicious carelessness in his deep voice:

"Jack Derringer gives out to me as 'ow you wos a cowpuncher, an' it gets me teetotally 'ow you plays your little game."

"Wall," returned the cattleman politely, "it's some difficult to explain, you not bein' a cowman. What is it you-alls is aimin' for to know the savvy of? Is it cuttin' out or brandin' or night herdin', hoss-wranglin', workin' on a trail outfit, or what?"

"'Orse-wrangler's a josser as does a bunk wiv the 'orses, ain't he?"

"No, siree," replied Broncho seriously. "You're some tangled in your rope. That's a hoss-rustler. Hoss-wrangler is what we-alls call the longhorn who keeps tab o' buckskins, pintos, an' sech-like obstrep'rous but some necessary parties."

"I'm all jammed in a clinch. Your lingo'll shift me off my bedplate afore long. What kind er flat-foot is a buckskin?"

The polite cowpuncher made no remark as to his inability to understand Bill's naval idioms, but explained:

"A buckskin's a sort o' cayuse——"

"I'm a leatherneck if you ain't enuff to make a blighter tin-hats.[12] An' wot's a cayuse?"

Broncho looked faintly astonished at the extraordinary ignorance of the man-of-war's man.

"A cow-pony," he said, half in sorrow.

"Is my upper-works collapsin', or wot? A cow-pony? Wot sort er bally hermofridite is that?"

"Why, a cow-hoss——"

"Cow-'orse? Am I 'alf-rats, or is you 'avin' a game? If so, governor, I guess you an' me'll part brass-rags——"

"Thar's generally a pretty fair mob of 'em in a round-up or trail-outfit; ten or twelve per man is the usual play," went on Broncho serenely, passing over Bill Benson's excited words, which, of course, were double-Dutch to him.

The bosun's mate sighed faintly.

"Go on; oh, go on," he said resignedly. "An' wot's brandin'?"

"Wall, thar's range-brands an' road-brands. Sometimes it's a wattle cut on the jaw, sometimes a slit dewlap, but mostly we-alls just irons 'em on the hindquarter. Brands that-away is mighty numerous an' variegated. These few I recalls for your eedification—The Running W, Laurel-Leaf, Circle, Lazy H, Pitchfork, Double-Bracket, the Two-Bar——"

"I've 'eard o' monkey brand, but I'm a blighted grabby if I ever navigates with a range-brand afore. Noo-fangled range-finder, I s'pose. A wattle-cut on the jaw I can keep stations with. It's a nawsty upper-cut that, I h'expec', likely to 'eat the bearin's of the josser wot cops it. Well, wot's the nex' course? Branding'll pass; it's too deep for my intellec'. Rub it off the signal-slate an' sachey ahead."

"Then thar's bound'ry-ridin', which is scoutin' round watchin' the cattle don't get strayed or drifted offen their proper range."

"I s'pose you does your manœuvrin' on a geegee most times?"

"On'y sech low and 'ornery mavericks as sheepmen foots it in the cow-country."

"Well, I never did take a cruise on er 'orse, but I takes my gal out one day in a shay. Lord! It were a go an' no mistake! I was got up to kill, and she—well, she was good gear an' you may lay to that. So we ups anchor and off we goes, makin' a fair wind of it, me a-cockin' a chest an' swayin' the main good-oh. It's then that bloomin' sarpint, Old Nick, starts in his little game, an' like another Eve, my Dinah gets her sailin' orders an' whispers kinder soft-like:

"'Make 'im go, Bill darlin', lick 'im an' make 'im go! 'An' me like a innocent babe, not twiggin' Old Nick's tactics, begins chucklin' like a hen, an' gives a pull on the yoke-lines.

"Well, what does this blighted 'orse do but give a flip out aft, an' go weavin' off like a crazy lunatic, an' we're soon navigatin' under forced draught. My Dinah gives a toot on her siren, an' I lays back on the yoke-lines; but that flat-footed, mud-scatterin' moke ain't takin' no notice, an' just claps on every pound o' steam.

"We goes by old Bluelights of the *Hannibal*, and a tiffy, like a torpedo-catcher on 'er steam trials. Bluelights 'e sings out,

"'Makin' 'eavy weather of it, Bill?' an' he hits the target that time if he never does afore.

"Right ahead there's a tramp loaded down to her Plimsoll mark with coals, an' goin' dead slow.

"I rings up the engines for 'ard astern with both screws, but it ain't no use; the next minit we rams him. Lord! It were a giddy-go-round!

"My Dinah an' me goes over the bows like bein' shot out of a 5-inch. She lands on the coals, which you can bet has a bad effec' on her flash rig-out; but I up-ends the sleepy skipper o' the coal tramp, an' the pair of us goes overboard, me a-claspin' 'im in my volupshus arms.

"We lands soft, an' he turns on me reg'lar frothin' at the mouth. I won't repeat 'is remarks, which is that powerful an' florid it's a treat and er eddication to 'ear 'im.

"Then 'e begins to wave 'is spars like a Norwegian flag[13] in a breeze, an' thinks I, 'It's time I tunes up my big bassoon in this bloomin' oratorio'; so I breaks in:

"'Refill y'r water-jacket an' cool off, me butter-backed, grimy-eyed blackymoor. Just keep them dingy paws o' yours outer detonatin' contact, or I'll cat an' fish them lovely black eyes o' yours.'

"That fair gives him the pip.

"'Sock it to 'im, Bill,' screeches my Dinah, from where she's repairin' 'er riggin' on the coal-tramp.

"The end of it all is, war is declared and 'ostilities commences. 'E starts in on 'is windmill racket, until I gives 'im one on that protrudin' ram-bow o' his an' drors fust blood.

"It's then a bloomin' bladder-bellied peeler comes steerin' down on us and interrupts the jamboree, an' that's the end o' my cruise be'ind a 'orse."

"Hosses," remarked Broncho musingly, "are a heap like human bein's. Some is reliable, an' some plumb onreliable.

"Some is mulish, an' that mean they'll eat your chaps offen you whilst you is consumin' of a drink; others, sech is their perverse nature, will go curvin' off on the run as if they're locoed; whilst many will buck their saddles off an' sunfish every time you-alls swings your leg over them.

"I has a white-eyed claybank one time that would pitch ontil this sinful world played its last jack-pot if I held my hand on his back that long—good old worm-fence buckin' at that. Yes, hosses is shore mighty various, but the worsest of 'em is virgin gold to a peanut ahead of any human that ever draws breath. Chucks! They don't run on the same range."

"That may be the way it looks from your side of the deck, but the bally fantasia that moke plays makes me sorter doubtful. I allows you lays it on too thick, mate," objected Bill Benson.

"I merely states it as my opeenion," observed Broncho politely; "an' now," he went on, "as it's gettin' some late, I guess I'll roll into my blankets."

"Down 'ammicks, boys," called the bluejacket to the others.

It had been arranged that he was to be on guard the first watch, Broncho taking the middle, and Tari the morning, Jim and the rover reserving themselves for the following night.

Soon the whole camp was asleep except the bosun's mate, who paced up and down the beach in a moody reverie. As the hours passed he shrank more and more from the dread event in which he was to take part during the middle watch; yet he had consented and given his word, and he was not the man to back out of an undertaking and leave his mate in the lurch, however much his feelings went against it.

Slowly midnight approached, and at last the dreaded moment arrived.

With an irrepressible shudder he went up to the sleeping cowboy and shook him gently, saying,

"Eight bells, mate!"

Broncho opened his eyes and sat up, his mind rousing itself from deep sleep to clear-headed wakefulness with the long habit of his calling.

"All quiet?" he asked in a whisper.

"Aye," replied the bluejacket, in the same low tone.

Broncho gave a keen glance round. Jack, with his right hand locked in Loyola's, was sleeping the sleep of the just, but the woman seemed to be crying softly.

Anxiously the cowboy bent over her.

"It's all right!" he whispered. "The poor gal's on'y a-whimperin' in her sleep, and I ain't none surprised."

Jim likewise, lying on his face, seemed dead to the world.

They then roused Tari, who sprang straight out of a heavy slumber to his feet without a word, and the three silent men crept softly away.

Tari glided ghostlike in the moonlight to the boat, and returned to the others with a coil of rope on his arm; and now all three approached the unconscious Hawksley.

Broncho had a ball of spun-yarn and a thole-pin in his hand. With these he scientifically gagged the terrified ruffian before he could make a sound; then, casting him loose from the tree, with Tari in the lead tugging on a rope made fast to the miserable wretch's wrists, and the other two on each side of him, they made an ominous-looking procession through the black patches of shadow and gleaming shafts of moonlight in the palm-grove.

Tari, his great harpoon like a wand of office in one hand and the rope attached to the prisoner in the other, sagging and tautening like a towline as the unhappy man hung back in terror and was jerked forward again, stalked ahead through the scrub and palms without a moment's hesitation as to his course, and in silence they threaded their way with stern eyes and grimly set jaws.

But what was that? Yes, there it was again! A human form dodging on their trail, taking advantage of every bit of shadow and gliding after them with the silence of a cat's tread.

For a second the pale moonlight glinted on a white, agonised face with big, frightened eyes, but firmly compressed lips.

It was little Jim. The one of all others the conspirators thought they had least to fear from.

But the boy was quick-eared, and his wits had been sharpened in the roughest school in the world.

All that long evening he had shivered under the knowledge that some deadly deed was in planning for the midnight hours.

Shrewdly he guessed the object of those long deliberations between the cowboy and the man-of-war's man. A word caught here and there of dread significance, and his hastily formed conclusions were confirmed.

Unable to sleep, racked with uncertainty as to what to do, as to whether he ought to inform the unconscious rover or let matters take their course, and nursing his grim knowledge, the boy lay quaking through the long hours of the first watch. Then at midnight, obeying the impulse of the moment, he counterfeited sleep to avoid detection; but on the three conspirators moving off he was unable to contain himself longer, and rising stealthily, he crept off on their trail, still undecided as to what he ought to do, but dragged after them by an unknown influence which gave him a sufficiency of nerve and cunning to avoid being discovered and yet left the problem still unsolved in his tortured brain.

Presently the little procession arrived at an open piece of ground in the midst of the forest, like a fairy glade, surrounded as it was by the stately trunks of the cocoa-palms standing majestically like the columns of a Greek circular temple. In the centre of this open space grew a gigantic tree, like a king circled by his courtiers.

Up to this monarch of the grove Tari led his captive, and halted.

Jim, as he slipped behind a clump of brushwood, recognised the spot as one which he and Tari had stumbled upon during their exploration of the afternoon, and he remembered that it was on the opposite side of the island to the signal palm, the lagoon coming in between.

The conspirators had chosen their spot well. It was far out of earshot of the camp, and seemed as if designed purposely for the object which they had in view.

Silently they went about their preparations, whilst the boy watched them from his hiding-place with a horror in his eyes.

Making use of a grummet, Tari, with the coil of rope round his shoulders, went up the tree like a cat. To any one who has never seen a native go up a tree in this fashion it is a most astonishing sight.

The rope circles the tree and the man's thighs, whilst he keeps his balance with his feet pressed against the trunk, progressing upwards by jerks. Each time, as he takes the pressure of his body off the rope, he slips the grummet higher up the trunk, tautening it up with his thighs before it can drop back again.

In this way Tari was soon at the top, and producing the boat's halliard-block and a salvagee strop from inside his shirt, he fixed them on the strongest branch he could find; then, reeving the rope, lowered one end to the ground. This Bill Benson and Broncho took hold of, and the Kanaka taking the other, they lowered him easily to the ground, thus testing at the same time the efficiency of their gibbet.

The doomed man was now led under the dangling loop, one of the executioners still keeping a firm hold on the rope to his wrists, whilst the others removed the gag.

Immediately the miserable wretch, dropping on his knees, burst into a piteous appeal for mercy.

The bosun's mate turned away, unable to stand the dreadful sight, but Broncho was made of sterner stuff, and listened to the raving, distracted words with an unshaken sternness.

"Have mercy!" whimpered the terrified ruffian. "Have mercy! I'll be your slave. Anything! I'll give you gold [eagerly], for I have it where I can lay hands on it. I swear it. By God, I swear it; only let me go!"

Slowly Broncho shook his head.

"Christ! Have you no pity in your soul? Think what you are doing! This is murder—cruel, bloody murder!"

"It's a shore-enuff proper-conducted lynchin'," growled the cowboy.

"What have I done to you? Lord God! What have I done? Free my hands and I'll fight you square, anyhow you like! Anything but this, this—this horrible death. I ain't fit to die. Lemme free an' have a chance in a square fight."

"I don't fight wi' skunks o' your breed!" came the scornful answer.

At this the wretch broke down utterly and exhausted himself in wild oaths of abuse; but after a string or two of these Broncho cut in impatiently:

"I allow you'd better throw off any prayer-stock you-alls wishes to cut loose. Your time's gettin' some scarce."

With a moan of terror the doomed ruffian threw himself down on his face, howling like a cur, and casting to the winds all further efforts at self-control.

Unmoved by this pitiful display of a cowardly soul, Broncho stepped up to the writhing form and pulled him to his feet; then, with a slow, deliberate care, adjusted the noose round the condemned man's neck, and called to the others to haul in the slack of the rope.

All this time, Jim, crouching behind the brushwood and shaking all over with fright, puzzled his poor head in a desperation as to how to act.

At the last moment the thought came to him. Already the three men were preparing to lay back on the rope, when right over their heads came a weird, unearthly voice:

"*Hangmen, beware! Do this deed and your time will shortly come! Beware! beware!*"

The effect was instantaneous. Tari and the bosun's mate dropped the rope and sprang backwards in wild alarm; only the undaunted cowboy stood firm.

Even the condemned man ceased his whimpering and looked up fearfully.

"Blazes! What were that?" cried the scared bluejacket in a hoarse whisper.

"Don' know," replied Broncho laconically. "A sperit mebbe, but no sperit palaver is goin' to jolt up this lynchin'. Take a holt and h'ist away."

"*Take care! take care!*" hissed the sepulchral tones again.

"My God!" groaned the prisoner, and would have collapsed, but a tug at the rope about his neck by Broncho's steady hand caused him to remain erect.

As for the superstitious bosun's mate, he crouched down as if fearing a blow, whilst Tari, with a wild cry of "Spirit debble! spirit debble!" fled madly from the spot.

Meanwhile, the small author of this terror-inspiring voice was tearing back along the trail with all the speed he could muster.

Breathlessly he burst into the camp, and darting to Jack's side, gasped incoherently,

"They're lynchin' him! They're lynchin' him!"

"Him? Whom? Why, it's Jim," exclaimed the rolling-stone, sitting up and blinking his eyes, his example being followed by the surprised Loyola.

"Come!" urged the panting boy. "Come quick! We may be in time. I give 'em a good scare. Follow me!" and off he went.

Jack was up in an instant, rapidly putting two and two together from the boy's wild words, and away he dashed in pursuit, with Loyola on his heels.

As they ran Jim managed to gasp out between his sobbing breaths a short account of Broncho's lynching, which drew an exclamation of concerned astonishment from the rover.

All this time Broncho was using his best eloquence to get the bluejacket to return to his grisly job.

"Brace up!" he urged, "brace up! You-alls ain't goin' to stampede the trail at a bunch o' ghost talk."

"I can't, man! Blawst me, I can't do it," groaned the terrified Bill Benson. "Gaud save us," he went on; "it were a warnin'!"

"Chucks!" growled the impatient and lion-hearted cowboy. "Rats to 'em, I say! Air you a quitter, Bill Benson? You, a British navy-man, a quitter?" and there was scorn keen as a razor-edge in his drawling voice.

"S'elp me Gaud, Broncho, I can't face it!"

"You heard 'em, Benson," put in Hawksley, seeing his chance; "you heard 'em. Don't let that fiend hang me, or may my spirit haunt you! May my blood be on your head and put a curse on all your days!"

"Silence, you gal-thief, silence!" hissed the angry cowpuncher, giving a jerk to the rope which nearly dislocated the wretched man's neck; then, addressing himself to the bluejacket, he went on:

"If you-alls baulk this ford, Benson, I'll put the coward's brand on you, shore as I'm tabbed in the stud-book Buckin' Broncho."

"It's no use," returned the man-of-war's man sulkily. "I ain't out to buck agin spirits—my courage don' run that swift. I ain't afraid as long as it's men, but ghosts top the limit o' my gristle. They overweights my firin'-battery absolute and entire."

For a second the cowpuncher glared in silence; then, slowly drawing his revolver, cocked it and covered the bluejacket with its sinister barrel.

"Mebbe this here argument'll revive you some," he drawled contemptuously.

Broncho was bluffing, bluffing desperately, but he had not spent the pay of so many seasons learning poker for nothing.

"Better catch a holt!" he went on significantly. "This here gun ain't out for play. It's a business proposeetion which it ain't wise nor healthy to monkey with."

After one wild, searching look into the stern eyes of the cowboy, Bill Benson gave in and reluctantly resumed his hold on the rope; whilst the unhappy Hawksley, seeing his last hope gone, burst afresh into a flow of terror-inspired lamentations and prayers.

At last the moment had come!

"Lay back on it!" hissed the cowpuncher, as the two executioners drew the rope taut.

In another second Hawksley would have been dangling in space. Already he was on the tips of his toes, when "Crack!" and the rope was cut through just above his head, and down he fell in a heap.

"Hold! What the devil are you doing?" cried a panting voice, and the next moment Jack burst into the open, a smoking pistol in his hand, followed by Jim and Loyola.

"You ain't wanted here, Jack Derringer," roared the baffled cowpuncher. "He's my steer, an' rope him I will! I'll take it kind if you'll quit blockin' up the scenery an' obstructin' this here execution."

"Why, Broncho, what's taken you? My old bunkie isn't going to turn into a butchering desperado, is he? Come, old son, this little game of yours has gone far enough."

"I stands a corralful from you, Jack, as you-alls knows; but you're playin' mighty near the limit. I asks you again to vamoose," returned the cowboy, sticking desperately to his guns; then he added more softly, "It's for your own good, pard."

"No good's going to come to me by any man's murder in cold blood."

"It's a fair an' square lynchin', Jack, and a sight easier death than the skunk desarves."

"Chuck it, Broncho, chuck it!" cried the rover. "It's no use. I can't allow it. The thing's impossible."

"On'y a jerk er two an' the gal's yours, Jack. It ain't your shout. I takes the responsibeelity. You-alls has no need to take a hand. He's my beef. Lope up the trail a hoss-length or two, Jack, an' the gal's free." Thus the cowboy tempted cunningly.

The blood rushed to the rover's face at the very thought. For a second a mighty temptation to let events take their course assailed him, and then, with a sinking misery in his heart, he regained his manhood.

"No, Broncho, no!" he jerked hoarsely.

"Think o' the hell you-alls is condemnin' the poor gal to! Think of her draggin' along her life-trail on the rope o' that hoss-thief," went on the tempter. "I allows you ain't the right to sp'ile her life this way."

The others watched the pair, waiting on the result with beating hearts. Would the cowboy's eloquence prevail? Would he after all be allowed to carry out his dreadful project? A word from Jack and the execution would continue. Every one realised the deadly temptation the cunning Broncho was so insidiously putting before his friend. Would the rover give in? Had he the right to spoil another life as well as his own? No one dared to answer the question.

Suddenly Loyola threw her head back, and going to the hideously tempted man, put her hand mutely into his, with a tender look of perfect confidence.

Jack caught the look, and knew that she was telling him that she would abide by his decision, whichever way it went. She trusted him, trusted him absolutely—that was what her eyes said—to do that which was right.

"What do you say?" asked Broncho, with an air of finality. "Shall I turn him loose an' bog the gal's happiness in an everlastin' quicksand, so as when the years o' hell an' misery pile up she comes to hate you an' your high-falutin' moralities worse'n him?"

"My God, Lolie, you won't? Oh, say you won't!" groaned poor Jack.

"Never!" whispered the girl, a smile of the supremest courage upon her face.

"Turn him loose," ordered the rover, in a voice which they could hardly recognise as his; then, rounding on his heel, he walked slowly out of the glade with bent head and miserable eyes.

A deep breath, almost a groan, burst from the lips of the onlookers. Jim sobbed audibly. The strain had been too much for the poor boy, now that he realised so fully all that his action had cost the man whom he loved most in the world. Bitterly he cursed himself. He would rather have seen

Hawksley hanged a thousand times. Utterly miserable and sick at heart, he flung himself upon his face on the ground, his whole body shaking with the strength of his emotion.

And Loyola—what of Loyola? With a strange, glorious light shining in her splendid eyes, she watched the receding figure of the rolling-stone; there was no misery in her face, only a perfect sweetness of content. Heedless of its consequences to herself, she only thought of her lover's courage, and her spirit leaped within her in a great exultation.

To her came the cowboy, asking sadly,

"I hope you ain't none raged with me, ma'am? I were playin' the hand for you and Jack."

For answer she placed her hand in his and murmured softly:

"I understand, Broncho—and I shan't forget," with which the cowboy's troubled face cleared wonderfully.

"An' my pard, Jack, ma'm'; I knowed all the time he were right. Any other maverick would ha' weakened, but he didn't. He's all grit, is Jack. I played up the hand for all it was worth, but I knew I was beaten when he fust called me."

At this praise of the man she loved the woman fairly beamed upon him; then her eyes turned slowly upon the unconscious form of her husband.

Following her glance, Broncho growled gruffly:

"Luck's hopped your way to-night, mister. I allow a thunderbolt's bein' constructed to put out your light, an' that's why Providence puts the hobbles on us humans an' blocks our game. I surmise they ain't none ready for you yet. Mebbe their heatin' plant ain't planned so as it reaches high enuff figures for you-alls, an' them pitchfork gents is busy fixin' it."

With which characteristic address he stepped to the side of its unconscious object, followed by Loyola.

The all-but-hanged scoundrel lay there strangely white and still, his legs crumpled up under him.

One glance of his experienced eyes, and the cowboy gave a queer exclamation of surprise.

"What is it?" cried the woman anxiously.

But, instead of answering, Broncho hurriedly felt under the man's shirt for the beat of his heart.

For nearly a minute he held his hand there, whilst Loyola and Bill Benson watched him with a growing look of apprehension; then he slowly drew back the eyelids and revealed a pair of glassy, expressionless eyes.

With a recoil of horror Loyola staggered back and fainted, the bluejacket catching her as she fell.

Hawksley was dead!

"Heart failure, I reckon!" muttered the cowpuncher grimly. "Seems his tickets for the great unknown were taken after all!"

And he turned to the unconscious woman, whilst the bosun's mate rushed to the lagoon for water.

FOOTNOTES:

[12] Tin hats = drunk.

[13] This is the name given by sailors to the small windmill noticeable on all Norwegian wooden ships, which is used to pump the water out of them.

CHAPTER X
"THE *BLACK ADDER*"

Jack, sitting hunched up with his face between his hands in a posture of utter despair, looked up dully as he heard the sound of approaching feet; then, as the gloomy procession came out on to the sands, he started to his feet with a cry.

First came Loyola, walking slowly with bent head and one hand on Jim's shoulder; but it was the sight of what was behind her drew the cry from his lips, for on the shoulders of Broncho and the man-of-war's man lay the body of a man.

The rover rushed forward.

"Hawksley's cashed in!" came in a solemn voice from Broncho, as he reached his side; but there was little need of the words. The fact was evident enough.

"You hanged him after all?" burst out Jack, with a queer strangle of reproach in his voice.

"No, pard; it ain't our funeral. The angels finished our job," explained the cowboy quietly.

The body was covered with the boat-sail and laid under the big palm; then the castaways flung themselves down to sleep, worn out by the tragic events of the night.

Nobody awoke until long after sun-up, and as Broncho was serving out their scanty rations, Tari appeared out of the scrub and slunk into a corner with downcast eyes.

Jack awoke to find himself blind again, but as he felt the woman's hand in his, he knew that she was at last free, and, notwithstanding his blindness, a great comfort flooded his soul.

At breakfast Jim explained his share in the tragic lynching to the astonished bosun's mate and Broncho, and the mystery of the supernatural voice was cleared up.

At midday the body of Hawksley was buried at the foot of the big palm in silence.

After the exciting events of the first twenty-four hours, life on the atoll progressed smoothly enough.

At first the shock of the tragedy seemed to stun Loyola's overstrained senses, but gradually, as the lazy, uneventful days passed, the memory of all the late horrors wore off, and a great hope of future happiness in Jack's arms filled her heart.

She began to pick up spirits and show more of that sunny disposition, with its infectious gaiety, which had been such a feature of her character before her unfortunate marriage.

At times a snatch of song would burst from her lips, which caused a smile of satisfaction to flit over the faces of the castaways, and she owned a devoted slave in each one of them.

"My, boys! but she's good gear!" commented Bill enthusiastically, one lazy afternoon, indicating Loyola with his pipe as he reclined under the cocoa-palms.

She and Jack, deep in talk, were pacing up and down the beach, hand in hand, for such was their custom on account of the latter's blindness.

She was telling him all the Island news, of new schooners, new stations, and new captains: of how old So-and-so had taken a new native wife, and Jack Bounce had been called down and thrashed by a new chum; of the stranding of the *Wee Willie* whilst Cap'n Ben was locked in his cabin killing imaginary snakes, and how the new trader on Pleasant Island had got a forty-four Colt bullet through the back from Nigger Bill, as a gentle hint to clear out; that Billy Cæsar, a noted chief in the Hebrides, had been wearing out his teeth on tough missionary again; how the blackbirder *May Allen* had lost a boat and her new recruiter in the Louisiade Archipelago, and numerous other small bits of South Sea gossip.

"She's shore a peach!" assented Broncho to the bluejacket's remark.

"Don't she smile be-e-autiful?" chimed in Jim, with an awestruck voice of admiration. "Lor, but she's a fine lady!"

"You can see that stickin' out a foot," agreed Bill Benson. "She'll 'ave a gunny-sack o' dibs too, bein' 'Awksley's widder. 'Eavens! but she is 'traps,'" and he turned up his eyes expressively.

"I don't surmise Jack'll let her handle any o' that Hawksley varmint's crooked-gained wad," declared Broncho. "He's powerful proud, is Jack."

"An' what about them maroonin' jokers on the *Black Adder*?" queried the bosun's mate reflectively.

"Does you-alls allow they're liable to come heavin' up on the scenery?" inquired the cowpuncher.

"Very pre-obbable," said the bluejacket. "They may 'ave the curiosity to see 'ow we're makin' out. If that Dago Charlie—him that were 'Awksley's mate an' did the maroonin' act—if 'e, I sez, comes protrudin' that snaky schooner our way, there'll be trouble, sure; but I won't panic much if 'e do come mine-droppin' under our bows. I just itches to draw a bead on 'im with one o' these Winchesters. Howsomedever, I fancies he's too busy lootin' copra stations an' fishin' other jossers' pearls."

"Let's bathe," proposed the boy suddenly; and rising languidly to their feet, they strolled off to the lagoon.

Here they were wont to disport themselves in the water four or five times a day, and to Jack especially this was a great pleasure, for he found that his blindness was no great inconvenience in the water.

As the lagoon of this atoll was completely surrounded by the growth, resulting from the toil of the coral insect, it was safe to bathe in it, without fear of the dreaded sharks which swarmed round the outer reef.

It made an ideal bathing-place. The white beach shelved gradually, and such was the transparency of the water that the bottom, with its clumps of coral, its glittering pearl-oyster beds, and its brilliantly hued fish, could be seen with ease.

Jim, the first few days on the island, fished with his usual ardour, and caught a number of queer-shaped marine monsters.

He was all keenness to cook and eat his catch, but Jack and Tari put their veto upon it.

As the rolling-stone explained, only the inhabitants of an atoll can tell what particular fish are poisonous and what are not, and on each atoll they vary according to the phases of the coral.

Tari stated that this strange poisoning of the fish changed according to the position of the planet Venus. This is the general belief among all South Sea Islanders, but of the two theories Jack's was more probably the correct one.

Jim, foiled in his fishing for fear of poisonous fish or fish with poisonous spines, turned his attention to shell-collecting, and he soon had quite a quantity heaped up, each one having the usual red spots which cover both shells, coral, and shellfish on an atoll.

It was a very pleasurable experience for the adventurous boy, this picnicing life on a coral island, and, though he said nothing, he felt keenly disappointed when departure was decided upon.

He dreaded a renewal of the open-boat trials and sufferings, and if the choice had rested with him there would have been no relaunching of the whaleboat.

After nearly three weeks on the island, of rest and recovering from the late trying times, they one day launched the boat out through the surf, and, with a good load of cocoanuts, headed away before the south-east trades for Papeete.

Hour after hour went by as the buoyant little craft ran gaily before the steady trade wind, with a new pioneer at the steering-oar in the shape of Mr. Bill Benson, late bosun's mate of Her Majesty's gunboat *Dido*.

"She weren't a bad little bug-trap as things go, an' no Callao ship neither," pronounced the navy-man, speaking of his late ship as they took their midday tiffin. "She was too top-'eavy, though, to my likin' for rough weather; the owner, too, was a bit wet on muslin. It was enuff to give one fits to see the way 'e carried on in that little 'ooker. Stunsails, mind you, on the fore, reg'lar old style. She could sail, too, an' weren't such a bad model, on'y 'er bally old nose sp'iled the 'ole effec'. I've passed many a Chinee junk in 'er under sail, an' some o' them ain't no slouches neither with wind to suit them.

"Her engines, though—oh, Lord! just a lot o' scrap-iron. You'd 'ear the tink-tink o' the bloomin' tiffy's 'ammerin' an' repairin' all day long. And b'ilers—oh, my! them wretched artificers spent mos' of their time crawlin' about on their bellies, tinkerin' of 'em.

"There weren't never no time wasted. D'rectly they wos cool enuff to boil a lump er ice, in them pore sweat-rags 'ad to go, creepin' an' crawlin' on dunnage wood so as their feet shouldn't catch fire; then presently out they'd come, legs first, cooked to a turn an' 'most senseless. An' the way she wasted steam through 'er numerous cracks an' chinks would 'ave made the bloomin' Chancellor o' the Excheq'r go muzzy.

"That were 'er on'y defec', though; otherwise she wos a' 'appy ship. Full er talent, too. Gunnery very fair, footer team first chop, the dramy a bloomin' constellation o' stars o' the first magnitude, finest squee-jee band in the Pacific, whilst our Jimmy Bungs[14] was er artist on the cinder-track. Wot more d'you want? But I guess my jaw-tackle's workin' too free. Give that cocoa-juice a fair wind, will ye, sonny," and he pointed to the pile of cocoanuts amidships.

"Do you-alls reckon that this war-canoe o' yours is browsin' around anyways handy hereabouts?" inquired Broncho.

"She was diggin' out for a bit er cannibalisin' through the Line Islands when I took my fancy dive."

"Then I surmise that we can diskyard the war-canoe from our hand as bein' wo'thless."

"I don't think we are likely to get picked up," said Jack, from the bottom of the boat. "The Paumotus are far from being popular with Island traders, and we are much too far to the west for any of the Cape Horners."

"That's so," admitted the bosun's mate. "We came through the Paumotus in the old *Dido*, an' did some fancy navigatin' at that, scrapin' our weeds off on coral reefs, an' jammin' through tide-rip channels with the wind jumpin' all round the compass. I went all cold up my back more'n once, muckin' through them bloomin' reefs."

"Ain't we goin' to stop at any of the islands on the way?" asked Jim anxiously.

"Not if we can help it," replied the rover. "I had a bit of trouble in the Low Archipelago once, and haven't forgotten it. You remember, Lolie, in the old *Moonbeam*?"

"Yes," muttered the woman, and shivered.

"Cawpse an' cartridge occasion, Jack?" inquired the cowpuncher in his off-hand way.

"Pretty near. Shooting in the South Seas is more noise than business though, sometimes."

"Every tuppeny bust-up is a 'orrible war. One copper-coloured coon with a slit skin will give t'other side a big vict'ry. Some er these Low Islands, howsomedever, is 'most perishin' for long-pig stakes, an' enjoys massacretin' whites now and agen if they gets the chaunce," said Bill Benson.

The afternoon passed in tobacco-smoke and siestas, and with the stars came back Jack's eyesight, which event always seemed to give him renewed life.

"Out of it, Bill," he cried, springing to his feet. "It's my wheel now, and your watch below."

"Them sidelights o' yours is the most mysterious be'aved optics I's ever shipmates with. I think you oughter adopt more drastic measures than them blighted bandages. Them eyes o' yours have run outer oil or somethin', or mebbe wants trimmin'," exclaimed the bosun's mate as he shifted places.

"The nerve's gone wrong somehow."

"It's that 'ere luminary that puts the hobbles on 'em. It was him cold-decked you, Jack," asserted Broncho.

"The moon's responsible for a lot of trouble in this world," said Jack. "You never know the way it will strike you, either. Some people who get moon-struck can only see in the daytime; others get their faces screwed up, and some go half-witted; but I'm hoping that perhaps when the moon changes my eyes will improve."

"Do you really think that, Jack? Oh, I do hope so, with all my heart," exclaimed Loyola earnestly.

"Wall, you've only three sun-ups to wait, Jack, if you allow that's your high kyard," announced Broncho.

"Mebbe they've got eroded an' won't render, but if it's the blessed moon you've manœuvred up against, I've heard tell that folks that is hoodooed that way, such as lunattics an' paralytic jokers, gets worse at the full moon. Don't you butter your dough too much on that idee," observed Bill wisely.

"The trades are going to leave us," put in the rover abruptly, after a keen look at the sky.

"Goin' to have more calm?" asked Jim anxiously.

"Well, doldrum weather, I expect."

"Ca'm weather kinder palls on one," drawled Broncho disgustedly, "'an it's shore onheathful, an' liable to make a gent feel moody an' bad; but if it's a forced play, we makes it ontil somethin' goes pop."

"Don't you jokers go manufacturin' trouble. Your joints'll tingle just the same when it does come alongside, an' if it do keep below the horizon, you're frettin' your brain-cases 'bout nothin'," said Bill reprovingly.

"'Last Post's' gone; it's about 'Lights Out,'" announced Jack. "Shy us over that almanac before you bed down, Jim. I'll take a star presently."

"I'm going to stand watch with you, Jack," declared Loyola decisively, getting up and seating herself by his side in the sternsheets.

So it was decided that these two should take the first watch, Bill Benson and Tari the middle, and Jack again the morning, as he could not trust either Broncho or Jim sufficiently with the dead reckoning.

The night passed quietly with but little wind. Loyola insisted on again bearing Jack company in his lonely vigil from four to eight, and after breakfast these two lay down in the bottom of the boat and slept soundly till near midday, awaking to find a big change in the weather.

The whaleboat was going close-hauled into a dead head wind. She was right off her course, heading a point to the east of north.

The Pacific sparkled under the strength of the tropical sun, and there was a heavy swell running from the nor-west.

On different quarters of the horizon rain-squall clouds hovered black and wind-torn.

The breeze blew fitfully, and occasionally came in stronger puffs, which heeled the whaleboat over till her garboard streak showed to windward.

It had evidently been blowing hard somewhere below the north-west horizon, to account for the long hills of water rolling in from that direction.

The atmosphere seemed very clear, and the surf, breaking on a line of reef about a mile to the north, showed up plainly, as if it was only a cable-length off.

In the west the rain was falling heavily and the sea was torn up by it, a well-defined line of white water denoting the edge of the squall.

Loyola, with the first instinct of a sailor, took a keen look to windward as she rose from her recumbent position.

"We're going to have a blow," she announced quietly, turning to the rolling-stone, who was slowly filling his pipe with a clumsiness caused by his blindness.

"Are we?" he muttered indifferently.

"You're right, ma'm," broke in Bill. "The wind broke off soon arter you turned in, an' 'as been very unsteady ever since."

"Coming out of the nor-west," went on the woman calmly; "a nasty quarter in these seas."

"Can you locate us at all, Jack?" inquired Broncho.

"What's your dead reckoning for the last four hours?" asked the rover.

"We've been headin' a point off north most o' the time," returned Bill Benson, "and ain't averaged more'n two knots an hour."

"St. Jean Baptiste can't be far below the horizon in the nor-west," said Jack, after making a rapid mental calculation.

"Pass me over the sextant and I'll get a noon sight," observed Loyola quietly.

Bill stared in astonishment, and ejaculated half under his breath,

"Blawst me, but she's a sailor's daughter an' no mistake."

"She was four years old when Big Harry brought her out to the South Seas in the old *Moonbeam*. When he lost his money he turned the yacht into a trader, and kept his daughter with him, as she had no mother, and she's been at sea most of the time ever since," explained Jack in a low voice, as this sea-maiden ogled the sun.

Silently they watched her. This taking of the sun to the uninitiated always seems a most mysterious and wonderful operation, and Broncho, Jim, and the bluejacket stared with eyes full of awe and admiration.

The sun was now close to the meridian, and presently the woman called out,

"Make eight bells!"

Jack laughingly beat the notes of the bell with a spoon on the barrel of his six-shooter.

"Throw me over the almanac and tables, Jim," cried Loyola coolly, and a minute later she announced their latitude.

"Think we're in for some dirt, Lolie?" inquired the rolling-stone casually.

"Sure of it! What you say, Tari?"

"Missee qui' right, big blow by-an'-by."

"I hope not," said the boy anxiously. "In an open boat there ain't no joke in it."

"I'm with you, Jim," declared the cowboy. "I'd rayther be lost in a blizzard a whole lot with a good hoss under me, than be upheaved an' junked about on this here onrestful sea."

Presently the wind died away completely, and the boat lay rolling helplessly on the swell, her sails flapping.

The afternoon passed slowly. Bill, in the bottom of the boat, lay face downwards, apparently dozing. Jim, next him, was listening with open eyes to one of Broncho's cattle-yarns. Tari, in the bows, slept placidly; and in the stern sat Jack and Loyola, conversing in low tones.

None of the boat's crew noticed the rapidly approaching change of weather. Loyola had her back turned to the heavy squall rising so rapidly, and neither Broncho nor Jim perceived it until the blind man cried suddenly,

"I smell wind!"

One glance was enough. Up sprang Loyola, and, seizing the steering-oar, with one long stroke she swept the boat's head round.

Then with a screech the wind fell upon them. The boat gave a violent lurch and lay down to it, the water pouring in over the gunwale. Broncho and Jim, taken completely by surprise, were tumbled to leeward on top of the bosun's mate, who was half drowned before they could extricate themselves, whilst Jack was awkwardly groping about in a vain effort to get in the awning.

The woman steered superbly, and her clear voice rang like a bell above the squall as she called to Bill to get hold of the sheet before the sail flogged itself to rags.

The rain fell in solid sheets, and the sea hissed as it beat upon it. The boat, rushing madly before the wind, rocked wildly, and dipped her rail under at each roll; whilst Jack, in a foot of water, baled furiously to keep pace with the rain; the other four struggled desperately with the maddened sail. Loyola, hanging on to the long oar with her strong young arms, stood swaying gracefully to the motion of the boat, as, calm and watchful, she held it steady.

The sunshine fled below the horizon to the south-east, chased by a mass of heavy, threadbare clouds, which came pelting across the sky.

The sail was quickly muzzled and close-reefed, and Loyola cautiously brought the wind on to the quarter, feeling its strength with practised hand.

But it was more than the brave boat could stand, and a sea washed over the rail which nearly filled her.

"Down that sail!" yelled Jack, whilst he and Jim baled with furious energy. "Down that sail!"

After the first tremendous downpour the rain fell steadily, but with less weight. Meanwhile both wind and sea commenced to rise, and though the whaleboat rode the big rollers splendidly, many of the smaller waves slopped aboard and kept the balers hard at work.

With the sail off her, Loyola swung the boat's head up into the wind, and held her with the steering-oar from falling off.

"Lemme relieve you, ma'm," called the man-of-war's man, clambering aft.

"I'm all right," answered the plucky woman. "Give the balers a spell."

"What's the glass say?" jerked out the blind man, panting with his exertions.

"Phew! but it's low, an' dropping too," replied Bill, squinting into the face of a small aneroid which they had saved from the *Ocmulgee*.

"Can you see under the squall?"

"No, it's black now, clear round the horizon."

"Wind seems to me to be increasing," commented Jack, feeling its strength with his face.

"It's just like the start of that blow we had in the *Moonbeam* off Rarotonga," called Loyola.

"That's bad!" commented the former. "I think, Bill, you'd better rig up a sea-anchor for us to ride to. What do you say, Lolie?"

The woman flushed with pleasure at Jack asking her opinion, and her eyes, shining with suppressed excitement, aroused in her by this struggle with the elements, beamed fearlessly into the heart of the storm.

"It's going to blow very hard, I'm sure of it," she answered; "but you know best, Jack."

Thereupon they wasted no time in acting on the rover's idea. Three oars were lashed together triangle-wise with a tarpaulin spread between them. This was weighted by the small boat-kedge. Then, with their strongest line attached, this contrivance was lifted over the bows and the line paid out as the boat drifted down to leeward. This had the effect of holding the boat's head up to windward, and caused her to ride easier.

There was nothing more to be done but sit still and hope that the gallant craft would succeed in weathering out the storm.

Leaving the post that she had held so well, Loyola seated herself beside Jack in the bottom of the boat, where they were protected in some degree from the howling wind.

Jack made her don a long oilskin coat to keep out the wind and rain, as, slightly clad as they all were, the wetting caused a feeling of cold.

Now that the strain and excitement of the first strenuous fight were over the woman felt somewhat limp and disheartened; but the presence of her lover by her side, blind and helpless though he was, proved a great comfort to her.

Shyly she sneaked her hand into his. He closed his fingers upon it reassuringly and whispered in her ear,

"I'm very proud of you, Lolie, steering through that squall."

Such was the noise of the wind that, though the castaways sat shoulder to shoulder with their backs to the gale, Jack, farthest aft, could only hear Loyola speaking next to him by putting his ear close to her mouth.

On the other side of Loyola sat Jim, the baler in his hand; whilst next to him Broncho and Bill Benson exchanged remarks, Tari being in his favourite place up in the bows.

"She rides well," muttered the bosun's mate, "an' if this kick-up don't stir up the mud too much, we'll see another dawnin' in this old low-degree turnip after all."

"You allows as how these perverse elements ain't goin' to get our scalps then," drawled the cowpuncher. "The deal comes a bit florid to me. The amount of *agua* we-alls contrives to gather at one time I regyards as liable to have baleful effects."

"An' my idees were about the same gauge. It's the gal who pulls us through the shindy. She's a bit o' dossy goods, wi' enuff nerve an' savvy to make an' ordinary josser pipe low an' subdued."

"You're shore right a whole corralful. I feels plumb useless an' no account when that 'ere squall rounds up on us, an' I near cuts loose a howl; but when I sees how she's playin' the game so ca'm an' easy, I cinches up my paltry feelin's an' whirls into the play with renewed sperit."

"Poor ole Jack, too," observed Bill. "That blindness o' his cuts him to the quick for sure. I watches 'im balin' with the blood runnin' from his lips where he's bitin' of 'em. 'E's an old bird, is Jack Derringer; keeps a stiff upper lip an' don' show much, but that blood lets out how fretted 'e is an' gouged up in 'is innards."

Broncho nodded in silence, for Jack's misfortune hit his old bunkie too hard for him to feel inclined to talk about it.

Suddenly a vessel was descried to windward, flying down upon them under a close-reefed topsail, flinging the surges to right and left of her and dipping to her cat-heads at each dive.

As she lifted her stern her deck could be plainly seen, crowded with men, who crouched under her bulwarks in glistening groups. Her low black hull battled in a field of raging foam, and her long topmasts swung madly across the heavens as she rolled.

She was evidently an Island schooner.

"Jack, it's the *Black Adder*," cried Loyola nervously, after one glance at the nearing vessel.

"Is she close?" inquired the rolling-stone.

"We'd be standin' by water-tight doors in the *Dido*," declared Bill.

"Near enough to throw the shorthorn steerin' with a thirty-foot rope," put in Broncho.

As the schooner surged by, her crew manned the rail, staring wild-eyed at the whaleboat.

Aft by the helmsman stood a long, thin man with a scraggy beard, and so near was the flying schooner that the movement of his jaws could be seen as he chewed steadily.

Suddenly he bent forward, and shading his eyes with one hand, gazed fixedly at the castaways.

"It's Dago Charlie!" gasped Loyola, with a horror in her eyes.

"By God, he's seen us!" yelled the bosun's mate wildly.

Sure enough the man began brandishing his arms in furious gesticulations, and a deep roar reached the whaleboat from the combined lungs of the stranger's crew.

"Bah! You swabs! We don't care that for you!" roared Bill Benson savagely, standing up and snapping his fingers.

"Thar's squaws among 'em," exclaimed Broncho with surprise.

"Island girls," muttered Jack.

The schooner had hardly got a quarter of a mile to leeward when she put her helm down and hove-to with a tarpaulin in the rigging.

"Goin' to lie by us till it moderates," said Bill. "Now he's spotted us he won't let us go if 'e can 'elp it. 'E knows it's the gallows for 'im if we gets clear, and 'e'll stand by to pounce on us. 'E'll get what he ain't lookin' for if 'e comes protrudin' here."

"What for of a play would it be if we-alls sends some lead after him, as a sorter hint to move on?" inquired Broncho.

"Wouldn't do!" pronounced Jack. "We'd get it all back with interest. If it moderates at all to-night we'll put the horizon between us."

"I'm jest pining to shoot him up some," declared Broncho bloodthirstily.

"Let 'im begin the action," said Bill grimly. "We'll finish it!"

Loyola said nothing, but cowered closer to Jack with big, anxious eyes.

"We'll give him the slip, Lolie, don't you fear," cried the rover heartily.

Slowly the hours passed. The gale continued to blow with unabated vigour, but the whaleboat rode it like a duck.

The castaways sat silent for the most part, and watched the schooner down to leeward with various emotions.

Jack, handicapped by his blindness, lay back with closed eyes, deep in thought.

Loyola, next to him, sat silent and troubled; whilst Broncho and the bosun's mate tried to converse, but gave it up after a few efforts.

Jim, with the baler in his hand, busied himself with keeping the boat free of water, for though she took no green water aboard, sprays and spindrift flew over in a continuous shower-bath.

As evening came on they ate their slight, unpalatable meal and struggled with damp matches to light their pipes in the screaming wind. Then, as the darkness deepened, they all sat silently expectant, waiting for the return of Jack's bewitched eyesight.

The rover sat up and sniffed round, turning his head slowly through the points of the compass with straining eyes.

They watched him, fascinated by this queer freak of fortune, Loyola in an agony of anxiety, the others curiously, but quietly confident.

Then, as the stars began to peep forth through the rushing clouds, they saw his eyes suddenly brighten.

"I can see again!" he murmured, almost below his breath; though they did not catch the words, all recognised that change in his face.

"Thank God!" burst forth Loyola half brokenly, for it was her great terror that some day perhaps his eyesight might fail to return with the nightfall.

A wave of intense relief rushed over the castaways, and as if some great weight had been lifted from their spirits, they commenced to talk, or rather shout, cheerfully.

The mere fact that their leader, if only for a few hours, was once more restored to his usual self, gave renewed confidence to all.

With a swift, winning smile, Loyola tenderly grasped the rover's hand and hugged it.

"So glad! so glad!" she cried joyfully.

"It's full moon to-night, Jack!" said Broncho casually, as if it were of no importance, though he knew full well how anxiously he, nay, all hands were looking forward to its advent as a slight chance of release for Jack from his horrible affliction.

"I know," replied the rolling-stone very quietly; then more brightly, "Now, let's have a look round. Ah! There's the schooner—rather too close, I'm thinking. How far do you make it, Bill?"

"'Bout 'alf a mile."

"About that, I think," agreed Jack; then he turned and looked keenly to windward.

"This dust-up will be over before dawn," he declared. "Let's see. The moon rises about eleven; the sky is getting clearer every minute. But that marooning hound needn't hug himself about that; he'll have to catch us first and fight us afterwards, and if he gives me half a chance to draw a bead on him before daylight, I'll put him out of action for ever, and think no more of it than stamping on a cockroach."

"That's bizness, Jack, that's the tactics! Kill the bloomin' swine an' all's serene. One of us ought to be able to 'it the bull's eye," asserted Bill keenly.

"Why, chucks!" exclaimed Broncho, "it's a cert if he comes mouchin' 'round he's due to get creased a whole lot. That yappin' wolf'll find it a heap fatiguin', chasin' round ropin' after this outfit. I allow he's some fretted now he pastured you-alls on the island so headlong an' thoughtless. That play o' his is goin' to make him sweat blood."

FOOTNOTES:

[14] Nickname for the cooper.

CHAPTER XI
"A SEA FIGHT UNDER THE STARS"

By midnight both wind and sea had dropped considerably. At one bell the castaways saw the schooner's fore-topmast staysail rise slowly as her crew manned the halliards, and a second later her mainsail raised its head.

Jack gave a quick look round, and then said sharply,

"In with that sea-anchor, boys; it's time we were flitting."

In a moment the inaction on the whaleboat turned to a keen, nervous energy.

Hand over hand the oars were hauled alongside, and the sea-anchor got in over the bows; then away they went to windward.

The boat lay over to it, heavily pressed under a close-reefed lugsail, wallowing, splashing, crashing into the seas.

Jack, at the steering-oar, sailed her a "clean full," whilst the rest of the castaways baled furiously.

All of a sudden a puff of white smoke flew away from the side of the schooner, and the faint report of a gun reached them.

"A snot from his twelve-pounder amidships," said Jack calmly.

The ball screamed past overhead, and plumped into the sea a long way off to windward.

"It'll be wild shooting in this jump of a sea," observed Bill.

"Shall I bring my pop-gun into action?" drawled Broncho almost indifferently, as he fingered his Winchester.

"Yes, let him have it; he's not going to drop lead over us without getting some back," returned the rover fiercely.

"Jump it into him, Broncho," cried the bluejacket eagerly.

"That I shorely will without any ondue delays," replied the cowpuncher, and taking a rapid sight he fired.

"It ain't easy shootin' in this here turmoil," he muttered, watching to see the effect of his shot. "Now he's scatterin' it loose," he went on, as a whole volley blazed from the schooner.

"Twelve-pounder again and rifle-fire," commented the man-of-war's man, as the bullets screamed overhead. "That vigorous josser will have to lower his sights a bit if he aims to do us any damage."

"I allow that shot makes him chew his mane; he's gettin' some acrid. He reckoned he was goin' to bluff us sports quick an' easy," muttered Broncho, pumping another cartridge into his gun.

"Now, my frenzied hold-up!" he cried derisively, and fired again.

"Get into the firing-line, Bill," broke in their leader sharply.

The bosun's mate needed no second bidding, but seized his gun eagerly.

"'Ere's 'santy' to you, Mister Dago Charlie," he cried out, and he pulled the trigger.

"Here she comes again!" yelled Jim, poking his head over the gunwale in his excitement.

As the schooner fired, all the castaways, with the exception of Jack steering, bobbed down in the bottom of the boat, as the latter cried:

"Lie low everybody," at the same time pushing Loyola down on to the floorboards.

This time there was a dull thud aft.

"Hulled, by God!" burst out the bluejacket.

"Torn my only pair of dungarees," said Jack coolly. "Rifle bullet clean through us."

"Not hurt, Jack?" asked Loyola piteously, her voice trembling.

"No fear, Lolie; just a graze, that's all."

"Chance shot!" remarked Bill. "What range is you sightin' at, Broncho?"

"Six hundred."

"Better make it five," advised Jack. "She's closed up on us a bit, but the sea and wind are moderating every minute. Tari, come and take the steering-oar. We'll bring all our battery to bear."

Whereupon the Kanaka changed places with Jack.

Seeing that he had utterly failed in his attempt to make the whaleboat heave-to, the marooner now ceased firing for a spell; but having put his hand in the fire, it was now too late to draw it out. It was his life against theirs now, and he crowded sail in pursuit with desperate purpose.

But the three riflemen in the whaleboat continued to pump lead in his direction, hoping by a lucky shot to cool his ardour sufficiently to make him sheer off.

Presently the schooner's maingaff dropped its peak.

"Halliards shot away!" exclaimed the rolling-stone.

Jim burst into a cheer.

"Easy, sonny, easy," said Bill gravely. "It's too early yet to begin shouting."

The *Black Adder* soon had her mainpeak hoisted again, but the whaleboat's success was too much for the pirate's temper.

Her helm was put up, and as she fell off her whole side burst into flame. The water was cut up all round the whaleboat by the shower of lead. It flew over the castaways, whining and humming through the air, and the boat quivered under the shock of three hits.

"Gee whiskers! Shrapnel!" exclaimed Bill concernedly.

"Slugs and pot-legs," agreed Jack, shaking off some blood which was running down his hand. "Any one hurt?" he continued.

"Why, you are, Jack!" cried Loyola in great distress.

"Only a scratch on the arm," remarked the former carelessly.

"Let me bind it up."

"No time now, Lolie. Well-aimed broadside that; 'bout four hundred, isn't it, Bill?"

"Aye."

"Plug those shot-holes if you can, Jim," went on the rover in a most unconcerned voice.

He knew that things were looking serious, but the last thing he wished to do was to show the boat's crew that he thought so.

"He shore cuts loose some lead that time," muttered Broncho. "The kyards is comin' some swift. Thar's nothin' tender about that 'ere maverick; he's plumb wolf from away back."

"More cartridges here, powder-monkey," laughed Bill cheerily to the boy.

Jim reached over to the bag, but Loyola was quicker, and held out her two small hands with all they could hold in front of the bluejacket.

"Thank you, mum; I 'opes as 'ow you didn't think I wos a-callin' of you a powder-monkey," said Bill, reddening.

"Why, don't you think I make a very good one?" smiled the intrepid woman; then excitedly, as the schooner's deck showed, "There's Dago Charlie! There he is, standing right forrard!"

All three rifles rang out.

The man sprang backwards and was hidden behind the bulwarks, but soon reappeared brandishing a furious fist.

What with the difficulty of accurate shooting at night and in the rough sea, neither side seemed to be doing much damage.

Jack, Broncho, and Bill Benson concentrated all their energies in the endeavour to pick off the schooner's captain, who exposed himself carelessly as he watched the whaleboat keenly through his binoculars.

"That 'ere dago is a heap too obvious on the scenery; if this boat would quit pitchin' so lively, we'd stop his sin-encrusted play some rapid," observed Broncho, as he took a long, careful aim.

"Two hours to daylight," muttered Jack, reloading. "I'd like to see him sheer off before dawn."

"So should I," said Loyola softly.

The woman was behaving with rare courage, and took no more heed of the flying lead than an old campaigner.

She and Jim had managed to plug all the shot-holes, and now that the sea was smoother they were able to take a spell at the baling.

"Lolie, you're a brick. Pluckiest little woman I've ever met," declared the rolling-stone fervently, as he knelt beside her.

"Have we any chance, Jack?" she asked sadly.

"Why, of course! You don't want to give in, do you, dearie? I should think you had seen about enough of the *Black Adder*."

"Me? I'd rather die than fall into the hands of Dago Charlie!" she cried vehemently.

"I thought so," observed Jack, with a keen look of approval in his eyes; and then went on almost gaily, "Then it's a fight to the finish, isn't that so, boys? We won't give her up, will we? No surrender to Dago Charlie for us?"

"Give her up? I'm a blasted grabby if we does any such thing," grunted Bill scornfully.

"I should smile," drawled Broncho. "What kinder skunks do you-alls think we is? I don't drop out o' this deal till my lamp goes out or that pesterin' snake yonder pulls his freight."

"We're never goin' to give you up to that fiend, mum," chimed in Jim, with a ferocious frown of valour on his face.

"Why," whispered the bluejacket under his breath to Jack, "the dago mighty near marooned us without 'er; an' if 'e got us now, it'd be over the side for us, and worse for 'er. 'E'll run no more chaunces like last time."

"You're right, Bill," agreed the rover; "that's my opinion."

The wind had now dropped to no more than a strong breeze and was veering into the north, and no longer coming in gusts.

The whaleboat sailed well, but was steadily being overhauled by the schooner, which, however, was some way to leeward.

The *Black Adder* now ceased firing, content with the knowledge that, barring accidents, she was sure of her prey.

But for the man at the wheel, none of her crew showed above the bulwarks, and after the castaways had wasted several rounds in a vain attempt to hit the helmsman, Jack laid down his gun in disgust and said,

"Let's cease firing and wait till he's a bit closer. It's no use throwing away ammunition like this."

"I agrees," assented Broncho. "As the kyards lay we-alls is simply wastin' chips. We'll hold our hand some."

"It's the perishin' day he's waitin' for," grumbled Bill, putting aside his smoking rifle and coolly filling his pipe. "He'll just keep station till sun-up, an' then the oratorio'll begin to play again."

The pursuer and pursued now raced along broadside to broadside, less than three cables' lengths separating them.

The *Black Adder*, though she was pinched up in the wind all she would bear, would not look up as close as the whaleboat, though she went faster through the water.

Jack's arm was now attended to and skilfully bound up by Loyola. A bullet had simply grooved through the flesh—not much more than a graze, but sufficient to cause a good deal of bleeding.

Jack, whilst his hurt was being doctored, thought hard. If something were not done soon, Dago Charlie's obstinate perseverance would prevail.

"We'll worry him yet," began the rover.

"Shore, an' euchre him too," said Broncho confidently.

"The wind's light enough now to help us," went on Jack. "Let's try some short tacking. We can go about three times to his one."

"That's good tactics, sure enough," commented Bill.

"Splendid!" cried Loyola. "Let's start at once."

"Right-oh! Ready about there, Tari. Bill, you ship an oar and help her round. We three will manage the lugsail."

The castaways had the boat round smartly, and away they went on the port tack, heading north-east.

The *Black Adder* was completely taken by surprise, and lost some valuable minutes before she followed suit and put her helm down.

Compared with the whaleboat, the schooner was a long time coming round.

Anxiously the boat's crew watched her as she rounded to with flapping head-sails, bowing her glistening black hull to the long swell with slow, dignified movements; then, as she felt the wind on the other tack, she lay over and came smoking after them, a frothing streak of white rolling away from her sharp stem.

She made a perfect picture for an artist as she cut through the gleaming path of the moon, carved out in a hard, clean outline of jet; and, forgetting her peril, Loyola could not help exclaiming upon the beauty of the scene.

"Just look at her! What other work of man can approach a sailing-ship for perfect grace and——"

"Ready about!" broke in Jack, with a queer smile and a muttered, "Sorry to interrupt you, Lolie," and round came the whaleboat again.

This time the schooner was prepared, and as she swung in stays she sent a ball from her twelve-pounder skipping after the chase.

The castaways saw the shot splash, and then with a whirr it ricochetted over their heads and plunged into the sea beyond them.

"Good shootin', and that ain't no josh!" commented Bill Benson.

"You're shore right, son," agreed Broncho. "That shot comes plenty close. This here Dago Charlie slings his scrap-iron too free an' easy: an' though we disdains these fam'liarities o' his, I shore regrets we-alls can't corral his game none. His scatterin' loose this-away is a'most liable to make a Montana sheriff apprehensife an' gun-shy."

"He ain't hit us yet," spoke up little Jim bravely.

"If he does he'll let sunshine through us, like as if we was a plate-glass winder," declared the cowboy.

Again the whaleboat tacked, and before the schooner got round, Tari swung her up once more on to the original tack.

Confused by the rapid manœuvres of the whaleboat, the marooner hesitated a moment too long whilst head to wind, and then starboarded his helm in an attempt to fall off on to the port tack again. But he was too late;

the schooner had not enough way on her to respond to her tiller, and in a moment she was all aback.

"My God! she's missed stays!" yelled the rover joyfully. "What luck! What all-fired luck!"

"Shall we-alls burn some more powder on him?" proposed Broncho eagerly. "I regyards this here as a speshul o'casion."

"I think we'd better hold on a bit, Broncho. The ammunition's none too plentiful, and we'll want every cartridge presently," declared their cautious leader.

"An' you thinks a show-down is some handy, Jack?" inquired the cowboy.

"Well, the wind's dropping fast; that's all in our favour."

"Perhaps he'll tire of this and sheer off before daybreak," broke in Loyola wistfully.

"I allow he's too mean-strain an Injun to break away afore he's rattled us some consid'rable more; but don't you fear, missy, we euchres him some way on the final deal," declared Broncho cheerfully.

"You bet! The time's comin' when we'll wag our tails an' send 'im navigatin' over the horizon quicker'n if a hornet's stung 'im," chimed in Bill heartily.

Thus with hopeful talk did each hide a sinking heart.

Taking her hand in his, Jack looked long and lovingly into Loyola's eyes.

"Whatever happens, dear, you and I will not be parted—that I swear," he whispered.

"Dear Jack," she answered fondly, and smiled back at him with a brave spirit.

"If it comes to the worst, we'll board and carry the wretched schooner," he went on valiantly. "Three white men, not to speak of you, Jim, and Tari, ought to be able to settle the mixed rabble on that pirate. Never fear, Lolie, we'll pull through somehow."

Fainter and fainter grew the wind as the dawn approached. Still the whaleboat doubled before the persevering schooner like a hard-pressed hare, and by well-timed manœuvring the castaways continued to hold their own, though the marooner hung out every flying kite that would draw.

Presently, with the magic quickness of the tropics, the dawn spread gloriously over the east and dimmed the brightness of the stars.

In the whaleboat a fresh anxiety showed itself on every face as the light of day grew swiftly.

Then, as Jack passed his hand wearily across his eyes and slowly shook his head, a groan of distress broke out amongst the castaways.

"It's gone," whispered the rover hoarsely; then, groping clumsily about, he slowly sank down in the bottom of the boat and sat there miserably, with bent head and closed eyes.

A fierce oath burst from little Jim's lips, an oath such as he had not used since the first days on the *Higgins,* and it started a flood of lurid, blood-curdling blasphemy from the over-tried cowpuncher, whose swearing vocabulary Bill Benson ably succeeded in providing with new words.

This fiery avalanche of oaths fell unheard by the small ears of Loyola, who, crouching by Jack's side, stared at the rover with dry, piteous eyes, whilst Tari, inscrutably silent as usual, steered on with twitching lips.

In the midst of it all, the sail flapped, then filled, then flapped again; the last of the wind had gone, and the whaleboat lay rolling on a long, glassy swell, which already the sun was covering with glittering sparks, like a mass of diamonds on the Pacific's wonderful blue.

The swearing ceased as suddenly as it had begun, and nothing broke the silence in the whaleboat for some moments except the dreary flapping of the lugsail.

Then Jack lifted his head and spoke:

"It's a flat calm, eh, boys?"

"A Paddy's hurricane clear down to the horizon," returned the bosun's mate.

"The schooner's in it?"

"Aye, an' kotched it first. She's over three cables' lengths away now, an' slewin' round without steerage way."

"By Jove, then, boys, we'll beat them yet," declared Jack excitedly. "Out with the oars and let's put the horizon between us as soon as we can. I can't see, but hang me if I won't show Dago Charlie I can row."

His words put fresh life into the castaways.

"You hits it, this time, old son, for shore," burst out the cowboy. "This hand shall be played with renewed sperit, an' that on-tamed wild-cat's goin' to be out-held, or I'm a sheepman."

CHAPTER XII
"THE PLUCK OF WOMAN"

Swiftly the sail was gathered in and the mast lowered, amidst a rattle of eager words. Only Loyola remained silent and downcast, for this blindness which attacked Jack so curiously with every sunrise hit her harder than any peril caused by the marooner's actions.

But Jack's keen ears noted her silence and realised its cause. Still seated as he was beside her, he felt clumsily for her hand; then, finding it, pressed it firmly, whispering,

"Cheer up, Lolie; my eyesight'll be all right directly I can get the correct treatment. Meanwhile, we'll just go on our way to Papeete and leave Mr. Dago Charlie standing."

"I'm trying to be brave, I'm trying to be brave," murmured the woman brokenly. "Only, only——"

"I know, dearie, I know," he broke in gently. "I know how it hurts you—yes, more than it does me, far more; but it'll all come right presently, don't you fear."

"But it does seem so hard, so very, very hard; and I was hoping so much——"

"Put not your trust in the moon," he laughed cheerfully; then went on, "You must steer, Lolie, as we want Tari to row."

The fact of being of some use seemed to hearten her considerably, and with a brighter face she took the steering-oar from the Kanaka.

"You stroke us, Jack," proposed Benson.

"'Xcuse me, boys, if my play with an oar is some wantin' in skill," observed the cowpuncher. "My eddication's been some neglected in rowin', an' I'm shore a tenderfoot at the game a whole lot."

Then away they went, Jack setting a steady stroke and Broncho at the bow oar pulling all he knew, but splashing freely with the clumsiness of a novice.

"I shore wishes this here were a paddle," he grunted. "I savvys paddles, but rowin' this-away comes plumb strange to me."

"Shoo, man, you're doin' fine! Reg'lar Varsity h'oar, I calls yer; fit for a captain's gig," declared Bill.

Jim, much against his wish, had been placed in reserve.

The whaleboat pulled easily over the long swell, and though worn to a degree, the castaways dipped their oars with the energy of desperation.

The blind stroke, drawing upon his wonderful reserve of strength, made the stout ash bend with his efforts, the man-of-war's man ably backing him up; whilst Tari, the indefatigable, pulled with the easy, untiring swing of the South Sea whale-hunter.

The moisture glistened on their stern-set, resolute faces as the sun beat down upon them with an eye-wearying glare.

The water rippled cheerily from the bends of the keen-lined boat, and swirled astern hissing and bubbling, whilst the ploughing oars churned up the calm depths of blue into a creamy yeast, leaving behind them at each stroke a miniature whirlpool, which seemed to move hastily away from the cruel blades, slicing their way so steadily through the transparency of the Pacific, and blurring its face as they drove the whaleboat onward.

An enthusiasm in this desperate race raised the watching boy's spirits to a gay fearlessness, and he burst forth into a well-known snatch:

"An' it's drill, ye tarriers, drill!
For it's work all day, without sugar in ye tay,
An' it's drill, ye tarriers, drill!"

"That's the style, Jim!" jerked the blind stroke approvingly. "Let it rip! That's the medicine!"

"Shore!" gasped Broncho.

"An' here comes the dago diggin' out after us," cried Bill. "They're pipin' fust an' second cutters away aboard the pirateer."

The *Black Adder* had lowered two boats full of men, which now came dancing over the swell in chase of the whaleboat, for all the world like two bustling centipedes.

"Jim serve out a cocoanut per man. Easy all, boys. Let's get our wind and a little refreshment, then we'll soon show 'em what we can do," said Jack, lying on his oar.

"That's the ticket! We'll stoke up an' revive ourselves before the final 'eat," declared Bill. "For it's a case of brace up an' get a wiggle on if we're goin' to stop that dago swab from bussneckin' round us."

"I'd shore like to put the hobbles on the rancorous hold-up," growled Broncho, as he sucked his cocoanut. "I feels kind o' gore-thirsty an' bulgin' with animosity this maunin'. I hungers for a show-down with them two boats. A long range duel makes me peevish a whole lot. My mood ain't in the saddle that-away, I wants to get clos't to my work. I jest itches to get my claws on to that 'ere maroonin' desperado and jolt him up some. I reckon he'd be some scarce o' tail-feathers when I'm through with him."

"Our game will be to draw the boats as far away from the schooner as we can," put in Jack; "and then, if the worst comes to the worst, we must fight 'em off. No, Broncho, no hand-to-hand rough-and-tumble if we can avoid it. Remember Loyola's a woman, though she's got a man's name and a man's nerve."

"It shore gets clean stampeded out o' my mind," muttered the cowpuncher.

"Then I'm blind and useless," went on Jack. "That leaves three men and a boy to tackle two boat-loads of cutthroats. No, no, our rifles are our only chance."

"Aye, Jack's right," agreed the bosun's mate. "We must revolute clear o' them jossers some'ow. We don't want it to come to fixin' bayonets to 'old 'em off."

Their small refreshment finished, the castaways took to their oars again with renewed vigour; but despite their desperate efforts, the schooner's boats began slowly to close upon them.

The cowboy, unaccustomed to rowing, with all his grit, was fast tiring out, and his oar began to cleave the water in uncertain jerks; he wasted his strength at the wrong moment, and began to find a difficulty in keeping time.

Jack still pulled an easy, mechanical stroke, putting a steady, unchanging power into his work, whilst Tari seemed almost as fresh as at the start; but Bill Benson, with the moisture pouring off his face, though pulling with strength and determination, was beginning to breathe heavily, and the strain upon him showed in the haggard look of his eyes.

Matters were looking very serious for the whaleboat's crew, and in that raging calm there was no hope of a helping sail appearing in sight.

Jim was sent to Broncho's thwart to help him, and everything not absolutely necessary thrown overboard to lighten the whaleboat; but still the dago gained upon them, until, as the sun neared the meridian, the schooner was almost hull down, whilst the boats were within a cable's length and a half of their quarry.

Loyola, with the rifles by her side, stood swaying gracefully to the swell as she held the boat's head on its course.

She made a lovely picture, standing there so straight and fearless, her little sun-browned hands grasping the steering-oar and the big slouch hat shading her dauntless eyes from the glare of the tropical sun.

From time to time she spoke to the toiling men with bright words of encouragement, which always brought a renewed strength to their aching muscles and produced a look of fierce determination in their tired eyes.

Then for a spell she would fall silent, and lose herself in her thoughts as she looked at the blind stroke, until her soul crept out of her sad eyes in a soft glow of infinite tenderness.

The tired, hard-lined features of the men softened as they watched her, then hardened again at the sight of the on-coming boats. The bosun's mate hissed a sea-blessing through his sternly compressed lips as he glared at the persevering dago; then, bringing his eyes back to the toiling shoulders of the blind man before him, he bent to his work with a queer expression of pity twisting up his face.

As for Jack, since their short meal he had rowed in inscrutable silence, his eyes closed, and only the fierce, unnatural strength which he put into the sweep of his oar-blade gave any indication of how deeply this blindness was cutting into his very soul. And, indeed, it was a bitter position to be in for one of such a self-reliant and masterful nature as Jack. The weak man whimpers when taxed by fate beyond his strength, but there was little weakness in Jack. Whimpering was not the method his wilful spirit thought of taking to ease its agony; no, he preferred action, and as a sharp report broke in upon his ears and the soft "Theeu!" of a bullet hummed over his head, he braced up with a queer laugh which had little mirth in it. No better tonic could have been dealt out to the man; the light of battle leaped into his sightless eyes, and washed away the misery—all gone, forgotten.

"Now for it," he muttered to himself grimly.

A man was standing up in the sternsheets of the leading boat, a smoking rifle in his hand.

"It's Dago Charlie," cried Loyola, looking over her shoulder, and she gave an irrepressible shudder.

"Loyola, you used to be a nailing shot with a rifle," declared Jack. "See if you can't stop that devil's game."

"Oh, Jack, I can't shoot at live men," declared the girl, in great distress.

"Why not, if they're shooting at you? and it's our only hope. Will you let that scoundrel win after all this long struggle without an effort to stop him? No, Lolie, I know you won't; you're too clean-strain to turn soft like that."

His words had the desired effect. In silence the woman let go of the steering-oar, and picked up one of the rifles at her feet; then, putting it to her shoulder in a workmanlike manner, glanced along the sights and fired.

A hoarse, shrill cheer from Jim announced a hit. The bow of the leading boat had toppled forward over his oar, and for a moment or so it ceased pulling, whilst the man was replaced.

Loyola paled to the lips as she watched the result of her shooting, but a bullet from the dago, which drilled a neat double hole through the brim of her sombrero, stirred her up afresh.

"Sit down directly you see the smoke of his rifle," counselled the blind man.

"Hell!" muttered Bill, below his breath. "There's more sand in that gal than the whole o' Southsea beach."

As for Broncho, his eyes sparkled in keen appreciation, and her nerve inspired a fresh life in his stroke. Gripping his oar, he lay back to it with such force as to near upset Jim off the thwart by his side.

And now a strange duel began between Dago Charlie and Loyola, marooner and marooned; and as the bullets came sizzling over the whaleboat, a fire of comment and encouragement broke out amongst the castaways, their fatigue all forgotten in the excitement of the moment.

If my reader has ever been under fire he will understand the feeling which fills one in such a position.

It is a difficult one to describe. Indeed, the hum of a bullet overhead affects most men differently; but unto all who are not cowards is given a strange uplifting of the spirit, unexplainable in words, but one which sends the blood coursing through the veins with a speed and vigour which no other form of excitement is able to rival.

The sensation of the gambler at the roulette table is mild compared to it; the fighter in the prize-ring has an inkling of it; the keen mountain climber thinks he has, but is mistaken: no, no one but he who has been face-to-face with flying bullets has experienced the mightiest thrill that one's senses can receive.

I have seen men whose nerves were of such steadiness that they could walk up and down, smoking, under heavy fire; but even they, when watched closely, exhibited unmistakable signs that this thrill within gripped them.

They were not smoking like a man does in his armchair by his home fireside. No; no slow meditative puffs here, but a quick indrawing and expelling of the smoke in rapid, ceaseless breaths, and there was a light in their eyes only to be seen in the firing-line.

Such a light could now be seen in each pair of eyes owned by the occupants of the whaleboat; even the blind ones gleamed with it.

Again the leading pursuer stopped to replace a wounded oarsman.

"Good for you, mum," cried Bill delightedly. "You deserves a marksman's badge."

"An' I puts down a bet on that," agreed Broncho. "That mutineer can't buck against you, missy. He finds you has an ace buried every time. I reckon the baleful effec's o' your cannonadin' puts a diff'rent tint on his views o' life."

"He thought he was goin' to get us so easy, too," grinned Jim.

"He notes now as how shore things don't exist. Providence, if in the mood, can beat four aces an' the joker," declsared the cowboy.

"Aye, an' a gal out-luck two boat-loads o' hell-scrapin's, easy as fallin' off a log," added Bill.

But Loyola was not going to have it all her own way: a shot from the pursuer made a long tear in her white dress, and the next one drew blood from her left shoulder.

"I can't stand this," declared Jack, his voice shaking. "You must stop firing, Lolie, and lie down in the bottom of the boat."

"Not I," cried the woman exultantly. "Do you think I'll hide on the flooring-boards now—now that I am being of some use; no, Jack, never!" and she shut her mouth with a snap of determination.

Jack fairly groaned in his distress, and with a tragic face bent to his work in silence.

But Loyola was all remorse in a moment when she saw how her words had hurt him.

"Oh, Jack," she cried out miserably, her passionate nature jumping from the heights of exultation to the very depths of self-reproach. "I didn't mean it, I didn't mean it! I'll do whatever you like, I swear I will. I'll lie flat in the bottom of the boat and never stir if you wish it."

The sensitive woman was greatly upset when she perceived how her quick, thoughtless words and refusal to obey Jack's request had made him feel his helplessness with a heavier weight than ever, and eagerly she tried to make amends.

But, at her words, Jack regained more of his old self. He knew well what it would cost her to lie down and take no part in the affray now that her blood was up, and though the thought of her being hit made him tremble, he gave in, saying:

"No, Lolie, you're quite right. Go on firing; you're our chief hope now, and I was a fool to think we could do without you."

"Dear old boy!" muttered the woman softly, below her breath. "I know what you thought and what you feared."

Then she rose to her feet and fired again, just as Dago Charlie was lifting his gun to shoot.

The castaways, watching the result of her shot, saw the buccaneer's gun drop from his hand, and, as he fell back into his seat, they cheered huskily.

"Copped it, the devil! Copped it this time," cried Bill. "Great shootin', mum. I'll sure cut the badge off my arm an' give it to you," referring to his marksman's badge.

"I reckon that maroonin' buckaroo's feelin' partic'lar pensif, not to say some perturbed," drawled Broncho, with a low note of satisfaction in his voice.

"Broncho, you and Bill cease rowing. Get your breath and come into the firing-line," broke in Jack sharply. "Tari and I can keep the boat going, and Jim can take the steering-oar. A little more shooting like that and the dago will get sick of it," he explained.

The two men unshipped their oars with alacrity, and, with Jim, clambered aft.

"What are you sightin' at, mum?" asked Bill deferentially. "You sure 'as the range proper."

"Two-fifty. They're not getting any nearer, either; do you think so, Bill?"

"No, mum, they ain't. They're just doin' a dockyard dip now. They ain't none eager to shorten your range, I'm reckoning."

Benson's first shot keeled over another man, and the leading boat stopped pulling again. Anxiously the castaways watched her. Evidently a heated discussion was going on.

Up got Dago Charlie in the sternsheets, and they noticed that his left arm was in a sling. A gigantic black faced him, gesticulating furiously with a windmill motion of his arms.

Then out came the dago's revolver, and the black sat sullenly down again.

"That ere mutineer gang seems near weakenin'," commented Broncho. "The lead we-alls deals out to 'em is kinder hard to chew on. They has four men in the diskyard, countin' the old he-coon, bein' three notches on Missy Lolie's stock and the hold-up Bill lays out."

The *Black Adder's* boats now drew together, and the whaleboat's crew watched them transferring wounded men from the first boat to the second without firing.

The operation was rushed through without much time lost, and then on came the first boat again with three new men in her; but a short cheer burst from the castaways as they noticed the second boat pull round and head away for the distant schooner.

But now a new man stood up in the sternsheets of the dago's boat and opened fire, and at his very first shot, over toppled Bill Benson.

Down went Loyola on her knees beside the wounded man, whilst Broncho snapped hurriedly at the marksman before he resumed his seat.

"Where's he hit?" asked Jack anxiously.

"He's only stunned, I think," replied Loyola, with a long sigh of relief. "The bullet has ploughed a groove through his hair, hardly cutting through the skin."

"Let him lie in the bottom of the boat, Lolie; you can do nothing for him. He'll come to after a bit, and soon be all right," declared Jack.

Dago Charlie was now only pulling leisurely, keeping up with the whaleboat, but taking care not to get any nearer.

Noting this, the castaways ceased firing except for an occasional shot, for their ammunition was beginning to get scarce.

Bill soon recovered his senses, and though at first feeling a bit queer and shaken, presently quite regained his old self.

All through that long, sweltering afternoon Jack and Tari pulled stubbornly, with tireless muscles, obstinately refusing to be relieved. Loyola had been compelled to lie down and rest in the bottom of the boat at Jack's feet, alongside Benson, and notwithstanding an occasional shot whistling overhead, so worn out was the woman from the trying time she had gone through, and lack of sleep, that she was soon dreaming peacefully in the land of nod.

Broncho, in the sternsheets with Jim, kept a keen watch on their pursuer, and was ready for him whenever the other man rose to fire. But the latter seemed to bear a charmed life; once Broncho knocked his hat off; then a bullet from the cowboy hit his rifle, and he had to take another; and a third time he was seen to put his hand up to his cheek, and feel where the lead had grazed his cheek-bone and cut a red line across his face, passing between his hat and his ear.

This last shot seemed to damp the man's ardour, and he evidently refused to stand up as a target for Broncho again, not knowing that he had shot the cowpuncher's belt-buckle away, and twice put lead into the whaleboat's stern-post.

Towards sunset, cocoanuts were served out again, and, whilst they refreshed themselves, the pursued discussed the situation.

"Seems to me he don' intend no more attackin'," observed the bosun's mate. "He's just keepin' station, relyin' on a breeze bringin' the schooner up presently."

"That's about it," agreed Jack. "Anyhow, bar a graze or two, we are better off than we were, whilst he's decidedly worse."

"I'm hopin' this sizzlin' sun is chawin' up that wounded arm o' his some," declared Broncho. "It comforts me a whole lot to think missy here has done put her mark on him, and I shore corrals in toomultuous delight if it goes to throbbin' an' achin' — —"

Broncho was interrupted by a sort of gasp from Jim, and the next moment the boy toppled up against him in a dead faint.

Tenderly the cowpuncher took the poor boy in his arms, whilst Loyola, with big tears in her eyes, sprinkled water over the pale, drawn little face, saying over and over again to herself,

"Poor Jim! poor little Jim!"

"What's up?" asked the blind man.

"Jim's strength has quit him, an' he's vamoosed into a faint," replied the cowboy.

"Why, what's this?" cried the girl, in consternation. "Look at his shirt; it's all soaked with blood."

"Blast me if the youngster ain't been wounded all this time," exclaimed Bill.

"An' never tole no one! He's clean-strain, is Jim," muttered Broncho hoarsely, as Loyola tenderly bathed the place and pulled away the blood-stained shirt from the wound.

"Where's he hit?" came the strained, husky voice of the blind man again.

"Bullet's glanced off 'is ribs an' made a nawsty gash," said Bill.

"The son of a gun! the son of a gun! An' he never tole no one!" repeated Broncho softly.

With quick, gentle fingers Loyola skilfully bound up the wound, using a strip of flannel torn from Bill's shirt, and Broncho's gay, silk kerchief, which the cowboy always wore, prairie fashion, round his neck.

Hardly had she finished her bandaging before the boy opened his eyes and looked round wonderingly.

"Wha's th' matter?" he asked faintly.

"W'y, you tried to outhold that wound o' yours, sonny, an' it overplayed you; but Missy Lolie has done bound it up an' blocked its little game," explained Broncho, smiling on him with a great affection in his eyes.

"Dear little Jim!" cried Loyola impulsively, flinging her arms round the boy and kissing him. "You'll feel better soon."

"Lay him down on the blankets," said Jack, in a low voice.

He and Tari still pulled steadily — they did not dare stop — and Tari kept the boat's head straight, no one being at the steering-oar.

With tender hands the boy was placed full length in the bottom of the boat, and Loyola insisted on his having a whole extra cocoanut served out to him.

This the boy drank off with feverish haste, betraying to the others the torments of thirst he must have been suffering the whole afternoon.

The milky juice put new strength into him, and declaring vehemently that he felt all right, he wanted to get up and take the steering-oar again; but this the others would not allow, and he had to remain lying where he was.

As the sun dropped below the horizon, a ripple was perceived upon the water right ahead.

"Wind at last!" cried Loyola, "and we'll get it first."

Jack and Tari put all their strength into a last spurt, whilst Bill and Broncho hastily stepped the mast and hoisted the lugsail, Loyola taking the helm.

Then darkness, the breeze, and Jack's weird eyesight sprang upon them together.

Gaily the tired rover pulled in his oar and looked eagerly about him; then he bent down, and by the light of the bright stars examined Jim's wound.

"I see you've been in good hands, Jim," he remarked, referring to Loyola's skilful bandaging.

"It's the touch of her fingers makes me feel better," whispered the boy, with a quick blush.

"Same here," declared Jack, with a curious smile. Then a sudden impulse took him, and, stepping aft, he looked deep into the woman's wavering eyes; and there must have been some magic in that one look of Jack's, for a flood of dark crimson crept slowly over Loyola's face.

For one brief second she felt his strong arm round her shoulders and his lips against her lips; then, with the low, whispered words, "Bravest and dearest!" he turned and joined Bill and Broncho, who were sweeping the horizon with the *Ocmulgee's* glass, searching for the *Black Adder*.

CHAPTER XIII
"PAPEETE"

Loyola sank back, shaking all over, her eyes gleaming with a wonderfully tender light, and fell into a deep reverie, which was rudely awakened by the flapping of the lugsail.

She had let the whaleboat come up into the wind.

"Now, Lolie," said Jack, stepping aft, "I'm going to relieve the wheel. You're tired out and must lie down and rest by Jim."

"Why, Jack, I've been asleep all the afternoon, and you've been rowing all day in the blazing sun."

"Well, anyhow, child, I'm going to steer now; but if you don't want to lie down, you can sit beside me," said the rolling-stone craftily.

This the woman was nothing loth to do, and slipping her hand into his, she nestled up against him with a perfect feeling of contentment, notwithstanding the fact that Dago Charlie still hung doggedly in their wake.

Presently a flare flamed out from the schooner's boat, against the bright light of which her men showed like little carved images of jet, outlined in red.

"Coyotes!" exclaimed Broncho, "he's afire!"

"Burning a flare to show the *Black Adder* where we are," explained Jack.

"It'll take the blighter h'all night to come up with us now," declared Bill triumphantly. "An' his boat ain't got the legs this whaleboat has. The luck's comin' our side o' the deck at last."

"We'd better set watches. Everybody must get some sleep to-night," observed the rover.

"Cert," agreed Broncho; "my eyelids is weighin' my eyes down as if they're loaded pack-saddles."

"An' mine is winkin' like an occultin' light," declared the bosun's mate.

"Of course, you, Lolie, and Jim are out of this," began Jack. "Suppose I take the first watch, Bill the middle, and Tari the morning."

"An' what about this nigger?" asked Broncho.

"Oh, you're the horse-wrangler; you're not on night-herd."

"And why should I be left out?" exclaimed Loyola, in an injured voice.

After a great deal of argument, in which even Jim joined, it was decided that if she chose Loyola could keep Jack's watch with him, whilst Broncho joined Tari.

So, this knotty point settled, whilst Jack and Loyola shared the sternsheets the others turned in on the flooring-boards, and were soon sleeping heavily the deep sleep of exhaustion.

The night passed uneventfully. The breeze held steady with a long, smooth sea, over which the whaleboat bowled along with the sheet well aft, making good speed and dropping the dago's boat fast; but slowly and surely the schooner crept up, though it was four bells in the middle watch before she picked up her boat.

Soon after a small coral reef with a few palms on it was passed to windward.

As the first light of dawn spread high over the east, the sleeping boat's crew were awakened by the wild, deep cry of the Kanaka:

"Sail-ho! sail-ho!"

In a moment these magic words had roused the tired sleepers into a wide-eyed wakefulness.

"Whar?" burst out Broncho.

"There she is! There she is, right ahead!" called Loyola breathlessly.

Jack seized the telescope, whilst the others broke out into a babble of exclamations, questions, and surmises.

"She's heading our way, I'm almost certain," declared Jack. "She's got square topsails, and her masts are in line, so I can't be certain of her rig; but I think she's an Island schooner, for a certainty."

"What for of a play would it be to let rip a volley at that paltry marooner. Mebbe it'd act as a signal-smoke to the stranger?" asked the cowpuncher, indicating the *Black Adder*, which was less than three cables' lengths off on their lee-quarter.

"First chop!" agreed Jack, picking up his Winchester.

"Just a sorter 'So long, ta-ta!' to the blighter," hinted Bill.

The schooner was busy sending up a big gaff-headed main-topsail, and the three musketeers aimed at the group of men tailing on to the fall of the sheet out-haul.

The three reports burst out together, and the group of men disappeared suddenly behind the bulwarks; a bullet had cut the rope they were hauling on.

"Good shot! good shot!" cried Jim hysterically, clapping his hands.

"That crowd hit the deck some sudden, I'm thinkin'," exclaimed Bill, grimly reloading.

"I guess that dago sharp's moppin' his feachers some, if he ain't fretted to the core an' grittin' his teeth with frenzy," chuckled the cowboy.

"Now, look out for squalls," cried Jack warningly, as the *Black Adder* put her helm up and yawed.

This time every fire-arm on the schooner seemed to have been let off. For a moment her decks were hidden in smoke, and the boom of heavy metal mingled with the sharp report of the rifles.

"Snakes an' coyotes, the pole-cat's been and overshooted!" burst out Broncho exultantly, as the storm of lead sang by above them.

"Thank 'eaven for that," grunted the bluejacket. "It 'ummed overhead like funnel-stays in a pampero."

Jack seized the telescope again, and looked long and earnestly at the approaching stranger; and whilst he had the glass up to his eye, the red rim of the rising sun showed above the horizon. In the excitement of the moment no one gave a thought to the spreading daylight, Jack least of all; and now he stood gazing, all unconscious that it was broad daylight and that he could see.

For nearly two minutes he stood there, the glass glued to his eye; then he slowly collapsed on to the stroke thwart, and blurted out with shaking voice,

"It's the French Government schooner from Papeete, Lolie—I'm sure of it—and heading this way. You're saved! you're saved!"

The woman stared at him with wide-open eyes, trying in vain to speak, and then fell back fainting.

The shock of the release from the strain of this desperate fight had proved too much for her intrepid spirit.

Tenderly they laid her down in the bottom of the boat and sprinkled water over her face.

"You bruck it too rapid, Jack," observed the bosun's mate slowly. "It's the recoil as knocks a woman."

"I was a cursed, thoughtless fool," groaned Jack, in bitter self-reproach.

"That 'ere put-upon an' hard-pressed gal has the sand an' grit o' forty of us men-folk," declared Broncho, with emphasis. "The way she stands this racket an' plays her hand has me bulgin' with admiration an' respec'."

"Me too!" gulped Jim, with big tears in his eyes.

Loyola was too wiry a woman to stay long in a faint, and in a very short space of time she opened her eyes and looked round fearfully.

"It's all right, Lolie, it's all right!" said Jack softly, as he bent over her.

Slowly she raised herself, looking wildly at him; then her eyes grew blurred, and with a heavy sob she held out her hands.

He seized them in his own and held them firm, his lips quivering.

"Oh, Jack!" she murmured brokenly, fighting for her self-control. "Oh, Jack!"

Nobody who has not experienced it can understand how a sudden unexpected release from long nerve-strain affects one.

Many are the stories of men rescued when hope of rescue had been almost abandoned, and of their strange behaviour on realising that they were saved.

One hears of big, strong men crying like babes and hugging each other; of men behaving as if their brains had been taken from them by the shock; who knew not what they did, all control being lost for a few wild minutes, of which they had no recollection whatever afterwards.

Thus, now that relief had come to Loyola's overstrained nerves, it was almost too severe a shock, and the brave woman felt herself on the verge of hysteria.

Tighter and tighter Jack gripped her hands as he watched her struggles against a breakdown.

"Bite on it, Lolie! Be brave!" he whispered hoarsely.

"Dagoman put um hellum down!" The utterance came from aft in the Kanaka's soft voice.

Tari's words seemed to break the spell. Loyola, with a shudder, snapped her teeth together and her eyes cleared. Jack drew a deep breath, and relaxing his grip on her nearly crushed hands, patted them gently.

Jim raised a tear-stained face, and with a sudden impulse seized the cowpuncher's brown fist and shook it wildly.

His action was catching, and in another moment the castaways were wringing each others' hands as if for a wager.

"Mercy! mercy!" gasped Loyola, smiling and once more her old self. "Jack's nearly squashed mine flat already."

All anxiety was now at an end, for already the French war-schooner was within a couple of miles, surging along under a heavy press of canvas, whilst the *Black Adder*, with sheets slacked away and a big square-sail set, was making herself scarce as fast as ever she could.

"The dago's hittin' it high on the back trail shore enuff," commented Broncho, as he watched the flying enemy. "That ornery maverick is quittin' the play without a sou-markee o' profit. He ain't out o' the wood yet, though. I'm allowin' the war-boat'll jump into his wheeltracks some swift when he savvys the vivid lead-slingin' he done cut loose on us. It shore oughter poke spurs into him."

As the castaways watched the two schooners with eager eyes, Tari leaned forward, and stretching out his disengaged hand, tapped Jack gently on the shoulder.

The latter turned round and found the Kanaka fairly beaming upon him.

"My *pleni* no more blind. Bad eye-debble him go 'way, no likee bullets. Tari heap glad."

Jack stared at him with open mouth, unable to speak, whilst Loyola, a whole world of tenderness in her big brown eyes, rubbed her cheek caressingly against his shoulder, whispering brokenly, "Thank God! Oh, thank God!" and her whole heart was in her voice.

"Hoo-jolly-ray!" screeched Jim, springing wildly on to a thwart. "Three cheers and a tiger! Hip! hip! hip! hurray!"

Meanwhile, Broncho was pump-handling Jack like a madman.

"You old son of a gun!" he growled; "you old son of a gun!"

Bill was just as excited.

"Blawst me if it ain't a blighted miracle; yes, that's just wot it is. But wot's done it? The blistered moon, the dago's flyin' lead, or the war-schooner juttin' over the horizon? Anyways, whatever done it, the dough's your way, Jack."

And now the Tahiti gunboat came swooping down upon them, a row of eager faces lining her rail.

When within a quarter of a cable she rounded to and backed her fore-topsail, whilst Tari ran the whaleboat up alongside her lowered gangway ladder, on which stood a little fat Frenchman in a spotless uniform of snowy duck.

"*Qu'est que c'est ce bateau là?*" he cried, flourishing a podgy fist in the direction of the flying pirate.

"*Black Adder,*" replied Jack shortly, and the notorious name drew a buzz of comment from the schooner's crew.

The next moment Loyola was handed up the ladder, and received, with the politest of bows and a shower of flowery expressions of delight and greeting, by the little French captain, who knew her well.

He was soon in possession of all the facts, and gave orders for the chase to be resumed, vowing with all the extravagant mannerisms of his race to bring madame's enemies to justice.

He was a kind-hearted little man, this sailor, as Frenchmen generally are, and the castaways were soon partaking of a luxurious repast in his tastefully arranged and comfortable cabin, whilst a snowy-aproned French steward waited on them with every delicacy that he could provide.

For some time questions flew thick, and Jack and Loyola were kept busy replying to the innumerable inquiries put by the little captain and a grave young man with a small moustache and gloomy countenance, who was introduced to them as the French Commissioner of the Paumotus.

It seemed that the castaways were indebted for their rescue to the fact that the Commissioner was on his way to open a small atoll for the pearl-fishing.

The French war-schooner was no match, however, for the slim-heeled *Black Adder*, which was soon hull down, and the impetuous little Frenchman was compelled at last, with many expressive shrugs of his shoulders at the sluggish speed of his vessel, to relinquish the chase and resume his course for the atoll.

The following day the island was reached, and the schooner dropped her anchor in the lagoon amidst a crowd of native boats, all eagerly awaiting her arrival; whilst ashore, a ramshackle lot of corrugated iron shanties were in course of erection, to act as stores for the enterprising vendors of grog and dry goods.

In a moment the schooner was surrounded by a clamorous crowd of Paumotu divers, who are without compare in the South Seas, being able to dive to tremendous depths and remain under water an extraordinarily long time.

The first person to step on board the schooner was a solemn-faced native Mormon missionary, whom Broncho eyed with great interest on being told by Jack who he was.

The gloomy young Commissioner was landed, and with a lazy simplicity he declared the island open for pearl-shell fishing before a mixed crowd of eager people on the beach.

For a week the schooner stayed at anchor in the lagoon, the whole of which time Broncho sat playing poker in the store of an old Yankee retired whaleman, from whom and the gloomy Commissioner he succeeded in taking a nice little pile of Chilian dollars, to his great delight.

Meanwhile, the rest of the castaways roamed the island, watched the diving, or whiled away the days in hammocks under the schooner's awning.

But at length the schooner was headed back for Papeete.

With a fair wind, a quick run was made to the famous island, and at sunrise one morning Jack and Loyola found themselves gazing eagerly at the well-known mountain ridges behind Papeete, with their bright green foliage and scattered cocoa-palms, and the magnificent Diadem rising rugged and glorious above them.

The schooner, running in through the Little Pass, brought up opposite the little islet of Motu Uta, once the residence of a queen, and afterwards a leper station.

Little more remains to be told.

Jack and Loyola were married about a month after their arrival, Bucking Broncho officiating as best man, whilst Bill Benson and a crowd of his shipmates—for the *Dido* had turned up unexpectedly—gave a go to the proceedings such as only British bluejackets are capable of.

As Jack and Loyola were so well known at Papeete, and had a host of friends in this Paradise of the Pacific, as it is so rightly called, the wedding went off with great *éclat*, natives, whites, and the French officials attending *en masse*.

Shortly after these festivities Bill Benson was carried away in his little gunboat on a hunt for Dago Charlie and his slippery schooner.

Jack and Loyola settled down at Papeete, the rover intending, directly he could arrange his money matters in far-off England, to start in the Island trade with a schooner of his own.

Jim and Tari remained with the happy couple as a kind of bodyguard, but after several lazy months in this happy land, Broncho began to long for the more active life of his beloved plains; and though the others did their best to persuade him to remain with them, he one day took his passage in the barquentine *Tropic Bird* for San Francisco, and, as he put it, "hit the trail for his own pastures."

It was a sad parting between the old shipmates.

Broncho's last words to Jack as they wrung each other's hands at the gangway, the San Francisco packet already heeling to the breeze, with the old original whaleboat splashing and bobbing at the foot of the ladder, were:

"So long, old bunkie. We've camped around together quite a spell. I jest loathes leavin' the outfit, but pull my freight I must. This old longhorn is jest itchin' to paw the earth again, an' lock horns in the old game. I hungers for the feel of a pony 'tween my legs, an' the smell o' the cattle. It's natur', pard, an' that's all thar is to it, though it shore twangs my heartstrings in toomultuous discord. Adios!"

Postscript 1.—Of the Yankee hell-ship *Silas K. Higgins* no more was heard, and as time went by she was at last posted on the black list of missing ships. Who can say what her real end was? Did she fall a victim to the terrible Cape Horn surges, or was it that word which the bosun spelt with a big M which caused her disappearance from the great ocean highway? The deep sea hid her and the deep sea does not blab.

Postscript 2.—Notwithstanding Bill Benson's statement as to the sailing qualities of his little gunboat, she proved to be no match for the Black Adder, and years of desperate doings intervened before Dago Charlie was at last brought to book for his many misdeeds.